I0594052

THE DEVIL'S CROWN

PART
2

THE DEVIL'S CROWN

A DARK ROMANCE

International Bestselling Author
MONICA JAMES

Copyrighted Material
THE DEVIL'S CROWN-PART TWO
(All The Pretty Things Trilogy Spin-Off)

This book is a work of fiction. Names, characters, places and incidents are the product of the author's imagination, or are used fictitiously. Any resemblance to actual events, locales, or persons living or dead, is coincidental. Any trademarks, service marks, product names or named features are assumed to be the property of their respective owners and are used only for reference.

Copyright © 2020 by Monica James
All rights reserved. No part of this work may be reproduced, scanned or distributed in any printed or electronic form without the express, written consent of the author.

Cover Design: Perfect Pear Creative Covers
Cover Model: Frankie
Photographer: Ren Saliba
Editing: Editing 4 Indies
Formatting: E.M. Tippetts Book Designs

Follow me on:
authormonicajames.com

OTHER BOOKS BY
MONICA JAMES

THE I SURRENDER SERIES

I Surrender

Surrender to Me

Surrendered

White

SOMETHING LIKE NORMAL SERIES

Something like Normal

Something like Redemption

Something like Love

A HARD LOVE ROMANCE

Dirty Dix

Wicked Dix

The Hunt

MEMORIES FROM YESTERDAY DUET

Forgetting You, Forgetting Me

Forgetting You, Remembering Me

SINS OF THE HEART DUET

Absinthe of the Heart

Defiance of the Heart

ALL THE PRETTY THINGS TRILOGY

Bad Saint

Fallen Saint

Forever My Saint

The Devil's Crown-Part One (Spin-Off)

The Devil's Crown-Part Two (Spin-Off)

THE MONSTERS WITHIN DUET

Bullseye

Blowback

STANDALONE

Mr. Write

Chase the Butterflies

AUTHOR'S NOTE

CONTENT WARNING: *THE DEVIL'S CROWN* is divided into two parts. It's a spin-off, but I recommend you read **ALL THE PRETTY THINGS TRILOGY** before starting this book.

THE DEVIL'S CROWN is a DARK ROMANCE containing mature themes that might make some readers uncomfortable. It includes strong violence, possible triggers, and some dark and disturbing scenes.

This warning is not a gimmick. This twisted tale is not intended for the fainthearted. So, if you're game…welcome to the madness.

God save your soul.

CHAPTER ONE

Alek

"You stubborn son of a bitch, you need to go to the hospital!" exclaims Saint for the tenth time, flinching as he looks at my thigh, which resembles ground beef.

"What…I need," I pant, attempting to adjust myself into a comfortable position in the back of the van, "is for Pavel to stop hitting every bump in the road."

"If you don't like my driving, you can walk," he replies with a shrug, peering at me in the visor mirror.

That isn't an option, seeing as I was beaten within an inch of my life. Actually, no, that's incorrect. I was beaten to death, only to be resurrected by the devil.

"She belongs to the Macrillo family now."

Clenching my fist, I hear Santo's words play over and over, which only flames my anger to biblical proportions. Ella is with him right now, being subjected to God knows what, and it's my fault. If only I hadn't lied to her. If only I'd told her the truth.

I just didn't think she'd sacrifice herself this way, sacrifice herself…for me. But that's what she did. Regardless of believing she meant nothing to me, she did this so we could all be free.

"Drive faster," I order, hissing when Pavel hits a pothole.

He responds with a smirk.

Saint sits by me, his T-shirt pressed over the bleeding wound in my chest, thanks to Raul imbedding a hoe into my lungs.

Raul was so close to gaining his revenge, but now that it was stolen from him, he'll stop at nothing to find me and finish the job.

I left Santo and his men at Raul's, clueless to what I was planning. Santo believes I saw our deal through, delivering Ella into his clutches, which is why he saved me. He was watching my every move. That is how he must have known where I was. But if I didn't need him alive, he'd be nailed to the lattice wall next to my half-brother with his cock shoved down his throat too.

"You need to calm down. You're bleeding like a motherfucker," Saint warns, shaking his head as I scoff at his fussing.

"Would you calm down if that vile asshole had Willow?"

When Saint's jaw clenches, that's enough of an answer.

I need to get out of this van and find Ella. Nothing else matters but getting her away from the Macrillo family. I have no idea what Santo has planned for her, which scares me beyond words. If he hurts her…

Thankfully, we're pulling into the driveway of Larisa's home. The moment the van stops, I attempt to open the door with bloodied fingers, but I fail terribly because Raul broke three fingers on my right hand.

The door slides open, and when I see Willow, I'm instantly ashamed. I have failed everyone and should be dead. Ella should be on her way home, and Willow and Saint should be free of me.

"Oh, Alek," she cries when she takes in my injuries.

"Help me, ангел," Saint frantically orders, gently looping his arm around me to help me out of the van.

"No, you'll get blood on your dress," I wheeze, recoiling when she does as Saint asked.

Of course she ignores me, and on the count of three, she and Saint lug my useless ass out of the van and support me so I can stand. Saint holds tight, and I lean into him, not wanting to crush Willow.

As they lead me toward the house, I dig in my heels. "No, I don't want Irina to see me like this."

Saint changes direction, and we begin a stagger toward the barn.

"Спасибо, мой друг," I express my gratitude to Saint, who merely grunts. He doesn't want my thanks. "дорогая, I'm so sorry…for everything."

"Shh, Alek, save your strength."

I have no idea why Willow thinks I'm weak when I'm feeling just fine. Currently, it feels as though I'm floating on air, and when I peer at my feet, I see that I am.

Saint and Willow are carrying me because I've lost the use of my legs. I can see my left femur bone as the skin and muscle have been flayed away. It doesn't hurt, however. I'm way past feeling any pain.

"Stay awake!" Pavel orders, slapping my cheeks as he takes over for Willow.

My chin lolls to my chest, and suddenly, I'm so tired. I want to return to the place I was before I awoke to this…this nightmare. It was quiet there. I felt at peace…something I haven't felt in a very long time.

Larisa's voice fades in and out, but her frantic Russian alerts me to my dire circumstance. If she doesn't tend to my wounds, she fears I'll lose my leg. Or worse still…my life. That's what I wanted, though. But not like this, not when Ella is unsafe. And not when I need to uncover what happened to Irina.

I fall backward onto something hard. It smells wretched in here. I then remember I defiled Ella in this very barn like a savage. She deserved so much better. She deserved silk and satins, but I merely took her like an ungrateful beast.

"Saint," I pant into nothingness because I'm swathed in darkness, and I'm so cold.

"Yes, I'm here." He sounds so far away.

"Promise me you'll save her." I lift my head off the workbench to search for him, but strong hands pin me down.

"No, I will not promise you that," he stubbornly rebukes, "'cause we're going to do it together."

"No, my friend, I cannot," I argue, shivering so hard, my teeth rattle. "I am…so c-cold."

"Oh, g-god, help h-him. Please." Willow's sweet prayers and tears are wasted on a monster like me.

"Do not cry, дорогая," I say, searching for her hand. Her warm fingers clench mine a moment later. "As I once said, don't waste your tears on someone like me."

"Fight!" Saint demands, angered I would give up this way. But I'm not strong like him. "If you die now, all of this would have been for nothing! Don't you dare dishonor those who sacrificed everything for you to live. Do this for Zoey! Do this for Ella. And do this for me."

"Aleksei, if you don't fight, you will die," Larisa states firmly. I didn't think she'd be opposed to the idea, but it seems as though I may be wrong.

She orders Pavel to go inside and grab a laundry list of supplies.

"Where is Irina?" I ask, desperately trying to fight off what feels like tens of thousands of hands touching me. They are suffocating.

"She's inside, sleeping. Max is watching over her." Willow's voice calms me somewhat.

Saint speaks to Larisa in Russian, but his words are a jumbled mess as his voice floats further and further away. "Ангел, go inside. This isn't going to be pleasant."

Yes, please listen to Saint. I don't want to subject Willow to atrocities that will scar her forever.

"I'll see you when you wake, Alek," she says as something wet and warm caresses my cheek. I soon realize it's a tear-laden kiss.

"I'll see you when I see you," I reply with what feels like a smile, but my face grows numb.

"This is going to hurt. A lot," Saint says while I hear the distinct sound of scissors cutting through material. "But you're Aleksei motherfucking Popov, and I've seen you handle worse. So stop being a little pussy and fight."

His pep talk has me wheezing. I was trying to laugh. But that soon turns to a winded gasp as I feel immense pressure and hear a brutal crack…then the pain follows. Pain I've never felt before. Gripping the bench beneath me, I try to stay still, but this feels like my bones are being ripped out of my skin.

"Ебать!" I scream, unable to breathe. But I can do this. I must.

"Sorry," Saint pants, and before I have a chance to ask what he's apologizing for, my world is no more because the son of a bitch has knocked me out cold.

I'll thank him when I wake. Or rather, *if*…

Every part of me is screaming. My mind. Body. Soul.

I will myself to slip back into the darkness because here, there's no pain. Only weightlessness. But if I stay a moment longer, I'm afraid I'll never resurface again.

So I force my eyes open, and little by little, I take in my surroundings, struggling to remember my last solid memory.

Ella…

I jar upright, causing a nauseating pain to follow the jolted movements. With a groan, I barely hold down my vomit. My vision is blurred, but I would recognize Saint, even if I were blind.

From the wooden rocking chair in the corner of the room where he sits, he peers up from writing in his leather journal, pen pressed to the page. When he sees I'm awake, he places the pen behind his ear and closes the journal. "About fucking time."

I attempt to speak, but nothing comes out.

Saint gestures with his head to the nightstand, where I find a glass of water. I attempt to reach for it with my right hand, but it's bandaged.

A slow perusal of my body indicates that most of it is bandaged. Using my left hand, I pull back the sheet and sigh in relief. Both legs are still there.

"You have Larisa to thank for that," Saint says, reading my thoughts. "She saved your life."

"No doubt," I hoarsely reply as I reach for the glass of water. Once I drain it, I wipe my dry lips with the back of my hand. "How many days have I been out?"

"Three."

Cursing under my breath, I attempt to swing my legs off the bed as I cannot lie here like a vegetable for a second longer. But they refuse to cooperate.

"You're on some hard-core painkillers. Give it some time."

"That is something I do not have," I counter angrily. "Each moment spent here is time when Ella is in harm's way."

"Don't underestimate her," Saint states. "She saved your ass."

"I know what she did," I bite back, frustrated that I'm

nothing but an invalid, unable to do anything while confined to this bed. "Have we got eyes on her?"

Pavel enters the room, looking at me with what might be called astonishment. "I can't believe you're alive."

"Thanks to your mother," I reply, shifting awkwardly to rest against the headboard. "What of Ella?"

Pavel pulls up a chair. "Nothing yet."

"What's that supposed to mean?"

"It means what it means. Santo won't let her breathe without him close by."

Well, that's unsatisfactory. "We need inside his house. We were able to do so with Saint under the ruse of being gardeners."

Soon realizing what I said, I give Saint an apologetic nod as that memory is one I'm sure he doesn't wish to relive.

He remains stone-faced.

"Santo isn't Oscar," Pavel replies frankly. "He's paranoid. He won't allow anyone he doesn't know within a mile of his residence."

"So what do you propose?"

"You need to be invited. That's the only way you'll get to her."

However, when he looks at Saint, I know there's a catch.

"And you'll get your chance. In six weeks' time."

"What's happening in six weeks?" I ask, preparing myself for anything. But his response reveals I haven't prepared for *this*.

"Frank and Ella's wedding."

Clearly, I've had a lapse in hearing because there is no

way Pavel has just shared this abominable news with me. But when he doesn't say a word, I realize I heard him just fine.

There's nothing further to say because words mean nothing. In this circumstance, actions speak, and we need to act fast.

Refusing to accept that my legs are on hiatus, I stubbornly cup the back of my thigh and swing it over the mattress, placing my foot on the cold floor. I repeat the same with my injured leg. With both feet planted on the floorboards, I attempt to stand but topple sideways.

Flailing, I punch the mattress in frustration.

"Get back into bed," Pavel orders, unimpressed with my efforts to stand.

"I will not," I angrily refute, slowly pushing myself back into a sitting position. "Ella is being held prisoner. I need to get her out of there."

Saint sighs, running a hand through his snarled hair. "She's okay."

"Okay? Define okay? And how would you know this?" I fire questions at him as though he knows a lot more than he's letting on.

After digging into his pocket for his phone, he unlocks it before tossing it onto the bed. "See for yourself."

Reaching for the cell, I look at the screen, and what I see is like a bittersweet kiss from hell.

A photo of Ella is before me, but she looks different. She looks…happy. A radiant smile graces those beautiful ruby lips, lips I kissed and cherished time and time again. Her face is glowing. It could be because her makeup complements her complexion, but it's not that.

Her hair is twisted into an elaborate bun and secured with a jeweled clip. Wearing a blue cocktail gown, she looks absolutely stunning.

Clenching the cell in my hand, I focus my attention on the man whose arm she's on—Frank Macrillo. He wears a tuxedo and a smug grin as he bends low, no doubt whispering sweet nothings in her ear.

She is merely playing a role, I reason with myself, but upon closer examination of this picture, I see that no, that smile, her grace, they're genuine. Nothing about this photo would indicate she's there against her own will.

I've been out for three days, and that's all it took for her to slip back into her role of doting fiancée.

"At least she's alive," I say after what feels like several minutes of silence, tossing the phone back to Saint.

"Yes, this is true. But you need to get better so you can move into your new house. We have much to discuss."

Arching a brow, I look at Pavel in confusion.

"Santo emailed through the paperwork. The million-dollar mansion which once belonged to Denka Orlov is now yours. With Serg dead, the world is looking for a leader…and that leader is you."

This was what I wanted. I fought so hard for my old life to be returned to me, but none of it matters without Ella.

Why does she look happy? She's not that good of an actress. Her happiness isn't staged. She's pleased to be on the arm of Frank once again. And what about Santo? Is she pleased to be with him?

"I'm going to kill them…kill them all," I growl with murderous rage.

"I know you will, but we need a plan. Going up against Santo is unlike anything we've done before. The Italian mafia is a whole different demographic. And let's not forget about Raul."

"They bleed just like everyone else," I spit, uninterested in Pavel's voice of reason.

"Before this happens, you need allies and money, and you need your reputation back. For this to work, you'll need to be the Aleksei Popov people remembered. You cannot be weak. If you show any weakness, it'll be exploited. Just as it's been in the past. You need for it to be believable."

Saint leans forward. "In other words, you need to be the ruthless son of a bitch you once were before you found your conscience. Can you do that?"

I'm worlds apart from who I once was, but they're right. Santo and Raul are the enemies—powerful enemies—and if I don't kill them, they'll kill me. It's survival of the fittest.

I thought I once ruled with an iron fist, but that was nothing compared to now. Back then, I had nothing worth fighting for, but now, everything is at stake. I'll be callous and calculated because that's what the people expect of the kingpin of Russia, which is who I am now.

With fire burning through my veins, I nod. "Yes. That will not be a problem. You do realize for that to happen, I'll need to return to my old habits?"

Saint's jaw clenches. "I know."

I understand his reservations, for a leader must have a

flock, and there is only one sensible choice. A woman who has been broken before.

Willow.

"I do not want Willow to be subjected to this," I say, meaning every word. "But she can reassure the others. I will not punish them. They can have their own areas of the house. They're merely for show."

The rocking chair sways backward and forward violently as Saint rises abruptly. "She's the only one who can make this decision. I won't decide for her."

We both know what she'll decide.

"I'll do it." Willow stands in the doorway with a fresh jug of water in her hands. She's clearly overheard what we just said.

Saint turns to her, his eyes pained. He knows what this means. She'll be on "display" whenever we're needed to showcase our social standing. The thought turns my stomach.

"It'll only be until we get Ella back," I assure both her and Saint. But that doesn't change a thing.

Willow will be expected to act as a submissive, and Saint will have to allow it for this to work.

"Santo is unaware of our past," I state, "which means he won't know he's being played."

"But your old inner circle does know of your past," Pavel says, reminding me that we have to tread with caution.

They know of Willow and my affection for her, which is dangerous. If they sense a hint of betrayal, it'll end badly for us all.

"They know of my affection for both Saint and Willow,"

I affirm, thinking this over. "They also know I can be very convincing when I want to be."

Saint scoffs, crossing his arms. "You mean, they know how people seem to fall at your feet, regardless of knowing your past?"

"That too," I reply, trying not to sound conceited. "We can play the angle that I needed my righthand man back after regaining my throne. And you two are a…package deal?"

I focus my attention on Willow. "This will mean they'll believe Saint and I are…sharing you."

"Like one big happy fucking family," Saint snaps, his anger palpable.

"However, if this makes either of you uncomfortable, I'll devise another plan. You've already done so much."

"Yes, this makes me *very* uncomfortable," Saint sneers, his fists bunched by his side.

"It's all make-believe, Saint," Willow says softly, but I can read her apprehension.

She's seen what these people are capable of. They won't be satisfied until she's shown complete submission because they believe she's the reason my empire crumbled to the ground.

So to welcome her back into my world would mean she'll need to show repentance for what she's done.

They are aware of my fondness for Saint because he was envied amongst my peers for his strength and loyalty. They won't question his return. But Willow will be a different story.

"What do you think, Pavel?"

Pavel seems to ponder on my question. "This will only work if everyone is on board. Who cares what they say? With you as leader once again, you can have whoever you want by your side. And in your bed. Figuratively speaking, of course," he adds when Saint turns a vicious shade of red.

"Ella is there against her will," Willow says, which pleases me. I don't want to believe another version of events, regardless of what the picture depicts. "And all I can think about is when you were held prisoner, Saint. I can't leave Ella there because what if there was no one to save you?"

She looks at Saint and only Saint because even though Willow is a strong, independent woman, if Saint was strongly opposed to the idea, she'd back down. And I respect them both for it.

"It's only until we can get her out of there," she reasons, working her bottom lip.

"And what will we need to sacrifice in the meantime?" Saint counters, eyes poignant.

Willow averts her gaze.

This is too much. I should have never asked. I'll think of another way.

"How bad do I look?" I ask, changing the pace.

"Like shit," Saint counters with a smirk. He seems pleased with the fact.

"Will I scare Irina?"

His smirk soon disappears.

"She's been in here watching over you," Willow reveals. "She doesn't speak much, does she?"

I shake my head, remembering the vile claims Serg made. "Can you ask her to come in here please? If she's afraid—"

"She won't be," Willow interrupts. "She's tough."

That she is.

Willow passes the jug of water to Saint, and a moment of confusion, fear, and love passes between them.

I realize how fortunate I am to have them in my life. They owe me nothing, yet here they are, willing to help me yet again. Not many would understand the relationship we have—I still don't—but we have an unbreakable bond. It shouldn't make sense, but it does. And each of us has a love-hate relationship with the fact.

We don't want to gravitate to one another, but we do.

"I know," I reply with a heartfelt smile.

Willow leaves the room, so I slowly make my way back into bed, pulling the covers over me. I lean against the headboard, catching my breath because this simple action was enough to leave me winded.

Saint places the jug on the nightstand, refusing to look at me. He hates what I've proposed, and I don't blame him. I hate it too.

I wish I could live my life in solitude without needing to impress others, but that's not how Russia works. I'm expected to act a certain way, and I refuse to be beaten by anyone ever again. I can't live a simple life. I tried. I was born a leader, and deep down, I feel most at home in the darkness.

If I were content being the "good guy," I would swap this lifestyle in a heartbeat. But this is who I am. This is where I belong.

Drugs, extortion, and other depravities are going to exist with or without me. As I see it, it may as well be with me because at least I hold some scruples.

Willow reappears, holding Irina's hand.

The moment I see her, I forget everything. She looks so small. Has she always been this thin? She chews the corner of her mouth, eyes glued to the floor.

Is she frightened of me?

"цветочек, I've missed you." I speak in Russian. I suddenly don't know what to say next.

I've put her in harm's way, so she has every right to fear or even hate me.

Willow smiles down at her. "Did you want to say hello to Aleksei?"

Irina lifts her shoulders in a half shrug.

My heart breaks to see her reject me this way. But I've betrayed her and quite possibly, added to the childhood trauma she already suffered.

"Not to worry. I just wanted to see you to make sure you're okay." I won't force her, but when she lifts her eyes to meet mine, I see the true extent of her strength.

"Irina 'kay," she whispers, wringing her hands in front of her. "Ski 'kay?"

"Ski okay," I affirm with a nod.

"Ski hurt?" she says, her lower lip trembling.

"No, цветочек. I'm all right. Just a scratch."

I need to broach this situation tenderly. I won't ask her now, but I need to know if what Serg said held any merit. However, what I do know is that I will not return her to the orphanage. I will call Mother Superior and ask for her blessing to adopt Irina.

I now have a home. A big home where I can keep her safe.

My lifestyle is far from suitable for a child, but I will try my best to be a good role model for her and ensure she has everything she needs.

Opening my arms, I offer her a choice. She can refuse, but when she lets go of Willow's hand and runs toward the bed, I understand how deep her love for me is.

She boosts herself onto the mattress, then throws herself into my embrace. I flinch because my broken ribs are still healing, but I don't let on that she's holding me so tightly I can scarcely breathe because this is all I want.

"I'll never let anything happen to you ever again," I promise, kissing the top of her head. She smells like her again.

As we embrace, I suddenly remember we're not alone.

Locking eyes with Saint, he appears to be pained, and I understand why. "Fine, we're in."

I nod in gratitude, drawing Irina closer to my chest.

Those who made the ones I love suffer are going to pay. I will inflict a lifetime of pain because Aleksei Popov is back… but unlike before, I have so much more worth fighting for.

CHAPTER TWO

Alek

"That is hideous," I spit from behind my large wooden desk as I peer up from my paperwork.

Nina Oblonsky, the interior decorator I hired, looks down from the ladder she stands on. The "artwork" she holds in her trembling hands resembles green vomit. "I thought you'd like it."

"Well, you thought wrong," I counter, pointing my gold pen at her. "Get rid of it immediately."

"It's modern, progressive," she argues lightly. She soon seals her lips shut when I stare at her, unimpressed. She came highly recommended by Ivan Elin, my neighbor, who I suspect has dealings with stolen automotives.

In my very own backyard, I have the telltale signs of a chop shop.

I shall let Ivan know what I think of his recommendation when I request his Rolls Royce as payment for wasting my time.

"I don't care what it is. If it's not removed from my office in the next three seconds, I'll ensure it and you are dealt with accordingly."

"Yes, of course, Mr. Popov." Nina quickly climbs down the ladder, taking her eyesore with her. "I'm so very sorry."

She makes a swift beeline for the closed door, but we're not done.

Placing my pen onto the desk, I stand. Thanks to my temporary limp, I now must use a cane for support. When I reach for it, the jewels on the gold cane topper catch the light emitted from the low hanging chandelier.

Some may see this cane as a weakness, but I do not. With my freshly pressed gray pinstripe suit and crisp white shirt and vest, I look the part of royalty. This cane is an extension of me and has proven to be quite the weapon—both literally and metaphorically.

Its ability to intimidate people into submission, like right now, is impressive.

"Ms. Oblonsky, did I permit you to leave?"

With her hand poised on the door handle, she turns over her shoulder, widening her green eyes. "No, I just thought—"

Raising my hand, I prohibit her from speaking another word. "Shh, shh. You'll soon learn when in my company, it's best if you don't do that."

She licks her red lips nervously. "Do what?"

With a smirk, I examine her slowly. "Think."

She came in here with an agenda because what interior decorator wears a white dress so tight that I can see she isn't wearing any underwear beneath? That bright red lipstick is also part of her ploy.

Just like every other woman and man who has come into my home, she has attempted to lure me in with her gimmicks. Short skirts. Expensive perfume and cologne. They all want to entrap the newly appointed boss of Russia and have a taste of the power.

But it's going to take a lot more than that because no matter what they bring to the table, I'll never be interested. Only one person holds my attention, and she's the reason I'm here.

It's been one week since I moved into this glorious home and reinstated my place at the top. It was met with resistance, of course, because many wanted to take Serg's place. But they were greeted with retaliation, and by that, I mean, I broke their noses, kneecaps, ribs whatever I felt was needed to remind them who was boss.

I told them I was on hiatus, but now that I was back, things have changed. I once worked within a circle, but now, I'm a lone wolf, and if anyone had a problem with that, they'd pay with their lives. Anyone is easily replaced because every single one of these assholes are disposable.

So, anyone who dares to come into my domain and attempt to play me, well, they will be made an example of. Just like Ms. Oblonsky here.

"Do you know what I do to women who disappoint me?" I pose, holding her gaze.

She turns around slowly. "I've heard—"

"What have you heard, Ms. Oblonsky? Please, enlighten me." My tone is calm, but this is the calm before the storm.

"I've heard rumors that you own ten virgins who are waiting at your beck and call."

Very good. Pavel's gossip has reached the right outlets then.

"And when they're no longer virgins, you dispose of them, only to replace them with two more."

Well, this is a little farfetched. But, I suppose, why allow the truth to get in the way of a good story?

Gripping the cane, I ponder her admission. "I don't suppose you'd fit the bill then, would you? I mean, you came in here, far from portraying yourself as a virgin. Am I right?"

She nods, guiltily.

"Is that why you brought that abomination in here?" I ask, gesturing to the painting under her arm.

Once again, she nods.

"You knew I'd hate it, and in turn, I'd punish you for your ill taste?"

She blushes, but nothing about this woman is bashful.

Nina is boring me. But to be fair, everyone does. There is no challenge. They all submit, but I don't want submission. I want to be pushed until I can no longer stand it. But I have a role to play.

Clucking my tongue, I decide to put an end to this spectacle because I need to prepare for tonight's gathering. "Very well. Who am I to deny punishment? Lift your dress. Let me see if you blush all over."

She suddenly appears confused. Was she expecting me to fall to my knees, duped by her ploy to get me hard? All she's done is put me to sleep.

When she realizes I'm serious, she lowers the painting onto the floor and suggestively draws up the hem of her dress. This show of hers grates on my nerves, but I feign interest in the grand reveal. Focusing on her bare пизда, I wonder if it'll stir a response in me.

It doesn't.

I could be offered all the pussy in the world, and it wouldn't make a difference. I am indifferent to everything. Since Ella left my side, everything has lost its flavor. I want, I crave only one drug and knowing she'll be here in mere hours has my cock hardening.

Nina believes this response is elicited by her and smirks. Just as she attempts to strip, I shake my head.

"I've seen enough. You may leave."

She freezes, clearly confused by my change of heart. But what she doesn't understand is that I don't have one of those. A heart, that is.

"Aleksei—" She falters, realizing her mistake.

"Did I give you permission to address me this way?" I ask bluntly. "My friends call me by my first name, and last I checked, we are not friends. You're merely a warm body to pass the time, and that is something I cannot spare, seeing as I need to find another interior decorator. Now get out."

"You're a real Мудак, you know that?" she cries, frantically pulling down her dress and retrieving her god-awful painting.

I smirk in response.

She slams the door shut behind her.

That was rather dramatic, but it had the desired effect as she'll no doubt tell anyone who'll listen about what a callous asshole I am. All this is necessary for me to rebuild my reputation, which is imperative to get what I want.

Tonight is the first step.

With Ella's wedding only weeks away, I needed to act fast, so I'm hosting a gathering at my home. Some call it a housewarming, but I call it strategy because I've invited anyone of importance, and that includes Santino Macrillo and his sons.

Someone who has regained their throne is expected to do this, so it won't raise any suspicions. No doubt, the tension will be thick as we're all finding our footing with each other. But as far as I'm concerned, I'm unrivaled because any challenge will be met with me cutting off their heads.

Hobbling over to my desk, I take a seat and decide to call Mother Superior to let her know how Irina is settling in.

When I asked for permission to adopt Irina, Mother Superior was apprehensive. I was the reason she was kidnapped in the first place. I was also the reason the orphanage belonged to a sociopath for a moment in time.

But with Serg dead, the signed deed died with him, and it was as if it never existed. Sloppy work on Serg's behalf as he didn't even have a backup plan. But I didn't expect anything less from that worthless piece of shit.

His mutilated corpse is my wallpaper on my computer. Far more creative than any artwork Ms. Oblonsky could ever present me.

Dialing Mother Superior, I smile when she answers. "Hello, Aleksei. How are you?"

My injuries are healing, but I'm still not comfortable

visiting the orphanage looking the way I do. Irina is accustomed to seeing my fading bruising, but I don't want to frighten the other children. Or Mother Superior.

"I'm well. I wanted to call to let you know I've found a wonderful au pair for Irina. She's from France. Her name is Celine. They bonded instantly." I decide to omit the fact Celine was the twenty-third candidate I interviewed for the position.

I've been very selective about who I chose for the job, but I'll have nothing but the best for Irina. How were they supposed to teach Irina English and Russian if their resume was full of grammatical errors?

Celine's kind and caring nature is what Irina needs.

"How wonderful," Mother Superior says. "I'm so pleased. How is Irina?"

"She seems to be settling in well. She hasn't quite grasped the concept that her room is hers. She believes she'll need to share one day soon."

Mother Superior chuckles. "I bet you've spoiled her."

Thinking about her pink bedroom and abundant toys, I smile. "Not nearly enough. You must come visit."

"I'd love to."

Clearing my throat, I decide to cut to the chase. "I know you said there was no paperwork on Irina, but I'm desperately trying to uncover her roots. Is there anything you can remember that may help?"

"I don't know what to tell you. All she came here with were the tattered clothes on her back. I have some photos I can email to you. Maybe you'll see something that I didn't?"

"Yes, that would be very helpful. Was a…complete physical examination done?" This is the nice way of asking if the doctors looked her over to detect any sign of sexual abuse.

"I will send everything I have to you," she says. I don't know why she's avoided the question, but it suddenly makes me nervous.

"Okay, thank you. Your attorney has had no issues with the deed?"

"No. Everything has returned to normal. Well, as normal as it can be after—" She doesn't continue, but I know what she was going to say.

After Sister Yali was slain.

This will always divide us because no number of apologies and no sum of money will ever be enough to excuse what I allowed to happen.

"Wonderful. I will call soon."

"Okay and please remember, the orphanage will always be your home."

A lump forms in my throat, and I quickly say my goodbyes before hanging up.

Taking a breath, I pull myself together. Mother Superior has every right never to speak to me again, but her kindness always has me feeling so unworthy of it, and that's because I am.

A knock on the door thankfully diverts my attention.

"Enter."

Pavel appears, looking at the blank space on my wall. "I take it you didn't appreciate Ms. Oblonsky's taste in art?"

Scoffing, I lean back in my leather chair. "Just add her to

the ever-growing list of disgruntled individuals who will work in our favor."

Pavel nods. "Very true. The more people who hate you, the better for us. Speaking of…are you prepared for tonight? One hundred and eighty-nine RSVPs came in."

"There is only one I'm concerned about," I reply, cracking my knuckles.

"You must take this slow, Aleksei. We are in favor with Santo, and therefore, we have the upper hand. You can't allow your emotions to cloud that. We need to be smart about this."

He's right. Until I can speak to Ella, I don't know what I'm dealing with. I need to know all the circumstances before I act, and tonight will allow this.

"What of Zoya?" I ask, needing a change of pace.

My mother is still MIA, which is troubling. She is far more unstable than I thought. On her own, she'll be looking for someone to support her, and I have a sneaking suspicion that person will be me.

With Serg gone, she needs another ride. But that won't be me.

"Nothing yet. Let us hope she'll find some poor asshole to torment and leave us be."

We both know that won't happen.

"I suppose I need to prepare for this evening. Have you spoken to the women?"

Pavel nods. "They'd much prefer it if you were the one who addressed them, seeing as you're supposed to be their master."

The thought sickens me, but it's a necessary evil to ensure

I stay on top.

Willow was able to acquire three women who had fallen on hard times. They were living in squalor while working at some strip club. She promised them a roof over their heads, a wage for their troubles, and food. She detailed what was expected of them, and that they were to submit to me because I was their master.

They needed to believe it. Otherwise, this plan wouldn't work.

When they agreed, she brought them here.

I've seen them a handful of times, but in all honesty, I have no interest in them.

Their beauty is unquestionable, but they're merely a means to an end. That's all. However, I know Pavel is right.

Tonight is their first real test.

No doubt, my guests will expect them to behave like trained circus animals. With me as their ringmaster.

"Fine. I'll go see them now."

"Don't sound so beaten up about it. Most men would be envious of your circumstances. Three beautiful women, waiting for your command."

"I'm not most men," I reply, standing. "Is everything organized?"

Pavel nods. "Yes. Security will be tight. All guests are to relinquish their weapons. If they refuse, they will not gain entry. We still can't be too sure who's friend and who's foe. However, we want everyone to feel welcome.

"Everyone on the guest list has been invited because they're useful to us. We need all of them on our side."

This already sounds painful.

"Very well. I'll see you later." Hobbling past him, I don't bother to tell him how much I appreciate his loyalty because he doesn't want praise. He has settled into his "old" role with ease and so has Max. Saint is well and does what he wants, which is fine by me.

Once out in the long corridor, I commence my walk toward the women's quarters. This mansion houses twelve bedrooms, more than enough for everyone to have their own. I've kept them away from Irina because I wish to shelter her as much as I can.

Celine has just moved in, which gives me some peace of mind. But Irina is smart, so sooner or later, she'll understand our lifestyle is far from normal.

The elaborate marbled staircase is my worst enemy, and I climb each step painfully slow. There is no element of surprise with this cane. Once I'm at the top, I take a moment to absorb everything.

The crystal chandelier is the centerpiece of the grand hallway. Multiple corridors lead off to the bedrooms and small living areas, but this communal space always takes my breath away. Denka Orlov's famous piano sits in the corner, a reminder of what happens to those who don't play by the rules.

Taking a left, I make my way toward the bedrooms. My bedroom is at the other end of the house—so is Irina's—but the hallway is almost a carbon copy of the east wing.

I raise my hand, about to knock, but then I realize masters don't knock.

Composing myself, I slip my mask into place and play the role I'm destined for. Opening the door, I'm surprised to see all three women within the one bedroom. They're sitting on the large canopy bed, the sheer gold curtains providing them some cover.

They stop talking when I enter.

Willow has taught them well.

Closing the door behind me, I enter the room at a leisurely pace. They quickly spring from the bed and kneel at the foot of it, eyes downcast.

This should please me, but it doesn't. All I wish is for them to leave.

However, if they don't believe the façade, they'll become a liability as the truth would ruin me. So I forget who I am and remember who I once was.

"What a delightful sight. I am most pleased."

The women are beautiful. Willow has chosen well.

I come to rest in front of the first woman. The strawberry blonde. I've forgotten her name. "Hello, персик."

She nods slowly, knowing not to speak unless given permission. Willow was once the pupil, but now, she's the teacher.

"You may address me."

She lifts her chin, her porcelain skin glowing under the lights. There is an innocence about her that has me fearful for her as the vultures will want to pick her apart. "Thank you, мастер. I'm here to serve you."

Swallowing down the bile, I nod my approval and move on to the next woman with hair as black as night. Her name is

Jada. I only remember this because her eyes are a lovely shade of jade.

"Are you well, Jada?"

She doesn't speak and remains submissive, which annoys me beyond words. This is so exhausting. At this rate, our conversation should be done come midnight. I don't know how I once took pleasure from this way of life.

I suppose conversing was not high on the agenda however.

"You can speak."

Jada raises her eyes and smiles shyly. "I'm good, мастер. Thank you for all that you've done."

Submissive zombies. That's the only way I can describe what I'm seeing. I would do anything for one of them to disobey me, but they won't.

I focus my attention on the last woman. Again, I cannot remember her name. "What is your name? Please answer me," I add, wishing for this exchange to be over with soon.

"Yuna, but you may call me whatever you wish," she replies softly, meeting my eyes. Her long dark hair is braided, drawing attention to her stunning cheekbones and pink lips.

Out of the three women, I feel Yuna has the most gall.

They're wearing matching sheer white gowns. I know they're accustomed to wearing much less at their previous job, but I still wonder if they'd like to wear something else. But I cannot offer them this option because in this world, a submissive is to act and dress a certain way.

These rules don't apply to Willow, though, because she isn't my submissive. To the outside world, she's my lover. Mine and Saint's.

I feel sickened by this thought.

Ella will see this, and I can only imagine how it'll affect her. She already believes I chose Willow over her, and tonight will only confirm this, which is why I need to get her alone as soon as possible.

I need to explain everything, and so does she, and once we're done catching up, I will tear the clothes from her luscious body and feast on her for a week.

Just the thought of it has me aching in my pants.

"Shall I suck your cock?" says Yuna. Looking up at me, she awaits my command.

Cupping her chin, I run my thumb over her bottom lip. "Thank you, Yuna, but no. I need to get ready for tonight's festivities."

She nods.

Bidding the ladies farewell, I exit their room, inhaling deeply as I close the door. How I've changed. In the past, I wouldn't have thought twice about exploiting these women however I pleased. But now, all I want is to enjoy a neat scotch in silence.

I can't be in this mindset tonight. To regain the respect of my "peers," I have to be the man I once was.

Let the games begin.

I've decided against the tie.

My navy suit is made from the finest material and lined

with elegant blue silk. I wear a white shirt with two buttons undone so my thin gold chain is on show.

My hair is slicked back. The longer strands emphasize the shorter sides.

Adjusting my cuff links, I opt for no jacket as it's too formal. This is supposed to be a party, after all. My gold pocket watch sits snugly in my vest pocket with the chain hanging loose, single Albert style.

I don't need to look into the mirror to know I look good. I paid my personal Italian tailor thousands of dollars to ensure it.

But this is all for show.

All I care about is seeing Ella and finding out what the hell is going on. With no time like the present, I reach for my cane and stroll out of my bedroom leisurely. The string quartet sounds delightful; a great choice to drown out the bothersome voices of my guests.

Irina is asleep, and I've asked Celine to stay with her in case she gets startled in the middle of the night. She tends to wander, which cannot happen tonight because I'm unsure of what the night will bring.

Focusing ahead, I see what can only be described as a vision. Willow waits for me at the top of the stairs with her back turned. Her red ball gown hugs her frame beautifully. She'd tied her long hair into an elegant twist, allowing one to gaze upon her graceful neck.

Saint stands by her side. He also looks wonderful in an all-black suit, shirt included. I'm not ashamed to acknowledge the beauty in both sexes, and both Saint and Willow are all class. He turns when he hears my cane stab at the carpet.

I understand he is far from impressed, but I will not allow anything to happen to Willow. I will kill every single one of these assholes before any harm comes to her—consequences be damned. When she turns, I'm left utterly speechless.

Her glamorous makeup draws attention to her stunning blue eyes and supple pink lips. I know I'm seconds away from being punched in the jaw by Saint, but I can't take my eyes off her.

"You look absolutely exceptional," I say, coming to a stop a few feet away.

"Thank you. You still know my size," she replies, running her hands down her ruffled skirt. She's referring to a time when the clothes she wore were ones I bought for her.

"It's something I'll never forget." I can't hide my nostalgia.

Saint rolls his eyes, which has me smirking. To have this weird harmony between us is awfully strange. I never thought we could ever co-exist this way. But here we are…

"You also look remarkable, Saint."

He raises his eyes to the heavens once again. "Let's get tonight over with. My asshole quota has already been met."

I couldn't agree more.

Offering my arm to Willow, she loops hers through mine and pulls her shoulders back as she gets into character. Saint flanks my other side.

"You never leave my side. If you must, stay with Saint," I instruct softly, not wanting anyone to overhear even though we're alone up here. "When I find Ella, I'm going to get her alone. I won't have much time. So please stay alert."

Both Saint and Willow nod.

Inhaling deeply, I focus on the task at hand, and that's finding Ella. No one can know of my plans, so I stand tall, basking in the wealth surrounding me because it feeds the narcissist I need to be.

With our first steps, Willow, Saint, and I descend the staircase, unhurried. We are the guests of honor, after all. Halfway down, I'm able to see my home filled to the brim with familiar faces. Not much has changed. They still look like the greedy sociopaths I grew to tolerate.

My tolerance isn't what it once was because I already want to kick everyone out. But I plaster my smile on my face, appearing overjoyed that my old associates are here.

"Here he is," says Charles Muller, an art dealer to the outside world, but in reality, he exports high quality cocaine across the globe inside his "works of art."

His services are quite genius, and he's discreet, which is why he's here. I need a new contact, seeing as Raul is off the cards, and my old supplier, Adam, is nowhere to be found. I thought once Serg was dead, he'd come out of hiding, knowing I wouldn't do business with Raul.

But alas, no Adam so therefore, no supply.

I suppose I could go into legal dealings and leave the drug world behind. But drugs are going to exist with or without me, so I'd rather it be with me because I feel most at home here.

"Hello, Charles. Good of you to come." I don't extend my hand because I will not let Willow go.

Charles nods with a smile. "I wouldn't have missed this

for the world. It's good to see you where you belong. Your home is extraordinary."

"Thank you. It's still a work in progress, but it's coming along nicely. Maybe we could discuss some artwork when you're free? I need someone with a good eye."

Charles appears overjoyed. "Yes, this sounds wonderful. I'll organize a date at your earliest convenience."

"Excellent. I look forward to it. Enjoy the festivities." I excuse myself because I can't tolerate playing nice for too long. I need to find Ella.

Willow holds on tight and stays silent, which is what's expected. To the outside world, she's on my arm to look pretty, and that's all. Saint is there as reassurance, and when my guests turn to look at us with interest, it seems the point has been made.

I work the room, greeting my guests and making small talk. A palpable tension hangs heavy in the air as not that long ago, I was seen as nothing but the enemy, a traitor. These putrid human beings easily discarded me, but now that I'm back on top, they want to pretend it never happened.

I can play the game, but I'll never forget how I was replaced without a second thought. There is no loyalty between us.

As we walk into the ballroom, I scan my surroundings, desperate to find Ella, but she's not here. Pavel walks over, and the stern look on his face alerts me to the fact something is wrong.

"She's not here," he whispers under his breath.

Inhaling sharply, I keep it together because we're on display. "All of them?"

Pavel shakes his head. "Santo is here. That's all."

Willow squeezes my arm gently, reassuring me. But there is only one person I need reassurance from, and it seems she's not here.

"Where is he?"

Pavel pulls his lips into a thin line, warning me not to make a scene. "Outside having a cigar."

Without thought, I let Willow go and silently order Saint to watch over her. This room is filled with circling vultures as they're all intrigued with the American beauty who was able to bring a leader to his knees.

They want to know why she's back and what role she plays in my life. As for Saint, their curiosity is sated because they're still afraid of him. The fact no one will look him in the eye confirms this.

Following Pavel, I attempt to act semi normal and not close to boiling point as people commend me on what a fine party this is. Or how delicious the caviar dip is. I'm half listening to their nonsense because none of it matters.

The only one that matters isn't here.

Stepping out onto the marbled terrace, I see Santo propped up against the balustrade, laughing at something Austin Bailey just said.

Both men have a taste in high-powered weaponry. However, Austin is a little fish compared to Santo, which gives me an idea. I'll revisit this later because now, I need to rein in the urge of throwing a smug Santo over the marbled banister.

"Gentlemen," I say with a forced smile. "Grand of you to attend."

Santo examines me closely. The last he saw me, I was straddling the line between the living and the dead. Thanks to Larisa's potions, my external bruising has faded. One is oblivious to how dire things were unless they saw it with their own two eyes as Santo did.

I left him with more questions than answers as he believed I would have been a little more grateful for him saving my life. But him saving me meant Ella was in danger. She still is.

Austin extends his hand, which I shake firmly. Thus far, no one has commented on my cane. It doesn't surprise me that Santo is the first one.

"I like this look," he says, laughing as though we're friends. "Very dashing."

We shake hands, and it takes all my willpower not to break his. "It serves many purposes," I cryptically reply. "I'm so pleased you could come. Where are the boys? I haven't seen them in so long."

I try to keep my tone casual.

Santo takes a pull of his cigar. "Those boys don't like to share," he replies with an arrogant smirk while I barely hold back the urge to elbow him in the face. "When I left home, they were arguing over who was going to play with the new… toy. So I'm unsure if they'll come. Knowing my sons, they'll end up making a mess."

I. Am. Going. To. Kill. Him.

Advancing, I'm only stopped because Pavel yanks on the back of my vest to halt my attack.

"Oh, what a shame. I was looking forward to catching up with them," Pavel says quickly, speaking for me because words have escaped me.

All I can do is glare at Santo, envisioning all the ways I'm going to kill him. He seems unaware of my rage.

The "toy" he speaks of is Ella. He flippantly refers to her like some plaything. I pale at the thought. I thought it was merely him and Frank I was up against. But it appears all the Macrillo men are involved.

Bile rises, and I press my fist over my lips to stop myself from being sick.

"Those boys are wild. They may turn up later. We'll see."

That's where he's wrong. If I don't see Ella tonight, I'll be storming Santo's house and taking back what is mine. I refuse to believe she enjoys being at the Macrillos' disposal. The things they would do to her…

"Where is this American beauty I've heard so much about?" Santo asks with a devilish smirk. "The room is rife with gossip. But no one has the balls to ask you what the arrangement is. Only you could pull something like this off."

"Like what?" I question firmly.

My defenses are in place because I don't like where he's going with this.

"Well, welcome the woman who ruined you back into your life and expect others to accept her. No one else would do this because they wouldn't have let her live. But not you. You're a big softie deep down, it seems."

"Far from it," I counter sharply.

Santo is testing me. He's the only person who has the guts to do so.

I knew my peers wouldn't be too accepting of Willow's

return as I parade her around like a show pony, revealing just how deeply I care for her. This act exhibits to everyone that she was far more than a submissive to me.

Now that she's back, they want to know what's changed because being vulnerable, which is what Willow made me, is seen as a weakness. Being weak opens me up to challenge, as some may not deem me fit for the role of ruler.

I need to put this belief to bed immediately.

"She knows her place. As do all my women."

Santo cocks his head, not convinced. "We shall see. I mean, the fact you refer to them as *women* intrigues me."

"How so?"

"They are merely here for our amusement. When you start identifying with them, it gives them ideas," he states with disgust.

Pavel subtly shakes his head, a silent warning not to act on impulse and throw this chauvinist over the railing. But how dare he come here and spew such deplorable views?

"What ideas?" I ask, feigning interest because a small crowd has formed.

"That their opinion matters," Santo replies without pause. "They're a warm body, and that's all. If you treat them as anything else, they believe they matter and that they're special. But they're not. Every hole is a goal, my friend. Some tighter, warmer, wetter, and sweeter than others, but in the end, there is always something better."

I stare, open-mouthed, not believing the filth I've just heard.

The onlookers snicker in concord, in the belief that what

Santo just said holds merit. They slap him on the back while I envision slapping his face against the marbled floor.

If these are his beliefs, then what has he done with Ella? She is seen as less than nothing, and I hate to imagine what she's endured since she also betrayed Santo.

I need to get her away from him without delay.

"I suppose that's where you and I differ," I say, silencing the boys club. "I value loyalty. And respect. It's imperative to have. One can easily fake it, but in the end, those with true emotions will fight with you and for you until the very end. You may see them as…easily replaced playthings, but I'm a collector of fine things. But kudos to you for not having any standards."

Santo's cocky demeanor soon deflates as I just insulted him to his face.

I dare him to retaliate because if he disrespects me in my home, I'll make an example out of him. I hope that he does.

But he doesn't.

He backs down, sensing his loss.

The laughter of others soon dies down when they realize they are at risk of being hurt and hurt really bad.

"Now, if anyone else has anything further to comment about who I allow to stand by my side, then speak now."

Eyes are quick to avert.

"Didn't think so," I quip. "And Santo, speaking of respect. I expect your sons to be in attendance. Call them."

With that, I turn on my heel, refusing to waste any more time on these vile humans.

Pavel walks by my side, and to anyone else, they'd think he

was stone-faced. But not to me. His slanted smirk highlights how he enjoyed the show.

"I have an idea," I whisper behind my staged smile.

Pavel waits for me to continue.

"This won't work with my old allies. They'll only see me as a failure, they *do*, and it'll only be a matter of time before someone challenges me for the top spot."

"What do you propose then?" Pavel asks, reaching for two glasses of French champagne from the silver tray held by a server.

He offers one to me, which is the perfect guise for me to conceal my plans as I raise the glass to my lips, and reveal, "We start from scratch. Out with the old. In with the new." And with that, the champagne trickles down my throat, the bubbles colliding with the excitement brewing within my stomach.

Pavel doesn't drink. He simply looks at me as though I've gone mad.

I suppose that's a fair response, seeing as I just proposed we kill half of Russia's underworld. But it's the only way.

Austin is little league because of people like Santo. But if I eliminate the competition, he will be grateful and trustworthy for my troubles, and I'll have a loyal ally for life. It's rather genius.

"You're mad," Pavel says from behind the rim of his glass.

I shrug, not bothering to argue because the point is moot.

This *is* insane, but there simply is no other way. I cannot have dealings with my old colleagues because they know too much. They've seen me at my worse, and with such an unforgiving audience, they won't forget.

They'll only see my hardships as failures and weaknesses, and will never respect me as they once did.

They may prefer me over Serg, but give it time, and others will favor someone else over me. Here, we sit on a throne of lies. The fake smiles, the staged laughs…it's all a power play as we sniff out the weak. I must pick them off before they strike first.

I invited those who matter, but that will soon be past tense as my interest now lies with the underdogs. Their loyalty will know no bounds when I offer them the world…on a silver platter.

We're all playing nice, but it's time to throw a wolf in among the chickens. And the first person to be sacrificed is Santino Macrillo.

Willow and Saint are by my side in an instant. "Everything okay?"

Nodding happily, I grin. "Yes. Everything is rather glorious. It's time Russia has a facelift."

Saint's eyebrows shoot up in interest. "You talking about taking out the trash?"

When Santo enters the ballroom with his feathers ruffled, I laugh. "The trash is about to take itself out."

Willow huddles closer to Saint, but she has nothing to fear. This is my world, and I only have one rule—kill anyone who stands in my way.

I spend the next two hours liaising with my new confidants, much to the distaste of my "peers." They don't ask how Willow is because they don't care. She is just another woman to them. They're uninterested in my past because I'm their future. Their meal ticket.

As I'm speaking with Concetta Capri, Pavel whispers in my ear that it's time to make a speech. Willow and Saint stand behind me.

Concetta comes from old Italian money. Her family's business dealings in real estate are worth a small fortune. However, their competition is Santo's friend, who sold me this house. They'd never challenge him because once you're in with the Macrillos, no one dares to question their place.

But that'll soon change.

"Please excuse me, Concetta. It seems I have an audience to address." I gesture for Saint and Willow to follow.

Concetta smiles happily, pleased that someone gave her the time of day. You see, that's how this hierarchy works.

On the outer, people like Concetta would hold importance, but in here, they're merely to make up numbers. The affluent look down their noses at them because they're not rich enough.

The ballroom is filled to capacity, but it's only one face I yearn to see. Why isn't she here?

Has harm come to her? Is she…?

Shaking my head, I can't fathom such a dire outcome for her. My heart will not permit it.

Focusing on this trivial nonsense, I make my way toward the feature wall and clear my throat. As heads turn my way, the room falls quiet.

Scanning the room confidently, I ensure each person understands this is my show, and betraying me will result in them paying with their lives.

"Friends," I commence with my arm extended out wide. "Thank you for coming. It feels like old times."

An uncomfortable laughter fills the static.

"But it's not. Things have changed. *I* have changed. There have been whispers that I'm not the same man I once was."

The audience gathered up close soon regret their choice to be up front and shift away. It seems my spectators weren't expecting a speech such as this one.

"And you're right. I'm not. I learned a lot from being exiled," I reveal, and suddenly, you can hear a pin drop. "I learned that a desperate man would do anything in order to survive. I know a lot of rumors are circulating over how I got here. So, let me set the record straight.

"Serg, my half-brother, was able to outsmart me, a fact I'm not proud of. But he was able to do this because all of you believed in him. You were quick to forget about loyalty and sided with whom you thought would prevail. But here we are.

"A smart predator waits, waits for the perfect time to strike. Why settle for one cub when you can eradicate an entire bloodline? Serg was impulsive, he was careless, and that's what got him killed.

"I took great pleasure in torturing him before I fed him his own cock, which he choked on. That's how he expired. I wanted to humiliate him until he took his last strangled breath."

I ensure to keep my eyes locked on every person as I scan the room. I want them to know that they're all Judases. They betrayed me without a second thought.

"Him being in power was always temporary because no one, *no one* can challenge me and win." This is a not so gentle warning. I dare anyone to try.

"I've invited you all here this evening to forget about the past. I forgive each one of you for disposing of me like nothing but trash. I forgive you for believing my half-brother could ever be me. It's water under the bridge."

Nervous glances among my guests reveal my little spiel has gotten to them. Good. I may speak of forgiveness, but this is merely a warning. No one better try to cross me because if they do, they'll suffer the same fate as Serg.

"Today is a brand-new day and a new era for us all. So let's raise our glasses and toast the future."

A waitress passes me a glass of champagne, which I raise high in the air, waiting for the rest of the room to follow. All do, bar one.

Henry Ballou deals in precious jewels. I know for a fact he fed Zoya's addiction for anything shiny. I never liked this asshole, and when he glares at me, arms folded, it appears the feeling is more than mutual. It seems my speech hasn't convinced him as he dares to defy me.

"Henry, you don't have a glass," I say lightly, gesturing

with my chin to the waitress to offer him one, but Henry jars out his hand.

"I don't feel like toasting," he replies bluntly.

Saint is at my back, ready to pounce into action if need be.

"We're at a party." I smirk.

"It suddenly feels like a funeral," he counters, which just irks me more.

"How so?"

Henry curls his lip, refusing to back down. "What I see is a shadow of my former friend. The Aleksei Popov I once knew is dead. In his place is this," he spits, pointing his finger at me in disgust.

"I'm just voicing what no one else has the balls to say. You've lost your nerve. You've grown soft. That whore behind you proves it."

Inhaling deeply, I keep my stance firm, alerting Saint to do the same. We mustn't strike. Not yet.

"It'll only be a matter of time before another pretty face comes along and takes you for a ride, and you'll drag us all down with you. We need a ruler. Someone who isn't afraid to get his hands dirty. Your brother did everything to better this town. He wanted change. He—"

I've heard more than enough.

The masses part as I calmly walk toward an unbending Henry. "Here, I offer you my own glass."

"I said no," he replies, his cheeks blistering red.

Tonguing my cheek, I measure the most appropriate response. It seems Henry missed the memo about what happens to those who challenge me.

With a casual shrug, I smile. "Okay then."

I allow him to gloat for a mere second, thinking he's won, as I down the champagne, and once the glass is empty, I ram it into his eye socket.

People near us yelp, jumping back not to get blood on their furs and couture, but continue watching with frenzied excitement as I continue my assault.

Henry's screams are guttural. I suppose broken glass in one's eyeball is awfully painful, but that doesn't stop me. Once the glass shatters into a million pieces, I use the jagged stem as a weapon and stab Henry in the jugular.

He cups his throat, eye wide as bright red blood gushes through his fingers. He gasps fruitlessly for air. I stand in front of him, unwavering, unmoved, and all I can think about is that he's spraying my brand-new suit with his blood.

He grips my vest with trembling fingers, using me as support when he falters on his feet. I stand motionless, wanting it to be my face he sees as he takes his last breath.

His wheezes sound like a tire deflating. It's rather unpleasant, and I look at my Rolex, bored by the bloodshed. When he finally flops onto his stomach with a wet squelch, I step back and reach into my pocket for my handkerchief.

He twitches for a few minutes before eventually stilling.

Once I've cleaned Henry's blood from my face and hands, I spit on his corpse. "Half-brother, Мудак."

A pool of blood collects around his prone form, so I step over him to avoid soiling my shoes. He's already ruined my suit. I'll have to pay Pavel's laundromat a visit.

Casually pilfering the glass of champagne from a guest's

limp hand, I carry on as though there isn't a dead body behind me. "To the future," I happily say, raising the glass high in the air.

People peer at one another, unsure if this is a joke or not. But they soon recognize this is no stunt, and if they don't drink, they'll end up in a bloody pool like Henry.

Nervously, the room erupts, and sing-songs, "To the future," as they uneasily throw back their drinks.

I smile, meeting Saint's eyes. He raises his own glass with a smirk, voicing his approval at my choice of methods to prove a point. I soon join him, never recalling a champagne ever tasting so sweet, so victorious.

If there were any doubts regarding my "balls," then let this be a lesson to anyone who wishes to question me ever again.

I'd rather rule with respect, but fear is just as good.

As I finish my drink, something strange happens. It's something minor, in light of what just occurred, but the hair on the back of my neck stands on end. I'm aware of everything as I desperately scan my surroundings, not understanding this response.

Nothing seems out of place. My friends are safe. So why can't I stop my heart from racing? My heart didn't miss a beat when I gouged out Henry's eyeball. But now, I can barely breathe.

Someone talks to me, but their voice fades into the abyss because nothing, nothing else matters but...*her*. She stands in the archway, looking confident, looking like royalty in a peacock-colored ball gown while I suddenly feel so unworthy.

She's here...Ella is here, in my home. She isn't a figment

of my imagination, and all I can do is stare at the woman who sacrificed everything to save me.

She must be able to feel the static in the air, the energy that has emanated between us since the first moment we met. I was only half living because only now do I feel alive.

Why won't she look at me?

"Go." Saint nudges me, breaking my trance-like state. I don't bother arguing because my feet lead me before my brain can catch up.

"What about the mess I made?" I say, realizing Henry is still soiling my polished floors.

"I'll take care of it in a moment."

I focus solely on her, refusing to accept she's on the arm of another. *She's just playing a role,* I reason with myself. Look at her, she's miserable. But when she laughs at something Frank murmurs into her ear, my rationale is tested.

Pulling it together, I notice Saint make a beeline for Ella as well. Willow is with Pavel no doubt. She's safe. What is Saint up to?

I soon find out when he approaches Ella, who's eyes widen when she sees him, but her horror transforms to shock when Saint deliberately bumps into a waiter, causing a trayful of drinks to spill down the front of Ella's dress.

Saint disappears as quickly as he appeared. Only Ella and I saw him.

Frank grabs the young man by the collar, scolding him for his clumsiness. But Ella shakes her head, placing her hand on Frank's forearm, saying something I can't hear. Frank begrudgingly lets the man go.

She has control over him? This hardly appears like someone who is held against her will.

I need to find out what the hell is going on.

Ella excuses herself, no doubt in hunt for a bathroom to clean herself up. Frank is about to follow, but Pavel appears, saying something into his ear. He nods, as whatever Pavel said has interested him enough to allow Ella to leave his side and seek the bathroom on her own.

I remain discreet, smiling and laughing at whatever nonsense my guests are saying, ensuring no one recognizes me making a quick beeline for the exit. Pavel and Frank are gone, so hopefully Santo is with them.

Saint stands by the door, hidden in an alcove. "She's gone to the bathroom down the hall."

Nodding my gratitude as this takes the guesswork out of finding which bathroom Ella is in, I quicken my step, blood coursing through me in excitement. I ignore everyone who tries to talk to me because the closer I come to Ella, the more desperate I become.

Turning the corner, I'm relieved to see no one loitering and bang on the bathroom door.

"I won't be a minute," Ella's sweet voice says from behind the door, but I don't have a minute. I've wasted too many, and I don't want to waste a second more.

Thumping loudly, I turn the handle in case she's forgotten to lock it. Of course, she hasn't. I don't want to announce my arrival as I'm frightened she won't open the door.

"Frank, I'll be out in a moment." She thinks her fiancé has come to check on her. So I continue banging as she knows he won't let up.

"What?" she snarls, the door jarring open widely, but when we lock eyes, her anger soon vanishes, as does the noise.

We're no longer a part of this world. We've created our own. Just Ella and me.

She looks so beautiful, but she always has been. She wears her long dark hair down, framing her delicate face. She wears heavy makeup, and I realize I've not seen her with it on before. I have the urge to smear the red lipstick from her lips because this isn't her.

I think of the carefree woman who preferred no shoes and a simple summer dress; *that* is Ella. This version is the one the Macrillos want.

She seems taller, and I realize she's wearing high heels beneath her ruffled skirt. This is all wrong.

Ella senses the shift and hastily attempts to shut the door, but I'm faster and wedge my foot and cane into the doorway, stopping her. She pushes against it, and bless her for trying to outweigh me, but I shove it open, sending her toppling backward.

I dive into the bathroom, slamming the door closed behind me. She backs away, eyes wide, and the action hurts me in ways I never thought possible. But I focus on the task at hand because we're running out of time.

"Come here," I order hoarsely.

She stubbornly shakes her head, which pleases me beyond words. If she won't come to me, I'll go to her because there is no way I'm spending a second longer without her body pressed to mine.

In three large strides, I'm on her, slamming my mouth over hers. She struggles against me, her small fists pummeling against my chest, but she surrenders when I bite her bottom lip, before running my tongue along it.

She tastes and feels like everything I've craved and I can't get enough. Tossing my cane aside, I wrap my fingers around her waist and draw her into my body. Just the smell of her is enough to get me hard. I want to fucking eat her alive.

She moans into my mouth, her tongue circling mine as we fight for dominance. But eventually, she concedes. Bunching up her skirt, I run my hand up her thigh, moaning when I feel the clip holding up her stockings.

She's wearing a lace garter belt, which I plan on using to tie her hands behind her back as I fuck her senseless.

Just as I rub over the outside of her underwear, something completely unacceptable happens. I feel a sharp sting, and not of the good kind because Ella just slapped my cheek, not in passion, but rather, disgust.

"How dare you!" she cries, her chest rising and falling rapidly as she gulps in mouthfuls of air.

"How dare I indeed," I reply with a smirk, elated to see her red lipstick smeared crudely across her mouth. "Hello, красавица."

"Don't call me t-that," she says, a tremble to her voice. "And don't ever kiss me again."

"There was a time when you didn't mind either," I counter, wounded, but I hide behind my wit.

"Well, that time is long gone. I need to go. Frank will be looking for me."

She storms for the doorway, but I sidestep, blocking her exit. "Since when did you become so subservient?"

"Since the man I had feelings for pretty much threw those feelings back in my face as he was still in love with the woman he bought!" she exclaims, furious.

So she still believes I meant what I said? Yet she sacrificed herself for my freedom. However, when she brushes a strand of hair behind her ear and the mammoth diamond on her left hand catches the light, I realize that maybe I've gotten this all wrong.

Maybe she did this for herself.

She doesn't look to be here against her will. Nor does she appear wounded or scared.

A heavy feeling threatens to drag me under. Could it be Ella returned to the Macrillos because she wanted to?

Yes, her returning saved my life and the lives of so many, but what deal did she make for Santo to let her live? He was intent on making her pay, but here she is, looking radiant and weeks away from marrying a monster.

"I don't understand," I say, willing my heart to slow down.

"Don't understand what?" There is a hardness to her, a cruelty which I forced her to become by trying to protect her.

"I never meant any of it, Ella. I was trying to protect you."

"By kissing another woman!" she cries, shaking her head in disgust. "By wanting to become a better man for someone other than me! How is that trying to protect me?"

She's referring to the conversation she overheard. It saddens me she could believe my lies so easily. She really doesn't understand the extent of my feelings for her.

"I kissed Willow to make you leave," I rebuke, angrily tugging at my hair. "It was the only way to keep you safe. Can't you see that?"

"You made me feel worthless."

"I had to," I argue, words suddenly escaping me.

"You didn't have to do anything," she replies. "But that's the thing about you, Alek. You do what you want, when you want, consequences be damned. I was just stupid to believe I ever meant anything to you."

"You do, Ella, for Christ's sake, you do! Stay with me and let me explain everything. I only organized this fucking party so I could see you. I needed to get you away from them."

My argument suddenly falls flat as I expected our reunion to go differently than this. I didn't expect her to look…happy. I thought I'd explain, and she'd understand why I did what I did. But it seems I know nothing at all.

"All of it was a lie," I clarify. "I wanted you to go back to America and forget about me. I wanted you to live a normal, happy life, for what life could I have offered you? I didn't know how to make you leave, so I hurt you, playing on your insecurities. I'm not proud of my choices, but I made them only because I wanted to keep you safe.

"I would have never given you over to Santo, never. This plan wasn't foolproof, but it was the only way I could save everyone. I was planning on sacrificing myself by willingly siding with Raul to make amends for the error of my ways.

"And I was okay with dying as long as I knew you and the people I care about were safe. But then you did something beyond brave."

"*If* what you say is true, then that was *my* choice to make, not yours," she says, slapping over her heart. "I'm sure you trusted Willow enough to let her in on your plan. But with me, I'll never compare to her because you see me as weak, as something you need to protect because I apparently need protecting!

"But who saved your ass, Alek? Was it Willow? Or was it me?"

Lowering my eyes, I nod, feeling utterly ashamed. She's right. "In hindsight, I would have done things so differently. I see that now."

"Well, that's the thing about hindsight. It's pretty fucking useless," she snaps, pulling back her shoulders. "Because in hindsight, I should have never allowed myself to be used by you. Now move. Frank will be looking for me."

"You're still going back to him after everything I just told you?" I exclaim, incredulous. "I never meant anything I said to Willow, but to you, Ella, I meant every word. Every time we touched, that was real.

"You stirred. You *stir*...feelings in me I've never felt before."

"How can I believe you?" she replies, deflated.

And that's the problem—all she has is my word, which apparently isn't good enough because I fooled her once. She won't allow it to happen again.

"Why did you offer yourself to Santo, if you feel nothing for me?"

She's unbending as she hacks into my heart, declaring, "I didn't do it for you...I did it for Irina, the kids, and Mother

Superior. They didn't deserve to be brought into this mess."

I hold my breath, hoping she doesn't say what I know she will.

"But more importantly, I did it for me. At least I know where I stand with Frank, with Santo, but with you…I'll always be guessing if I'm enough."

"Ella!" I cry out, exasperated. "Listen to me. You *are* enough. You're more than I deserve."

I'm prepared to fall to my knees and beg she forgive me for making her feel anything but a queen. But it's too late.

"You're right," she states, staring me down. "I *am* more than you deserve. We're done. You easily discarded me. I don't care what your motives were because we could have worked together. But you chose to lie to me, to hurt me in ways unimaginable. I won't be second best."

"You aren't!" I grip her forearm, pleading she believes me, but she doesn't.

Ripping from my hold, she curls her lip. "Well, you are. I thought I wanted a future with you, but I don't."

Words escape me.

"I have nothing waiting for me back in America. Here, I know my place, and I'm okay with it. Frank loved me once. We can find that love again."

"Do you realize how desperate, how pathetic that makes you sound?" I question, furious she'd allow herself to be used this way. "You're merely a plaything for the Macrillos!"

"I'm pathetic?" she scoffs. "Isn't that a little hypocritical, considering you're in love with someone you bought to be your sex slave!"

She isn't holding back. I deserve this. But it still hurts.

"And what was I to you?" she poses, challenging me to express my feelings. "When you didn't know who I was, when you thought I was Sister Arabella, wasn't I just another conquest? At least I know where I stand with them."

She's daring me to argue, and yes, at first, she was. But not now. Now I…I what? I love her? Is that what this feeling digging a hole through my chest is called?

"If you believe that, then we're really done." I wipe my mouth with the back of my hand, removing her lipstick-stained kisses as they're nothing but lies.

"Glad we can agree on something. Tell Willow and Saint I said hi." She's seen them both by my side while she's on the outer. No wonder she won't believe me. It always seems I do choose them over her.

I look at this woman, the woman who was filled with love and self-sacrifice and no longer see her. In her place, I see the shell of the person I've ruined beyond repair. She is allowing herself to be used because that's what she believes she deserves.

"You want him? You want *them* and not me?" I ask, needing her to say it. I know Santo only agreed to let her live if she gave him something in return.

She pauses, working her bottom lip, and I think maybe, just maybe she'll tell me this is all a bad dream. But this is real life, a life I must learn to live again.

"Yes, I do. You're a liar. And a murderer. You're a bad man. And I won't fall for your lies like everyone else you have fooled. You're nothing but an insecure asshole with mommy issues. You want to show the world you're big and strong, but you're not. You're weak. And you're pining after someone who will *never* love you. How can she? You ruined her life the moment you bought her like nothing but chattel.

"You make me sick. I don't want you. And I never will."

The fight in me simmers because nothing is worth fighting for anymore.

She willingly went to Santo because I broke her heart. I broke her. She may have saved me, but her motives weren't entirely selfless. She did this for herself too. Better to be "loved" by someone, than not be loved at all. But Santo and Frank don't love her. They merely see her as their property, and she allows it.

Fearful I'm about to be sick, I retrieve my cane and limp out the door. If this is what caring for someone entails, I want out.

CHAPTER THREE

Ella

I stand tall and unbending until Alek's footsteps eventually fade into nothingness. The moment he's gone, I lock the door and slide down it, allowing myself to crumple.

Drawing my knees to my chest, I hug them tight, silently crying tears I fought so hard to keep back. Hurting Alek was the only way to keep him safe, which is ironic, considering that is what he did for me. But the tables have turned, and now, I must protect him.

It saddens me that he believed my lies so readily, but didn't I do the same?

I believed he kissed Willow because he wanted to, that he wanted her more than me, which is why I decided to hand myself over to Santo. If he cared for Willow, then I would do anything to save her, and the people he loved dearly.

That's how much he means to me.

Even though I believed he didn't want me, I happily

walked up to Santo's door and gave him what he wanted. I knew what that meant for me, and I was okay with that. But then I soon discovered that things weren't as they seemed.

The Macrillos were only siding with Alek and helping him with Serg because they wanted to gain Alek's trust, hoping he'd help them. To the outside world, The Macrillos are untouchable, but on the inside, it's a completely different story.

The family is on the cusp of being bankrupt and because of this, even though they once only dealt in weaponry, Santo decided to try his hand in drug distribution as well, but Serg was in the way. Santo had the Italian mafia helping him with grade A drugs, but Serg had taken over Russia.

No one would buy from Santo, no matter how pure his product was. So Santo needed to get rid of the competition. Alek and he wanted the same thing, but Alek just didn't know it.

Serg didn't want to get his hands dirty, seeing as Serg was respected and Alek wasn't by most. He cut a deal with Alek, so he could put the blame on Alek for Serg's death if anything went wrong. His plan was for Alek to kill Serg so he could manipulate Alek into going into business together.

Alek's reputation is still notorious, regardless of what he's done. And Santo needs that.

He may have most fooled, but people are starting to talk, and the Macrillo name is losing face. Santo needs a partner in crime, and what better person than the ruthless Alek who just gouged out the eyeball of one of his peers without breaking a sweat.

He needs Alek's name, but more importantly, he needs Alek's knowledge to help him build this new empire, and then once he's back on top, he'll kill Alek, as there is room for only one leader. He needs Alek to watch and learn.

Serg would never go into business with Santo, but Alek was desperate and needed help, which is why Santo went to Alek with a hidden agenda. He knew Alek had ties to the orphanage and that I was hiding out there.

But that wasn't the only reason he asked Alek to help him. He needed Serg gone to implement his plan. And once Serg was disposed of, they'd go after Raul so the drugs from the Italian mafia were the only ones being distributed in Russia.

This would encourage Alek to believe he and Santo were allies, but in reality, he would be biding his time, waiting to take out Alek and rule Russia.

Santo can't do it alone. He has no idea about drug dealings in Russia, but Alek does, and he plans to exploit that. He'll learn from Alek, only to discard him once he's done.

And I can't allow that to happen.

I only know about this plan because Santo's feelings for me stem deeper than I thought. So deep, he's delusional to the truth that I hate him.

I offered myself over to him, certain he'd kill me for my betrayal, but he did the complete opposite. He kissed me. He told me he missed me and that he wanted me to be his mistress. Of course, I refused, but when he locked me in the basement and had one of his men torture me until I couldn't stand it anymore, I surrendered.

My plan was to escape as soon as I saw an out. I just

wanted the pain to end.

However, drunk, Santo came to me, apologizing for his brutality, revealing his grand plan and what he intended to do to Alek. He shared all this, thinking I would somehow be impressed, and he could win my love by killing the man who found me and "gave" me to Santo.

I told Santo that Alek had forced me to surrender myself to Santo, promising a world of pain if I didn't. And Santo believed me. He thought he had Alek fooled, that their partnership is for Alek's benefit as well as his. But the truth is, I'm fooling them both.

Santo forgot about his confession about Alek, but I hadn't. So I agreed to become his mistress and the only way to do that is to marry Frank. Mila can't know about this arrangement. She would never allow her youngest son's former fiancée to be the mistress of her husband.

The scandal would ruin them.

So this is the only solution for me to be involved with the Macrillo family without suspicion. I marry Frank and entertain his father behind his back.

Tears roll down my cheeks because I'm disgusted that to prove my loyalty to both men, I've had to subject myself to their devious tastes. I've flirted with both and allowed them to touch me, kiss me, and I hate myself for it. But the moment I saw Alek tonight, I pushed aside my regret because I'll do anything to save the man I love.

And I do. I love Alek so much that I can scarcely breathe at times. So this is a small sacrifice I'm willing to make because this is only temporary.

I could have told Alek the truth, but his life, all our lives are in danger if we don't have eyes on the inside. If I learned anything from this entire experience, it's that being in the inner circle and playing both sides is a winning formula.

That's how Serg was able to trick Alek. He had Renata. And now, Alek has me.

I'll learn everything there is about the mafia, about who Santo has ties with, and when I have enough information, I'll tell Alek. Now, all I have is the drunken confession of an old fool. I need proof. And I need to earn the Macrillos trust because I plan on killing every last motherfucking one of them.

If I tell Alek now, what happens? He has no real allies. Santo is stronger than him. He has more influence. Alek needs to reinstate his position back on top so he's unstoppable. Right now, he's a sitting duck. Henry's defiance proves this.

Alek has four friends, four loyal friends who will lay down their lives for him, but it's not enough. They can't win against Santo. Not now. But in time, they will.

As utterly insane as this sounds, Alek needs Santo. Santo will take out Raul because he needs him out of the picture. Alek can't do that on his own. He tried, and he almost lost his life. He needs allies, and Santo is that man.

Santo thinks he's using Alek, but I'm using Santo to help Alek. It's a Machiavellian plan, but it'll work. Until I have everything I need to overthrow the Macrillos, I have to play this game. And Alek will believe me, he'll believe that I don't want him anymore because he doesn't believe himself worthy of love.

He sees himself in the worst possible light when, in reality, he's the most selfless, most honorable man I've ever met. What he does to protect the people he loves proves this. He doesn't see his worth because when he looks into the mirror, all he sees is the man he once was.

It was nice to hear him confirm what I always knew to be true. I just needed to see it for myself. I was riddled with jealousy when he kissed Willow, and it clouded my judgment. But I always knew Alek was trying to push me away to save me.

I thought I was doing the same by handing myself over to Santo. I just didn't realize Alek devised a plan with Raul. If I did, I would have insisted Santo find Alek earlier. He was lucky to get there in time. Santo saved Alek's life, only with intent to steal it once he's milked him for his worth.

This plan is far from perfect, but until I can think of something else, it'll have to do. Besides, if I run now, I'll be running for the rest of my life. And Alek's life will forever be in danger. I knew there would be consequences when I handed myself over to Santo. And now, I must deal with them.

Now that I know Saint and Willow are still here, I could always talk to Saint. But we hardly left on good terms. I believed his world was trying to steal mine. Besides, they're Alek's friends. Not mine. I only have myself to ensure this plan succeeds.

With my pointer and middle finger, I gently touch over my lips as Alek's taste lingers on my mouth. His kisses are nothing I've experienced before. He takes my breath away, but I'd happily expire because I can never get enough of him.

This spark has been present since the first moment we met. From the moment I laid my eyes on him, I was under his spell, a spell he isn't even aware he casts. Something about him is magnetic. He turns heads wherever he goes, and it's not just his looks. It's him.

He radiates confidence and control and men and women alike are drawn to him because of it. He's done some god-awful things, but that just makes him all the more captivating because he doesn't make apologies for his actions.

He accepts the consequences and faces them, head-on.

I didn't realize how hard I'd fall for him because I didn't think that type of love existed in real life. But with Alek, it was almost involuntary. His steel-blue eyes are so expressive, but in the same token, they are guarded.

His life has been far from normal. He killed his stepfather at such a young age. That should disgust me, but it doesn't. It reveals Alek to be a survivor.

His stepfather beat him, abused him. Alek did what he had to, to survive just as I'm doing now. In the end, all of us will fight for our survival, whatever the consequences. So I can never see Alek as anything but a survivor.

A loud knock on the door has me jumping up and racing over to the sink. I turn on the faucet and wash away my smudged lipstick as it's evidence which can't be denied.

"Ella? Are you in there?" Frank's voice displays his annoyance that he's had to come looking for me like a bad dog who strayed too far from its owner.

Pulling it together, I reply loudly, "Yes, I'll be out in a bit."

The handle rattles. "Open the door."

Looking at my reflection in the mirror, I tell myself to woman up as I have a role to play.

Drying my hands on a hand towel, I take a deep breath before opening the door. Frank stands with his hand braced on the doorjamb, unimpressed he had to ask. He tilts his head, examining me closely.

I gulp in panic.

"You've been crying."

It isn't a question. It's a statement.

With heart in my throat, I nod, forcing more tears to surface. "Yes, I feel horrible. I've ruined this beautiful dress," I reply, thinking on my feet as I return to the sink, allowing Frank in.

His polished shoes sound against the floor as he walks toward me. Not making eye contact, I dab at the front of my dress with a towel, faking care when, in reality, I just remembered I was supposed to be in here, cleaning the stain.

"Don't worry about it," Frank says. I once found his slight Italian accent sexy, but now it makes me want to be sick. "You look better without it on."

I fake a smile because this is supposed to be a compliment, but on the inside, I'm holding back the urge to slap him.

"Can we go?" I ask. I don't know how long I can play this charade with Alek so close by.

Frank's brown eyes narrow. I should know better than to ask. "No, Aleksei has requested a private audience with my father and me."

"Why?" I question far too quickly but then soon backtrack. "I don't like him."

Frank grins, his boyish dimples giving anyone who doesn't know him a false sense of security. "Good. You're not supposed to like him. The only person you're supposed to like is me."

Before I have a chance to reply, he's on me, pawing me as he kisses me with far too much tongue. His heavy-handed cologne makes me want to puke. He grips my breasts, squeezing hard, while I resist the urge to knee him in the balls. I may as well be kissing a dead fish because I feel absolutely nothing.

He doesn't set me on fire by merely being in his presence. Nor does he have me wanting him with every fiber of my being. I think of Alek, and how his kisses make me forget everything but him. How his kisses make me feel loved, wanted, and not owned like a piece of property as I do with Frank.

Frank mistakes my gusto for him, not Alek, whose mouthwatering taste still lingers on my tongue.

"Oh, you bad girl," he whispers against my lips, drawing up the hem of my dress.

I panic, not wanting to insult Alek any further by having sex in his bathroom. "Not here," I coyly reply, stopping his retreat with my hand over his.

But he slaps my hand away angrily. "Since when do you have a say?"

I'm about to blow my cover and bite off his tongue, but the door opens, and Santo appears. His sharp green eyes narrow into slits when he realizes what he's walked in on. Frank doesn't let me go, grinning smugly when he sees his father's reaction.

Frank plays dumb, but I'm certain he's aware of his father's affection toward me. He wouldn't say a word though. As far as he's concerned, he's the one who's won, seeing as I'm wearing *his* ring and not Santo's.

I quickly untangle myself from Frank's arms, embarrassed and ashamed as I look like nothing but a whore. I go about dabbing down my dress, refusing to make eye contact with either of the Macrillo men.

"Let's go, son," Santo commands, his tone stern. "We need this alliance."

He doesn't say anything further, not wishing me to know why. But I already know, thanks to his drunken late-night confession.

An annoyed grunt gets caught in Frank's throat, but he eventually concedes.

"Come, Ella." It's Santo who addresses me.

The last thing I want to do is face Alek with Santo and Frank by my side, but this'll allow me to uncover what Alek wants to discuss.

So with one final attempt to salvage my dress, I fold the towel and place it onto the counter. When I meet Santo's eyes, all I see is annoyance, but he doesn't say a word.

Frank offers me his hand, wanting to appear the perfect gentleman as he escorts his fiancée, but we both know he is far from that. However, I play my part because it's only a matter of time.

Santo leads the way while Frank and I follow to where I'm presuming is Alek's office. I don't know what he's planning, and after what just happened between us, I can't imagine it'd be good.

"Don't be nervous, *bambina*," Santo says softly, trying to console me. "He can't hurt you."

Frank has no idea about Alek "returning" me to Santo. He believes I returned on my own free will. That I saw the error of my ways and returned because I missed him so much.

Santo and I are the only ones who know the truth, a fact that excites Santo. He enjoys guarding a secret no one else knows. Mila isn't convinced, but as long as I stay out of her way, she doesn't care.

The farther we walk, the shallower my breaths become. I don't know how Alek will react to seeing me with Frank, but I can't imagine it'll be good. We turn the corner, and I see Pavel standing outside a large door. My heart begins to race, but he remains passive, not letting our secrets spill.

He opens the door, and when we walk into Alek's huge office, it's sensory overload. The décor is so Alek—smart, sophisticated, simple. He doesn't need to show off his power with flashy things. His presence is enough.

And when he remains propped up against the front of his large desk with a scotch in hand, his presence almost suffocates me. He doesn't meet my eyes. He dismisses me as though I don't exist.

Saint and Willow stand in the corner of the room, and as soon as I make eye contact with Willow, I instantly look away. She's smart. I know if she looks close enough, she'll see what lies I hide.

My attention suddenly focuses on something I missed because from first glance, I'd believe my eyes were playing tricks. But there is no mistake. Three women in sheer white gowns are seated on a sofa, awaiting command.

My stomach drops. Why has Alek called us in here?

The door closes behind us, sealing us in.

Alek doesn't speak. He simply sips his scotch coolly.

Santo and Frank also stand without emotion, as this is a show of strength. Who'll crumple first?

My knees begin to tremble, and I feel faint, but I don't let it show. To Alek, I'm on the arm of my fiancé because I want to be.

Santo finally caves. "What did you want to talk about, my friend?"

Alek smirks, but nothing about it is welcoming. "How are you enjoying the festivities?" he asks, his Russian accent sending goose bumps all the way to my toes.

"Very fine," Santo replies, playing along. "You always knew how to throw a good party."

Alek nods, taking a long swallow of his scotch.

He still won't acknowledge me, which hurts. I know I forced his hand, but I wish he didn't believe me. I wish he'd do to Santo and Frank what he did to Serg. They deserve that and far worse. But what happens then?

He still has three other sons and the wrath of Mila to deal with. When he takes them down, they *all* must go. Otherwise, he'll forever be looking over his shoulder.

"I'm glad you're having fun. And what about you, Frank?" Alek moves his attention to Frank.

The hatred simmering behind his blue eyes turn them to a midnight black. He wants to flay the skin from his bones, and that pleases me so. It means he cares. It means there's still a chance he'll fight for me.

"Grand affair," Frank replies, drawing me closer into his side.

I want to recoil, but I can't.

"What about Henry?"

"What about him?" Frank counters. As if someone being stabbed in the throat with a broken champagne glass is a common party trick.

"You didn't find his response to me regaining my position a little troubling?"

Saint shifts, shielding Willow with his body. I was stupid to believe she ever had feelings for Alek. Their love is suffocating in a good way.

"Yes, but this is to be expected. Not everyone is going to be happy about you returning."

Alek nods, appearing to digest what Frank just said. "You're right, which is why I called you both in here. I don't expect things to go back to the way they were. When I was in control of this city, no one dared to challenge me.

"But times have changed, which is why I must too. I need allies I can trust. I hope you're one of them."

Santo nods, grinning from ear to ear as he believes Alek has played right into his palm. "Of course, my friend. You have the alliance of the Macrillos. If anyone dares to defy you, we will have your back."

"Very good." Alek hums, slowly running his finger along the rim of his glass. "You're the biggest weaponries dealer in Russia. I deal in drugs," he bluntly says. "We co-existed in the past because we were never a threat or in competition with one another. We stayed out of each other's business. But I want that to change."

What is he doing? Is he proposing what I think he is? Is he willingly getting into bed with the devil?

Santo allows Alek to finish, but his excitement is clear. This is what he wanted. This is what he'd hope would happen once Serg was gone. Alek, however, isn't aware of Santo's attempt at dabbling in drug distribution.

Alek needs allies to rebuild his name, and he believes Santo can help. But how can he go into business with him knowing what he does? Unless business is suddenly more important than me. I made my choice, and now Alek has made his.

He needs associates more than he needs me.

My stomach roils, and I think I'm going to be sick.

"What are you proposing?" Santo asks, pretending this is Alek's idea. He won't rouse any suspicion so when he strikes, it'll be an ambush, one Alek will never see, as this is *his* plan after all.

"I want Raul gone," he spits ruthlessly. "That asshole is a dead man walking. And I need your help. You were able to infiltrate his house once, which I thank you for. I need you to do it again."

Santo runs his hand over his gray stubble, appearing deep in thought. "And if I agree? What do I get?"

"Austin Bailey's head."

Santo bursts into laughter. "Oh, you never fail to amaze me."

Alek doesn't smile. "My plan is for a new dictatorship. No

more allowing the little fish to swim by, unharmed, because they steal from us. Austin may deal his hand-me-down guns from the IRA to low-life criminals, but that's money out of your pocket.

"We never worried about that market because why bother with something so small? Their business didn't affect ours. But that's not the point. I never thought that son of a bitch Serg could overthrow me, but he was able to because I was complacent. It also was because we have disloyal sons of bitches among us.

"I want to stamp out all competition, no matter how small, and have a close network of colleagues who specialize in their field. This way, there is no…temptation for a rebellion."

What Alek is proposing makes sense. This allows him to control who's in power and erases the risk of an uprising. But this means he'll be putting his faith in Santo, practically handing him his business on a silver platter for Santo to steal.

Oh god…

"Of course, you will be the main distributor of weaponry, which you will obtain from Pavel. If you deal with anyone else, they must go through me first. Me, I will be the only drug lord in Russia. Anyone else will be eradicated. I will deal to everyone. No discrimination like last time. Pimply college kids and desperate junkies now all get their drugs through me.

"I will manufacture their product with any cutting agent. They won't know the difference. They'll be so desperate to score, seeing as the riffraff dealers are no more, that they'll settle for anything, which increases my profit margin immensely.

"Which is why I need Raul gone without delay."

"Who will you get your product from?" Santo innocently asks, but I know he's only implementing his game plan.

Before Alek has a chance to reply, Santo adds, "May I suggest someone?"

Alek nods.

"I have close ties with some Sicilians. You could sample their product? If you're pleased, they could supply you. The shipments come in cargo once a month with olive oil. It'll be discreet, and you won't need to deal with anyone from Russia.

"Getting supply offshore makes sense. And they're new. Fresh beginnings are what we both need."

Alek, no, please don't fall for this. Please see through his ruse.

"How do you know this?" Alek questions, his gaze stern.

"Because they're family, and nothing else matters more to us Sicilians."

"What do you get if I agree?"

Santo grins, realizing he's reeled Alek in. "I don't want any of your profits. If this plan of yours succeeds, I'll have more than enough of my own, but I want a say in who stays and who goes.

"I know The Circle was a tightknit group. Although they're no longer, I want in as they did."

Alek ponders Santo's terms. "So you will introduce me to your…family and help me kill Raul, and in return, you want to pick and choose who will remain my loyal servants?"

Alek has chosen this term with intent. He wants Santo to know that neither he nor any of the remaining players once the cull is complete will ever be his equal. It may seem Alek is in partnership with Santo, but Alek works alone. He isn't interested in sharing his throne, which is why Santo plans to kill him.

Santo nods. "Yes. That's all I ask. As I see it, what you're proposing will mean there will be very few…bosses, I guess you could say, in their expertise. We all have to co-exist as we once did. I don't want to deal with some *stronzo* if I don't have to."

This is all lies. Santo wants to handpick men who will side with him once he kills Alek. He'll choose men who favor him and won't question the change of leadership once the time comes.

Sweat begins to collect along my brow. This is catastrophic. Is Alek doing this to punish me? I don't understand why he'd agree to any sort of partnership with the man who was going to kill me.

But when Alek finally meets my eyes…I understand. I see it clearly.

Alek was prepared to fight, fight for me, fight for us. But he readily believed my lies, and now when he looks at me, all I see is death. Death of many. And the death of us.

I hurt Alek, and even though he is confident in all aspects of his life, when it comes to his feelings, when it comes to love, he is insecure and unsure. He told me he was left wounded and seen as weak after he opened his heart to Willow, and now, I've just done the same to him.

I've obliterated any hope of redemption for him. He has just taken three hundred steps back to the cruel, unfeeling drug lord he once was.

I wanted this. I created this monster. Oh, god…what have I done?

"You have a deal," Alek says, eyes still fixated on me. He wants me to know that every life he takes is in part, my burden as well as his.

Santo claps while Frank hums in happiness. This is the deal of a lifetime, one they wanted to orchestrate, but Alek has done that for them.

"Shall we discuss the finer points?" Santo eagerly suggests.

Alek finally releases me from the spell he holds me under as he returns his attention to Santo. "No, this is a party, after all."

Frank turns his head, peering at the almost naked women who I'd forgotten were even there. "So let us celebrate."

This evening, I uncovered via covert gossip that Alek's parties back in the day were notorious for drug-induced orgies. Surely, that has changed.

"How about you introduce us to your renown дорогая?"

I bite down on my tongue, prohibiting the string of curses I wish to throw at Frank. He is openly flirting with another woman with his fiancée in tow.

Alek's jaw clenches as he gently places his glass onto the edge of his desk. "Come, дорогая."

There is no way. But when Willow obeys, I swallow down my bile. Have I got this all wrong? Have they returned to what they once were?

Alek said he was lying, but when he caresses her cheek tenderly, I'm suddenly unsure. I don't know anything anymore.

She has her back turned to us, but I can see Alek's response to her. He still craves her. He always will. Saint stands with a poker face. So different to the man who came to blows with Alek, protecting the love of his life.

This world changes people as customary rules don't apply.

"How about you share?"

I have the urge to stomp on Frank's foot, but all I can focus on is Alek touching someone other than me.

I can't breathe.

I can't cry.

I am numb.

"Not with her," Alek says with affection. "She is mine."

Santo nods, understanding Alek's rationale. Isn't he doing the same with Mila and me? "Yes, of course. But what about the other treats? Surely, they're not just for show?"

"What's mine is yours, my friend," Alek says, his double meaning wounding me, which is what he wanted.

"Saint, take Willow to my bedroom. Both of you be waiting for my return."

Alek has hinted that their relationship runs three ways. Both men share her. Or more accurately, *she* shares *them*. Saint is a very attractive man, and Willow is stunning. Society may see this throuple as unconventional, but in this world, one would be jealous of Alek, sharing his bed with both of them.

There are no labels here, as there shouldn't be.

Once Saint reaches Willow side, the look of love shared between them goes unnoticed by Frank and Santo because they would never understand a love so pure as the one Saint and Willow share. But not by me.

I'm envious of that kind of love because I almost had it. Almost.

Saint leads Willow from the room, and when they pass me, Willow brushes her fingers over the back of my hand with the gentlest and most discreet of touches. Santo and Frank are too busy gawking at the three women to notice, but the simple reassurance brings tears to my eyes.

She knows. She can read my heart breaking at this situation. She knows because she's lived it too.

She and Saint are gone a second later as is Pavel. I'm now left alone with the wolves.

"Come," Alek says to the three women, who spring to his command.

However, they waver on their feet. Are they drugged? Drunk? I don't know, but they're certainly eager as they drop to their knees in front of Alek. They peer up at him, submissive, something I could never be.

Alek glances at each one, gently running his fingers through their hair. When they moan at his touch, I want to cut out their tongues.

He lifts the chin of the blonde with his pointer finger. "Who do you obey?" he asks her in English, and I realize he's done this because he wants me to understand every word.

"You, мастер," she replies.

"Yes, I am your master." Alek grins while I hold back my tears of anger as I just uncovered what мастер means. "Do you want to please me?"

"Yes."

"Good girl, персик. How will you do that?"

She seems to weight his question before turning to the woman with soft black hair and kissing her sluggishly.

Alek peers down at them, his eyes void of emotion. A spark of hope flickers. Maybe he isn't turned on by this deviancy because it's not them he wants. I cling to this small shred of hope because I can't handle the alternative.

Frank lets me go and steps forward, needing a closer look at the spectacle in front of him. This allows Santo to huddle close to me, undetected with Frank's back turned. But Alek's back isn't, so the action isn't missed.

Alek tips his face to the ceiling and inhales deeply, remaining this way for seconds. I'm trembling all over, and Santo mistakes my response as arousal. He bends down and kisses the tip of my shoulder before running his finger along the side of my neck. I smother my pain.

Alek slowly returns his focus to us, watching the way Santo touches me behind his son's back. I can't read his emotions because he merely looks bored. I want him to lunge forward, consequences be damned, and break Santo's hand for daring to touch me in his home.

I want him to show ownership over me because that would mean he cares. That would mean there is still hope for us once this is all done with.

But as he continues looking at me with indifference, I know I've hurt Alek beyond repair. Mission accomplished; so why do I feel so dead inside?

Santo reaches around me and begins to massage my ass. I stare deep into Alek's eyes as I owe him that. I wish for him to see the anguish I feel at having to do this, but after our meeting in the bathroom, where I hurt him, he believes this display to be reciprocated.

I feel sick.

The woman with the black hair turns to her friend with the braid, knotted to perfection, and commences kissing her. The slender blonde doesn't waste a moment as she slowly unfastens Alek's zipper. With eyes still locked on mine, he threads his fingers through her glossy hair and coaxes her to take him into her mouth.

She doesn't need the encouragement however and eagerly begins to bob her head as small pleasured moans spill from her. I've never wanted to kill anyone more than I do her. But I have no right. I brought this on myself.

Alek asked if I wanted the Macrillos and not him, and I said yes. He's merely giving me what I wanted. But I don't want this. Seeing another woman please the man I love is torture like I've never experienced before.

Watching the corded veins in his throat pulsate as she increases her rhythm has me biting the inside of my cheek to keep from crying out, begging for this to stop. He's enjoying another woman sucking his dick while the men who are supposed to be the enemy and I observe.

He fists her hair, coercing her to take him deeper, and she complies. She places one hand on his upper thigh for support while the other she slips between her legs to pleasure herself.

She seems to be enjoying this more than the receiver. I know how Alek tastes, feels, so I understand her contented whimpers of passion. The women break their kiss, wanting a piece of the prize too.

Alek wraps his fingers around the throat of one woman and coaxes her to stand. When she does, she presses her lips to his. He kisses her roughly, an animalistic growl leaving him. He tugs at the strap of her dress, slipping it from her shoulder. She repeats the action to the other side, resulting in her dress pooling at her feet.

She has a large tree tattooed down the length of her spine. The roots are imbedded deeply into a cliff's ledge, and I suddenly wish to be standing on that ledge because if given the chance, I would jump.

I'm beyond broken.

The remaining woman stands and strips naked. She gently pries the woman away from Alek's mouth only so she can feed him her full breast. He hungrily suckles it while reaching for the other woman and slipping his fingers into her sex.

It's like a feast of the senses, and the main meal is Alek. One woman sucks his cock as he fingers another and suckles the breast of the third. The moans from the women have bile rising up my throat, and I place a hand over my mouth to stop myself from being sick.

"If my son wasn't here, I'd throw you up against that wall and fuck you," Santo whispers into my ear.

Frank has his hand down his pants, pleasuring himself at this live porno show happening just feet away.

I don't reply. I can't. Everything has escaped me but this hollow feeling sinking within my belly. I can't stand it anymore.

"Care to share?" Frank says, his voice thick with yearning.

Alek releases the woman's breast but doesn't stop playing with the other woman as he addresses Frank. "I'll only share if you do."

Gasping, I narrow my eyes at him. There's no way I'll be treated like nothing but a whore. But then I realize I need to get off my pedestal. I'm exactly like these women, consenting to be used by two men.

Tears fill my eyes.

It seems I'm nothing but a plaything to everyone in this room.

Alek looks at me, confusion flickering across his hard features as he notices my eyes are wet with tears. But I won't give him the satisfaction of letting him see me cry.

"No, Ella isn't to be shared with anyone." It's Santo who speaks in place of Frank.

Alek's lips twist into a sinister grin. "She looks like an acquired taste anyway."

Unable to hold back my tears, one tumbles down my cheek, betraying my hurt. I don't wipe it away. I want him to know he wounded me, but that's okay because I hurt him too.

What was once pure and good has now turned into…this.

Santo kisses my cheek. "Go wait in the car, *bambina*."

In this situation, I hate that Santo is the one who cares most about my feelings. Alek snickers cruelly, and as he pushes the women away, only to toss the blonde onto the couch, I know the Alek who once cared for me is long gone.

Frank and Santo are like ravenous beasts, charging for the remaining women. As pants hit the floor and women's bodies are bended to please, I stagger for the door, turning over my shoulder one final time to see the man I love breaking what's left of my heart as he claims a body that isn't mine.

CHAPTER FOUR

Alek

Popping another antacid tablet, I rub my chest, hoping this heartburn will go away. But it doesn't look promising.

Last night still lingers on my tongue, and I want it gone. Reaching for my glass of scotch, I toss it back, eager for the strong liquor to drown out the memories of me consorting with three women, but it doesn't. It only highlights their moans of pleasure.

"What do you think?" Pavel asks sharply.

I have no idea what he's talking about, and he knows it. I need to focus, but all I can see are Santo's fucking hands and lips all over Ella. She didn't shy away. She looked me straight in the eye, daring me to react.

But I don't understand how she expected me to behave.

She told me she didn't want me anymore. That even though I pushed her away for her own safety, it didn't make a difference. She couldn't forgive. She'd moved on.

Undoing another button on my shirt, I look at Saint, Willow, and Pavel. "Is it hot in here?"

Saint shakes his head, smirking. "That's your guilty conscience." He's right.

Although I never slept with anyone last night—having chickened out at the last minute—tasting another woman, well, three women, has left me with this utter guilt. It doesn't matter that Ella isn't interested in me anymore because that doesn't change my feelings for her. Even though she willingly shared with me that she wants both Santo and Frank, I still want her.

"She isn't there because she wants to be," Willow says, forever the optimist.

"I appreciate you trying to make me feel better, but she blatantly told me otherwise. I hurt her, and now she's dealing with that pain by living with two men." I clench my jaw so hard, my teeth rattle under the force.

"We've all said things we don't mean," Willow reasons. "I saw it, Alek. Something's going on."

Leaning back in my seat, I rock gently. "What's going on is that Ella can't forgive me. She now knows the truth, so if what you say is true, then why didn't she tell me? She looked quite comfortable to me."

Willow works over her bottom lip in thought. "She's doing it for a reason. I refuse to believe otherwise."

I wish I had Willow's optimism, but she wasn't there when Ella told me she didn't want me. I hurt her horribly, and this isn't fixable. I wish it was, but I'm a realist...which is why I'm really going to kill Santo and Frank Macrillo.

The deal I made with Santo may have seemed like I bended to his demands, but the truth is, I need him to trust me unconditionally. And when I've achieved this, I'm going to kill him.

I'll use him to dispose of Raul, become friends with his contact as I need a new supplier once Raul is gone, and when I bleed Santo dry, I'll ensure he and his son are wiped from the face of this earth. He thinks my plan is to keep the big hitters in play, but he's wrong.

It's all the little fish I want on my side.

At the moment, people are cautious, wondering if I'll have a change of heart. In this job, having one—a heart, that is—is seen as a weakness. I need to eliminate the naysayers because if they're not with me, they're against me.

And what better way to commence my purge than by paying a visit to my dear friend Raul.

I have no idea how Santo proposes we get to Raul, but he promised to make it happen. He came through last time, so I hope he does so again. At the time, he *was* filled with bloodlust over the pussy he just ate, so he could be full of shit. But he wants this as much as I do.

His greed won't allow him to fail as he benefits from this deal too.

He thinks I fell for this whole spiel of not wanting to interfere. He merely wants to oversee who I choose.

Bullshit.

I'm not stupid. I know he'll play this hand at first. He'll gently suggest his opinion, stating he only has my best interests at heart, but sooner or later, he'll enforce his ideas, only concerned for his own selfish needs.

Taking me out so he can rule is no doubt his endgame, but he'll be dead before he even has a whiff of victory. You see, I'll have the loyalty of the underdogs, and after being shunned by men like Santo, they'll be more than eager to have their revenge.

However, Santo doesn't know this, which is why I'm playing double agent.

To him, it'll seem I'm keeping the main players in business while eradicating the small-fry, but what he won't know is that I'm building an army of misfits, ready to strike at my command.

The old-school outlaws don't believe they can be outsmarted, and didn't I? They believe they're irreplaceable, but they're wrong.

In the words of Saint, it's time to fuck shit up.

In the meantime, I need to keep Santo in the dark. He can't get wind of any of this. Otherwise, the plan is void. This means, for appearances' sake, I need to act like the old Alek so as not to rouse suspicion among my peers. Last night cemented this.

Frank and Santo had their fun with Jada and Yuna like the "good ole days." I'm sure they'll be unable to keep their mouths shut about how father and son tag teamed in my office. They'll spill the sordid details to their friends, and word will spread like wildfire.

This was all about strategy. About re-establishing myself as king.

A starving man doesn't ask what meal it is; he simply

gorges himself full. If I give Santo what he wants, he won't ask questions, and I'll outsmart them all in the end.

"It doesn't matter anymore," I say, referring to Willow's last comment.

"Like hell it doesn't," she argues angrily. "You're just going to give up?"

Sighing, I reach for the bottle of scotch and pour myself another glass. "I don't know what I'm going to do," I answer honestly. "I need Santo on my side at the moment, and I know Ella. Well, I know that she's stubborn. She won't do anything unless she wants to, which is why I believe she's there because she wants to be."

"Well, you're a jackass," Willow counters unapologetically. "I read the letter you left her. You clearly care for her."

That letter is now void.

"I hurt her terribly," I say, throwing back my scotch. "She's gone back to what she thinks is love. She was in love with Frank, real love. I think she hopes her feelings will come back. Or maybe she'll settle for something like love.

"I don't know. What I do know is that there is no other explanation for her to be there. If there was, she would have told me last night. Serg is dead. Irina, Mother Superior, the children, they're all safe. She has no reason to stay there. She has no reason to marry that Мудак. But she is."

Willow looks at Saint, whose silence affirms his belief in my words.

Ella had the perfect opportunity to prove me wrong last night. She wouldn't marry Frank and live in the Macrillo house just to spite me. She isn't that stupid as she knows once she's in, there's no leaving. Which is why I have to believe she's there because she wants to be.

I would fight for her, but she's given me nothing to fight for.

The thought has me wanting to down this entire bottle of scotch, but I can't. I promised Irina I'd take her to the playground.

"I'll be back later," I announce as I come to a stand, not wanting to deal with this.

Pavel sighs, but he doesn't press.

I know he wants to discuss our plan of who's staying and who's going, but I don't want to deal with any of that right now. I just want to spend the afternoon with Irina.

Saint stands, but I shake my head. "Spend time with your ангел."

They've both done more than enough for me. I count my blessings every day. If they decided to leave now, I would wish them well, but I know they won't.

Willow's lips are pulled in tight. She's unhappy I won't listen to her theory, but the truth is, I don't want to give myself false hope. I just need to accept this for what it is. The sooner I do, the easier it'll be to digest that Ella doesn't want me anymore.

But that doesn't mean I will back out on my plan. Regardless of her feelings, I'm going to kill Frank and Santo. I don't expect her to come running back to me, as I know she'll hate me more than she already does when she uncovers what I've done, but there is no way I'm going to stand back and allow this union to take place because she's in danger.

All may seem well for the moment, but sooner or later, the Macrillos will find a shinier toy, and Ella will be yesterday's news. And when that happens, she'll be discarded like trash.

This is one way I can save her from more heartache.

Reaching for my cane, I walk from the room and down the hallway toward the kitchen where I know Irina will be. She's taken an interest in watching Pierre, my personal chef, prepare our meals. It gives me great pleasure to see her sitting at the kitchen counter, watching Pierre chop vegetables with skill.

"Hello, цветочек. Are you helping Pierre again?"

Pierre grins. She trashes his kitchen on most days, but he doesn't mind.

"Ski!" Irina jumps down from the stool and runs over, demanding hugs.

Even though I'm still unsteady on my feet, I drop to a half squat and pick her up. It's awkward with my cane, but I manage as I'll never stop hugging her.

"Ready to go to the playground?"

She nods happily, her rosy cheeks warming me.

Pierre passes me her pink Disney Princess backpack, packed with her favorite snacks.

Just as I'm about to leave, she places her small palm on my cheek. "Ski sore. Irina walk." Before I can protest, she wriggles, implying she wants to be put down. She gestures she wants to carry her own bag.

I smile at her, offering it to her. Once she's looped both straps over her shoulders, I offer her my hand, and she happily accepts.

We commence a slow hobble toward the door, Irina giving me all the time I need. I can't wait until I can walk without the aid of this infernal cane. As we reach the garage, Olio, the new security Pavel hired, waits for me.

He has my car keys in hand. "I will drive you," he says, but I shake my head, snaring the keys from him.

"Not today, thank you."

His worry is clear as venturing out unprotected is unwise, but I want to be alone with Irina. I need to ask her about the vile claims Serg made. I need to know if they're true. There is no easy way to ask this, but I don't want anyone there when I do.

Once Irina's buckled up her seat belt, I hobble over to the driver's side of my BMW SUV and toss my cane into the passenger seat. It takes me a while, but once I'm in, I press the remote to open the garage door.

Putting the SUV into drive, I exit slowly, taking in my surroundings before I leave. My home is secure, but one can never be too sure. As expected, the coast is clear, and I make my way down the driveway and out through the double gates.

Once they're closed, I start the half-hour drive to Irina's favorite playground.

A children's audiobook sounds over the speakers, filling in the static because I need to gather the nerve to ask her something that has me clenching the steering wheel. If she says yes…

"Irina," I say, looking at her in the rearview mirror.

She meets my eyes and smiles.

Clearing my throat, I commence. "I don't want you to get

upset, but can we talk about what happened in…the dark?"

Her confession about being scared of the dark disturbs me immensely because what Serg said he did to Irina in the dark is sickening. But if it's true, I will get Irina the help she needs.

Her smile fades, and she quickly turns her head to look out the window.

"I know you don't want to talk about it, but it's very important that you do." I don't know how to broach this. I'm sure there is some protocol to follow, but I need to do this my way.

"Did Serg, the man who took you from me, did he…hurt you? Touch you?" I swallow down so many vile emotions because this isn't about me. It's about Irina and finding out what happened to her.

Irina doesn't reply.

"цветочек, I just want to help. I won't get angry. Whatever answer you give me. I just need the truth."

Irina swings her feet, her tiny kicks reverberating against the leather seat. She doesn't want to talk about this, which has me believing there is truth in what Serg said.

Cursing under my breath, I control my temper because losing it now would be the worst thing I can do.

"Ski choo-choo," Irina says, and even though I'm not angry with her, I can't hold back the bite in my reply.

"I can't read to you now! I'm asking you a question. Answer me."

I instantly regret the words the moment they leave me, but I'm just so frustrated. Not with Irina, but rather, myself.

I'm so angry with myself for failing her.

Peering at her in the rearview mirror, my insides sink when I see her eyes wet with tears. "Ski mad?"

"Not with you, цветочек."

"Ski bring Irina b-back?"

Afraid I'll drive us off the road, I signal and pull up by the curb. Once the SUV is in park, I turn over my shoulder to look at Irina. "Never. My home is your home, Irina. Always."

She nods, sniffling. "Choo-choo help Irina," she reveals, while I listen closely, unsure what she's trying to say. "Choo-choo keep dark away."

Thoughts are racing a million miles a minute as I attempt to decode what she just shared.

"The book I read you?" I ask, trying every angle until I find the right answer.

Irina shakes her head before pointing at the railway track to the right. "Choo-choo come, bad man go away."

I frantically compile a list of things that could mean. "Bad man? Serg?" I ask.

Irina shakes her head.

Is she referring to her past?

"Bad man is your family?" I question, and Irina nods sadly. "Your папа?"

She nods again, confirming the bad man is her father.

A train is somehow linked to her childhood, something she sees as her saving grace. Once the train came, her father would go away?

Could it be when she heard the sound of the train horn, her ordeal would be over? Could it be because her mother, sister, brother, someone she trusted caught the train to work maybe, and when the horn sounded, she knew it meant they'd be home soon after. And so did her father.

Did he use the horn as a marker, knowing how many minutes he had left to abuse his own flesh and blood? Is this why she is so obsessed with Thomas Tank Engine and insists I read it to her over and over again? Does she feel safe when I read it to her?

I am going to find this piece of shit and end him in the most brutal of ways.

"Irina, what is папа's name?"

She bites down on her bottom lip. I know this is painful for her.

"You've done nothing wrong. Absolutely nothing," I assure her. "I'm going to protect you from him. He'll never hurt you again. I promise."

Irina sniffs, her lower lip trembling.

Before I can ask her anything further, my cell chimes. I decide to give Irina some time because I don't want to press too hard and do more damage than good. Not recognizing the number, I press the button on my steering wheel to answer the call through my Bluetooth. When I hear Frank's voice, a shot of utter wrath pulses throughout my body.

"Hi, my father asked I call you." I don't speak because the less I talk to this motherfucker, the better. "He said tonight is the night."

"Care to be a little more specific?" I bark, not interested in his theatrics.

"It's Chow's anniversary," he reveals when he realizes I'm

far from impressed with his call. "There is a small gathering at the family's Buddhist temple. He won't expect an attack, which is why we strike. He'll be unarmed."

There is so much to process, but all I can think is how can Ella have feelings for this son of a bitch. He is so stupid, desperately trying to impress daddy by talking big. I'm doing the world a favor by ending his miserable life.

"Did you hear me?" he asks when I don't reply.

"Yes. Text me the details. I'll be there." And I end the call.

Who knew? Raul is a Buddhist. I thought they didn't believe in violence. And Chow's anniversary is today? That seems like a lifetime ago. But I suppose his death wasn't an occasion I marked down in my diary to celebrate the milestone in years to come.

Seems rather perfect, ending his life on the anniversary of his father seeing as I was the one responsible for his father's death. I don't feel a slither of remorse.

"Sorry, цветочек. Shall we go to the—" However, I pause when I look into the rearview mirror and see Irina with her hands covering her eyes, humming under her breath. "What's wrong?"

I immediately regret asking her those questions. Was it too much, too fast?

When she doesn't reply and continues humming, I unsnap my seat belt and frantically exit the car. Opening her door, I squat so we're at eye level as I gently remove her small hands from her face. She doesn't fight me.

"What's the matter?"

She cups her mouth, and whispers, "Bad man."

"I'm a bad man?" I ask, heart in my throat. I shouldn't have asked her those questions. I should have sent her to a professional who knows what the fuck they're doing. I'll just end up messing her up more than she already is.

But when she shakes her head, I suddenly realize she isn't talking about me.

"The man on the phone? He's the bad man?"

She nods while I resist the urge to curse uncontrollably.

"He make Ski mad. Irina protect Ski from bad man. Irina doesn't like when Ski sad."

Bless her kind heart.

"I will take care of the bad men. I promise. I'll never let anyone hurt you ever again." Pressing my lips to her forehead, I kiss her gently.

She leans into my touch with a small whimper.

Ensuring she's buckled in tight, I close the door and get back behind the wheel. The entire drive to the playground has my mind racing.

There is no way I'll allow Ella to take on the Macrillo name. I won't stand by and permit their marriage to take place, regardless of Ella's feelings, or lack of, for me.

Parking the car, I examine our surroundings carefully. I take note of where cars are parked, who's swinging off the playground equipment, joggers, and dog walkers. I treat everyone as the enemy. Reaching into the glove compartment for my gun, I conceal it at the small of my back under my shirt.

Irina squeals in excitement, the SUV rocking with her enthusiastic bounces. She knows to wait for me and stays seated until I open her door. I unbuckle her belt and lift her out of the car. I want to carry her, just until I can confirm the place is safe. But she wriggles, wanting to walk.

Her independence pleases me as I want her to grow up strong and confident without needing another to survive.

I grab her backpack and my cane, and we commence a not so slow walk toward the playground, hand in hand. Irina doesn't want to push me too hard as she knows I'm injured, but her excitement gets the better of her, and she looks up at me with those big eyes.

"Okay, go," I instruct in Russian with a smile. I don't need to tell her twice, and she takes off in a quick sprint, heading straight for the swings.

With her pink backpack lobbed over my shoulder, I make my way to the bench seat, which allows me to take in the playground from every angle. I take a seat, placing the bag next to me.

My phone chimes, but I don't look at it. Not here. I cannot risk taking my eyes off Irina. I made that mistake once before. Never again.

Irina kicks her small feet in the air, desperate to go higher. When she notices me watching, she waves while I almost launch from my seat.

"Both hands!" I sigh in relief when she quickly complies.

Being responsible for another human is exhausting, but when I look at Irina, it makes the hard work worth it. I think of my mother, and how she didn't share the same sentiments. She only cared for herself. Being in the position I'm in now, I realize what sort of person that makes her.

A parent has a role to fulfill, and leaving your child to fend for themselves is a cowardly act. It has me despising her all the more. I wonder where she is. If she thinks I'll forget about what she did, she's sorely mistaken.

"Aleksei?"

Peering to my left, I see Austin. He is walking some small white fluffball, which yaps at me.

This meeting is purely a coincidence. Austin has no reason to fight me. He needs me. And I need him.

"Well, hello. Please, sit." I move the pink backpack so he can do so.

Austin swallows nervously, but does as I say. "Thank you for inviting me last night. Your home is lovely. I had a great time."

"You're most welcome," I reply, keeping my eyes on Irina.

The white dog sits at Austin's feet. Loyal and obedient. Maybe I should think about getting one of my own. "I wanted to express my disgust over what Henry did. It was quite inappropriate." His Irish accent is quite charming.

"Which is why he's now dead," I counter, waving at Irina as she runs over to the slide. "I don't like yes-men, Austin. I like someone who isn't afraid to stand up for what they believe in."

For this to work, I need Austin to be ruthless, not trying to please me with what he thinks I want to hear.

"What do you think of Santino Macrillo?" I ask, not interested in small talk.

Austin pales and tugs at the collar of his polo. "He is—"

Clucking my tongue, I shake my head at his vagueness. "That won't do. Hesitation gets one killed, or in your case, it has you coming in second best. Quite frankly, I can't stand the son of a bitch and I'm thinking it's time for a change."

Austin has every right to be wary. I would be worried if he weren't. But I need to put money where my mouth is. This could be a trap for all he knows.

"I need someone I can trust. And I don't trust Santo. My colleague, Pavel, he has access to some fine artillery."

"I know who Pavel is," Austin says with enthusiasm.

Pavel's reputation is notorious. He isn't interested in dealing his stock to multiple buyers. He is happy selling to the highest bidder and letting them do all the hard work. Santo was that man, but that's about to change.

"Good. Then you know he was selling to Santo while you were forced to deal in IRA hand-me-downs. But that's going to change." I don't know what ties Austin has to the IRA, but if he's connected to them, he has a little power.

Not enough to outweigh Santo. Well, not yet.

Irina's little legs pump up the stairs as she climbs up for the slide for the third time.

"I have a proposition for you that will benefit us both. This old hierarchy won't do. Henry's disloyalty is a perfect example of why. It's time for a detox. And what better way to start this cleanse than by putting a bullet in Santo's head."

Silence.

Giving Austin a moment to digest what I've just shared, I unzip Irina's backpack and reach for the baggie with sliced carrots. I offer one to Austin.

His fingers tremble as he accepts.

I chomp down on my own carrot, the crunch seeming

amplified in the sudden quiet. We must look a pair. Me, with my child's Disney Princess backpack eating a carrot, and Austin with his fluffy mop of a dog.

But this is exactly what I want. To the outside world, we look harmless. However, what I'm proposing is anything but that.

"I couldn't do that to Santo. I mean, if anyone found out—"

"You disappoint me," I interrupt. "You're clearly not listening to what I'm saying. No one will find out because anyone who objects to what I have planned will be dead. I am assembling a new team of men and women I trust. And I want you to be a part of that team. I know it's a lot to take in, but if you agree, I'll make you a very rich man."

"And how does this benefit you?" Good. *Now* he is asking the right questions.

"Everything goes through me. I'll take a small cut, and we work together to build a better Russia."

Irina is hanging upside down from the monkey bars, swinging happily.

"So you want to control where the business comes from, and in turn, who you choose, will report to you?"

"In a way," I reply. "In your case, Pavel will deal whatever weaponry you need, and then you'll sell them to whoever you like. How you run your operation is your business. I won't interfere with that. But I control who provides you with your product. I need to keep a close eye on everyone. We wouldn't want a repeat of last night, would we? This is why I need a fresh bunch of colleagues. I know you're tired of brown nosing in hopes of working your way to the top. I can promise your name will be notorious across the world."

Austin could double-cross me, but he won't.

His greed and the prospect of being who Santo is, is too enticing. When you've been treated like the underdog all your life, you'll do anything to be on top. Santo is standing in the way of Austin being a king. He won't betray me because what reason does he have?

He isn't going to side with Santo. Or anyone else, for that matter. Half of the guests last night didn't even know Austin's name. He has no influential allies. But I'm offering for that to change.

"I will reach out to others. Art, jewels, real estate, automotive, waste management, construction, restaurants, pornography; these are just a few business ideas I have, and I need someone I can trust to oversee these ideas.

"We all want the same thing; to make money and to see those pretentious assholes groveling on their knees."

I haven't heard Austin chew his carrot. I hope he hasn't passed out from shock.

"Once we rid the Santo's from this world, their allies will become yours because they don't care who they buy their drugs, guns, sex from. As long as they fill their need, they'll do business with whoever will give them the best deal."

Some asshole kid pushes Irina from the swings, which is my cue to end this conversation so I can break his hand. Kid or not, no one touches my цветочек.

"Think about it," I say calmly, standing and shouldering Irina's backpack.

"What if I say no?" he asks, curious.

Looking at him, I smirk. "You won't."

And he won't because if he does, he knows he'll end up in a shallow grave alongside Santo.

Leaving him to process what I just shared, I walk to where Irina is dusting the dirt from her dress. Just as I'm about to give the little jerk who shoved her an earful, she does something which has me grinning from ear to ear.

She shoves him back. "I'm not scared of you," she says in Russian, placing her hands on her hips, mastering the Wonder Woman stance.

Looks like she didn't need me to come to her rescue after all. My brave little girl can hold her own. I can only hope my new associates can do the same. Otherwise, they'll end up like the little boy Irina shoved. Only, they'll be pushed off a cliff.

We're on our way to the Buddhist temple, ready to kickstart a new chapter in my plans to reign. Santo has given us a meetup point. Pavel and Max are riding ahead as Pavel wants to scope out the place in case we're walking into a trap.

Therefore, it's just Saint and me in my SUV.

"What's wrong?" I ask, turning down Bach on the radio.

Saint's leg bounces as he stares out his window. "Willow," he replies.

I figured, but I didn't want to assume.

"I'm just worried about her. I hate leaving her alone."

"I'll call Pavel and tell him to pull over. I'll ride with him. Take my car back to the house and check on her."

"No, she'll be okay. She's tougher than she looks. Just old memories playing on my mind."

How they've both grown. Their relationship is an equal playing field, which is what all couples hope for. We both learned long ago Willow doesn't need a knight in shining armor to save her. She can save herself.

The GPS instructs us that our destination is five minutes away. Saint's phone chimes with a text. He reads over the message. "Pavel said everything seems legit."

A wave of relief washes over me, not that I was afraid of being ambushed but rather, I was afraid Raul wouldn't get what's coming to him. The significance of this kill is enormous and will change everything. Once Raul is gone, I can put my plan into motion and meet with Santo's drug contacts.

The sooner this happens, the sooner Santo dies.

"Remind me why we can't kill Santo and Frank?" Saint quips, cracking his knuckles.

"Because we unfortunately need them. Besides, a special form of torture is to be inflicted on Frank. I haven't thought of what yet."

I'm unable to think of them together without wanting to stab something.

"He's going to suffer in the most excruciating of ways. But before that can happen, I need to find out everything he knows. I want to kill them both...so bad," I say between clenched teeth.

"But I cannot until I get what I need from them. Henry's

insolence is an example of why I need to work with Santo. Until I can—"

"Build up your street cred?" Saint offers as I search for the right words.

"Yes, thank you," I reply with a smirk as his lingo always humors me. "Until I can do that, I need to play nice."

With a sigh, he nods. "Keep your friends close and your enemies closer, I guess."

"Precisely. It won't be for long. I spoke to Austin today. It didn't take much convincing. He will want to make a name for himself and prove himself to the IRA. They will be a very strong ally to have. I need an in. And Austin will be that.

"The others will follow suit. This is all about strategy. Like a game of pok—" I don't finish my sentence because no one needs to be reminded how good at poker I am.

I take a left and see Pavel's black truck ahead.

A black Bentley is parked close by. The Macrillos are also here. I wonder if Santo's other sons will join in with the family affair. I don't have any issues with them, but when I kill their father and brother, that'll soon change.

Parking my SUV away from Pavel and the Bentley, I examine the upmarket neighborhood and realize this is a horrible idea. How are we supposed to pull off a murder without alerting the neighbors?

Saint senses my worries. "Santo wouldn't organize this if he wasn't sure. Remember, this benefits him too."

He's right, but it does nothing to ease the tension humming through me.

With no time like the present, we exit the car and make

our way toward Pavel and Max standing on the sidewalk. No doubt the black duffel Pavel holds has an array of weapons.

It's hard not to reminisce about old times with us four standing together. But how we've all changed. Life certainly has a warped sense of humor because when Santo, Frank, and Lorenzo, Santo's eldest son, step from their car, I can't believe I'm siding with these assholes instead of killing them.

Reminding myself it's only short term, I pull back my shoulders and tamp down my murderous urges. "This is rather public," I say when Santo approaches.

Lorenzo is the spitting image of his father. Frank looks more like his mother, a fact I'm sure he isn't too happy about. One would have to be blind not to see that Lorenzo is the favored son. The way Santo huddles close to him and leaves Frank to lag like a lost puppy must irk Frank immensely.

"Yes, it is, which is why it's perfect," Lorenzo replies, speaking in place of his father.

"How so?" I coolly question.

"No one will expect an attack, and this gives them a false sense of security."

"There will be a lot of innocent people inside," Saint says, far from impressed with Lorenzo's plan.

"And?" He looks at Saint like he's nothing but a bug he wants to squash with his Italian loafer.

But he's messing with the wrong man.

"And motherfucker, you want to start a war with Raul's people? This needs to be discreet. No innocent person is dying on my watch. We clear?"

Lorenzo steps forward but is restrained when Santo grips

his upper arm.

Saint smirks in response, daring Lorenzo to touch him.

"There's only one entrance—the front door," Santo reveals, deciding to intervene. "We walk through it and kill Raul."

I tongue my cheek, needing a minute to process this "plan."

"I mean no disrespect, Santo, but this is rather idiotic."

Saint scoffs, as I'm sure he'd have used a different word.

"But Saint is right. We need to remain undetected. I do not want anyone knowing we're responsible for this. I don't want Raul's men hunting me, intent on revenge."

"Oh, I didn't realize you wanted anonymity. I mean, I thought this would be good for your—"

"Street cred?" I offer while Saint chuckles beside me.

Pavel sighs, clearly annoyed he has to think of everything. Opening up his duffel, he retrieves three gas masks. He tosses them to me, Saint, and Santo. I catch mine, tilting my head to see what else he packed in his bag of tricks.

He hunts for three small round grenades. I now understand what we need the masks for.

"One entrance means there's only one exit. Pull the pin and toss these gas grenades into the temple and we wait outside, ensuring Raul doesn't leave. The smoke will last for approximately two or so minutes. But once it clears, you won't have time to loiter. The place will be crawling with cops and Raul's men."

"Won't this grenade kill them?" Frank asks, while I refrain from raising my eyes to the heavens at his stupidity.

"It's a gas grenade, so no, it'll merely blind them and make it hard to breathe. That's why there are gas masks," he explains like it's a no-brainer.

"How many people are inside?" I ask Santo.

"No more than twenty. Two are Raul's bodyguards."

As far as plans go, Irina could have come up with a better one, but we're here now. "Those two assholes need to be put down immediately," Saint says, putting on his gas mask.

"Make it quick, Aleksei," Pavel warns and doesn't waste a minute as he coolly walks up to the temple. Santo quickly puts on his mask and orders his sons to wait outside.

I wonder if Buddha is leading me to nirvana with this impromptu opportunity. I mean, what a terrible accident it would be if Santo's mask accidentally on purpose came loose in battle, and he choked on the poisoned air.

No one would suspect foul play.

When I think of his hands all over Ella, I almost blow my cover and stab him in the throat with the hunting knife I saw in Pavel's bag. But I can't. I need him. If I didn't, he'd already be dead. I just need to be patient.

Once Pavel pulls the pin from one grenade and rolls it along the temple floor, we spring into action because we have mere seconds. Saint rushes ahead as it takes me a while to follow thanks to this infernal limp, but I chase close behind as I put on my mask.

Pavel repeats the same action with another grenade before giving Saint the last one in case we need it. He jogs away, nodding in good luck as he passes me.

Saint enters the temple while Santo draws his gun before following suit. Screams erupt, and seconds later, plumes of smoke billow from the temple. Men and women rush from the door, their arms covering their noses as they gasp for air.

They pay no heed to me as I enter coolly, gas mask in place because when one is fighting for survival, outside stimuli does not matter. Once inside, my eyes take a moment to adjust to the candlelight amplifying the smoke in the air.

Chaos runs rampant, and when I see two bright sparks, it's evident Saint or Santo found Raul's bodyguards. People push past me, desperate to exit, while I simply walk down the aisle with my eyes on the prize.

I can't hear anything, thanks to the terrified shrills, and my vision is obscured, thanks to the thick smoke. But Saint is like a pit bull, and within seconds, I vaguely make out his form coming toward me, dragging someone down the aisle by the collar of their shirt.

Saint doesn't have to help me, but as he gets closer, it's evident he's enjoying this as much as I am. The darkness inside him will never go away. It's a part of him, and hurting bad people is the only way to justify the need to feed it.

He could never live a "normal" life because we've both seen and done too much for that life to be enough. I suppose this is why he and Willow are helping me. They need the violence, the mayhem to help them feel alive.

It doesn't make sense to most, but to us, this is how we survive.

As Saint gets closer and the smoke clears, I see he is dragging an unconscious Raul behind him. Santo has a large gold statue of Buddha in his hands. Is he really pilfering? I can't imagine he'd take it for his own personal collection, seeing as he's a devout Catholic.

I find it rather puzzling that he's stealing like a common thief. It's not like the Macrillos need the money. But I don't have time to process that right now because Saint gestures with his head toward Raul. Peering around the temple, I smile when I see the gold altar. This will be my stage.

Santo races for the door, Buddha in one hand while he digs into his pocket for his cell with the other.

"How long do you think I have?" I ask Saint as he changes direction and hauls Raul toward the altar. My voice sounds like Darth Vader.

"No more than five minutes." He yanks Raul up like he weighs nothing and slams him onto the solid altar. Raul doesn't wake.

I wish I had more time to make this motherfucker pay for what he did to me, but I don't. Looking at the photo of Chow, I reach for it without a slither of remorse for my actions and smash the frame against the side of the altar. It shatters, causing the glass fragments to rain around me.

A pointed shard catches my eye, which is perfect.

Digging into my pocket for my handkerchief, I bend down and pick up the shard with it. Once I wrap it around the end which serves as my handle, I stand over an unconscious Raul, and without hesitation, I stab him in the chest.

His eyes pop open before he springs up like he's possessed. It takes his groggy brain a moment to realize what's happening, but with time working against us, I decide to speed up the inevitable. I don't have a gun or knife because I have something better, something which I only have thanks to Raul.

Tossing my cane in the air and catching it like some magic trick, I grasp the middle and use it as a bat, striking Raul in the temple with the heavy jeweled topper. *This* is what I meant when I told Santo it served many purposes.

Raul wavers and collapses onto his back, disoriented. I don't give him a second to recover before I commence to beating him with my cane. His attempts to fight me off are futile because I'm a man hell-bent on revenge.

Each time I hear a bone snap, I holler in excitement. My breaths are amplified because of the gas mask, only fueling the murderous rage inside me. I break Raul's kneecap just as he did to mine and then rip the shard of glass out of his chest, stabbing him in the thigh and dragging it downward, slicing him open.

The thin cotton of his pants do nothing to cushion the blow, and his hiccupped gasps for air alert me that his lungs are close to relinquishing, just as mine were. Once I get to his shattered kneecap, I stop, only to tear open his slashed pants material and use my fingers to split apart his skin.

I see tendon and muscles and tip my head to the heavens, humming in victory.

Raul is going into shock, so I don't have long. With bloodied fingers, I take off the gas mask so he can see who's about to end his life. Reaching for the picture of Chow, I slam it against his chest and shake my head.

"You were so desperate to avenge your father. So now, you can be with him. You failed. I win."

Like a coward, he surrenders and closes his eyes as I yank

out the shard of glass and slit his throat with it. His blood spurts from the wound, covering me. The hot metallic sting is like coming home to a pair of well-loved slippers.

I never left this world. I was merely on a sabbatical.

He stops twitching in under a minute; the injuries to his body too extensive to survive. Examining the mess I've made, I smirk. It's done. I would have preferred more time, but he is merely an entrée to who I really want.

The assholes in question come running through the door, duffel in hand as they begin to raid the temple of anything that isn't nailed down. There is a lot of gold in here, which I'm sure will fetch them a small fortune, but I find this behavior… strange. Why would a billionaire steal petty goods?

As Santo stuffs his bag full of trinkets, I calmly say, "I think it's time I met your family."

He looks at the altar, the blood drip…drip…dripping onto the floor, a reminder of what I'm capable of if he doesn't obey. He thinks he's safe, but he's living on borrowed time.

My time to reign has finally come.

CHAPTER FIVE

Ella

"Come on, *bella*," Frank whispers into my ear, nudging his hips into my back so I can feel his disgusting erection.

I groan in response, faking sleep because morning sex is the last thing I want right now or ever.

Frank grumbles angrily before I feel the mattress shift. I keep my eyes squeezed shut until I hear the shower in the en suite start. A relieved breath leaves me. Burying my face into my pillow, I fist the sheets beneath and let out a guttural scream. The pillow mutes my cries, which I've held in for the past few days.

Santo and Frank are conspiring; their hushed voices confirm that whatever they're up to can't be good. I can't shake the feeling it has to do with Alek.

From the snippets of conversation I've overheard, it seems Raul is dead, and Alek was the executioner. They made it clear he killed cruelly and without remorse, and that he is far more dangerous than they originally thought.

Santo wants to speed things up because he doesn't trust Alek. But what he really means is that he's afraid he'll end up like Raul. This frightens me because it doesn't give me much time to investigate. I wanted to present Alek with information I compiled so he could deal with it swiftly and accordingly.

But now, I have a feeling this will be over a lot sooner than I anticipated. I can't allow this to have been all for nothing, which is why I need to talk to Santo.

Frank is merely the errand boy. Santo is the one calling the shots, and if I want to help Alek, then I need to get what I can out of Santo. I scream into my pillow once again, knowing what that means. Nothing in this house is for free.

The en suite door opens, hinting Frank is showered and ready for the day. I can't fake sleep any longer, so I groan and turn sleepily onto my side.

"*Buongiorno, principessa,*" Frank mocks as I gradually open my eyes.

"Morning," I reply, followed by a staged yawn. "You're going out?"

Frank is in a smart white linen shirt and black pants; attire which means business.

"Yes, I have to organize a few things for tonight."

This has my attention.

Shifting and leaning against the headboard, I pull the blankets over my chest as my silk nightgown doesn't leave much to the imagination. "What's happening tonight?"

Frank sits on the edge of the bed to put on his black socks.

"We're having guests," he replies ambiguously.

"Oh? What guests?"

He pauses and turns over his shoulder, arching a brow. I know better than to ask questions. "Maybe if you acted like a fiancée, I would tell you things a fiancée should know. But lately, it seems you'd rather be anything but my wife-to-be."

He's pissed because I've denied him sex since my return. But I literally want to vomit the moment he comes near me.

"I told you I've got my period," I softly argue, knowing this excuse will only work for so long.

With an annoyed sigh, he slips on his leather loafers. "Well, you have other ways to please me. But I suppose I'll have to burn off some steam another way then."

Clawing the sheets under the blankets, I remain stone-faced. "I'm sorry, Frank. You know I'm not myself when I'm hormonal."

Frank stands abruptly and looks at his appearance in the large wall mirror. "Oh, sweetheart, I know, which is why you're not needed tonight. Stay here and rest."

"What?" I ask, pulling back my shoulders.

"You said you're not yourself, so you shall stay here until you are," he cruelly replies, running his fingers through his immaculately styled hair.

"Frank," I argue, but he's just played me at my own game.

"I'll have Rosa bring up some breakfast."

This has me ripping off the blankets and chasing after him as he walks to the door. "You can't keep me locked in here," I cry, as that's what he just hinted at. For Rosa, his servant, to bring me breakfast means I'm not allowed to go downstairs and retrieve my own.

I make the mistake of gripping his elbow, begging he stop and turn around. Withdrawing from my hold, he spins violently, and before I can retreat, he slaps me.

Staggering back, I cup my cheek, mouth ajar. This is the first time he's hit me. Whatever small shred of influence I had over him has gone. He seemed overjoyed when I told him I was back and had made a big mistake.

I thought I had him fooled. Clearly, I'm the one who's fooled. This isn't good. I'm only here because I'm of use to the Macrillos. But if they grow tired of me, I know this won't end well.

"Don't ever forget your place," he spits, his eyes turning black. "I own you, and I'll do what I please to you. You never should have left me. This is your punishment for doing so."

Retreating with wavering steps, I hold my breath, terrified he's about to display his power over me in unthinkable ways. But when he looks down at his gold diamond watch, I exhale in relief.

"If I wasn't late, I'd let you make it up to me. Maybe later. Have a nice day, *bella*." And with that, he's out the bedroom door. The lock clicks in place, confirming I'm a prisoner until Frank says otherwise.

Running for the door, I fruitlessly turn the handle in hopes it'll open. It doesn't.

"Frank!" I bang on the woodgrain. "Let me out! You can't keep me locked in here! Frank!" My cries go unheard, or more accurately, ignored because Frank can do whatever he wants to me while I live under the Macrillo's roof.

Kicking the door angrily, I brace my hands against it and lower my head between my splayed arms, catching my breath. This is bad.

I thought I outsmarted Frank, but being locked in here proves that I haven't. I know I would be in his favor if I slept with him, but I can't. I don't want anyone's hands on me bar Alek's. It was naïve of me to think I could do this without having to sacrifice whatever is left of my soul.

Pushing off from the door, I collect my clothes and decide to shower and think over what my next step will be. I'm useless to Alek if I'm locked in here. I may as well tell him what I know and hope we have enough information to beat the Macrillos before they get to us first.

I feel like a failure. My plan would have worked if only I gave Frank what he wanted.

The lock on the door clicks, and I turn quickly, hopeful Frank has changed his mind. When the door opens, however, it's not Frank; it's Santo. He enters swiftly, not wanting to be seen entering the chambers of his son's fiancée.

"Are you okay, *bambina*?" he asks, rushing over. When he gets closer, he freezes, staring at my reddening cheek. "He hit you?"

Nodding slowly, I lower my eyes.

"Oh, Frank," he mutters under his breath. "What did you do to provoke him?"

I bite the inside of my cheek to stop myself from spewing obscenities at him. How dare he assume I did something that would warrant such a punishment. And even if I did do something, nothing ever excuses a man for raising his hand to a woman.

This proves what cowards the Macrillo men are.

Gathering my composure, I rivet my attention to Santo, giving him puppy dog eyes. "I won't sleep with him," I whisper, playing a dangerous angle, but it's the only leverage I have. I can't fail Alek. His life depends on it.

"Oh, *bambina,*" Santo coos softly. "You've not laid with him since your return?"

I shake my head slowly.

"Why?"

"Because it's not his hands on me that I want."

Santo's eyes widen. I've caught him by surprise.

Even though he's made his intentions clear, we haven't crossed that line—yet. I don't know why he hasn't. I thought he would have. I never questioned it because I don't want him to. But now, I realize this is the only card I have left to play.

"No?" he questions, needing me to reconfirm.

"No, Santo. I don't want Frank." Little does he know, I don't want him either. The only hands I want are Alek's, and that's the reason I'm prepared to do whatever it takes.

"You don't know how happy that makes me," Santo says, smiling. "It kills me, wondering what he's doing to you. But now I know. We have to be careful. We can't let anyone know."

He commences a slow walk toward me. I stand still while my heart threatens to rip free from my chest.

"It's almost over," he reveals. "My plan to become king of this town is coming to fruition quicker than I thought."

"How so?" I ask, barely able to catch my breath.

"Aleksei is wild and unpredictable, which makes him

dangerous. And I can't work with that."

My heart is beating so frantically. I place a hand over my chest, afraid I'm about to have a heart attack.

"Tonight, my family is coming to meet Alek. We will find out everything we can. I was going to drag this out, but we can't wait."

"Wh-what does that mean?"

"It means, Aleksei Popov's days are numbered," he replies with a smirk. "I thought I needed him, but after speaking with my family, we just need the basics, and then we can fill in the blanks as we go. His impulsive nature makes him hard to trust. Even though he's come through when he said he would, I can't take the risk. Too much is at stake. It would be easier with him, but after what he did to Serg, to Raul, it's evident he'll have no issues doing the same thing to me."

Vomit threatens to rise, but I quash it down. "When will this happen?"

Santo reaches out and brushes the hair from my cheek. "It all depends on how much Alek is willing to share tonight. My *famiglia* is very powerful. They're the Italian mafia. They rule Italy, and now, they'll rule Russia as well. They didn't want to step on anyone's toes as we need buyers for their product, but with Alek the way he is, he is a risk we can't afford. It won't be easy at first, but please be patient with me, *bambina*, and when I rule, I'll buy us a house where we can be ourselves.

"We're both prisoners here. But it won't be long now. That's why I've decided to speed things up. I can't bear to be away from you any longer."

Tears spill down my cheeks, which Santo wipes away with

his thumb. He mistakes my tears for those of happiness. "This is all for you. I will kill the man who handed you over like nothing. He wasn't aware of my feelings for you. He didn't care what the repercussions were. He simply saw you as a paycheck."

My heart breaks because my plan has backfired—epically.

I need to warn Alek about tonight, but how? Locked in this room with no phone or computer access, I'm useless. If Alek gives Santo the information he needs, they'll kill him. Even though he's always on alert, he won't expect this so soon.

Alek is using Santo as well. He needs him alive just a little longer to gain what he can to cement his position back on top. This is why he won't kill him yet. But Santo has seen how impulsive Alek is—he's afraid of him, which is why he's going to kill him. There is a change of plans, and now, I must act accordingly.

God, forgive me.

"Thank you, *tesoro*," I softly whisper, peering up at Santo from under my eyelashes. "You are so good to me. I want to be there tonight to support you. But—"

"But what, *bambina*?" he asks, lifting my chin with his pointer finger.

"But Frank has ordered I stay locked in this room," I state, incredulous he took the bait.

"My son has a bad temper. I'm afraid I'm to blame. I can't override his decision. You know how it'll look if I do."

Shit. This won't do. If I don't warn Alek, he'll be walking into a trap.

"I know," I reply, frowning. "But I want to see you take

what's rightfully yours. You've earned it. Santino Macrillo, the kingpin of Russia, has a nice ring to it. And me, his beloved—" I pause with intent, and Santo plays straight into my hands.

"My queen." He fills in the blanks, rubbing his thumb along my bottom lip.

"You can't blame me for wanting to see you succeed," I reason, darting out my tongue to lick over his thumb. "And ending the man who hunted me like prey."

It works like a charm.

"Of course not. I will see to it then," he affirms confidently.

"And Frank?"

"You let me take care of my son."

Smiling happily, I bow in gratitude, as I know Santo will appreciate the gesture. But it seems he appreciates something else more.

"Now, how will you take care of me?"

Before I can reply, he wraps his hand around my waist and draws me against his chest. He examines me closely, and if I thought this monster could love, I'd say he was looking at me with love in his eyes. But he sees me as his possession. Nothing more. Nothing less.

"I haven't brushed my teeth yet," I say, panicked when he leans down to kiss me.

But him bending to my request doesn't come for free.

He walks us toward the bed, shoving me face-first onto the mattress. "It's okay. It's not your mouth I want."

Panicked, I try to scamper away, but Santo laughs, clearly aroused by the chase. He comes up behind me and lifts my short nightgown. He cups my ass, humming in approval before he tears off my underwear.

It's all happening so quickly. I don't want this.

When I hear him unfasten his belt, panic sets in, and I cry out, afraid as I look over my shoulder. "Please, Santo, not yet. I—"

"You what?" he snaps, his angry erection tenting from the front of his gray slacks. "You're just a cocktease? Is that it? Maybe I'll keep you locked in here after all."

Alek's face flashes before me, and I'm reminded of what happens if I don't comply. If I remain locked in this room, there will be no one to warn Alek of Santo's plans. Yes, I know he won't come alone—he'll have Saint, Pavel, Max, and maybe Willow.

This also means they too are at risk of being harmed.

I'm the only one who can protect them. And I can't do that in here. But not like this.

Santo presses his knee into my lower back, pinning me down as I attempt to recoil away from him. He only presses down harder as I fight desperately.

"No!" I cry out, flailing, but he doesn't listen.

"No? So, you're a liar? Is that it? You're playing me and my son? If I find out that you are, I will kill you and everyone you love," he warns, and it's not an empty threat.

Does he know about Alek and me? If he does, he will make sure Alek and the people Alek loves pay with their lives.

So with hollowed tears, I surrender. I stop fighting and turn back around, offering myself to Santo as I lift my hips. He doesn't need an invitation and drops his pants as he mounts me from behind. When his weight presses down on me, I go to another place.

It's quiet here. There is no violence, no pain.

When Santo spits in his hands and lubricates my entrance, I squeeze my eyes shut and think of Alek. I think of the way he makes me feel. Of how his touches are filled with nothing but love and tenderness. He is seen as a monster, but he isn't.

He is everything to me, which is why I'm doing this.

The bed begins to rock as Santo ruts into me, his grunts echo his ecstasy while my hollowed cries resonate my pain. Every part of me demands I fight him, but what happens when I do? I only wanted to make things better, but this is what happens when I think I can outsmart the Macrillos.

As Santo's pleasured grunts fill the room, I grip the sheets beneath my fingers, burying my face into the mattress, hoping to suffocate myself so I no longer have to feel him inside me. He latches onto the back of my neck, forcing my face farther into the bed.

"*La tua fica è il paradiso,*" he grunts, commending me for feeling like heaven. To me, however, this is hell.

I don't bother gasping for air. I want to die. But I can't because staying alive isn't just for Alek; it's for me as well. A murderous rage I've never experienced before fills me. Once this is over with…I'm going to return the favor. Santo wants to take without permission, so I will do the same.

However, only his life as penance will do.

No matter how many showers I've had, I can still feel him slithering inside me. I can feel his hands clawing me, punishing me with what he believes is love.

Gripping the bowl, I dry-heave into the toilet, hoping to expel some of this disgust inside me, but nothing helps. It only makes me feel worse.

Santo finished in under a minute, then he wiped his seed from my lower back, kissed my shoulder, and promised to see me tonight as he left the room. The door remained unlocked—although, I wish it wasn't. Being locked away suddenly didn't seem so bad.

It kept the monsters away.

Unrolling some toilet paper, I wipe my mouth and toss it into the bowl. I flush the toilet and come to a shaky stand. I'm sore down there because Santo wasn't gentle. Everything hurts. But I need to focus because there is no way I'm going to spend another night in this house.

I hunt through the lavish garments in my walk-in closet and pick an elegant red dress—the color reflects the fire burning inside me.

As I look at myself in the mirror, I shake my head, disgusted I didn't fight harder. I should have done something, anything. Instead, I allowed that monster to take me against my will. I rub more makeup over my upper arm where Santo's punishing grip left bruises.

The back of my neck throbs. Even though I can't see, I know I'll have bruises there too, so I wear my hair down to cover them.

Quickly dressing, I find the beautiful silk dress is the perfect camouflage to conceal how I'm feeling inside. On the outside, I look composed and put together, but on the inside, I want to fucking kill Santo. I want to take from him how he did from me.

I don't feel sorry for myself. I'm fucking angry I didn't kill him when I had the chance. I choked, and it's something I'll never do again.

The door opens and in strolls Frank. He's dressed in a button-down shirt and a pair of black slacks. He looks casual, but nothing is relaxed about tonight's proceedings. When he sees me slip into my red heels, he hums in approval.

"I'm glad my father persuaded me to change my mind. You look ravishing. Good enough to eat."

My heels put me almost at eye level with Frank, so I stand tall when he walks over to me and kisses my cheek—the one slathered in makeup to conceal the handprint he left behind.

"Didn't your mother teach you not to play with your food?" I quip, not checking my sarcasm at the door. I have nothing left to lose.

Frank chuckles, nudging my cheek with his nose. "This smart mouth of yours will only get you in trouble."

"Oh, I hope that it does," I purr, wanting him to think he's in with a shot. My victory will taste all the sweeter when I neuter him after I'm done with his father.

Frank smirks, appreciating my flirty sass. "C'mon, *bella*,

we can finish this later. Now, we have guests to entertain."

Fixing my hair to cover the bruises on my neck, I accept Frank's arm as he escorts me from the room and down the spiral staircase. Joyful voices speaking Italian sound from downstairs. Santo's family must be here already.

We enter the parlor room, and what I see angers me all the more.

Three men in expensive silk suits are huddle around Santo and Mila, laughing and liaising as though they're not breathing the same air as a monster. The younger man of the three strangers stops talking when he sees us enter. The halt in conversation has Santo turning toward the doorway.

We lock eyes and flashes of him on top of me, in me, rob me of air. I keep my cool, however, as Mila is watching. Even though she's aware of her husband's infidelities with others, she doesn't know of ours because this is a family affair which would never be allowed.

Santo remains poker-faced, but I can smell his smugness. He got to me before his son did. How that must make the old man beat his chest in pride.

Thankfully, a server comes over with a tray filled with champagne glasses. I resist temptation and only take one glass.

"Zio Vincenzo, I want you to meet my fiancée, Antonella." The older man with dark brown eyes walks over and kisses both my cheeks.

This must be Santo's brother.

"Pleased to meet you," he says in Sicilian dialect.

"And you," I reply in the same dialect, impressing him.

"*Sei Italiano?*"

"My father is," I reply. "He's from Napoli."

I can see Santo from the corner of my eye, beaming proudly. It makes me sick.

"Come, Christian," he orders the younger man who resembles him. I guess this is Vincenzo's son.

Christian looks out of place compared to these stuffy old men. He also doesn't seem to appreciate his father hovering as he glares at him when he passes him. But he does as he is instructed and gives both my cheeks a kiss. He looks the same age as Frank. He doesn't seem a threat, but the fact he's here proves otherwise.

"It's wonderful to meet the woman who was able to capture my cousin's heart."

Frank draws his cousin in for a tight hug, but it's all for show. They're not close.

"Stop with this romantic nonsense," says Vincenzo, embarrassing his son.

Christian tongues his cheek, not appreciating his father's tone. I can't shake the feeling he's only here because he bears the Macrillo name.

"*Ciao, mi chiamo Fausto,*" says the last man. He appears to be the same age as Santo and Vincenzo, but there is no mistake that he is the head patriarch. The air of authority follows him as he kisses my cheeks.

So, this is the Italian mafia. The men who plan on taking Alek down.

Gulping down my champagne, I realize I'm in way over my head. I thought this would be…easier. Renata made it look so simple. But I suppose she didn't have to contend with the Italian fucking mafia.

I don't fail to notice Mila observing my every movement. As a rule, we stay out of each other's way. She doesn't like me, and the feeling is more than mutual. Even before Santo showed any interest in me, she had it out for me.

I thought it was because she believed I wasn't good enough for her baby boy. But now, I think she knows Santo likes me more than he should. She sees me as a threat to her precious kingdom, but she can have it. Once this night is through, I'll be out of here. I just don't know how yet.

Looking at the grandfather clock, I see that it's after seven. Alek should be here soon. I don't know how I'm going to do it, but I need to tell him his life is in danger. He needs to kill Santo before Santo gets to him first.

A shiver surpasses me as I'm afraid. This has all turned to shit in the span of twelve hours. This world is so foreign to me. I want out, and when the air charges and sparks with a pulsating current, it seems I'm about to get my wish.

All attention rivets toward the doorway, all in tuned to the man who turns heads wherever he goes. Alek enters the room, and all I want to do is cry in happiness. He's here. Even though I'm still furious at him for consorting with those three women, I can't deny my happiness overrides my anger. For now.

His dark hair is slicked back, showcasing his chiseled features and those steel-blue eyes. He's clean shaven, but like always, a hint of a five o'clock shadow pokes through. He reeks of authority in his navy fitted slacks and a white crisp shirt.

His cane makes him look all the more intimidating.

Saint and Willow are close behind him. Both look stunning. I wonder where Pavel and Max are.

"Ah, my friend," Santo says happily, walking over to Alek and offering his hand.

They shake, and I can't help but feel deflated as Alek hasn't sought me out. He's behaving as though I don't exist, but I suppose that's to be expected after our last meeting.

How things have changed since then.

"Please, I want you to meet my brother, Vincenzo; his son, Christian; and my brother-in-law, Fausto." Santo waves his family over, wanting to get introductions out of the way early.

"Pleasure to meet you, Aleksei," Vincenzo says in Sicilian.

"English please, Vince—"

"The pleasure is all mine," Alek replies in Sicilian, cutting Santo off.

All men stare at Alek, impressed he can speak their dialect. Did they really think he'd come unprepared?

Fausto shakes Alek's hand firmly. Two alphas in the same room—this will not end well.

I quickly avert my eyes, knowing I'm openly ogling Alek. I catch the gaze of Willow who watches me closely with a concerned look on her face. She's here for appearances' sake, but neither Saint nor Alek would put her in harm's way which makes me believe they don't intend on tonight ending in violence.

The need to speak to Alek is even more imperative.

Frank's grip on my arm tightens as he draws me into his

side. I don't know what's caused this sudden possessiveness, but when I meet Alek's eyes, I realize he's the reason. He doesn't seem to care that we're in a room full of people because he looks at me as though we're the only people in the world.

He openly examines me from head to toe, his heated gaze lingering on my face as he works his way back up. I remain passive, not wanting to alert that anything is amiss with so many eyes on us. His hunger turns to fury, however, when he focuses on Frank's fingers digging into my upper arm.

I want nothing more than to wrap myself in Alek's arms and explain everything, but I can't. His blatant stares haven't gone unnoticed by Frank, so I have to tread with caution.

"Let's eat," Santo says, breaking the sudden uncomfortable silence.

Alek smirks, utterly cocky as he knows he owns this room. Even the Sicilians seem impressed by him. Vincenzo slaps Alek on the back as he says something I can't hear even though Alek's attention doesn't waver from me.

He continues to stare at me with a look I can't quite place. It appears he's attempting to solve a puzzle without all the pieces.

Frank angrily walks from the room, his fingers still digging into my arm. "Ouch," I cry, trying to break free from his punishing grip, but he doesn't let me go.

"This dress makes you look like a slut," he cruelly spits, shaking me. "Go upstairs and change."

"Hardly," I bite back, eyes narrowed as I pry his fingers off me. "And no, I will not go change. If you don't like my dress, don't look at me. I'd prefer it if you didn't."

Before he has a chance to reply, I march ahead and enter the ballroom alone. One of the maids escorts me to my seat, and I begrudgingly sit, as I don't want to break bread and pretend I'm not dying inside. I don't know how I'm going to get through this dinner without stabbing Frank or Santo with my fork.

Everyone else enters.

I keep my eyes peeled to my silverware, nervously arranging the perfectly aligned forks and knives, but I need to do something with my trembling fingers. The chair next to me scrapes along the floor, and Frank's suffocating cologne hits my nostrils.

He grips the back of my neck and yanks me toward him to snarl into my ear, "You're going to regret your words, *puttana.*"

Angrily peeling his fingers off me, I sarcastically reply, "Nice. Calling your fiancée a whore. Good to see your mother taught you manners."

"Don't you dare speak about my mother that way," he whispers, squeezing my leg under the table.

"Or what?" I challenge, turning slowly to face him.

The gloves are off. I can no longer pretend I want anything to do with him. I wish I could have lasted longer, but I can't. Not after what Santo did today. I refuse to be a victim, so it's time I fought back.

"Thought so," I mock. "Now, get your *fucking* hands off me." I jar my leg away from him, daring him to scold me in front of our "guests."

He clenches his jaw, but he doesn't make a scene.

Alek enters last, so he missed the altercation, but when he peers over, he senses something is amiss. He is ushered to his chair—left of Santo, who sits at the head of the table proudly. When Willow and Saint remain standing behind Alek, I purse my lips, confused.

Santo says something to Alek as though it's normal protocol for two people to stand while we dine on this four-course meal. I risk a glance at Willow, but she keeps her eyes peeled to the floor—like a good submissive.

Saint is on high alert, watching everyone's movements, ready to spring into action if need be. I need to get one of them alone so I can tell them what Santo has planned. But I'm beginning to think that's going to be impossible with Frank breathing down my neck.

The maids scurry into the ballroom, hands filled with traditional Italian foods. The table is decorated beautifully, and if I wasn't here against my will, I would appreciate the effort put into tonight's dinner. But when an antipasto is placed in front of me, all I want to do is vomit.

Pushing the plate away, I instead reach for the bottle of *vino*. However, a small whimper escapes me when Frank pinches my waist so hard, tears sting my eyes. No one sees as he's discreet and does it under the table, but Alek hears my small cry.

Santo continues talking to him, but Alek pays no attention as he's too busy looking at me. I want to jump up and tell him everything, but if I do that, they're all dead. So I bypass the *vino* and reach for the sparkling water instead.

My hand trembles as I pour myself a glass. Frank seems

overjoyed he's instilled the fear of God into me.

Conversation is spoken in mostly Sicilian. It's all small talk, but soon, that'll change. Santo made clear tonight is a strategic move. He wants to milk what he can from Alek, hoping it'll be enough for him and his family to turn rogue.

They don't want to prolong this transaction as they can't trust Alek, but I know what that really means—they're afraid of him.

I don't touch my food. I simply sit quietly, a spectator to the conversation around me. Frank is pleased by my submission, and once the third course is served, his touches turn gentle as he gently caresses over the back of my knuckles.

My chest heaves as I attempt to conceal my heavy breaths. His touches make me want to be sick. When he lifts the hem of my dress, I jolt upright, biting back my tears. I'm moments away from losing it.

When the tiramisu and espresso is served, I silently repeat over and over that it'll be over soon. Once they're done, Santo will casually suggest a cigar and brandy in the den where they will no doubt lay out their plan.

Women won't be allowed in the boys' club, which gives me the perfect opportunity to strike. I just need a few seconds alone with Alek, Saint, or Willow to alert them that things are not okay.

It'll be over soon...

I haven't been able to look at Alek throughout the entire dinner, afraid he'll sense something is wrong. If he does, I don't know what he'll do. Or what he *won't*. And that's what terrifies me.

"More coffee, Mrs. Macrillo?" asks Georgina, a maid I've come to like and trust in the short time I've been here. I hate that they have servants. It's completely unnecessary, but I'm suddenly struck with an idea. I keep my excitement under wraps.

When Georgina addresses Mila, I risk a glance at Mila but wish I didn't. She is glaring at me. What can she see?

"No, thank you, Georgina. I might escort Antonella to the bathroom." She comes to stand, hinting this isn't optional.

Alek pauses conversing and listens with interest. Santo appears anxious as this is awfully strange.

"You hardly touched your dinner. You must be unwell."

I don't have a choice and come to a shaky stand. "Please excuse me," I say in a voice I don't even recognize and follow Mila as she escorts me from the room.

As I pass Willow, she lifts her gaze and those expressive eyes console me; they tell me it'll be okay because she knows, she knows I'm a prisoner because she was once too. I'm suddenly filled with hope.

With face downcast, I continue following Mila who leads me to the downstairs guest bathroom. She opens the door, gesturing I'm to enter first. I do and brace for anything. Once the door closes, Mila is on me, pulling back my long hair.

"Get off me!" I snarl, gripping her fingers in my hair, trying to pry her away. But she has a tight hold.

"You will not embarrass this family, are we clear?" she says, yanking my head back at a painful angle. "I see the way my husband looks at you. Don't think I haven't noticed. You will not hurt my son. You'll be a good wife to him. Stay away from Santo."

"And if I don't?" I quip through clenched teeth as she pulls my hair harder.

"Then you'll be very sorry," she threatens. "This is your first and last warning. I don't like you, and I know my son will grow bored of you soon, but until then, I must tolerate you."

"Why not get rid of me now?"

"Because you've already brought enough shame to this family. If this wedding doesn't go ahead, then it'll only disgrace us even more. Let's hope those childbearing hips bring me many grandsons. I don't know what's so special about you. Maybe it's because you're nothing but a шлюха who sleeps with any man who looks your way. I told Santo for Alek to deliver you without a scratch, you'd have to have tempted him with something, and the way he watches you has confirmed my suspicions."

Oh, god. This is bad.

Santo doesn't need another reason to kill Alek. If Mila noticed Alek watching me, has Santo?

"You will know your place in this family. Otherwise, things will end badly for you, Antonella. I haven't dug deep but don't force me to."

If she does, she'll find out about Alek and me.

So I nod quickly. "Okay. I understand."

"Good girl. Your disobedience tonight is the last time you act out. Otherwise, it won't only be my husband sneaking into your bedroom. My sons share everything. And they do as I say." She lets me go and shoves me into the wall.

I bang into it, flinching as this just adds another bruise

the Macrillos have left.

Mila curls her lip, repulsed. "Fix yourself up. You look a mess." She opens the door, composed, not bothered by what just unfolded in here seconds ago.

Once the door closes, I hug my middle and fold myself in half. No wonder Frank is so cruel. Both his parents are monsters.

Frank's brothers share everything, including women, it seems. Does this mean Frank does the same with his brother's wives?

I could crumple in a heap and cry. Or I could fight.

Looking at my reflection in the mirror, hunched over, looking like a victim, I slowly straighten my spine and brush back my snarled hair. I can't cry any more tears. I don't want to. Alek once called me brave. I intend to stay that way.

Once I no longer look a fright, I open the door, ready to end this once and for all. However, when I find Frank waiting for me outside the door, I can't hide my surprise.

"Are you all right, *tesoro*? Mother said you're unwell," he asks kindly, his Jekyll and Hyde persona in full swing. "That's why you've been acting so strange."

"I'm fine," I reply firmly. "I wish to go upstairs."

I need to get away from him so I can ask Georgina to slip a note to Alek. I trust her. I know that she won't rat on me. If she can't get to Alek, Saint or Willow will do.

But Frank shakes his head. "No, my father has asked we join him in the den."

"Why?" This is unheard of.

"Because he's challenged Alek to a game of poker." My

stomach drops.

Why would he do that? He knows Alek's past. He knows what he did to Willow. Santo is up to something.

"He likes you," Frank says, startling me.

"Who?" I gulp, tugging at the jeweled cross around my neck.

"Alek," he replies like that should be a no-brainer. "I saw the way he was looking at you. It pleases me that he wants what's mine."

I don't have time to react before he bends down and places his mouth over mine.

Bile rises, and I keep my lips slack as he attempts to kiss me. "I'm sorry for this morning," he whispers against my mouth. "You just know what buttons to press."

Pulling away, I can't hide my horror. Is he really blaming me for his violence?

"Come, you know my father doesn't like to be kept waiting." He loops his fingers through mine and leads me to the den. I don't know what I'm walking into, but it's not good.

Frank opens the door and ushers me in. The moment I enter, I see Alek sitting at the poker table, coolly leaning back in his chair, sipping a drink. Everyone sits at the table, bar Saint and Willow. Mila isn't here.

Santo turns over his shoulder, smiling fondly at me. "Are you feeling better? Mila said you weren't feeling well."

"I'm fine," I reply curtly, incredulous he can speak to me so casually after what he did.

I try to make my move and stand near Willow, but Frank leads me in the other direction, toward the empty chair. He takes a seat, expecting me to stand behind him like a good little *fidanzata*.

Clenching my jaw, I remain passive, not wanting to alert anyone to the inner turmoil brewing. It won't be long until it explodes out of me.

"So are we ready?" Santo asks, arranging his chips into stacks.

Willow shifts uncomfortably. The memories of what happened the last time Alek played poker must still be too raw.

Alek chuckles arrogantly. "Sure. You ready to lose?"

Santo grins, raising his crystal glass in salute.

I don't know anything about poker, so it's all very foreign to me as they start playing. They play their cards close to their chest, none of them giving anything away. Alek has always had the perfect poker face.

I'm fascinated by the way he approaches this game with utter confidence. If I were playing, I'd be fooled into thinking he had a winning hand every time he laid a card down. Santo wins the first game. His prize—twenty thousand dollars.

As some machine shuffles their cards, Fausto makes his move. Playtime is over.

"Aleksei, Santo has explained to us that you're in need of someone you can trust. With Raul gone, you need someone who can fulfill your demands."

Alek nods, his poker face still in play. "Yes. That is correct. However, I will not go into business with an amateur."

Fausto looks as though Alek has slapped both his cheeks with the insult. "I can guarantee our product is the very best."

Santo doesn't speak. He simply deals the cards to the players, allowing Fausto to say his bit.

"You must understand, trust is everything to me," Alek says, peeking at his cards, which remain on the table. "My empire collapsed in the past because I was too…lenient," he settles for. "But I've learned from my mistakes."

"We live, and we learn," Christian says in Sicilian. There is something I can't put my finger on with him. He seems different from the rest. He's hiding something, something I feel he doesn't want his family to know.

Alek nods, reaching for his cards and organizing them leisurely. "This is true. And I've learned that if anyone betrays me, if anyone doesn't agree with my way, then I kill them."

Fausto's thin lips lift into a pleased smile. "There is no other way. We want the same thing. My family has been doing this for a very long time. We're discreet."

"How?" Alek asks as they commence playing.

"Back home, we own all the major waste management companies."

I have no idea if this is code for something.

"Every Tuesday, we leave deliveries. We pick up deliveries. We give our customers special garbage bags for a fee of course. Our cartel act as trash haulers, and to the unknown, we are just keeping the streets clean. We have influence over certain routes, and we're not afraid to get our hands dirty if any competition believes they can challenge us."

"That's all good and well in Sicilia, but what about here? Russia isn't Italy. How do you propose to work this operation here?" Alek asks, pushing some chips into the growing pile in the middle of the table.

"That's where our partnership works in both our favors," Fausto explains. "Your reputation is notorious. Tales of the brutal Aleksei Popov have reached Sicilia. We work together to regain your allies and win over who we need."

"How do you propose we do that? In case you hadn't heard, I'm the anti-hero everyone loves to hate." Alek's sarcasm knows no bounds. He doesn't care he's sitting with the Italian mafia, who would kill him without a second thought. The fact seems to provoke him all the more.

"Alek, together, we're unstoppable," Santo says cockily. "You can trust me. We both benefit from this partnership. I have the drugs, and you have the connections, the knowledge to distribute those drugs."

Santo is trying to sell this idea to Alek because yes, both need one another in this transaction, but as far as trusting him, that's total bullshit. He will dispose of Alek the moment they get the information they need to succeed on their own.

Alek mulls over Santo's words, and when he lifts his eyes, focusing on me, I take a small step backward, suddenly afraid.

"Okay, let's do it."

The men look at one another, their surprise soon turning to happiness as they believe they've won. "*Meraviglioso!*"

The celebration is short-lived however.

"I'm a gambling man," Alek says, reaching for his glass. "You said I can trust you, so how about you all put your money where your mouth is?"

The men don't see a problem with it and push all their chips into the middle of the table. But Alek has other ideas.

"Let's make things interesting. Money is so…mundane. Let us bet something far more exciting."

"What did you have in mind, my friend?" Santo beams, slapping Frank on the back happily.

"How about"—Alek taps his chin, appearing in thought—"how about Willow for…Antonella."

My mouth drops open, as I can't conceal my surprise. "You motherfu—"

Alek smirks, daring me to continue. I glare in response.

Santo shifts in his seat uncomfortably. Frank's spine straightens. Willow remains docile.

"As you know, I won Willow in a game of poker. She's my lucky charm."

I narrow my eyes at Alek, furious at him. Just what is he playing at? Does he propose to "win me" so he can take me away from here? Suddenly, the idea doesn't seem so bad.

Frank shakes his head, but I see Santo place his hand over Frank's bouncing leg. "What are the terms?"

So this is what it feels like to be treated like nothing but a commodity. I now realize that regardless of how much Alek has changed, Willow will always remember that he was the man who bought her.

"How about winner takes all the money and a night with these beautiful women?"

The men lick their lips like the hungry wolves that they are as they ogle Willow.

Christian's attention is on Saint. "What about him?"

Alek shrugs and questions, "What about him? You want him too? That'll cost you extra."

Saint's jaw clenches. There's no way he'd allow this, so they clearly have a plan. I can only hope it's to win me as their prize. My anger turns to hope. Maybe Alek hasn't given up on me after all.

"Name your price," Christian says, making clear he wants both Willow and Saint. But the way his gaze travels up and down Saint's form, I dare say, Willow is just a bonus as Saint is the real prize.

"If I lose, I give you Willow, Saint, and the name of my biggest buyers. This proves my trust in you." Oh, god, Alek has just signed his death warrant. "But if I win…you tell me how you run your operation. I want to know where you get your product from, as I assume you don't manufacture it yourself.

"This seems fair as there are more of you playing than me. The odds *are* in your favor."

This seems sacrilegious. If they tell Alek this, essentially, he could make a deal with their supplier behind the mafia's back, cutting them out.

"This proves *your* trust in *me*," Alek adds, throwing Santo's words back at him. "This seems fair. Don't you think?"

The men look at one another around the table, clearly conflicted by Alek's proposition. They both have a lot to lose. But Alek doesn't lose. When he won Willow, his life changed forever, and I can guarantee, he plans to do the same with this proposal.

"Yes, all right," Santo agrees, nodding. "You've got a deal."

"Wonderful. And I almost forgot, seeing as you're getting two of mine, I want Ella for two nights. Not one." A flush spreads up my neck when Alek arches a dark brow.

"*Papa*," Frank argues softly. "Not Ella. She is mine."

"Hush, son," Santo says, revealing this is a done deal.

Frank isn't upset about my reputation but, rather, his own. He knows he'll never live this down. Alek will remind him of all the things he did to his fiancée. A form of torture for a proud man like Frank.

It's a stare-off between Alek and Santo—two alphas, battling for the top spot as they recommence their game.

I watch with bated breath, unsure who's winning. When Fausto curses and throws down his cards, it seems he's out of the game. This continues for grueling minutes that feel like hours until only two players remain—Alek and Santo.

Alek smirks cockily while Santo shifts in his seat. The game is clearly in the bag for Alek. He wouldn't look so certain otherwise. But when Santo lays his cards down on the table and snickers, I realize I know nothing at all.

Alek's lips lift into a lopsided grin when Santo reveals his spread. "I'll be damned. Looks like you beat me."

"Looks that way," Santo says, clapping happily.

Frank's shoulders drop, relieved I won't be made a whore by the Russian drug lord.

There is animated chatter among the men, congratulating Santo on his win while I stare wide-eyed. What just happened? Alek wasn't supposed to lose. He was supposed to win. He was supposed to get me out of here. He wasn't supposed to trade Willow and Saint like nothing but cattle.

But now, he's condemned me, Saint, and Willow.

I can't breathe.

Santo draws the chips toward him, happier than a pig in

shit. He's won the information he needed, money, and two of Alek's closest confidants. The bad guy won. I don't understand this.

"Let us have a drink before you spill all your secrets," Fausto quips, coming to a stand. He is elated their plan to milk Alek of his secrets has come about so soon.

Christian walks over to Saint, and when he attempts to caress his cheek, Saint strikes out in the blink of an eye and elbows him in the nose. It crunches under the impact. Christian howls, cupping his bleeding nose.

The men's joy soon turns to dread. Alek beams proudly. Santo looks at him, utterly confused.

"This was a test, as such. You didn't stipulate that they'd have to behave," Alek explains, amused. "Shame on you for not being more thorough. You have your hands full with these two.

"What did you say, Christian?" Alek pretends to search for the right words. "We live, and we learn?"

Christian narrows his eyes as he hunts through his pocket for a handkerchief. This isn't over. Not by a long shot.

Alek is playing them at their own game. He knows Saint and Willow can look after themselves. The deal was never for them to submit. Alek has outsmarted Santo and his family, playing on their greed, eagerness, and stupidity.

"Let this be a lesson for future business transactions. We don't leave room for negotiation. You won Saint and Willow, but we didn't set the guidelines for what we agreed on. For instance, if you said you'd wanted to fuck, demoralize, or abuse either of them, I wouldn't have approved," Alek states, using this loss as a win. "Your negotiation skills are sloppy. Fueled by greed. This isn't smart business, and I won't enter into a partnership with careless men."

Santo isn't happy, but he nods. Besides, all he wants is the information. Saint and Willow were a cushy bonus. "You're right, Aleksei. This won't happen again."

I don't understand it, but in this world, someone's word seems to be enough.

"I expect you to treat my friends as you would me—with respect."

As far as deals go, Santo and company have lost, and they won't be using Saint and Willow to gratify their devious ways. They will suck it up because this is their fault for not setting their own rules. Alek set this plan in motion, knowing Saint and Willow would be safe if he lost.

He wanted to teach Santo a lesson; that's why he lost. He wouldn't have made the deal otherwise. Make no mistake, he will always be alpha. If Santo goes back on his word and hurts Saint or Willow, their partnership is done. And Santo would never allow that to happen, so he'll behave.

But what about me? Where does this leave me? If he won, he could have saved me. Did he even try to win? Was I ever taken into consideration when Alek made this deal? I soon find out that I was.

"Lucky for me then," Frank snarls, glaring at Alek. "If you won, I'm sure you wouldn't have shared the same respect for my *fiancée*."

Alek leans back in his chair, eyeing me without emotion. "She looks like she bites. I probably would have asked for a rematch if I won."

Santo chuckles while I grit my teeth, ready to kill this motherfucker with my bare hands. How dare he.

"I now see why you're unrivaled. You're smart. Resourceful. We will make a great team," Fausto says, nodding at Santo happily. "We can teach one another so much."

How wonderful; everyone wins. Alek has proven he's got the biggest dick, and Santo and his *famiglia* get the information to use as collateral against Alek when the time is right. I should let them kill him.

Suddenly, realization hits—all of this was for nothing.

Alek didn't need me to save him. Fausto is right; he *is* smart and resourceful. He would have figured this out on his own. By trying to help him, I've condemned myself to hell. I could blame Alek, but I only have myself to blame for thinking I could pull this off.

Frank's chair tumbles over as he stands abruptly. Santo's eyes narrow into slits—a silent warning to behave. They've got Alek where they want him.

"Let's go," Frank growls, gripping the crease of my elbow.

"Don't be too long," Santo orders. "We have much to discuss with Aleksei."

My body is a live wire, and Frank's hands only ignite the fuse. I don't fight him because I want to be as far away from Alek as I can. The moment we're out of that room, I exhale, my body shuddering as I attempt to breathe.

Frank either hasn't noticed my impending meltdown, or he doesn't care. He hauls me up the stairs toward our bedroom and practically tosses me inside. My mind is racing, as is my heart.

"That smug *bastardo*!" Frank curses, tugging at his hair as he paces the room. "I should go back down there and kill him for embarrassing us in our home!"

As I slump onto the end of the bed, my mind goes into self-preservation mode because how am I going to get out of here? My grand plan just unraveled. Knowing Alek would be waiting for me at the end of this was the only reason I persevered.

But now, I have no one.

Tears I've tried so hard to keep at bay break the surface because I've never felt more hopeless than I do right now. I bite my cheek to stop from crying in front of Frank, but I can't stop them. Fat, ugly tears roll down my cheeks as I gasp for air.

"Why are you crying?" Frank shouts, angered that I'm not more sympathetic to his complaints.

"I-I-I—" I'm trembling so badly that I can't form a coherent sentence, which infuriates Frank all the more.

"Anyone would think you're upset he lost. You probably are. You probably couldn't wait to spread your legs for him, you dirty whore!" He rushes over, and before I have a chance to fight him off, he pulls me up by my hair.

Crying out, I twist and turn, desperately attempting to break free. But Frank only yanks harder, craning my neck so far back, I'm certain he'll snap me in half.

"You dressed like a slut for him, didn't you? You're not getting any from me, so you're getting it from someone."

"Fuck you!" I scream, fighting like a wild cat.

"Fuck me?" he angrily spits, stunned I would talk back.

"You need a reminder of who's boss."

He lets me go, only to push me into the wooden dresser. A pained gasp leaves me as I fight for air. Frank doesn't allow the reprieve, however, and is on me, walking me toward the wall with his hand locked around my throat, making it impossible to breathe. He pins me to the wall.

"Tell me who you're fucking!"

I frantically slap at his hand as I gag, unable to take in air. But he doesn't let me go.

His eyes are crazed when he lowers his face so that it's inches from mine. "Tell me!"

My eyes flicker. I'm on the cusp of passing out, but it doesn't end this way for me. I refuse to be a victim at the hands of another Macrillo man.

Running on fumes of adrenaline, I raise my knee and connect with Frank's balls. He gasps and lets me go, buckling in half. Shoving past him, I run for the door, but he reaches out and snares the back of my long dress, dragging me toward him.

"No!" I scream, flailing for my freedom.

Frank kidney punches me, which has me dropping to my knees, gagging and wheezing. "Look what you made me do! Just answer my question, and I'll forgive you."

But there is no forgiveness here. This toxicity was always bound to end in blood. So with nothing left to lose, I lift my chin and seal my fate forevermore. "You're right; I am fucking someone else."

Frank inhales sharply, closing his eyes as if needing a minute. He's going to need more than a minute.

"I didn't come back because I wanted to," I reveal, gripping my middle as it hurts to breathe. "I left you, Frank, because I could never be your wife. You're a spoiled mommy's boy who is trying so desperately to be like his father. Santo asked Alek to bring me back because—"

"Because he loves me!" Frank says, wishing to live out his fantasy. But I soon shatter that with a sharp shake of my head.

"No, you fucking moron. Because he…loves *me*."

Frank's mouth parts, his eyes displaying the horror within. It only fuels me further as I come to a shaky stand.

"You asked who I was fucking? Well, surprise, it's your f-father!" I proclaim breathlessly, the truth finally setting me free.

Frank staggers back, shaking his head. "You liar! You fucking liar!"

"No, it's the truth. I returned to be your father's mistress. I was to marry you, only for your precious *papa* to fuck me behind your back," I crudely state. "Looks like he'll always be bigger and better than you. And *bigger* he is."

Frank vibrates, his face turning red and spittle foaming at the corner of his mouth. "He would never do that to me!"

His pain is like a drug to me, and I violently flip my hair over my shoulder, revealing the back of my neck. "No? Who gave me this then?" I say, exposing the bruises his father left behind.

My body, mind, and spirit are broken and bruised, but if this is my end, then I will ensure I go out with a bang.

"He fucked me in our bed. Doggy style. And I loved it. I loved every—"

I never get to finish my sentence because Frank advances with a roar and punches me in the face. Hot blood gushes from my nose, and all I can think is that it'll ruin my dress. My mind is lost, lost to this family as all they've done is abuse me until breaking point.

Frank punches me in the stomach and ribs, sobbing like he is the one getting the shit kicked out of him. His tears please me because I know I've hurt him. I have no doubt he's going to kill me, and I accept my fate, knowing what destruction I've left behind.

I've destroyed Frank. The fact has me laughing manically. This must be what it feels like to lose your mind.

"You whore! You lying whore!" Frank screams, kicking and punching me over and over again. By this stage, the fight in me dies, and I welcome death as I crawl on hands and knees toward it.

I want to tell him about Alek. I want him to know being here has nothing to do with the Macrillos and everything to do with Alek, but I can't. If I do that, they'll go after him. Tears stream down my cheeks when I realize I won't ever see him again. I won't ever be able to tell him that I love him with all my heart.

Frank picks me up and tosses me into the vanity table, perfumes and makeup cluttering to the floor. My head crashes into the mirror, breaking it. Glass shatters all around me. I slump over the vanity, gasping and gurgling on blood. I think I've bitten through my tongue.

No one can hear us because every room is soundproof. No knight in shining armor is coming to my rescue.

"We'll see who's bigger," Frank snarls, yanking up the hem of my dress forcefully as he comes up behind me. He shoves my face into the vanity, muting my screams.

His words, coupled with his actions, kickstart my heart, and a surge of utter fury animates me back to life. I was content that I had destroyed Frank by revealing his father's devious ways, but no, I will not allow another man to take from me against my will.

With bloodied fingers, I frantically fumble for a weapon, something, anything, and when my hand passes over a silver nail file, I take that as a sign from above. Mother Superior said He works in mysterious ways, and now is no exception.

Just as Frank rips off my underwear, I spin around and violently stab him in the side of the throat with the nail file. Frank's eyes widen before he staggers back, cupping his throat, which is gushing blood. The nail file trembles in my bloody hand when I realize what I've just done.

As Frank fumbles to find his footing, I think of his father, pinning me to the bed facedown as he forced himself on me. I think of how Frank was seconds away from doing the same thing. With that thought surging through me, I chase after him and stab him again, this time in the chest.

On instinct, he presses a hand over the wound, which only has the hole in his neck spewing forth a river of red. He gurgles, desperately trying to disarm me. He's losing blood fast, which makes him weak. But when he realizes he's going to die if he doesn't stop me, a surge of power overcomes him, and he launches forward, crazed and covered in blood.

"I'm going to fucking kill you!" he wheezes, frenzied.

We wrestle with the nail file, both wounded and fighting for our lives. At this moment, he truly is a monster—both inside and out. He elbows me in the face, and I fall backward onto the floor. Just as he comes charging after me as I scurry across the carpet, nail file in hand, he loses his footing, tripping and hitting his head on the sharpened corner of the dresser.

He is dead weight as he collapses on top of me.

Screaming, I frantically pummel his chest, trying to shove him off, but my muscles have given up, and he doesn't budge. I'm certain he's going to come to at any moment and punish me for disobeying him and sullying his mother's Persian rug. But then I realize he's not moving…or breathing.

Squirming frantically, I manage to roll out from under him and scamper away. He flops onto his stomach with his face pressed to the floor. A bright red puddle stains the white carpet where he bleeds out. But there is no movement.

Drawing my knees toward my chest, I lean against the foot of the bed and stare at Frank's still body, watching for any signs of life. But there are none.

"Oh m-my go-god," I cry, dropping the nail file with horror at what I've just done.

Leaning forward, I tremble uncontrollably as I press my fingers to his neck, checking for a pulse. His skin is hot and sticky because of the blood. But no matter how many times I try to wipe it away, it only resurfaces, confirming what I know to be true.

Frank is dead…and I killed him.

Unable to accept this fact, unable to accept what I just did, vomit rises, and I'm sick all over myself. I'm a murderer.

I killed a man. Yes, he was a bad man, but I ended someone's life. Doesn't that make me a monster as well?

What do I do now?

Hysteria rises, and I think I'm about to faint. Just as I grip the bed for support, the door opens, and my crime is exposed to the angel who stands before me. I now see why Saint calls her this. That's the last thought I have before I surrender to the madness; lost and never to be found.

CHAPTER SIX

Alek

I don't know what's happening, but quite frankly, I don't like it. Frank has been gone for far too long, which means Ella is in trouble.

Something isn't right. Tonight, she lost her spark, and all I saw was fear.

I lost the game on purpose. If Santo had seen my cards, he'd have known *I* had the winning hand, not him. But I could tell by the lift of Santo's lips that he thought he had a winning hand, so that was why I made the deal. I knew his victory would make him careless.

The plan was to give Saint and Willow a reason to be here and uncover whatever the fuck Santo was hiding. Him stealing from the temple made no sense. It had me thinking he's hiding something, which I needed to uncover.

Saint and Willow's presence allow them to be my eyes on the inside. But more importantly, it allows them to get to

Ella. And that is the real reason I bet the way I did. Willow is convinced Ella isn't here because she wants to be, so I thought on my feet and came up with this plan to find out the truth, once and for all.

To hopefully save my Ella.

I couldn't ask her, nor could I make it obvious how much it killed me to stay away from her. If Willow was right, Ella would pay the price, and I feared they'd already hurt her. She looked broken, which is why I needed to do something extreme like gamble with Saint and Willow's life.

I hope they can forgive me, but I knew Santo was too greedy to set any rules. This was the loophole that saved them. Besides, Santo would be terrified for his life and likely send Saint home within an hour of them being here.

What Santo really wanted was information, which I gave him. But it was all bogus. There is no way I'd tell them anything about my business. I don't trust them, and I know they'll use it to dispose of me. But I do need the mafia on my side.

And for that to happen, Santo will need to have an unfortunate accident that cannot be connected to me so I can continue this business relationship because the mafia are smart.

I could have won tonight, but that wouldn't give me what I wanted. Santo would sulk, and Ella would be in even more trouble. I had to be cruel because I saw the way Mila watched us. She knows something isn't right.

I wanted more than anything to win against Santo because I would have kidnapped Ella. There is no way I'd allow her to return here, but I can't do this with Santo on my ass. I need to be smart.

No more running.

And besides, if Ella is here because she wants to be, winning her would result in me not giving her back, regardless of her feelings. And I don't want to force her. I can't force her to forgive me. Or to love me.

This was the only sensible way not to arouse suspicion, but now, I'm fucking suspicious.

"This is wonderful," Fausto says, smoking his cigar. "This partnership is going to flourish. I just know it."

Nodding coolly, I keep my emotions under wraps. "I couldn't agree more."

I need an out. I can't leave on my own accord because they will sense something is amiss. Saint enters Santo's office, and the hollowed look on his face instantly has me sitting taller in my seat. Something is wrong.

"Pavel called. You need to bounce." He offers no further explanation, but I don't need to be told twice.

Coming to a stand, I fake regret that I have to cut our evening short. "Apologies, Santo, but duty calls."

Santo also stands, shaking his head. "I understand. I feel for whomever you're about to pay a visit to," he says, assuming I'm leaving to take care of business.

But I know Saint, and I know this is an excuse to get me out of here.

Fausto kisses both my cheeks, then places me out at arm's length to look at me. "It was a pleasure. We will organize a time when you can sample our goods. No time to waste."

I don't bother with small talk and shake hands with

the rest of the men. "Remember our deal," I instruct Santo, reminding them that if anything happens to Saint or Willow, his head will be the only suitable form of payment for going back on his word.

"In good faith, how about we make another deal? I give you Saint and Willow in exchange for ten thousand dollars," Santo barters, revealing his true needs.

Again, his desperation for money sets off alarm bells.

But if I do that, it defeats the purpose of losing. They need to be here to uncover what they can without suspicion. But when Saint clenches his jaw, I understand he may have already uncovered too much.

When Willow excused herself to use the bathroom and Saint followed, Santo's greed got in the way as he left them unmanned. I can only hope they used Santo's carelessness to their advantage and got to Ella.

But what of Frank?

He manhandled her from the den, and all the while, I had to stop myself from breaking every finger in his hands for touching her. If I made a move, we'd all be dead.

"Are you sure?" I question, needing this to be seen as Santo's decision in case something has happened.

"*Si.* I don't want to overstep any lines."

Bullshit.

If he wanted Saint or Willow, he would have no qualms with this arrangement, but he wants the money more.

I'm about to argue as a deal is a deal, and I don't go back on my word, but when Saint discreetly gestures with his head that it's time to go, I nod.

"Okay. I'll wire the money to you immediately. Thank you," I say even though it kills me to express any gratitude to him. "They are both treasured to me."

"I understand. Antonella is as well. To Frank," he quickly adds, but it's too late. It's obvious he is possessive of her and sees her as his.

The thought has me envisioning all the ways I plan on killing him. But now, I need to find out what is wrong.

"Send me the details when you're ready to do this."

The mafia men smile happily, even though Christian looks disappointed his uncle backed out on the deal. I decide Saint should show him at a later time what he missed out on, meaning he should break every bone in his body before slitting his throat.

Saint already suffered enough at the hands of Oscar. Anyone else who thinks they can do the same will suffer dire consequences.

Leaving the men believing they've won, we follow a maid to the front door. Willow quietly waits for us, wearing Saint's jacket. It's about five sizes too big. What the hell is going on?

No one speaks a word as we make our way toward the cars or, rather, car. Max and Pavel both drove tonight—remaining outside—in case we needed two cars, and it seems we do. I don't question where Pavel is as we get into Max's white car.

"Drive," Saint orders even before the door slams shut.

Max puts the car into gear and coolly drives down the driveway. But the way he clenches the steering wheel, I know there is nothing nonchalant about this entire situation. The gates open, and Saint sighs, appearing doubtful that they would.

Only when we're off the Macrillo property do I turn over my shoulder to look at Saint. Willow is huddled into his side, tears welling in her eyes.

"What's going on?" I beseech for someone to tell me what happened.

Saint tightens his hold on Willow. The jacket she wears shifts, allowing me to see that the front of her white dress is stained bright red.

"дорогая! Are you all right?" I frantically ask, heart in my throat. If they hurt her…

But Willow nods quickly. "I'm f-fine. It's not my…blood," she whispers the last word while I feel my blood drain from my face.

"Whose blood is it?" I demand, flinching from the harshness of my tone, but I suddenly can't breathe. "So help me God. Saint—"

"It's Ella's," Saint answers, cutting me off.

"О боже, нет," I cry, my body vibrating in absolute fear.

But what Saint says next has me understanding his motives for why we needed to leave immediately. "And Frank's. He's dead. Ella killed him."

His shortened sentences are like a stab to my heart, and I clutch at my chest, afraid it'll rip through my rib cage because it's broken. It's fucking broken.

"Where is she?" I'll get to the bottom of this later. Right now, I need to know she's all right.

"She's with Pavel. But Alek…" Saint kisses Willow's temple as she whimpers. "She's hurt badly. I had to carry her out discreetly because she was unconscious. Luckily, Ella made friends with one of the maids who escorted me to an unused exit. From what I could see, Frank beat her to within an inch of her life, and from the torn underwear, he—"

"Enough!" I exclaim, placing a fist over my mouth to stop my vomit. "Max, please drive faster."

Willow shakes her head, angered and afraid. "She put up a fight. She'll be okay," she says for both our sakes. The fact she's covered in blood affirms that she helped Saint get Ella out of there.

"And Frank? What did you do with him?" I ask, jaw clenching when I think about how I want to string him up and kill him again.

"I threw him off the balcony. He's hidden in the hedges underneath, but it won't be long until they find him. The bloodstains on the carpet are a dead giveaway that something ugly happened."

"We're all in danger," I state, my brain racing a million miles a minute. I need to come up with a plan—and fast.

"They'll think Ella escaped on her own," Saint says, and he's right. At first, they will. But it's only a matter of time until they work out the truth.

"Santo won't rest until he finds her and kills her for what she's done."

"We can hide her," Willow says, always coming to the rescue of others.

"That'll only work for so long. We're talking about retribution for the death of the Macrillos' youngest son. This is war," I declare, not believing those words are coming from my mouth.

I wait for Saint to argue, to tell me I'm overacting, but he doesn't, and that's because he knows I'm right.

"What will you do?" she asks, nervously biting her thumbnail.

"There is only one thing I can do. I need to leave Russia and go where no one can find us until I can work out a better plan.

"You need to do the same," I order Saint. "They will be coming for us. They'll be coming for us all. We don't have much time."

My time to reign was short-lived because now, I'm a fugitive. There is no way I'll fail Ella again. I have a target on my back because I saw the way Mila looked at me. I thought I was discreet, but she knows I have feelings for Ella. Ella couldn't have gotten far without help.

And they'll eventually figure out that help was us.

The tires screech as Max speeds toward my house. He doesn't even have a chance to turn off the motor before I open the door, throwing my cane across the lawn with a roar. It only slows me down. Racing for the front door, I almost tear it from the hinges as I frantically search for Pavel.

I don't want to scare Irina, so I don't call out.

Seconds later, he appears at the top of the staircase. "She's in your bedroom."

That's all I need to know as I take the stairs two at a time, my limp nonexistent because I'm running on pure adrenaline.

"She's in and out of consciousness," Pavel quickly informs, chasing me. "I've given her some strong painkillers."

I can't speak. I can't even think clearly. All I want to do is see her and make sure she's okay.

Bursting through my bedroom door, I thought I prepared myself for this, but I haven't. Nothing could have prepared me for this.

A broken figure lies in the middle of my bed, but there is no way it can be Ella. She is barely recognizable. Her body looks beaten, and her face…her swollen face is covered in so much blood. Running over to the bedside, I come to a sudden stop when I see the full extent of her injuries.

Tiny slits cover her face that look like they were caused by shards of glass, and the cuts are seeping blood. Her dress is torn, and her feet are bare. Her hair is snarled, almost standing on end like it's been pulled. Every part of her body looks bruised and bloody. Her chest rises and falls sluggishly as she struggles to breathe.

I see this clearly, but my mind refuses to accept this as truth. This can't be Ella. This broken woman cannot be her.

Slumping to my knees by her bedside, I brush the matted hair from her face with trembling fingers, but it sticks to the coagulated blood. "Прости меня, любовь моя. Я подвел тебя."

Forgive me, my love. I failed you.

I can't stop the guttural cry as I lower my chin, defeated. Gently gripping her limp hand in mine, I silently promise to protect her with my last dying breath.

"You can go to my mother's. No one will find you there," Pavel offers, but I shake my head.

"No, I refuse to put another life in harm's way. I have to disappear."

Squeezing Ella's cold hand, I beg she takes my strength to heal.

"I can help with that, but it'll take time to organize passports, ID—"

"And that is something I do not have. Time. I've already wasted too much," I say with regret.

"What will you do?" asks Pavel, realizing this is one thing he can't fix.

"There is only one thing I can do. I need to leave Russia. I need to take to the seas."

This is the only solution I can think of at the moment. It'll buy me time, and it'll keep Ella safe. We're not safe on land or in the skies. But at sea, we have a fighting chance.

Turning over my shoulder, I look at Saint who nods.

He knows this is our best shot because this is how he brought Willow to me. Yes, they encountered a few bumps along the way, but they survived. I have a yacht and supplies, so we can leave tonight.

"Pavel?" I ask, needing his advice as he's never failed me before.

"They might not figure it out," he says with a frown. "You can pretend not to know. But do you want to take that risk? Go now when you've got the chance."

Willow swallows as I can imagine this conversation brings up many unpleasant memories for her. "Doesn't that show your guilt? Leaving?"

"Yes," I reply honestly. "But by leaving now, I'm escaping the inevitable. They *will* work it out, дорогая, which means you can't be here when they do. Saint, you and Willow must also leave. Back to America. You must go far away from here."

"And what about you?" Willow asks. "We leave, and you'll be on your own."

I appreciate her concern, but I need to go into this selfishly. The only person I can look out for is Ella. Which leaves me with another question—Irina.

I can't leave her behind. The last time I did, she was almost killed. But how can I take her with me?

"No. We'll stay here," Saint says, surprising me.

"No, that is out of the question," I argue because they'll be sitting ducks here.

"This isn't negotiable," he contends firmly. "What, you propose to stay lost forever?"

"I'd hope not," I reply. "But I cannot make any promises. As long as there is a threat to Ella's life, we will remain hidden."

"We make up an excuse for why you had to leave so suddenly and hold down the fort until your return. Besides, you need someone here to keep tabs on the Macrillos. How else will you know their comings and goings?"

He's right. But I can't, in good faith, ask them to stay here while we work out a plan.

"We continue like it's business as usual," Pavel says, appearing to agree with Saint's idea. "You left Russia on a tip of where to find your mother. This will be a plausible excuse… for now. We'll keep in contact while you're away and work out our next move. Saint is right; for appearances' sake, someone needs to be here."

"No!" I exclaim, shaking my head firmly. "I will not ask this of you. You're putting your lives in danger. I cannot allow it."

"You're not asking us to do anything," Saint reasons stubbornly. "This is *our* choice. We run, and all of this would have been for nothing. I'm sick and tired of the bad guys winning. This ends now."

"And besides," Willow says softly. "Who will look after Irina? You can't take her. That's not safe for a child."

"You will look after her?"

Willow nods. "Of course. I'll look after her like she is my own."

This is all too much, but I'm running out of time and options. Someone would have discovered Frank's body by now.

"I can never repay you for everything you've done for me. For us," I add, looking at the three people who've always stood by me. "I'm indebted to you for the rest of my life."

Saint shakes his head, not interested in favors being owed. "You owe us nothing. Just don't die. And keep her safe. You make contact as soon as you can, and then we can figure out our next move."

I may have given up trying to figure out why they're helping me, but I will never take it for granted. Without them, I'd be dead.

"I packed a few of Ella's things. I didn't have much time, but I grabbed what I could," Willow says, gesturing to the black overnight bag by the bed. "It should be enough for a few days."

The tremble in her voice betrays her anguish. The memories, memories *I* forced onto her, have resurfaced, reminding her of the ordeal she endured because of me. She knows firsthand because she was Ella once upon a time.

Leaning forward, I press a soft kiss to Ella's brow. "You're safe, красавица. No one will hurt you ever again."

Coming to a stand, I realize there is something I must do before I leave. I need to say goodbye to Irina. My broken heart can't take any more pain. But I must explain to her that I will be back. I just don't know when.

"I'll pack for you," Willow offers, looking up at me with nothing but sadness reflected in those gentle eyes.

With caution, I cup her face and run my thumb along the apple of her cheek. "Thank you. You give me faith there is a God because only He could create something as perfect as you."

Leaning forward, I kiss her temple, wishing to express my gratitude.

She leans into my touch without repulsion. I'll never tire of her advancing instead of recoiling. "Go see Irina."

Even without words, we're in sync with one another. I truly have found my soul mates in Willow and Saint.

Without a moment to waste, I quickly make my way toward Irina's bedroom. It's late, which means she'll probably be asleep. But I can't leave without saying goodbye.

I quietly open her door an inch and peer in. Celine is sitting on the couch, watching TV. When she sees me, she jumps to attention. I make her nervous.

"Mr. Popov," she whispers, walking toward me as I enter.

I've told her countless times to call me Alek, but Celine won't hear of it. She is respectful and kind, which is why I know Irina will be safe with her and Willow watching over her.

"Irina just fell asleep. She had a wonderful evening helping Pierre in the kitchen." A small smile floats across her lips. "Is everything all right?"

I wish I had the time to explain what's going on, but I don't. Time is the enemy, and the longer I'm here, the more of a chance it gives Santo to hurt Ella. I need to be quick, but how do you do that when you're saying goodbye to your child?

It makes no difference that Irina isn't my flesh and blood; family is what you make it, and Irina is my daughter. She chose me as her father, and that makes me the luckiest man alive.

"I have to go away for a little while," I explain, peering over at Irina, sleeping soundly in her pink princess bed. "Saint, Willow, Max, and Pavel will remain here. Would you be okay with continuing your duties as usual?"

"Of course," she replies, clearly concerned to why I'm fleeing in the middle of the night. "What should I tell Irina?"

Rubbing the back of my neck, I think of a suitable response as my cheeks billow. "Tell her I'll be back soon."

Celine nods, knowing better than to ask questions.

Walking quietly to the bed, I peer down at the little girl who has shown me how to love. I didn't think I was capable of the emotion, but Irina proved me wrong. She's taught me so much.

Sitting on the edge of the bed, I run the back of two of my fingers across her warm cheek. "I'm so proud to be your папа. You are a gift. You give me a reason to go on. Be safe, little цветочек. I'll be back soon. Папа loves you."

Bending down, I kiss her forehead, which are wet with my tears.

Am I doing the right thing?

Leaving the ones I love seems so cowardly. If anything were to happen to any of them, I'd never forgive myself. But I have to do this because Ella…what I feel for her scares me. I don't know what it is. Love seems so inept to describe how I feel when I'm around her.

Brushing the hair from Irina's face, I promise to return and soon.

Wiping away my tears, I turn around and smile at Celine. "If you need anything at all, ask. Whatever you need, it's yours. I'll ensure you get a raise for your troubles."

"No, Mr. Popov, that's not necessary," she says softly. "I love Irina. I love it here."

"And I appreciate that, which is why I want to look after you." She knows better than to argue and simply bows in gratitude.

But I lift her chin with my pointer finger. "Don't bow for anyone."

She licks her lips, her cheeks flushing a scarlet pink at my command. It's ironic, but I mean it. She needs to hold her head high. Oh, how I've changed.

But I can ponder on my growth when we're on my yacht and sailing the hell away from here.

Irina's colored crayons catch my eye, and I decide to leave her a note. I don't want her to think I've abandoned her. This feels so final, but reaching for the pink crayon—Irina's favorite color—I write in Russian on the back of one of Irina's colored in pictures of Thomas the Tank Engine.

I promise to keep you safe. I love you with all my heart.

Folding the picture in half, I pass it to Celine. "Please give this to Irina when she wakes."

Celine places the picture into her pocket and nods. "I'll see you soon."

I reply the only way I can; the only way which is the truth. "I'll see you when I see you."

Taking one last look at Irina, I leave her bedroom, the heavy weight in my chest threatening to suffocate me. If I don't go now, I never will.

When I enter my bedroom, I see two bags by the door. Mine and Ella's. "I wanted to change her clothes, but I don't want to disturb her," Willow says, wringing her hands in front of her.

"It's okay. Best we let her sleep."

I don't know why she won't wake. She needs medical attention, but this requires more time that we are running out of. Rushing over to the bed, I bend down and gently scoop Ella up into my arms. She whimpers but remains asleep.

Willow tears the duvet off the bed and covers Ella with it. "Be safe," she whispers, her fear clear. We all face the unknown.

With Ella enveloped soundly in my arms, I lower my lips to Willow's and kiss her softly. It's not that of a lover's kiss but rather, a kiss of love. I owe her everything.

She kisses me back chastely, and when I taste her salty tears, I pull away, wiping them away with my thumb. "I love you, дорогая. With all my heart."

A similar sentiment to what I left for Irina.

Willow smiles and once again gifts me in ways I don't deserve. "And I love you, Alek. Come back to us soon."

Nodding, I walk over to Saint—my strong, loyal comrade. He is the epitome of an alpha male. I understand why Willow chose him over me. I will only ever be half the man he is. He doesn't appear to want to rip my head off, which is why I lower my lips to his and kiss him as I did with Willow.

This is why this works. I love them equally.

He doesn't recoil. He accepts this for what it is. It doesn't make sense to most, but to us, it does. "And I love you, Saint."

With a sigh, he cups the back of my neck and draws us brow to brow. It's a brotherly embrace, and it fills my broken heart with hope. "Never underestimate my hatred for you… but I guess now…I've accepted that I hate to love you."

I'm hit with his trademark fragrance—spicy, sweet, and floral—mixed with Willow's scent of a vanilla kiss.

"And for that, I'll eternally be grateful. Thank you. Thank you to all of you."

We break apart, and I nod at Pavel.

Although I value our friendship, what I share with Saint and Willow is an entirely different kind of love. Besides, if I put my lips anywhere near him, he'd have no qualms slicing them off with his pocket knife.

But to me, love is love. Whether that love is with a man or a woman, there is no wrong answer when the heart is involved.

"Let's go, Aleksei," Pavel instructs, walking toward the door. "I'll drive you to the port."

Taking one last look at the two people who changed my

life forever, I commit them to memory, afraid this will be the last time I see them. "Please look after Irina."

Willow nods, wiping away her tears with the back of her hand.

Saint draws her into his side, kissing the top of her head. And this is the last image I wish to have of them—embracing and in love.

Turning around, I cradle Ella tightly in my arms and leave behind my world, in hopes I can return one day soon.

CHAPTER SEVEN

Ella

"**N**O!"

Jolting upright, I'm prepared to fight for my life because the last thing I remember was…

My brain hurts. So does my body. But it's my soul I'm most concerned for.

Brushing the matted hair from my face, I take in my strange surroundings because I have no idea where I am.

I'm in a king-size bed covered in the finest linens, and the bedroom is just as luxurious. To my left is a door that is ajar, revealing a bathroom. The curtains are drawn over the large window in front of me, so I don't know if it's day or night.

The need to use the bathroom suddenly overwhelms me.

I peel back the blankets, only to see I'm in an oversized white shirt that is not mine. Drawing the collar to my nose, I inhale deeply and am engulfed in heaven and hell. I'd recognize this fragrance anywhere—Alek.

But why am I in his shirt? And where the hell am I?

My body creaks as I slowly place my feet onto the carpet and come to a wobbly stand. The room is swaying, so I take small steps toward the bathroom. Once inside, I quickly use the toilet, sighing in relief when I see the marbled shower feet away.

I desperately want to use it as I feel gross, but the need to find out where I am and whom I'm with has me flushing the toilet and washing my hands in the sink. Innocently looking into the mirror above the basin, I yelp and turn over my shoulder, convinced a monster stands behind me.

But when I see that no one is there, I realize that monster is me.

Slowly turning back around, I grip the sink, staring into the bloodshot eyes of a stranger. This looks like me, but it can't be.

My face is black and blue with swirls of red. My nose is swollen, as is my left eye, which I can barely see out of. Dozens of small cuts on my face are red and inflamed. Leaning closer into the mirror, I peel back my bottom lip to see indents of my two front teeth incised into the flesh.

Clenching the porcelain, I'm suddenly hit with a searing pain, the same pain I felt when Frank beat me to a bloody pulp. With a wounded hiss as two of my fingernails are snapped clean off, I unfasten two buttons on my shirt and lift the material away from my skin to see my body is badly bruised.

Tears of fury fill me because I am SO FUCKING ANGRY!

I was…raped, humiliated, threatened, and beaten within

an inch of my life. I should have fought harder. I should have done more.

But when I think about my motives, about why I did what I did, I realize there is one running theme—Aleksei Popov.

I did all of this because I thought I was protecting him, but he showed me what a fucking idiot I am for thinking I meant anything to him when he lost a game of poker on purpose.

Alek knew Saint and Willow could look after themselves, and him losing was to teach Santo a lesson. Not once did he take me into consideration. He knew Saint and Willow would be safe, but what about me? If he won, none of this would have happened.

His cruel reply plays over and over in my mind. *"She looks like she bites. I probably would have asked for a rematch if I won."*

That motherfucking asshole.

Cupping water in my palms, I wash my face, flinching when the hot water burns my sensitive skin. Helping myself to a new toothbrush on the counter, I brush my teeth gently as my mouth stings. Once I'm as clean as I can be without showering, I turn off the water and dry my face with the plush hand towel.

The military precision of items in here pisses me off, so I childishly knock over a few bottles on the counter and rearrange the towels on the rack so they're no longer aligned. The disarray makes me feel somewhat better.

My tangled hair is a lost cause, so I twist it into a bun, securing it with an elastic I find in one of the drawers. A small pair of scissors catches my eye, so I stow them into the hemline of my underwear. Someone dressed me because the last thing I remember was I wasn't wearing any underwear, thanks to Frank ripping them off.

I clench my teeth at the thought, ignoring the searing pain running up to my temple.

Ready for battle, I tiptoe through the bedroom, deciding to take a peek out the window to familiarize myself with my surroundings before I strike. However, when I draw back the curtain and see blue seas, my plan falls flat on its face.

I'm on a boat?

As I look around at my plush surroundings, it's evident I'm on more than just a boat—I'm on a yacht.

Honestly, I could be walking into anything, but I don't let that deter me as I continue sneaking through the bedroom toward the glass door that I presume leads to the upper deck. I brace my hand on the handle and open the door quietly. The sunlight blinds me, and I hiss, shielding my eyes to adjust to the harsh light.

Taking a moment to look over the railing, I take a deep breath of the fresh air, filling my starved lungs. I'm surrounded by nothing but water. With careful steps, I climb the stairwell, seeing another level of the yacht.

But I can investigate that later because now, I need to find out who's steering this yacht.

With heart in my throat, I grip the handrail, and when I get to the top step, I take a steadying breath. I crane my neck, hoping to see who's on board, and when I see the broad back of a man, I curse the day *he* walked into my world.

Undoubtedly, this is Alek, looking the part of captain in

khaki chinos and a light blue shirt. His hair whips in the wind as he stands by the large wheel. The computerized panel to his left indicates this yacht can steer itself, but the control freak that he is won't allow it.

His feet are bare, and out here, under different circumstances, one could be forgiven for thinking he looked laidback, but nothing is relaxed about this scenario because I need to know why I'm here…wherever the fuck *here* is.

With slow, silent feet, I tiptoe toward him, hoping the crashing of waves will mute my footsteps. He doesn't turn around. He hums to Bach, which plays over the radio. When I'm within a few steps of him, I dig out the scissors, and I exhale in relief…which is my downfall.

I should have known the smallest change in the environment is enough for Alek to catch me out.

"You're awake," he calmly says, which infuriates me further.

Without a flicker of remorse, I lunge forward, intent on stabbing the asshole for…being such an asshole. Alek spins around, catching my wrist, and disarms me instantly.

"Let me go!" I screech, fighting him off, no matter that every muscle in my body protests angrily. His hold isn't firm, but I'm fighting injured, which puts me at an even bigger disadvantage.

I glare at him, hating how my heart skips a beat when we lock eyes. Him being here comes a little too late. Where was he when he had the opportunity to save me before I killed Frank?

Realization passes over me, and I freeze, sickened.

I killed Frank.

His blood coats my hands. Oh, god.

I can feel his dead weight on me. His hot, sticky blood coating my skin.

I'm going to be sick.

"красавица, are you all—"

Alek doesn't have a chance to finish his sentence because I push him off before running over to the railing and dry heaving into the sea. My body shudders as I force myself to expel anything, but I simply dry retch.

Maybe I can purge the sickness within. But nothing will ever cleanse me of my sins.

"You haven't eaten," Alek says from behind me. "You've got nothing to throw up."

"Thank you, captain obvious," I snarkily reply, wiping my lips with the sleeve of Alek's shirt.

Alek gently places his hand on my shoulder, but with his touch, all I'm reminded of is Santo and his hands, his unwanted strokes all over me. "Don't touch me!"

Instantly, I spin around, intent on breaking every finger on Santo's hands for touching me when I didn't want him to. But Santo isn't here.

Alek stands before me, hands raised in surrender with nothing but confusion etched on his face. "It's me," he coos as though that's supposed to make me feel better.

"And that's the problem!" I cry, clenching my fists by my side. My anger is directed at the world, and sadly for Alek, he's the only person here. "Where are we?"

"We're on my yacht. You've been in and out of

consciousness for twenty-something hours. I tried my best to tend to your wounds," he explains, hands still raised. "But now, I see your internal injuries are far worse. Are you okay?"

"Am I okay?" I scoff sarcastically. "Why do you care? The time *to* care has passed because if you did, we wouldn't be here."

I've wounded him. Good.

"How about you get cleaned up? I can make us something to eat."

"I'm not hungry," I retort, but my grumbling stomach makes a liar out of me.

Alek lowers his arms cautiously. I wonder what he sees when he looks at me. Does he know what Santo did? What I allowed him to do?

Curling my lip, disgusted with myself, I turn my back and storm down the stairs toward the bedroom. I don't want Alek to see my tears. I don't know why I'm so angry with him. I'm just so fucking angry. At everything. At me.

Tearing off my shirt, I toss it to the ground and make my way into the bathroom, desperate to shower in hopes of washing this filth—on the outside *and* the inside—off me. Once I'm naked, I step under the shower spray, sighing when the hot water trickles down my body.

But the pleasure soon turns to pain when the droplets resemble Santo's tongue, licking every inch of me clean. Screaming, I place my hands against the tiles and bow my head, allowing the water to fall over me as I sob guttural tears.

No wonder I've been out of it for days. Who the hell would want to wake to this?

I reach for the lavender soap and begin to lather it over my body. I scrub myself raw, but it doesn't wash away the filth coating my skin. Nothing ever will. A part of me is broken, and that part can never be repaired. Santo stole so much. As did Frank. And at this moment, I realize Alek has as well.

Once my tears have dried, I wash my hair and face, not even bothering to look at the products in the shower caddy. Everything has lost its smell, its ability to rouse me. Life moves in monotone.

Switching off the water, I dry off and wrap the towel around myself as I hunt for something to wear. I'm surprised to see my things hanging in the wardrobe and folded neatly in the drawers, underwear included. All my thoughts are so scattered, and even though I know Alek has all the answers to clear the fog, I don't want to talk to him right now.

I just need time.

I dress in plain underwear, my jean shorts, and a T-shirt. Even though it's warm out, I slip on an oversized sweater. I want to cover as much of myself as possible. I don't bother with shoes and run my fingers through my wet hair.

Even though I told Alek I wasn't hungry, the mention of food has my stomach growling at the possibility. I'm also parched. Maybe Alek will get the hint and leave me alone.

Hoping he does, I make my way toward the middle level where there is a kitchen and living space and slide open the door. It's huge in here. Far bigger than I anticipated it would be. The living area looks like one you'd find in any home.

It's fitted with a huge plasma TV, a comfy leather sofa, and a coffee table.

The kitchen has a dining area to the left of it. There is a large table with a flower vase on top of it and eight wooden chairs. It's cool down here, and the gentle hum reveals the AC is on. I never knew a yacht could be so luxurious. I open the stainless refrigerator and salivate when I see the water bottles.

Lunging for one, I can't open it fast enough, and when the cold water hits my throat, I gulp it down greedily. Only when the bottle is drained do I come up for air. Wiping my lips with the back of my hand, I hunt through the well-stocked shelves for something to eat.

Everything suddenly looks so good, but Alek's comment about not eating has me thinking I should probably start with something light. Closing the fridge, I open the bread box and snare a jar of unopened peanut butter from the pantry.

The plates are stacked neatly in the cupboard, and I shouldn't be surprised it's fine china. Opening the top drawer, I grab a knife and go about making my sandwich. My growling stomach can't wait. I grab a banana from the fruit bowl on the counter and peel it before cutting it into slices and laying them over my thick layer of peanut butter.

I press the slice of bread over my banana and peanut butter goodness and take a large bite of my sandwich. I actually hum in delight because nothing has ever tasted this good.

Leaning on the counter, I take everything in because this seems to be my new home for the next week? Weeks?

When I hear footsteps pound down the stairs, I quietly eat my sandwich, averting my eyes. It seems we're the only ones on this yacht, which has me wondering what happened to Saint, Willow, and Irina. But I'm not ready to go there—not yet.

Alek is pissed off, but he's also worried, which makes no sense. He wasn't worried when he purposely lost the game of poker. Or when he insulted me in front of everyone. My anger just seems to grow. I know it's misdirected and not all Alek, but I can't help it.

Alek hurt me; he always hurts me. If only he'd trusted me and didn't feel the need to send me away like some damsel in distress, then we wouldn't be here. I don't know what I feel for him anymore. I just feel numb.

I continue eating in silence, content on being left alone.

Alek calmly walks over to the bar and pours himself a drink. He doesn't offer me one. The tension is so thick that I can barely breathe.

"So how long are you planning on ignoring me?"

I don't take the bait and continue chewing.

"Ella, I'm talking to you."

Inhaling deeply, I know he won't go away unless I answer him. "That's all you seem to do," I reply, keeping my cool. "Talk. As I see it, the time to talk is over. Now, if you'll excuse me, I'd like to eat my sandwich in peace."

Just as I'm about to take a bite, Alek grips my wrist, stopping me. Lifting my eyes, I don't check my irritation at the door.

"Being a brat will not work in your favor," he warns, tightening his hold.

Laughing in his face, I mock, "I've fallen out of favor with you long ago."

His eyebrows shoot up into his hairline, revealing genuine shock at my admission. But what did he think? I'd drop to my knees and thank him for saving me? It's too little, too late.

"I know I've hurt you," he confesses, his hardness waning.

"You don't know anything."

"Well, tell me," he presses, running his thumb over my pulse.

The simple touch sends a current all the way to my toes, but I won't be sidetracked. What he did was wrong, and I would be stupid to simply forget our past.

Fool me once…

Stubbornly, I keep my lips sealed shut.

"I know they hurt you. I saw what they did to you," he reveals, his face twisting into a nasty scowl.

"Then why didn't you do something when you had the chance?" I challenge, refusing to back down. "But once again, I was second, oh sorry, third best."

"Please, let me explain."

Ripping from his hold, I toss my sandwich onto the counter and stand on tippy toes, needing to be eye level when I tell him to go fuck himself. "Just save it. I don't want to hear it. I don't want to hear your excuses."

"They're not excuses," he says between clenched teeth. "It's the truth."

"Fine then, tell me you didn't lose on purpose," I defy, wanting him to know that I'm already privy to the truth.

"Goddammit, it's not like that."

"It's exactly like that!" I cry, shoving at his chest.

He staggers back a couple of steps, stunned I pushed him. "Yes, you're right, I did know Santo had what he thought was a winning hand. I read people…well, I seem to be able to read everyone but you! I thought you'd be happy to get out of there. Do you think I was happy to lose to that son of a bitch? But I did it because my plan was to give Saint and Willow an excuse to be there so they could get to you!" he exclaims as if that's supposed to excuse him.

"I would have been happier if you won and trusted me!" I shout back.

"This was the only way I could get to you without putting you at risk. I needed an inside man."

I know all too well what happens to inside men.

"Oh, bullshit!" I argue, shaking my head. "Why not win and trust me?"

"Because I didn't know if you were on my side!" he counters quickly.

And there it is, the truth, the truth I didn't need to hear because I already knew Alek didn't believe in us, in me. It seems I'm a convincing actress after all. But honestly, it didn't take much persuading.

"You said—"

I promptly stop him. "I said a lot of things. We both did."

"Why did you stay with him?" Alek asks, baffled. "I don't understand. You can't…forgive me? Is that why?"

My insides twist, and the small amount of food and water I just consumed threatens to come back up. "It doesn't matter now," I reply because the reason is now void. All of this was for nothing.

"Like hell it doesn't!"

Alek advances, and suddenly, I'm overwhelmed with images of Frank hurting me. On instinct, I cover my face and curl into my chest, preparing myself to be hit. But it never comes.

"I would never raise my hand to you, красавица." His sincerity is reflected in his tone, but my good sense yells at me not to be naïve because the harm he's caused to my heart is so much worse.

These external wounds will heal, but the ones inflicted internally will be open forever.

Feeling tears I don't want to cry well to the surface, I quickly turn around and head for the bedroom. There is so much more to discuss, but for now, I know what I need. Alek once again put his faith in others, seeing an ally in everyone but me.

I risked everything for him. What an idiot I am.

CHAPTER EIGHT

Alek

"**S**anto seemed to buy it, but it won't be long until he finds out the truth," Pavel says into the satellite phone as I focus ahead. It's a new moon, so we're sailing in almost darkness.

As expected, my house was one of the first Santo and his sons visited, demanding answers. Pavel stuck to the story that I fled to Ukraine on a tip that my mother had been spotted there. But that will only be plausible for so long.

The Macrillos are out for revenge.

Running a hand down my exhausted face, I decide to moor the yacht for the night and attempt to get some sleep once I get off the phone. We're in the middle of nowhere, and according to the nautical charts, no boats usually pass through here.

"Any thoughts on what you're going to do?"

I wish I had the answers, but I don't.

Ella needs to be far, far away from harm's way before I can strike. Until then, she's at risk of being found. Only when she's safe will I go back to Russia and end the Macrillo bloodline. But until then, we're fugitives.

"All I can think about right now is getting Ella to safety," I share with Pavel. "I can't do anything until I know no one can hurt her. Only when she's safe will I come back and finish this once and for all."

"And until then? What happens to business?"

This should concern me, but it doesn't. Worrying about what happens to my empire is so low on my list of priorities that I fail to remember why it mattered at all.

"We stick to the original plan," I reply because to ensure Ella's safety, I need every single ally in my corner. "They know I trust you; therefore, they'll do the same. Call if there are any problems, and I will set them straight."

That won't be necessary, however.

Underdogs don't argue; that's why they're the underdogs. Pavel is offering them the opportunity to change their status, so there is no way they'll disagree.

"Okay. If you think this is best."

I don't know that. I don't know anything, but I don't stand a chance fighting against the Macrillos if I'm worrying about Ella. She needs to be hidden where no one can find her. I just need to find where that place is.

"Call if anything changes," I say. "Is everyone okay?"

"Yes, for now." And with that ominous response, Pavel hangs up.

He isn't being melodramatic because he's right. For now,

our excuses will appease the Macrillos. But when they exhaust every avenue, they'll circle back to the most likely scenario and press harder until someone cracks.

Gripping the wheel, I refuse to ponder on that thought for too long. I will have thought of a plan before that happens. I just hope that epiphany hits me soon.

The still waters allow the perfect conditions to moor for the night, not that that will be for long. Even though I'm utterly exhausted, I can't sleep. Every time I close my eyes, all I can see is Ella's broken, bleeding body.

None of that would have happened if I had protected her. I failed her. She has every right to hate me, and hate me she does. Today, she wouldn't even look at me. I knew damage had been done. I just didn't anticipate how much so.

I thought once I explained, she'd understand, but I was wrong. She sees my decision as yet another betrayal.

I need to know what happened between her and Frank for it to have ended the way it did. But something monstrous happened to Ella. The physical scars aside, she is harboring something so heinous, she can't even stand to be in the same room as me.

My mind thinks the worst, and what Saint said, about her underwear being torn…it all points to something unthinkable happening. I saw her bruises the night of the poker game. Even though she tried to conceal them, I saw, which is why I decided to lose the poker game.

I hate that I didn't trust her, but it would have been foolish of me to think she was doing this for me. I wish that she was, but I'm still no closer to uncovering any of this.

With a sigh, I hobble down the stairs, my limp not getting any better as I refuse to use my cane like some invalid. I quietly open the bedroom door, thankful to see Ella's sleeping form on the bed. The glow from the TV allows me to see her curled in a fetal position with the blankets thrown off to the side.

There isn't anywhere else to sleep because the spare bedroom has a foldout sofa fit for an elf, so I strip off my clothes and slip into a pair of sweats. It's already warm enough with the sweats, so I don't bother with a T-shirt and slowly get into bed. I don't want to frighten Ella, so I turn my back to her and move as far away as I can, giving her some space.

I'm on the edge of the mattress, but just the sound of her gentle breaths is enough to lull me into a sleepy state. She once teased maybe one day we'd take our impassioned lovemaking to a bed. Now that that is a reality, I've never felt more detached from her than I do right now.

We may share a bed, but we may as well be worlds apart.

Just the thought of losing her forever has my heart twisting into knots. I don't think I'd survive it. I wish I was better experienced with this sort of stuff, but I don't know how to deal with all of these foreign feelings.

I'm an emotional mess. And not knowing how she feels about me pains me in ways I've never experienced before.

Rolling onto my back, I toss an arm over my eyes, wishing to block out these insecurities that just seem to grow worse. Everything is such a mess.

"No, please no." Ella's whimpers have me slowly removing my arm as I turn to look at her.

Her face is pinched tight as she thrashes her head from

side to side. "Get off. Please, get off me."

Shooting upright, I lean over and gently touch her shoulder. "Shh, Ella. You're safe."

But my touch seems to rouse her demons.

"No!" she shrieks before rocketing up, her labored breaths no doubt matching her racing heart.

She brushes the hair from her face as she looks around the room frantically. When she realizes where she is, her breathing calms, and her shoulders drop.

However, when she turns and sees me sitting beside her, she scoots away so quickly, she falls off the bed. Quickly scampering after her on hands and knees, I peer over the edge of the mattress to see her tangled in the blankets.

"Let me help you."

Just as I'm about to reach over, she asserts, "No, just leave me alone."

"Don't be ridiculous," I press because her stubbornness isn't getting her anywhere.

I tug at the blanket, helping to free her, but you'd think I just pulled it back over her head. The moment she's free, she springs to her feet and backs away from me. The wall prohibits her from moving any farther.

Her retreat just adds to the hole in my chest. "Why are you acting this way?" I beseech she give me some insight into why she hates me so. "Talk to me."

Her face is illuminated in strobes of light, thanks to the action flick on TV. It only highlights her agitated state. "I have nothing I want to say."

She spins, making a mad dash for the bathroom, but not

this time.

Launching off the bed, I jump over the twisted blankets and reach out, snaring her wrist. She rips free and spins, and with a cry, she slaps my cheek. "Don't touch me!"

"Ella," I press, ignoring the sting to my face because it pales in comparison to the one in my heart. "What happened to you? Please tell me."

"What do you want to hear?" she screams, tearing at her snarled hair. "How I allowed myself to be used? By Frank. By Santo. By you. And the worst thing is, you knew, didn't you? You knew they were hurting me?"

"I didn't know how badly until I saw the bruises—"

"Yet you still decided to lose," she interrupts, eyeing me angrily.

"Goddammit!" I cry, needing to punch something because I am so frustrated she won't listen to me. "I was never going to leave you there. Even if I had to take you against your will. I didn't know—"

"Didn't know what?" she presses, daring me to continue to make excuses.

"I didn't know if you still…liked me," I settle on. The words feel like glass cutting through my windpipe as I confess my fears.

She scoffs, unmoved by my honesty. "And that's the problem, Alek. I liked you too much."

I don't fail to notice her use of past tense.

"What does that mean?" I beg she open up so I can fix it and make it right. But we are way past a quick fix.

"It means I don't even know how you feel about me. Your

actions show you care, but then you go and act as though I'm some damsel in distress who needs rescuing. Why can't you treat me like an equal? Why can't you trust me?

"It was so easy for you to send me away. So easy for you to lie to me. And I know you did this because you thought you were protecting me, but all you did was make me feel helpless."

"I never meant to do that. The need to protect you had nothing to do with you, but everything to do with me and the situation you were in because of me," I argue, wishing she'd understand why I did what I did. Yes, the plan wasn't foolproof, but I couldn't let anything happen to her. "I was trying to keep you safe. Just as I am now. You've started a war with the Macrillos. Why did you kill Frank? What did he do to you?"

She shakes her head, pulling her lips into a thin line.

I know she doesn't want to talk about it, but I need her to. Bottling this up will kill her inside, and he will win.

"He may be dead," I state, fists clenched by my side. "But he'll always have control over you if you let this fester. All you'll think about is him, about what he did, about what you could have done differently, and you'll be his prisoner forever.

"Believe me when I say, if you don't expel your demons, they will rule you for the rest of your life. And sooner or later, you'd wish he killed you instead."

Tears well in her eyes, and as much as it kills me to see her cry, this is the first step of her healing. Her hard exterior will crumble. It's holding on by a thread.

"Why are you helping me?" she asks, her lower lip

trembling.

"Oh, красавица, for you to ask this of me breaks me. I would do anything for you. I know this is hard to understand, but everything I've done has been for you. Sending you away was the only way I could ensure your safety.

"If anything happened to you—"

"What?" she poses, wiping away her tears. "If anything happened to me, what would you do?"

Heat creeps up my neck because I know what she's asking. She wants me to tell her that I love her. But they're merely words, ones that don't even skim the surface of how I feel about her.

"You can't even say it," she says with a broken smile. "Are you afraid it'll make you weak?"

"No…I'm already helpless when it comes to you," I confess honestly. "Will saying three meaningless words prove to you how much you mean to me?"

She doesn't reply.

"I can't say them because I don't know what it, what…love is," I say, the taboo word feeling like poison on my tongue. "I've left my home, my friends, Irina, my empire behind because of you. Doesn't that count for something?"

"I never asked you to," she retorts, but her fight has simmered.

"Yes, you were too busy fighting for your life because of your *fiancé*," I sneer, peering down at the engagement ring on her finger.

"Fuck you," she spits. "You have no idea why—"

"Why what?" I bellow, arms out wide. "I'm all ears. That's

all I've been. But you're treating me like the fucking enemy."

And what she says hurts so much, I take a step backward, needing a moment to center myself in fear of falling.

"You are."

"You cannot forgive me?" I ask, knowing I'm far from perfect and understanding she feels as though I put her last. But it's because of her I did this. And even though that's the god's honest truth, it's not enough.

"I can't," she whispers sadly. "Too much has happened, and when I think of you, about us, all I see is violence, greed, lies…I don't associate happy memories with you…just fleeting moments in time. I'm sorry."

Jarring my hand out, I beg she stops. I don't want her apologies. Or her canoodling me and my feelings. The bad outweighs the good, and I understand that. I wish it were different, but it's not.

"Very well," I say, pulling back my shoulders and tamping down this decaying feeling within. "Once I ensure your safety, you'll never have to see me again."

"I'm sorry, Alek."

"Don't be…you can just add this to your fleeting moments." My quip wounds her, but this is the only way I can deal with her telling me that I'm not enough.

This entire time, she believed she wasn't enough for me, and that's why she won't listen to reason. But the truth is, *I* was the one not worthy of her love.

"We're about a day away from the closest port. We will pick up supplies, and then I will make arrangements for you to disappear until I can eliminate the Macrillos."

Her eyes widen. But the time to care for my well-being has passed. "Just drop me off somewhere. I can make my own arrangements."

"If that were true, I wouldn't be a fugitive in my own country," I reply calmly, but she reads the comment for the crack that it is. "The sooner this is over with, the sooner I can get on with my life. And you can do the same."

I want her to fight me. I want the spirited woman I've come to cherish to rear her head and tell me that I'm wrong. But that woman is no more. She is broken. We both are. And together…we're on a collision course bound to destroy the other the moment we collide.

"I'll sleep in the living room," she offers, reaching for a blanket.

But I shake my head. "I'm not tired anymore. I'll continue with our journey so we can arrive at the port sooner."

She suddenly looks guilty, but there is no need. This always came with an expiration date. I was too caught up in the hope of a fairy-tale ending to see that. But now, the future is clear. It seems only violence can sharpen my senses because the plan, the epiphany I was so desperately searching for, has struck.

Turning, I leave Ella in the bedroom and take the stairs to the upper deck. I need to make a call. It's late, but I know Pavel will answer.

"What?" he sleepily says with a yawn.

Me? I've never felt more alive. "Plan is you call Austin Bailey and tell him I need sanctuary for Ella."

"In Ireland?" Pavel asks, his surprise clear.

"Yes. His ties to the IRA will ensure Ella's safety if anything happens. In return, we cut a deal with them—a steady partnership in exchange for harboring Ella until I can eliminate the Macrillos. A slice of Russia will be too good of an opportunity to pass by. It's time for a new Russia where I rule with an iron fist. If they're not with me, they're the enemies and will pay, as will their families for defying me."

"As far as plans go, this is actually very good." It's a relief to hear him say that. "We move into different territories, only to grow stronger as we align with the most powerful."

"Exactly," I reply. "This is a new era. Traditional Russia needs a change…and that change is me."

To any old-school game player, what I'm proposing is sacrilegious. Consorting outside the "inner circle" is unheard of. And that's why it'll work.

Pavel will continue working over the underdogs as we grow stronger quietly, only to take down the existing adversaries who stand in our way. I have a vision. And I'm prepared to make a deal with the devil if I have to.

However, looking down at the ring I wear on my pinkie finger, I smile—I *am* the devil. Welcome to my hell.

"And what if the Macrillos get wind of this somehow? We still don't know if we can trust Austin."

"Catholics in Protestant territory? I don't think so. Besides, how will they find out? It's not like they're associates of Austin. Never underestimate a man's desire to succeed."

Austin will agree as this benefits him, *and* the IRA. This alliance benefits us both.

"Does Ella know of this plan?"

Sighing, my high soon fades because if only I told her of my plans from the get-go, we wouldn't be here.

"Not yet. I'll tell her in the morning. Can you organize someone to meet me in Latvia? I need some new identification for us, just in case."

"Yes, of course. I will organize everything and send word on where to meet."

"Perfect. I'll call you once we get to the port. Keep me updated with any news."

"How is she?" Pavel asks, which surprises me. He isn't one to meddle, but Ella has touched us all.

"Her bruises are healing, but her internal scars have caused the most damage as have I," I declare with regret. "The best thing I can do is leave her be."

Pavel is quiet, which is never a good sign. "Best for whom?"

Not in the mood for this type of talk, I cluck my tongue. "Good night," and I hang up.

The heaviness returns, but I push it aside. I have a plan, and that's all I intend to focus on. I need to get Ella to safety where I will disappear from her life—a fleeting moment that will soon be forgotten.

CHAPTER NINE

Even though my injuries are healing, the heaviness in my heart just seems to worsen with each passing minute.

Alek hasn't spoken to me. Not that I blame him. We're broken, and I don't know if we can fix it. But I meant what I said; even though I love Alek, I'll always associate this sorrow inside me with him. His world has taken so much from me that I don't even know who I am anymore.

I don't blame him, though. I blame myself because every choice was mine to make. Alek never asked me to do any of this. It was all me. If I had the chance to start over, I don't know what I'd choose.

My heart is broken for so many reasons, and this is why I've built up my walls. I don't want to tell Alek what happened because I don't want pity. It'll kill me to have him look at me any differently, to have him look at me like a victim.

I wish I could stop thinking this way, but no matter what

Alek says, his past actions prove he will always see me as some damsel who needs rescuing. If I tell him what happened, what Santo and Frank did, he will blame himself and forever be trying to make it up to me.

I appreciate him wanting to protect me, but for this to work, I want to be his equal. I don't want him to be fighting my battles constantly. I took care of Frank on my own, didn't I?

Pushing him away is the only thing that feels right in a world that is filled with so much wrong. I know it doesn't make sense, but I just want to heal on my own. I don't want to answer his questions because I don't want to relive those experiences ever again.

I'm on the cusp of wanting to forget it ever happened, and then on the flip side, I'm so fucking angry I didn't do more. I'm so messed up. Any shrink would tell me I'm repressing my feelings instead of dealing with them. But I just can't deal— period.

I'm guessing we will reach the port soon. I'm not entirely sure what plans Alek has for me, which is why I'll need to talk to him. The thought has me piling my hair onto the top of my head into a messy bun because I'm suddenly burning up.

My hand, or rather, my ring gets snagged in my hair, reminding me that I'm still wearing Frank's engagement ring. Prying it off my finger, I'm tempted to throw it overboard, but decide to stow it away in case I need it as a bargaining chip.

This thing is worth a small fortune.

When the yacht suddenly decreases in speed, I jump up from the bed and look out the window. In the distance, I can see fishing boats and what looks to be a small fishing town. I have no idea where we are. Curiosity gets the better of me, and I decide to venture onto the upper deck so I can get a closer look.

Not bothering with shoes, I slip my cardigan over my green summer dress and head upstairs. The sky is sliced with slashes of orange and red hues because it's dusk. It's in the darkness where I now feel most comfortable.

The daylight is too bright, too…revealing.

I stop on the top step and grasp the railing, needing a moment to admire Alek because I can only do so in secret. Just because he's toxic to my heart, that doesn't erase my feelings for him. I still love him so much.

His muscled, bare broad back glows under the twilight skies as he stands at the wheel, steering this vessel like a pro. His dark hair catches the breeze. When he shifts, I see something which shocks me—he has a tattoo.

Praying hands are inked on the back of his left arm.

The image has me gripping the railing, suddenly unstable on my feet. The meaning behind it baffles me. Why praying hands? Is this for me?

Scoffing, I tamp down such whimsical thoughts and make my way toward the front of the yacht, avoiding Alek. The gentle breeze is lovely, and I hold the guardrail, lifting my face toward the heavens. Inhaling, I take a much needed breath.

Being out here in the open gives me some peace. If only it were enough to soothe the demons within.

As I take in my surroundings, nothing gives our location

away. I'm guessing we're out of Russia because people will not only be looking for me, they'll be looking for Alek as well.

Giving in, I shout to be heard, "Where are we?"

He could be childish and not reply, and I would deserve it. But he's not. "Latvia. We will dock here for a couple of hours. This should be enough time for you to buy whatever things you may need for the rest of our journey."

Rest of our journey? To where?

"Where are we going after here?" I ask, biting the bullet.

"You're going to Ireland," he replies, revealing this isn't a round-trip ticket for me.

"And what am I supposed to do in Ireland?" I ask, annoyed.

"Stay alive," he bluntly states, indicating he's in no mood to talk.

With a sigh, I realize I can't avoid the inevitable any longer and turn around to look at Alek. He stands tall, unruffled while I suddenly feel hot. The front of him is just as impressive as the back. His chest is defined, his abs rippling as he turns the wheel. His khakis sit low on his waist, and his defined V-muscle draws emphasis to the sprinkle of dark hair leading from his navel and down into his pants.

He is a vision, and I know he feels, he tastes, as good as he looks.

Getting my mind out of the gutter, I concentrate on what's important. "So I'm expected to stay with strangers and hope they don't kill me? Is that right?"

"Yes," he replies, eyes focused ahead. "If you have a better plan, then please, enlighten me. But seeing as speaking seems to be off the table, I went ahead and organized this without you. I'm only following the rules you set."

"Oh, fuck you, Alek," I spit, not appreciating his sarcasm. "Just leave me here. I'll work something out myself. I don't wish to be indebted to you for the rest of my life."

And this is why I don't want to talk to him. Every conversation just seems to end in a fight.

With a slanted smirk, he finally meets my eyes. "We're done, Ella. You made that fact perfectly clear. So once I kill Santo and his sons, I'll be out of your life forever. I don't want anything from you…well, not anymore."

Tears sting my eyes, but I don't give life to them. "Who's in Ireland?"

"The IRA."

I open but soon close my mouth. I need a minute.

"How is this option any better than staying with the Macrillos? You're just shipping me from one crime family to another."

"I never asked you to stay with the Macrillos. Nor did I ask you to marry that ублюдок, Frank. But now, I'm *telling* you; you are staying in Ireland until it's safe for you to leave," he orders sharply. "And so help me god, if you disobey me, I will keep you bound and gagged until we arrive."

His threat isn't empty.

"You'd probably enjoy it, you sick asshole," I snarl, thinking of when I walked in on him spanking Renata's bare ass.

"You're right," he counters with a lopsided grin. "I would."

I should tell him everything, spill the reason I stayed and agreed to marry Frank. But if I tell him that, he'll uncover what Santo did. A shiver passes over me.

With a huff, I turn back around and decide to ride the rest of the journey in silence.

When we sail into port, I can't take in my settings fast enough. We're surrounded by other boats, which is why we can't stay long. We're fugitives, and seeing as Latvia was once a part of Russia, we're still close enough to the mother country to be seen by the enemy.

I imagine once we leave here, Alek will take an indirect route to get us to Ireland to avoid running into any trouble.

I hate that, once again, I have to rely on Alek to come to my rescue, but I'm so far away from home, I don't know what to do. I could call the American consulate, but Santo often bragged he had allies in high places.

What if one of those allies were working at the consulate and got wind of what I was doing? I need to be as far away as possible from the Macrillos. They won't stop until they find me, and this time, Santo won't fall for my charms.

So Ireland doesn't seem like such a bad plan, but I feel somewhat…robbed. *I* want to be the one who ends Santo's life. It's my right to torture him as he did with me. Maybe that'll be my closure? I honestly don't know.

What I do know is that going to Ireland feels like I'm running away. I don't know how far away it is from here, but I can imagine it's not close.

The realization of being stuck with Alek for a week, two weeks, alone on this yacht suddenly hits me, and I grip the railing, scared. My resolve to ignore him weakens. I literally have nowhere to go unless I fancy swimming to Ireland. Or I can think of another plan.

Alek steers the yacht into a space before turning off the motor. Deciding to put on some shoes, I turn but am distracted as I watch Alek slip into a short-sleeved blue shirt. His deft fingers fasten each button with no hurry, and watching him dress is suddenly just as sexy as seeing him undress.

He leaves three buttons undone, exposing the sparse dark hairs on his chest. His golden skin seems to glisten under the sunset skies. When he turns his cheek, catching me gawking, I quickly avert my eyes and make a beeline for the staircase, almost throwing myself down the stairs.

With shaky fingers, I slip into my white boat shoes and untie my hair. Alek must think it's safe here, but with my hair down, I can try to conceal the healing scars on my face, which will make me stand out from the crowd.

I need to blend in, and looking like a reanimated corpse will not achieve that.

Once I'm ready, I reclimb the stairs but stop at the second level when I see Alek swing out a ramp and attach it to the dock so we can disembark. He's so confident in everything he does.

Inhaling, I hope to breathe in his courage and walk through the living room to where Alek is. He does a double take when he sees me, but is soon to recover and fiddles with some latch on the ramp mechanism.

I stop a few feet away, but his cologne catches the wind, which has me involuntarily moving closer so I can bask in his scent.

"Here," he says, digging into his pocket and producing a

wad of euro. "Buy what you need."

I don't want to accept it, but with no other choice, I take it, ensuring our fingers don't touch. "Thank you. I'll pay you back."

His stiff upper lip is a sure sign I may as well have told him to go fuck himself. "Don't bother."

"No," I press. "Remember, I don't want to be indebted to you—long or short term."

He nods. "Suit yourself. You can wire it to me."

So that's how it's going to be. Once this is done, this is *done*. No chance of ever catching up for old times' sake when I can repay him this wad of euros. But this is what I wanted. Wasn't it?

I'm suddenly not sure.

And this is why I can't be anywhere near him. He confuses me. He also infuriates me like no other man has before.

Needing to get off this yacht, I shove past him and test the ramp to ensure it's safe for me to walk on. It's solid enough, so I race down it, thankful when my feet hit land.

Looking around, I see what appears to be local markets selling souvenirs and clothes, but what interests me more is the delicious smell wafting through the air. Some people are browsing, but my attention is drawn to the woman to my left, who is eating what looks like a trifle.

The cream mixed with the red swirls of something has my stomach rumbling. I know I should probably eat something a little more substantial, but after everything I've been through, from now on, I'm going to eat dessert first.

I see a stall selling these delicious-looking treats and

make a beeline for it. There is no one in line, so I point at the picture on the wall with a smile. The older lady nods with a toothless grin and goes to work, making my trifle. Or what I'm guessing is a trifle.

She passes me the plastic glass piled high with the sweet-smelling goodness where I pay her, ensuring to tip her ten euro. She nods in gratitude, saying something in Latvian I'm presuming. I can't wait and hungrily dig the spoon into the cream and bring it to my nose.

It's cream and curd cheese. The brown layers don't look like a spongy chocolate cake. Poking out my tongue, I sample my spoon, humming in utter delight when the flavors of cream, cranberry, and a sweet rye bread give my taste buds an orgasm.

Digging my spoon in for a bigger helping, I pile the dessert high and take my first big bite. It's like heaven in my mouth, and I can't silence my moan.

For the next few minutes, I'm lost in culinary bliss and don't realize I have company until I look up and see Alek watching me. I pause midbite, suddenly embarrassed. We were supposed to blend in, and here I am, making love to my trifle.

Swallowing down my mouthful, I watch as Alek saunters over, eyes never wavering from me. Heat creeps up my neck, and I look down, ensuring my skin isn't blotchy, giving away my sudden awakened state.

He stops in front of me and cocks his head to the side. He looks pissed off, but he also looks...aroused. I stop breathing when he reaches out with his thumb and wipes it along the corner of my mouth, showing me it's coated in white cream.

Utterly mortified, I quickly wipe at my mouth with the side of my finger, embarrassed I ignored social etiquette. But that's all forgotten when Alek places his thumb into his mouth and sucks slowly. It slips free, leaving a sheen on his bottom lip that I have the sudden urge to lick clean.

"ням," he says, which leaves me wondering what he said.

When those steel-blue eyes sharpen and turn predatory, I quickly remember I'm supposed to be weaning myself off him. Yes, the attraction will always be there. That's not the problem between us. The problem is the communication part, the part where I'll never be his counterpart.

Relationships need to work on an equal playing field. Otherwise, Alek will always see me as his submissive, seeing as he likes control so much. And I don't want that.

Alek senses the shift in the air and clears his throat. The moment is over, which is good. So why am I disappointed?

"Meet me back here in an hour," he instructs, catching me completely off guard.

"You're not going to follow me around, making sure I don't run with scissors?"

He purses his lips, confused by my choice of words. "Why would you do that?"

A burst of laughter threatens to spill from me because sometimes, he can be so stuffy. But it's one of the things I like, *liked* about him. He speaks so eloquently. Each word as if crafted by the devil himself.

"Don't worry," I reply, waving him off. "Okay, an hour. I can do that."

"Buy yourself some clothes, supplies, but no phone," he orders softly, peering from left to right. "Remain incognito. I'll see you soon and be car—" But he soon stops himself.

Telling me to be careful would mean he cares, and that's just too much for both of us to deal with right now. We both turn away from one another and head in opposite directions.

My appetite is now shot, so I place the remnants of my dessert into the trash and go on the hunt for some supplies. Someone packed my clothes, and I dare say that someone was Willow. She knows firsthand what somebody on the run needs and has packed the essentials.

But it won't be enough as I don't know how long I'll be at sea.

There are no Gap or Old Navy stores in sight, but the stalls are well stocked with local products. Perusing the different stands, I purchase a pair of jeans, some denim shorts, T-shirts, and some cotton underwear.

A red swimsuit catches my eye as I pass by a stall. The older lady notices me eyeing it and quickly pulls it off the hanger. She offers it to me with a smile, speaking to me in a language I don't understand.

There are no changing rooms, so I hold it up against my body and look into the full-length mirror in front of me. Once upon a time, I'd have no problems wearing this. But now, all I can think about is how much skin will be exposed.

My confidence has been ruined, which is why I decide to buy it. Even though the yacht has AC, it's stuffy when I occasionally venture outdoors. I don't want to tan, but some vitamin D may be beneficial for my health.

I also buy a sheer white sarong, as this will help with the anxiety I feel at being so exposed.

The rest of the stalls have beautiful fragrant handcrafted soaps and perfumes. Even though there is soap on the yacht, I can't pass by the lovely bars of lavender and lemongrass and purchase two of each. There are stunning perfume decanters crafted with what looks like fine glassware.

I open each stopper and smell the utterly enchanting samples. Each fragrance is earthy, warm, sweet, and I love how local produce has been used to handmake each scent. I buy three bottles, smiling when the man kisses both my cheeks in gratitude.

With my hands filled with shopping bags, I see that I have fifteen minutes to spare. I couldn't possibly purchase anything else, but my stomach grumbles, hinting the shopping spree can end with some delicious local cuisine.

I walk toward a food cart, intent on buying whatever those dough-looking things are in the window but yelp when someone grips my wrist.

"We need to go. Now." Alek's firm tone has me nodding quickly as I know something is wrong.

I hide behind my hair and keep my eyes peeled to the ground as we walk briskly through the crowd. Alek still has a secure grip on me, almost dragging me toward the yacht. I exhale in relief when we practically run up the ramp, watching as Alek frantically gets everything in order.

"Go into the bedroom!" he orders, and I do as he says because his urgency warns me that something dire looms.

I'm shaking so badly when I enter the bedroom that the

bags rattle in my hands. I place them in the corner of the room before drawing the curtain an inch so I can look out the window. I don't see anything out of place. All looks calm until, in the distance, I see three men in uniform come running through the crowd.

My heart threatens to rip from my rib cage as they get closer and closer to the stationary yacht. They're shouting words I don't understand with phones pressed to their ears as they point our way.

Finally, the motor kickstarts to life and moves so quickly, I hold the wall to keep my balance. This doesn't deter the men. They seem to increase their speed before jumping into a speedboat, and although I don't read Latvian, it's clear by the writing on their boat that they're the police.

We have a good head start, but their boat is smaller and faster than ours. At this rate, they'll catch up to us in no time. I need to do something. I refuse to hide.

Using the walls for support, I exit the bedroom and grip the staircase railing as I frantically climb the stairs to the upper deck. I'm nearly at the top when the yacht hits choppy waters, and I almost lose my balance.

Yelping, I hold the railing for dear life and find my footing. When I hear Alek cursing in Russian, the need to help him has me climbing the remaining stairs briskly, ignoring my safety. I use the railings to walk my way over to him as he desperately steers the yacht.

He turns over his shoulder to see how close the police are but sees me instead. "I told you to wait in the bedroom! Go now. It's too dangerous up here!"

He's angry that I disobeyed him, but as I see it, we have a better chance of working together to survive this. "No! Tell me what I can do to help."

When he looks intent on arguing, I hold up my finger, warning him not to because this isn't negotiable.

He must be able to read my stubbornness because he asks, "How good of an arm are you?"

"I was a pitcher for my high school softball team," I share with a confident grin because this is something I can do.

"Excellent," he replies, gesturing with his chin toward the chest feet away. "There is a fishing net inside. I need you to throw it into the water on my command."

With a sharp nod, I waste no time and drop to my knees, opening the white chest. The fishing net along with some flares and life jackets are inside.

Quickly gathering the net, I hold it in my arms securely. "What now?"

Alek looks over his shoulder at me and nods. "Good girl," he commends. "Now, keep low so those assholes can't see you and unravel the net along the floor. It can't be tangled when you throw it into the water."

"Got it!"

Doing as he ordered, I duck low and run toward the back end of the yacht. I roll out the fishing net, ensuring it's laid flat. This is a lot harder than it sounds as I have to do this on my hands and knees. But once it's done, I turn over my shoulder and give Alek a thumbs-up.

He smirks in victory, and it titillates me.

I watch as he pulls down a level, decreasing the speed of

the yacht. We're still moving at a steady pace, but he's done this so the speedboat can get within reach. Peering over the edge, I see they're still too far away.

My heart is in my throat, but I'm not scared, I'm excited. Pulsating energy animates me in ways I've forgotten, thanks to the Macrillos robbing me of who I am. But now, knowing I can help Alek, that I can take down the "bad guys," has my vigilante self hollering in exhilaration.

It's time to take back my life. Step by step.

Alek's focus switches from steering the yacht, to looking over his shoulder to see where the police are. They're catching up to us, but I'm assuming this plan has to be executed without error. I begin to doubt myself.

What if I fail?

"Ella!" Alek cries. "Get ready. On my command."

Oh, shit. I don't have time for self-doubt.

Gathering one corner of the netting in my trembling hands, I duck low, my attention riveted on Alek. His astute gaze switches from the front to the back of the yacht. They're close. I can hear the motor on their boat roaring loudly behind. I can also hear zipping through the air.

"Oh, my god!" I cry, covering my head with one arm. "Are they…shooting at us?"

"Steady!" Alek orders with a grin. He's enjoying the chase immensely, which means he knows we're going to win.

My clothes are soaked with sweat, and my breathing is labored. I wonder if I'm having a panic attack. But there's no time to break down.

"Now, Ella! Do it. Now!"

Alek's voice and his faith in me have me pushing my doubts aside as I lift the netting and toss it over the edge of the yacht. It sails high through the air, catching the breeze before the spotlight from the speedboat illuminates the net crashing into the water.

I don't know what I'm looking for, but Alek's plan comes to fruition in three seconds when the propeller of the motorboat gets tangled in the net and kills the engine immediately. The motorboat jars to an abrupt stop, which sends two of the three policemen careening into the water.

The remaining man aims his gun, and a spark of light has me dropping to my stomach to avoid being hit by the bullet he just fired. Alek yanks on a lever that has the yacht roaring to full speed and away from danger.

I stay sprawled on my stomach for minutes, catching my breath. I did it. I stopped them. Tears of happiness spill down my cheeks, and this time, they're tears I don't wipe away.

When the night grows silent, I release the pent-up breaths I was holding and exhale, long and hard. When my head stops spinning, I lift myself into a sitting position and stay seated on the deck. Alek doesn't ask if I'm all right, and that's because I am.

We worked as a team, which is the only thing I've ever wanted. He didn't treat me like some fragile flower; he put his trust in me. We worked together, and suddenly, an epiphany hits—this is what I should have done from the very beginning.

Instead of trying to deal with Santo myself, I should have told Alek in the bathroom when he cornered me. But I wanted to prove to him that I was capable of doing this, just as Willow was. I know it's silly, but I wanted him to see me as a fighter as well as a lover.

Coming to a stand, I decide to shower as I need some time to think. I was so angry that Alek didn't trust me or treat me as an equal, but what just happened proves that he does.

"I'm just going to shower," I say, not wanting to make a fuss, and clearly neither does he as he nods.

Walking down the stairs with my head hung low, I realize I'm on an emotional roller coaster. The highs and lows just continue to confuse me.

Stripping off, I walk into the bathroom, feeling somewhat lighter. I don't know how to explain it, but escaping those men has a small piece of my heart, a piece which I believed was lost forever, stitched back together.

The cool water helps soothe the burn, but my body is an electrical current, and I can't quash this humming within. As I pass the lavender bar of soap I bought at the market over my body, my needy center begs I touch it to help appease the building pressure.

The excitement of the chase, of escaping with our lives intact, has left me incredibly...horny. I'm shocked at the revelation and quickly rinse off. Stepping from the shower, I avoid my reflection in the mirror as I dry myself with the fluffy towel and brush my teeth.

Once I'm dressed in my sleep shorts and tank, I decide to sleep and forget about the growing heat in my shorts. I thought that after what happened with Santo, I would never experience this sort of sexual arousal again. But no one is forcing me; I want this.

Pulling back the covers, I slip into bed, the rich Egyptian sheets sliding against my heated skin. Too hot to sleep with the blankets, I arrange the sheet over me and turn on my side, my back facing Alek's side because I can smell him on his pillow, and it doesn't help my current predicament.

Leaning up on my elbow, I punch my pillow a few times as it's too lumpy, but the pillow's not the problem. With a huff, I collapse into it and beg sleep comes…and it does until I'm awakened by the shower running.

At first, I believe I'm dreaming, but as my sleep clogged brain comes to, I realize I'm not. Alek is showering, and apart from the running water confirming this, he has left the bathroom door open, allowing me to see in.

Instantly, I avert my eyes, embarrassed, but I soon get over my shame as I want to see more.

His back is to me, which exposes his hardened torso and glorious, firm ass. His legs are muscular and strong, and I envy every waterdrop which clings to his golden skin. He shifts, reaching for the soap and gives me a glimpse of his thick cock.

He isn't hard, but the sight has me rubbing my legs together, attempting to soothe the painful burn which has resurfaced.

He runs the soap over his body, washing thoroughly, and as he washes between his legs, I imagine it's my hands helping him get clean. Stepping under the spray, he rinses his body, the suds trickling down and into the drain.

He stands with his face tipped toward the waterfall head, brushing back his wet hair with both hands. His biceps ripple, as does his abs when he shifts to turn off the faucets.

Horrified by what I'm doing, I squeeze my eyes shut and fake sleep, not wanting Alek aware that I caught him showering. I can hear the towel move backward and forward across his skin as he dries himself. I can smell the minty toothpaste as he brushes his teeth.

The light switch flicks off, and Alek's soft footsteps pad across the carpet as he walks to his side of the bed. I know he won't sleep for long. Just enough so he can steer us to safety. The mattress dips as he gets under the covers and turns his back to me.

With a contented sigh, his breathing grows shallow within minutes, hinting he's fast asleep.

I need to follow suit, but I can't. I'm on high alert. I feel like I've just drunk ten coffees in a row, and I know the only way I can settle down is to give in to my needs.

Rolling onto my stomach, I turn my neck in Alek's direction and am greeted with his broad back. I can see his tattoo clearer. He doesn't need to be inked from head to toe. This simple tattoo suits him and just levitates his hotness to another level.

With blushing cheeks, I slide my hand down into my shorts. My skin is so hot that I hiss when I touch it. I'm already wet, so I slip a finger into my pussy. I bite down on my tongue to mute my pleasured moans.

I focus on the dips and muscular planes on Alek's back and the way his wet hair curls at his nape. The sheet rests just above his ass, allowing me to see his tapered waist and dimples of Venus. Every part of him looks like he's been chiseled out of marble.

I add another finger and pump my hips into the mattress,

desperate for the friction to help me come. I've never done anything like this before, but I'm not ashamed. I feel liberated. I feel like I'm taking back my body after it was violently stolen from me.

This has me biting the corner of the pillow as I continue looking at Alek, fingering myself. His touches, although possessive, have always been welcome. He never forced anything on me that I didn't want. At the orphanage, when he asked me if I wanted him to spank me, it's like he could read my mind because I never wanted anything more.

I've never been this sexually deviant with anyone before, but with Alek, he brings this side out of me, and that's because he worships me like no one ever has. When he kisses me, touches me, he makes me feel like I'm made solely for him, and the way he wants me with such passion, that's the biggest turn-on of all.

I fervently drive my hips into the mattress with a measured pace, not wanting to wake Alek as I play with my swollen clit. And the covert nature of such a wicked act has my orgasm tackling me so hard that my screams are muffled into the pillow.

I come so hard, tears leak from my eyes, but I ride this wave because something releases inside me, and I'm not just talking physically, but emotionally as well. Once I come down from my post-orgasmic bubble, I collapse into the pillow and sigh, content.

Instantly, I feel better as this was the only cure to appease the ailment within.

The sleepiness I was chasing overcomes me, and I give in, knowing my nightmares won't be as predominate tonight.

CHAPTER TEN

Alek

The yacht is cruising on autopilot because I fear I'll kill both Ella and myself with my inattention this morning. And that's because all I can focus on is the fact Ella was pleasuring herself in our bed last night.

Yes, I pretended to be asleep because I knew she was spying on me in the shower. It was an honest mistake leaving the door open. I was so preoccupied thinking about how close we were to getting caught that I completely forgot to close the door.

But when I heard the mattress shift, I knew she was watching me, and the fact pleased me more than I care to admit. I didn't put on a show. I just wanted to get out of the shower and hope that maybe what happened would have helped Ella open up somehow.

But she staged sleep when I entered the bedroom, shooting my hopes to hell.

I figured being close to her would help me sleep a few hours because yesterday proved I need to give one hundred and ten percent all the time. But sleeping was the last thing I wanted to do when I heard the muted whimpers and unmistakable sound of Ella's fingers bringing her pleasure.

It took every ounce of willpower not to turn around and replace her fingers with my mouth, but I couldn't. I won't touch Ella. I can't. She's made it very clear that she doesn't want me anymore, so with no other choice, I was forced to listen to her breathy whimpers and the sliding of her fingers as she came.

I have the worst case of blue balls and need to use my cane but not for my leg. I've been walking with an even worse limp since I woke early this morning. I didn't trust myself, so I took a cold shower—with the door closed—hoping it would help, but it didn't.

So to keep busy, I've made enough breakfast to feed a small army.

Sitting at the breakfast bar, I stare into my black coffee, wishing it would give me the answers I so desperately seek. It doesn't look promising.

Ella's soft footsteps up the stairs do nothing to help my predicament, and when she enters the room wearing a red swimsuit and denim shorts, it only cements the fact that I'm so screwed. Her hair is twisted into a high bun, and her sunglasses sit on top of her head.

When she notices me staring, she stops dead in her tracks. "Oh, sorry. I thought you were up top. I'll come back."

Just as she turns to leave, I leap up from the barstool,

heart in my throat. "I made breakfast. Please eat." Not my most eloquent of words, but at least I constructed a coherent string of words.

She purses her lips, moving them from side to side in contemplation before she nods.

The urge to feed her is unbearable, but I rein it in. I sip my coffee casually, appearing nonchalant as she walks around the breakfast bar to look at the spread of food on the far counter.

"Wow, I'd ask if we were expecting company, but after last night, I doubt it. What happened? Why were the police chasing us?"

Jesus Christ, what happened was that we almost got caught. If it wasn't for Ella and her perfect aim, I'd hate to think where we'd be.

"We stopped at that port because I asked Pavel to organize some new IDs for us in case we needed them," I explain, owing her the truth. "His contact was someone he trusted, but it seemed Santo got to him first."

She visibly swallows. "What does that mean?"

"It means he threatened to kill me if I didn't hand you over," I bluntly reply because there's no sugarcoating this.

"And what did you do?"

Finishing my coffee, I calmly place the cup onto the breakfast bar. "I killed him, of course."

She pales and presses a hand over her throat. "Is that why the police were chasing us?"

Nodding, I lean my elbows on the counter and interlace my fingers. "Yes. Someone must have seen what I did and contacted them. If it wasn't for your precision, we wouldn't be here. You never told me you played baseball," I add, trying to lighten the mood.

It doesn't work.

"How did Santo get to someone Pavel trusted? I mean, Pavel doesn't trust easily."

And she's right.

"When I called Pavel this morning and told him his contact had gone rogue, he was most surprised. He knew Josef for fifteen years and never once doubted his loyalty, which means Santo is playing dirty. Pavel hypothesized that Santo was holding something he loved as collateral. It worked with me, didn't it?"

When Serg had Irina, I would stop at nothing to save her. I assume Josef was doing the same thing. But we will never know for sure.

"Originally, I wanted to stop at that port to grab enough supplies for the long haul. The further away we are, the safer it is. But now I fear, I may have done the complete opposite. I thought the IDs would—"

"You were right," Ella says, interrupting me. "That was a smart move. You wouldn't know it would backfire."

Her reassurance doesn't make me feel any less guilty, however.

"This means Santo is circling everyone we know, looking for the weakest link to rat us out. We have to be careful with who we trust from now on. We won't be so lucky next time."

"And you trust the IRA?" she asks, ignoring the food as our conversation seems to feed her curiosity.

"Yes, I do."

"Why?"

Of course, she is skeptical. She doesn't know what I have planned. It's time she does.

"Because my plan is to take over Russia, using the underdogs as allies. Everything goes through me. Guns. Drugs. Money. I'm the source. This is the only way I can ensure no one will dare to try to overthrow me again.

"My old associates see me as weak. They remember who I was, how I ruled, but I don't want to be like that anymore. For this to work, I need a new circle, and what better way to do that then band with a group of misfits who would do anything to be on top."

If not for her chest rising and falling, indicating she is breathing, I'd fear she was dead. But I know this is a lot to take in.

"My plan was to befriend Santo for when I took out Raul, I took out the best drug source in Russia. There are others, but I want someone who can handle my needs. I want a quality product. And I want to be the only person distributing it."

"The mafia," she gasps, understanding what I mean.

"Yes, that's another reason I lost the poker game. I needed those assholes on my side. I was using them to benefit me. I'm not stupid, Ella. I know once Santo got what information he needed from me to distribute his drugs, he'd have me killed. I just needed to get there first.

"I would have had the mafia wrapped around my finger so that when Santo "disappeared," they would continue supplying to me. In this case, blood would not be thicker than water. Trust me."

Ella looks like she's going to be sick. And when she places her hand over her mouth and rushes out the door, headed for the railing, it appears that she is.

"Ella?" I ask, cautiously walking toward her.

She is hunched over the edge, gasping for air.

"Did I say too much? Forgive me."

I wait in the doorway, unsure if she wants me to leave her be. I don't want to go, but I understand if she needs time.

"I'm so stupid," she says so quietly that I almost missed it.

"No, you are not. Why would you say such a thing?"

I wait, giving her the time she needs to face me, and when she does, I grip the doorframe, afraid of what she's going to say.

"You were always two steps ahead of him. Of everyone," she says, confusing me. I have no idea where she's going with this.

"You asked why I stayed with Frank, and the reason is…you," she confesses while I stare wide-eyed. "I handed myself over to Santo because I knew it would help you. I knew how much Irina, Willow, Mother Superior, everyone, I knew how much they meant to you. And I couldn't live with myself knowing any harm would come to the people you love because of me.

"At first, I thought you didn't want me, but I soon worked out that you did what you did to protect me. I was angry that you could have fooled me so easily, but when I was able to do the same thing to you, that anger turned to sadness.

"We should have just trusted one another and worked together. Last night proved that."

I don't know what to say. I wanted the truth, and here it is. I just don't know what to do with it.

"Santo wanted to be your new BFF because he wanted to gain your trust, hoping you'd help him. The family is on the cusp of being bankrupt," she shares, which has me cursing under my breath.

No wonder they were raiding the temple like common thieves. They are.

"Santo decided to try his hand in drug distribution to help make more money. But Serg was in the way, which is why Santo helped you at Raul's house. You're more valuable to him alive than you are dead.

"No one would buy from Santo, no matter how pure his product was. But they'd buy from you. He needed Raul and Serg out of the picture and so did you. With them gone, he could manipulate you into going into business together.

"He needs your name and reputation, but more importantly, he needs your knowledge to help him build *his own* empire, and then once he was on top, he was going to kill you. He needed you to watch and learn."

This was what I wanted to believe was true. I wanted this to be the reason Ella agreed to marry Frank. But now that I know the truth, it does nothing to calm me down.

"You stayed because Santo blackmailed you?" I ask because surely her knowing all this information meant she was their prisoner.

But when she averts her gaze, it seems I am so fucking wrong.

"No," she softly replies. "I was undercover. I wanted to

gather all the information I could about his plans, the mafia, anything of use to you so you could strike and bring him down. You needed an inside man and I wanted to help. I was in a position to.

"Just as you thought sending Willow and Saint into Santo's house was a good idea because they were meant to be there is the same reason I acted the way I did. No one would suspect me snooping around because I was Frank's fiancée.

"It wouldn't arouse any suspicion, and I could come to you when I had information. But everything got so messed up," she confesses with a tremble.

Running a hand over my mouth, I take a moment because I'm dumbfounded.

She saw how successful Renata was at playing double agent, but Renata is now dead.

"I couldn't tell you in the bathroom at your house because I didn't know anything of use. I didn't come that far just to give up. Even though I wanted to."

"Oh, Ella," I say, shaking my head. "I appreciate you doing that for me, but you should have told me."

"You don't think I know that now?" she cries, stubbornly wiping away her tears. "I just wanted to prove to you that I'm not some silly girl who needs rescuing. I saw an opportunity, and I took it. And it would have worked if—"

"If what?" I press when she pauses and gnaws on her bottom lip.

"The morning of the poker game, I argued with Frank," she shares. "He threatened to keep me locked in our bedroom. I couldn't let that happen. I had to warn you about Santo's plans because I was afraid you'd give Santo the information he needed, and he'd have you killed.

"Santo saw how impulsive you are. He's afraid of you, which is why he would have killed you if you fell for his ploy. He was going to drag it out, but he said your days were numbered. He said he and his family just needed the basics, and if you gave them that, they'd have killed you that night."

That stupid, insignificant piece of shit.

"Renata was able to help Serg…I wanted to help too."

"Renata is dead," I blankly state, while the whites of Ella's eyes show.

I appreciate her doing this, I truly do. But this could have been avoided if she trusted me. But then I realize, why would she? I haven't given her reason to because I didn't trust her.

I could have told her about our plans instead of sending her away because she's right; even though she is far from being a damsel in distress, my first instinct is to protect her and not put her in harm's way. We both tried so hard to protect the other, but in the end, we made more of a mess than doing good.

Miscommunication and the irrational urge to defend each other has caused so much pain. But peeling back the layers, I see this for what it is; we did what we did because our feelings for one another *are* irrational, so much so, we would do anything to keep the other safe.

Just like me leaving Russia, and Ella sacrificing herself— an absolute Shakespearian twist.

"What happened with Frank?" I press, but when she grips the railing behind her, I know sharing time is over.

I'll give her the time because today was progress, but I will continue to push until she cracks. Now that I know what I do, I can only imagine what happened, how far she was goaded to have done what she did.

She's not ready to tell me, and honestly, I don't think I'm ready to hear her truths.

"I want them dead. All of them," she whispers angrily. "Mila too."

The Macrillos have wounded Ella, so much so that her stance on murder has now shifted. Only something heinous could have changed her mind.

"I know you want me to go to Ireland, but I want to be the one." I watch with interest as she clarifies, "I want to be the one who kills Santo. You wanted revenge on those who hurt you…and now, so do I."

My first instinct is to deny her. The thought of her going anywhere near Santo turns my stomach, but how can I deny her? She's right. I stopped at nothing to find Serg and deliver him the fate he so deserved. Denying her would not only be hypocritical, but it would also be wrong.

Grappling with my mixed emotions, I sigh. "Ella, I understand, I really do, but this is beyond dangerous. I don't have a plan. The only thing I cared about is getting you to safety, and then I would have worked out the rest."

"So that's a no?" she questions, angered and also let down.

After us both realizing if only we trusted one another from the very beginning, none of this would have happened, this is a kick in the teeth.

"No." I shake my head. "This is a let me think about it.

I won't knowingly send you into danger. Unless there is a rock-solid plan, the answer is no. But I won't deny you your vengeance."

She folds her arms across her chest, appearing pleased with the compromise. "Good. So what happens now?"

With so much doom and gloom surrounding us, we've forgotten we're surrounded by blue seas and nothing else. "Now, you're going to eat."

When she looks like she's about to argue, I hold up a finger, warning her this isn't negotiable. "And then I might take a swim."

"A swim?" she asks, a flicker of a smile lighting up her face. How I've missed seeing her smile.

"Yes. It's a lovely day. Seems a shame to let it go to waste."

"Okay," she agrees, which pleases me.

I've hated this hostility between us. I can only hope we've turned a corner.

When she walks toward me, indicating she wants to come inside, I stand firm, needing a moment to admire her. Her wounds are her battle scars, and although I wish I could have taken the beating for her, those scars show the world she was stronger than whatever tried to beat her.

I *have* underestimated her strength because her self-sacrifice saved us all. If she didn't make that deal with Santo, we'd all be in a very different situation. For starters, I'd be dead.

She stands before me, nervously adjusting the strap on her swimsuit. It's a modest piece, but the way it clings to her torso, her breasts, it amps up my desperation tenfold. I want her as I've never wanted anyone before.

I can barely function because I'm not a patient man. And denying myself her is like denying my lungs air to breathe. But this doesn't change anything. She still sees me as nothing but the past. Just because we've uncovered a revelation doesn't change the fact she intends to get on with her life once this is done.

But the hunter in me won't shift. It provokes her to challenge me.

"Red's your color," I say with a smirk, unable to stop myself from visually eating her alive.

"Well, being a sleazy old perv is yours," she rebukes with sass.

Her comment only feeds my deprivation.

"Old?" I fake heartache as I place a hand over my chest.

She smiles once again as I move out of her way so she can enter.

She walks past me, her scent almost folding me in half. I don't recognize this perfume. It must be new. Whatever it is, I like it. I like her. And it's evident how much I actually like her when she places a strawberry into her mouth and my cock twitches at the simple action of her eating a piece of fruit.

The juice of the strawberry trickles down her chin, and when she wipes it away with an innocent flick of her tongue, I quickly excuse myself before I come in my pants like a pubescent teen.

I enter the bedroom and change into my swimming trunks, refusing to think about Ella upstairs in nothing but a swimsuit, eating strawberries. Goddammit. How can the simple act of eating be such a turn-on?

I suppose she simply needs to exist and that's enough to get me hard, well, harder.

Adjusting myself, I hobble up toward the upper deck and kill the motor. This is just as good as any spot to swim. I then walk down the stairs, toward the back of the yacht where the swim platform is.

This luxury yacht was a package deal with the house. Denka Orlov didn't need it anymore. So the realtor threw it in for an extra twenty grand. It troubles me that Santo might be able to track me somehow because the realtor was his associate, but I hope the yacht's name change will steer him off course.

I named it Yali, after the fallen sister who died too young.

With that, I step toward the edge of the platform and dive into the depths. The water is cool, but it's the perfect antidote for the warm sun. I swim deep, as I love water and only come up for air when I must. When I break the surface, I float on my back, staring into the clear blue sky.

It's so peaceful out here, but my mind is constantly running in the background.

Ella deserves her revenge. I just don't know how I'm going to give her that without her getting hurt.

The encounter with the Macrillos will be embroiled in violence and bloodshed, and seeing as she's public enemy number one, they'll be gunning for her, not me.

I need to speak to Saint as he knows firsthand how to deal with a headstrong, determined woman. I see the way he and Willow operate as a team. He, too, wanted to shelter her from harm's way, but when he saw she wasn't one to take orders, he had to adjust.

I'm a dominant by nature, so doing that with Ella sends my head into all sorts of trouble.

She liked me to control her in the bedroom, but when it comes to independence, she won't be told what to do. I still can't believe she knowingly threw herself to the wolves. What a brave woman she truly is.

A splash alerts me that I'm no longer alone.

Craning my neck, I see Ella come up for air as she combs her wet hair from her face. I don't make a fuss and continue to float, wishing my worries would follow suit and drift away.

Ella keeps her distance, which is probably best for us both. But I'm still so in tune with her. It's like she moves, I move. She breathes, I breathe. She hurts, and so do I.

"What happened to your leg?" Her distant voice indicates she's not close. Maybe this is where she feels most comfortable to converse.

"Raul imbedded a garden rake into my thigh and flayed my muscles into shreds. He also broke a lot of bones," I add because this all scales to why I have a limp. "Does my limp disgust you?"

"God, no," she quickly replies, surprising me because she answered without hesitation.

"It should. It disgusts me," I share. "Seeing as I couldn't go to the hospital as too many questions would be asked, Pavel called his mom, and she pieced me back together again. She did the best she could, considering she was working with a god-awful mess.

"There really isn't anything that woman can't do," I say in

awe of her. "She's saved my life numerous times when she's had every right to let me die."

"Maybe that's because she knows you're not the bad guy," Ella states, again, catching me off guard.

"The limp shouldn't be permanent," I reveal, not that it matters to her. "It would be gone by now had I had some physical therapy on it. But I had other pressing matters to deal with."

Like finding her…

With that thought, I dive underwater, wishing to be lost to the stillness of the sea. I wish I could be lost forever, but that would be the easy way out, and thus far, my life has been anything but easy. So I resurface, noticing Ella swimming closer to me.

I tread water, watching the way she moves so gracefully. I wish I could put a lid on these emotions, but the wanting, it's just getting worse.

"What happened to Renata?" she asks, as I revealed she's dead.

Brushing back my wet hair, I reply honestly, "My mother shot her, and although the shot wasn't fatal, Serg using her as a shield for his protection is what killed her in the end."

"That's horrible. I know what she did was unspeakable, but no one deserves that."

"You're right," I agree with a sharp nod. "But that's what distinguishes us from the animals."

"And what of your mother? Did she get away?"

Just the mention of Zoya ruins my paradise. "Yes, but honestly, she is the least of my troubles. Her day will come.

Besides, word would have spread about what I did to her precious baby boy, which is enough torture for now."

"I heard whispers," she reveals. "But what happened to Serg?"

Relishing in the memory I relive often, I share, "I nailed him to a wall where I cut off his cock and fed it to him. He died, choking on his own appendage. One of my greatest kills."

I suddenly realize what I said and frown. "Sorry, I didn't think. Forgive me."

Speaking so flippantly about killing someone while Ella is struggling with what she did to Frank is heartless. I don't want her to think taking someone's life is easy. It's easy for me because I've done it so many times.

"It's okay," she says, treading water a few feet away from me. "Why did you decide to do that?" *That* meaning feed him his own cock.

It still pains me as I confess, "Because he implied, he… well, he suggested he molested Irina. And that he wasn't the first."

"What?" she gasps, slowing down her treading.

"Yes, when I found her, she was dolled up like no little girl ever should be. If I could kill that долбоёб again, I would." I clench my fists, rage overtaking me.

Ella blanches before turning around and swimming back toward the yacht.

"Shit," I curse as I should have thought before I spoke. "I'm sorry, Ella."

I quickly swim after her, angry with myself for revealing too much. Of course, this is too much to take in.

She lifts herself onto the platform and snares a towel from the lounge chair. I boost myself up onto the platform seconds later, heart in my throat as I'm worried she's going to stop talking to me again. She rubs her skin raw as she dries herself, refusing to look at me.

"I'm sorry. Please forgive me for saying too much."

However, when she shakes her head, gnawing on her bottom lip, it appears I've misunderstood this entire situation.

"Forgive *you*?" she cries, her cheeks flushing an angry red. "*I'm* the one who should be asking for forgiveness. I'm such an idiot. I've started a war with the Macrillos.

"You've left Irina behind when she needs you the most just to save my ass…again. If only—"

"Hey," I say, stepping forward. "Stop it. You didn't force me to do any of this. I'm here because I want to be."

I won't allow her to shoulder the blame. I saw the state she was in. The people to blame are the Macrillos.

I want more than anything to reach out and touch her, but I don't. It's hard to remember I gave up that right when I allowed her to get hurt.

A voice over the CB radio interrupts us, and when I hear what they say, I swiftly run up the stairs toward the radio. Picking up the fist mic, I ask them to repeat what they just said because there has to be some mistake.

But when they confirm that we're in the direct path of an upcoming monster storm, confusion turns to panic. I thank them and quickly consult the digital weather charts on the control panel.

"блять!" I curse, frantically checking the radar in hopes

it'll say something different. It doesn't.

"What's the matter?" Ella asks, clinging to the towel, sensing something is wrong.

"That was another boat. They just put out a distress call for all boats in the area. An unexpected storm is headed our way."

"Oh, my god. Is it bad?"

Nodding, I sidestep to look into the sky. The clear blue skies have turned a wrathful gray. "We have to slow down."

"Can't we change course?"

"There's no time." The wind begins to pick up speed, and the temperature has dropped about ten degrees in minutes, confirming my claims. "She's strong. We can ride it out. Don't worry."

The truth is, however, no matter how good of a sailor one may be, storms are unpredictable. We are now at the mercy of the sea gods.

Ella turns and runs down the stairs, which is a good move. She'll be safer indoors than she will be up here. Flicking the switches, I decrease the speed, looking at the satellite to see how far out we are. We have about twenty-five minutes.

"Here!" Ella yells, startling me because I thought she'd gone to safety. But when she offers me a T-shirt and my boat shoes, I realize there is no way she'd let me do this alone.

She's slipping into her sneakers anxiously, her fear palpable. I want to assure her it'll be okay, but as the storm mass begins to grow on the satellite screen, I actually don't know if it will be.

Once dressed, I run over to the chest and retrieve the two

life vests. I also grab the flare gun just in case. This is just my luck. For us to get shipwrecked. I suppose it worked for Saint and Willow, but eventually, I found them, helpless and with no means to fight, which is what will happen to us.

But the difference is—we will never get out alive.

"Put this on!" I order, tossing the vest to Ella. She quickly secures it over her head as I do with mine.

When the heavens open, it's only a matter of time before we sail into dangerous waters. Ella huddles close to me under the canopy to stop from getting wet. I take the wheel, watching the screen carefully for any changes ahead.

Ella does the same, and when she sees the huge blob we're sailing into, she yelps. "Alek, we won't make it."

"Yes, we will," I promise.

"Have you ever sailed in these sorts of conditions before?" she shouts to be heard over the howling wind.

"There's a first time for everything." I try to play aloof, not wanting to scare her.

A thunderclap cracks loudly, and Ella screams and grips my forearm. So help me god, we are getting out of this, and when we do, I'm going to beg Ella for a second or rather, third chance. Our story doesn't end this way.

The rain pelts in from every direction, making it impossible to see. And as the swell begins to grow, I have to use the navigational panel as my eyes. The CB radio crackles, and just as Ella bends down to pick up the fist mic, it goes dead.

The yacht begins to rock violently, and although sturdy, the monster waves begin to drag us under. I grip the wheel, keeping it steady as I steer us as best I can. The wind is loud, and when a lightning bolt hits the deck, it's apparent we're headed straight for the eyewall.

"What can I do?"

"Just stay close to me," I instruct because I can't steer this yacht while wondering if she's safe or not.

"That won't be a problem," she says, pressing her body into mine.

As the swell continues to grow and the waves crash into the yacht, I begin to wonder if this is really it this time. Is this where it ends for us?

The weather just worsens, and the conditions are so bad, I can barely see my hands on the wheel. I hold on tight, steering as best I can, but when an enormous wave comes crashing down onto us, and I hear Ella scream, I let go.

"Ella!" I shout as she's no longer by my side. "Ella!"

Panic strangles me as I shield my eyes, blocking out the rain as I frantically look for Ella. I don't have a second to spare because the high waves threaten to drag us under. The tread on my shoes helps me from sliding as I go on the hunt. I grip the railing to keep from falling into the water as the yacht rocks violently from side to side.

My heart is beating so fast that I'm afraid I'm going to have a heart attack. I've never felt this level of fear before. When Irina was taken, I was scared, but more than anything, I was angry as I knew I'd see her again, but now, I don't have the same reassurance.

"Ella!" I bellow, cupping my mouth, hoping my voice will carry.

A lightning bolt lights up the sky, allowing me to see Ella, hanging on for dear life. Her arms are extended over her head as her body hangs over the edge of the yacht. If she loses her grip, she will fall overboard.

"Ella! I'm coming!" Forgetting anything but getting to her, I fight against the brutal elements, determined to win. I lose my footing and slip, but I grip the railing and regain my balance.

She arches her neck, and when she sees me, she screams something which gets lost in the roar of the waves. Using the railing as a guide, I get to her within seconds. Without hesitation, I bend low, and when I have a firm hold on her wrists, I slide her toward me.

When she's within reach, I lock my arms around her and drag her toward my chest. She clings to me, our life jackets in the way, but she holds on tight. "Thank you!" she half sobs into my ear.

I brush over her hair, her back, needing to make sure she's okay. The relief I feel is indescribable. I can celebrate later because now, I have to steer us to safety.

Helping her up, I keep a tight hold of her hand as we make our way back to the helm. I grip the wheel, but we suddenly hit a wave, and it spins so quickly, I lose hold.

"Alek, I'm sorry!" Ella shouts, her wet hair stuck to her face. "I never meant for any of this to happen."

But I shake my head. "I don't want words of a quitter. We fight."

"How?" she cries, peering at the twenty-foot wall of water ahead.

I refuse to surrender, and at this moment, I realize if we die, Ella will never know that I…love her. I always have. I was so terrified of saying it, but now, I want to say it a thousand times over. However, it's too late. We will go to a watery grave with regrets.

But I won't accept that.

"Alek, I—"

But I'll never know what she wanted to say because when the sky lights up, revealing the cable connecting the satellite tower snapping free and heading straight for Ella, I shove her to safety before the world turns to black.

CHAPTER ELEVEN

Ella

"Please wake up," I whisper for the...I don't even know because I've lost count. Every second Alek is nonresponsive feels like years.

The storm has passed, and I don't know how, but we're alive. However, I wouldn't be if Alek hadn't pushed me to safety. His heroic actions got him knocked unconscious when he saved my life. It all happened so fast.

The waves were unlike anything I've ever seen before, which is why I decided to drag Alek downstairs, afraid he'd get washed out to sea if we stayed outside. I couldn't carry him, and each time his head bumped down a step, I begged for forgiveness.

The slippery flooring helped as I hauled him into the living room. I lay him on the carpet, as he was too heavy to lift onto the couch. Positioning a cushion under his head, I took off his life vest, dried him off with a towel, and placed a blanket over him.

I waited anxiously, biting my nails as I watched his chest rise and fall. He was breathing, but he wouldn't wake. And he's been this way ever since.

The satellite phone and CB radio don't work, thanks to the tower hitting Alek before crashing into the wild waves. The autopilot also seems to be damaged. We're stuck out here alone. I have no way to contact anyone for help, which is why I'm desperate for Alek to wake.

I can't see any blood, but he took a hard hit to the head when he fell onto the deck. Not to mention the satellite tower knocking into him like a steam train at full speed. I fear his injuries are internal, which is so much worse because I can't see them.

Gripping his cold hand in mine, I give him my warmth, my strength because he needs to wake so I can tell him how sorry I am.

He's saved me time and time again. Without question, he's put my safety above his. He left Russia behind so he could protect me. And what he did, sacrificing himself for me…I need to apologize for taking out what happened to me on him.

I now understand the saying you hurt the ones you love because I lashed out. I was angry and scared, but Alek didn't deserve any of that. I just didn't know how to vocalize my pain because how do you relive the worst moment of your life without breaking down?

I'm a victim, yes, but I prefer to see myself as a survivor because I *will* survive this. I won't allow what Santo did destroy me because I refuse to let him own me that way. For every silenced voice out there, I'll fight for them, for us.

I'm forever changed because of this experience, and I'll take it a day at a time. I know I'll have good days. I'll have bad days. But to me, the most important thing is that I'm living those days the best way I can.

Stroking over Alek's cheek with the back of my hand, I release this anger inside me. I understand why he made the choices that he did. We can't change the past, but we can the future. I accept that at the time, he thought he was making the right choices. He didn't make them with malicious intent. He thought he was doing the right thing.

I want to get past this so we can move on. But I hurt him, so I hope that we can.

A pained groan escapes Alek's lips, shattering the silence.

"Alek!" I cry, shooting up into a kneeling position. "Alek, can you hear me?"

He stirs, shifting his head against the cushion. He flinches, indicating he's in pain.

Jumping up, I run over to the sink and pour him a glass of water. I slip a dissolvable aspirin I found in the first aid kit into the glass.

"Here, drink this," I say, dropping to my knees next to him. I wait for him to open his eyes, and when he does, relief like I've never felt before overwhelms me.

He seems to be taking everything in slowly as I can imagine things are fuzzy. When his focus lands on me, his eyes widen as if remembering what happened.

"Are, are you all right?" His voice is hoarse.

With a nod, I give him the glass. "I'm okay...thanks to

you." I would offer to help him drink it, but I know better.

With slow, pained movements, he lifts himself into a half-sitting position so he can drink the water. He gulps it down in one swig, pulling a face at the aspirin-flavored water.

Once he's done, he places the glass onto the carpet and shifts, propping himself up against the sofa. "Tell me everything that happened."

Sitting cross-legged next to him, I nervously tug at the elastic band around my wrist. "Well, we were caught in a storm, and I would be dead if you didn't push me out of the path of the satellite tower. It knocked you out cold.

"I dragged you down here, afraid you'd be washed out to sea."

"How long have I been out?" he asks, rubbing the back of his head.

Looking at the clock on the wall, I shrug. "Like four hours."

"Fuck," he curses, throwing the blanket off him. "I have no idea where we are. With the satellite tower down, we have no way of knowing our coordinates. The CB radio is dead too? And the autopilot doesn't work because it has no coordinates to navigate to?"

I nod.

With a huff, he attempts to stand, but wavers and grips the edge of the sofa for support.

"Let me help you." I race forward and loop an arm around his middle, coaxing him to rest his weight against me.

"Thanks," he says, leaning into me.

He towers over me, but he's weak and needs help when he

comes to a wobbly stand. It feels good being the one helping him instead of the other way around. We hobble toward the stairs, needing to stop a couple of times for Alek to catch his breath.

The climb to the upper deck takes about ten minutes, but when we get to the top, Alek clings to the railing and pulls away from me, indicating he's okay to do it on his own. His retreat stings, but it's to be expected.

Just because I've decided to forgive doesn't mean he feels the same way.

I watch as Alek hobbles to the control panel and begins to play with all the buttons and levers. When nothing sparks to life, he reaches for the CB radio. It clicks over a few times, hinting it too is dead.

He grips the panel and lowers his chin, appearing in thought. "This is my fault. I'm sorry. I shouldn't have sailed through the storm. I thought we'd be okay."

"Hey," I say on a rushed breath, gripping his forearm. "We *are* okay. Thanks to you. We've got enough food and water on board to last us for weeks. Hopefully, we will pass another boat soon."

He nods, but he's deflated.

"Alek, this isn't your fault," I reassure him.

But he doesn't want to hear it and gently removes his arm from my hold. "I'm going to shower."

I want to talk, to tell him I'm sorry, but decide he needs some time alone to process our current situation. So I nod, letting him go do his thing.

He limps toward the stairs, taking each one with what

sounds like a frustrated thud. I understand his anger because our predicament is far from ideal, but we won't starve to death, so that's one thing working in our favor.

Walking to the front of the yacht, I grip the silver railing and peer out into the vast nothingness, which gives me the false belief that we're the only people alive. It's so quiet, and after the noise that has chased me for so long, the silence is actually a nice thing to bask in for a while.

I know Alek needs a phone to keep in contact with home, as he's worried about Irina. And also, about the Macrillos.

Right now, we need a miracle.

That doesn't look to be anywhere near, so I decide to make us something to eat, and then we can think of a game plan. When in the kitchen, I open the refrigerator and look at all the ingredients. I want to make something special for Alek, but I'm sure after being knocked out cold, he can probably only stomach something light.

I have all the ingredients for an antipasto dish, which isn't too heavy, and we can snack on it. Not an ideal dinner, but at least it'll put some food into Alek's stomach. So, grabbing everything I need, I place all the ingredients onto the counter and grab the wooden chopping board, which works as the best serving dish.

I commence rolling the cured meats and arranging them into neat piles on the board. I then hunt the cupboards for small ramekin bowls to pile in the olives, artichoke hearts, sundried tomatoes, and other vegetables in vinegar.

Cutting the various cheeses into cubes, I arrange everything so it's all symmetrical. Peering down at my handiwork, I can't deny I'm impressed. This would be ideal with fresh, crunchy bread, but I decide to grill the frozen baguette as the perfect substitute.

As I'm waiting for the baguette to defrost in the microwave before grilling it, a musky cologne comes drifting up the stairs. When Alek appears freshly showered, I take a moment to appreciate him because I feel like I'm seeing him in a new light.

No matter what Alek wears, he oozes confidence and control. Even in simple black pants and a white shirt, he looks like the ruthless ruler I've grown to…

Retiring that thought for now, I focus on the baguette and not Alek moving behind me to retrieve something from the freezer. When I hear a bottle unscrewing, I assume he found the bottle of vodka. The clinking of glasses as he pulls them from the cupboard reveals he doesn't wish to drink alone.

He rounds the counter and takes a seat at the breakfast bar. "Drink?" he asks, holding up the iced bottle of vodka.

"Sure, but I don't think you should be drinking after sustaining a head injury," I say, removing the baguette from the microwave and placing it under the grill.

Alek ignores me—like I knew he would—and goes about pouring two glasses of vodka. He slides one across the counter to me.

"Trust me, I've sustained worse," he replies, before raising his glass in salute and draining it dry.

He pours himself another serving while I reach for my glass and take a small sip. I blanch and puff my cheeks out because that's some strong booze. It doesn't affect Alek as he downs his second glass.

"So, I think we're approaching Estonia or on the way to Stockholm. The winds would have pushed us north. But this is a guess," he says, running his finger along the rim of the glass. "And a rough one at that."

"You're worried about Irina?"

"Very," he replies with a sharp nod. "I hate being so… powerless. It's not in my makeup to be at the mercy of others. Even when things were dire with Serg, I still had options, but now, I do not. We have no other choice but to wait until we reach a port or pass another vessel.

"But even then, I'm putting my faith in fate, in the unknown, and when you're a gambling man, that's a hand you don't usually win with."

"I feel like this is all my fault," I say, not wanting sympathy. I want him to know I'm aware he wouldn't be here if it wasn't for me.

"It's not your fault, Ella. It's life. What is the American saying?" he asks, moving his lips from side to side in contemplation. "When life gives you lemons, you make—"

"A whiskey sour," I reply, forfeiting the lemonade option because we need something a little stronger to deal with this shitshow.

His lips twitch. "This looks lovely. Thank you."

I remove the bread from the grill and crack open a clove of garlic with the blade of a knife. Alek watches as I rub the garlic onto the toasted side of the baguette. The rich smell of garlic and hot bread has my stomach rumbling.

Placing the bread onto a plate, I grab the olive oil and

balsamic vinegar—the perfect duo to accompany hot bread. Passing Alek a small plate, I gesture for him to dig in.

Watching him stack his plate with food pleases me greatly. I don't know why, but there is something oddly satisfying about feeding the man you care for…which leads to my dilemma.

I want to tell Alek everything, but I don't know where to start.

Deciding I need a little more Dutch courage, I reach for the vodka and take a long swig from the bottle. Alek pauses from chewing, a small smirk on his handsome face.

"Alek, I…" I clear my throat as my voice is suddenly hoarse.

He waits for me to continue while I wonder where my Dutch courage is.

I just need to say it without thinking about the repercussions. If he says it's too late, at least I know, and I can take this bottle of vodka and nurse it in the bedroom alone.

"I wanted to say—" But my sentence remains in limbo because Alek turns his head as if listening intently to something in the distance.

"Did you hear that?" he asks, standing up slowly.

I shake my head because I didn't hear anything.

He seems to have regained his balance but still has a limp as he hobbles toward the middle of the room, listening closely. Just when I think his head injury is playing tricks on him, I hear a faint horn sounding in the distance.

"I definitely heard that," I exclaim, running toward the window.

I know better than to be seen, so I part the curtain an inch and look out. When I see a bright light, I turn over my shoulder and say, "I think it's another boat. It's far away, but something is definitely coming toward us."

We should be happy, but we don't know if this vessel is friend or foe.

Alek storms over to the coffee table and shoves it aside. He quickly rolls back the rug that conceals a small compartment. He punches in the code and opens the door, which houses an array of weapons and stacks of money.

"Here," he says, offering me a small gun. "Do you know how to use it?"

I shake my head nervously, eyes wide.

He retrieves one of his own, placing it at the small of his back. "This," he says, pointing at some lever on the side. "This is the safety. When it's in this position, it means it's on. You can't shoot. But when you flick it this way"—he flicks it, moving its location—"it's ready to use. Aim and shoot the bad guys. Got it?"

I open and close my mouth because I'm afraid I'm going to fuck this up.

"Hey, you've got this, okay?" he assures, walking toward me and placing the gun into my hand.

It's lighter than I thought it would be.

Taking a closer look at it, I marvel at how something so small can cause so much destruction. Aim and shoot, he said. It's that easy to end someone's life.

Memories of Frank assault me, and I blanch because his death was a lot more complicated than a bullet ending his life.

It wasn't quick. It was bloody. Brutal. He suffered, suffered because I killed him.

"Ella," Alek says, gently placing his hand over mine on the gun. "If you don't feel comfortable doing this, it's all right. I understand this is difficult for you."

Peering up at him from under my lashes, I shake my head. "I want to help."

I'm actually happy he wants to work together, instead of sending me away to safety. I can't now cower when given the opportunity to show Alek he can rely on me.

He squeezes my hand with a half-smile. "This is just in case. Stay behind me, okay? I wish I didn't have to flag them down, but this may be the only chance we get at passing another boat."

He's right. But I'm wary of strangers, especially after what happened in Latvia. That was someone who was supposed to help us and look what happened.

Alek lets go of my hand, ensuring I'm okay with this plan as he watches me closely.

"I trust you," I say with a nod, placing the gun into my back pocket.

He surprises me when he reaches out and brushes his knuckles along the apple of my right cheek. His touch is welcome, and I lean into it, which seems to catch him off guard. He doesn't know I was seconds away from apologizing before we were interrupted.

I hope we live long enough for me to finish what I started—in every sense of the word.

Alek leads the way to the upper deck, ensuring I'm close

behind as he looks over his shoulder. When he sees that I am, he walks over to the yacht's spotlight. He quickly switches it on and off three times, before he repeats the same action with longer flashes. Then he ends the sequence with three more short flashes—I know this is Morse code for SOS.

The boat is heading toward us, and as it gets closer, I can see it's also a yacht. Smaller than ours, but it still seems luxurious enough that whoever is on board has money.

"Who do you think they are?" I ask Alek, my frightened voice amplified by the silence.

"I wish I knew," he replies, keeping a close eye on the approaching vessel.

They signal back with their spotlight that they've seen us. Dread fills my stomach as they get closer. I huddle into Alek, feeling somewhat better being near him.

"Here we go," he mutters under his breath when the yacht reduces its speed and approaches us.

He adjusts his shirt to cover the gun concealed at the small of his back and waits for the occupants of the yacht to show themselves. Their boat is different from ours. Their helm is enclosed with dark glass, so I can't see who's behind the wheel.

I wait with bated breath, adrenaline coursing through me.

The yacht engine switches off when we're side by side. A man steps out from behind the glass. A woman follows close. They walk toward the railing, facing us. Even though it's dark, the light from the spotlights allow me to see that both look to be mid-thirties.

They're dressed casually and look "normal." But I've come to learn that looks are very deceiving.

"Are you in trouble?" asks the man with what I'm guessing is a Spanish or Portuguese accent.

Alek nods. "Yes, we got caught in the storm. My satellite is out, so I have no idea where we are."

The woman stands by the man, watching us closely. She wears a black bikini top and denim shorts. Her skin is golden, and her black hair sits piled high on her head. She is stunning, and I protectively move closer to Alek, marking my property if you will.

She smirks smugly in response, and I instantly don't like her.

"Oh, *amigo*, you're lucky we passed you when we did. You're not in the route of many boats. We too suffered some storm damage but not too much. The nearest port is about three days away. We're headed that way to pick up some supplies. You can follow us."

I don't sense any malice in the man's words, but experience has taught me not to trust so easily.

Alek's body language reveals he'd rather do this alone, but we're stuck. We're at the mercy of these strangers because even if they point us in the general direction of the closest port, without any navigational devices, we risk veering off course.

"I'm Rodrigo," he says with a wave. "And this is my girlfriend, Maria."

She nods but stays quiet.

"I'm Oleksander and this is Arabella."

Alek is smart to give pseudonyms similar to ours. This way, when used, they won't sound completely foreign, and we don't risk the chance of not responding when addressed. I guess in my case, however, I once answered to Arabella.

"Oleksander?" Rodrigo asks. "Your accent had me guessing you were Russian, not Ukrainian."

Oleksander must be a common Ukrainian name.

Alek coolly extends his arm around his back, his hand ready to reach for the gun if need be. "Ah, yes. This is what happens when you're a nomad. You adopt all accents," he says in a perfect French accent.

Who knew he spoke French.

Rodrigo laughs, and again, I don't feel like he's a threat. "This is true. Okay then. Let us be on our way."

He turns toward the helm, but Maria stands firm, eyeing both Alek and I. It seems she's just as suspicious of us as we are of her.

Rodrigo says something to her in a language I don't understand, kissing her puckered brow. She eventually concedes and follows him. As their yacht fires back to life, Alek gently coaxes me to follow him as we prepare to follow two strangers in the middle of the night.

"What did he say?" I whisper, trying not to move my lips, afraid Maria can lip read. I assume Alek understood him because he moved his arm, no longer needing to be within reach of his gun.

"That we're no threat to them," he replies, keeping his eyes peeled on the yacht.

"What language was that?"

"Portuguese."

"Are *they* a threat to us?" I ask the obvious.

Alek's silence is answer enough.

As the yacht pulls out in front of us, Alek steers so we're following. He shifts and flinches, indicating the aspirin didn't do much to help with his pain.

"Teach me how to steer this thing so you can lie down," I say, as the autopilot no longer works.

"I'm fine," he stubbornly replies, but he looks far from fine.

"So, you're not going to sleep for three days?" Apparently, that's how far the closest port is.

Alek huffs in annoyance, which means he knows I'm right.

"I have a plan," he reveals, surprising me because I didn't realize there was a plan B. "I need to get onto their yacht and find out our coordinates. If we're traveling back toward Russia, we need to change course. Three days until the nearest port seems like a long time, but I don't know how far the storm pushed us out.

"Relying on these people, these strangers for three days is too long."

Nodding firmly, I agree with Alek's plan B. Something about Maria rubbed me the wrong way, and it has nothing to do with her eye fucking him. Well, not entirely.

"Can I at least get you some more aspirin?"

Alek finally breaks eye contact with the yacht as he looks at me. I can see his confusion as to why I'm playing nice. I want to tell him why, but decide we need to focus on one drama at a time.

"Thank you. And some scotch."

"Oh, what was that?" I cup my ear with a smirk. "A nice

big glass of water?"

With his head injury, mixed with painkillers, there is no way I'm giving him any more alcohol.

He grins, almost sending me to my ass, reminding me how handsome he is when he smiles.

I quickly take the stairs, heart in my throat because I've missed that playfulness. Since this entire shitshow started, I haven't laughed, and I've forgotten how good it feels. Maybe it doesn't have to be all doom and gloom.

Maybe there is hope for me yet.

Grabbing some aspirin and a bottle of water, I venture back upstairs. A yawn tackles me from out of nowhere. I mute it behind the back of my hand, but Alek heard it.

"Get some sleep."

"No," I argue, handing him the aspirin and water. "I'm fine."

I ignore the fact that I now sound like Alek.

Alek pops the lid on the aspirin bottle and throws back god knows how many before downing them with a large swallow of water.

"There's no point in both of us being tired," he reasons, and he's right.

Sooner or later, he's going to be dead on his feet, which means he might make decisions he wouldn't normally make. Fatigue does that. I need to be on my A game for both of us.

He senses my defeat.

"I'll wake you if I need you. I promise."

Another unexpected yawn escapes me, indicating the prospect of sleep is too good to pass up. "Okay. But only for a minute.”

A cushioned lounge sits to Alek's left, which is where I curl up and welcome sleep. Alek knows better than to argue by insisting I go to bed. When apart, bad things happen, and now, with the unknown once again facing us, we can't take any risks.

My eyes are heavy, but I open them nonetheless, certain I've been asleep for only a few minutes. But when the bright sunlight blinds me, I realize it's been much longer than that.

It takes my eyes a moment to adjust to the daylight, but when they do, I suddenly wish I was blind.

Lounging feet away is a bronzed goddess, wearing skimpy bikini bottoms, and that's it. She doesn't seem at all concerned that her boobs are sunny side up, bouncing to whatever song sounds through her earbuds.

Rising to a sitting position, I brush my matted hair off my face and look at Alek. Thankfully, he is lost in another world, paying no attention to the naked Maria feet away.

“Hey,” I hoarsely say, stretching.

My voice snaps Alek from whatever thoughts are plaguing him. He turns to face me, smiling. “Good morning. How did you sleep?”

“Better than you,” I quip, which has him grinning.

With Maria in earshot, I mouth, “Location?”

He discreetly shakes his head. Maria has no problem

disclosing what cup size she is, but she's tightlipped about revealing where we are.

"I'll make us some coffee."

"No need," interrupts Maria, removing her earbuds. "I already made us some when you were sleeping."

I don't remember asking her if she wanted coffee because when I said us, I meant Alek and I. But it seems she beat me to the punch.

Why is she even here? But the better question is, where is the rest of her bikini?

"Olek, are you hungry?" I purposely direct my question toward Alek because I would rather starve to death than eat with little miss perky boobs.

When he pulls his lips into a thin line, indicating Maria's coffee came with breakfast, I roll my eyes and stand. "I'm going to shower."

Maria says something in what I'm assuming is Portuguese, which has Alek laughing. That laughter is usually reserved for only me.

"Ella—" Alek starts, noticing I'm unhappy that I woke to some naked woman making breakfast for him, but I ignore him and make my way downstairs.

Mumbling under my breath about how I hate the world, I angrily rip off my clothes and step into the shower. Alek is merely playing along because he is a master manipulator and knows he can use Maria to his advantage. But it still pisses me off that every woman—or man for that matter—with a pulse has to flirt with Alek.

I'm suddenly hit with an idea.

Once clean, I dry off and quickly change into my swimsuit. I tie the sarong around my waist and slip into my gold sandals. Using my large sunglasses as a headband, I style my hair into a messy bun. I want it to appear like I didn't go to any effort, but I have, and the reason is because Alek said he needs to know where we are, and I plan on finding out.

With Maria openly flirting with Alek, I can't imagine her relationship with Rodrigo is rock solid. So I plan on playing her at her own game.

Spraying some perfume along my neck, I apply some sheer lip gloss and pucker my lips. It's time to lose the company because this yacht is only big enough for two.

I venture upstairs confidently, taking great joy in seeing Alek do a double take when he sees me. I lower my sunglasses as I walk toward the front of the yacht, ignoring Maria whose ass is now exposed to the sun.

Rodrigo is sitting on the lounge on his yacht, legs crossed as he drinks a coffee. I casually grip the railing and tip my head back, jutting out my chest. It has the desired effect.

"Good morning," Rodrigo shouts while I wave.

"I don't suppose you have any real coffee over there?"

"Of course. Want to come on board?"

Lowering my sunglasses, I look over the top of them and give him a sassy wink. "I thought you'd never ask."

He stands eagerly. "I'll turn off the engine and come get you."

But I shake my head. "It's okay. Just slow down. I'll swim to you."

We're not traveling fast, so swimming won't be a problem.

I wonder how Maria got over here.

Rodrigo nods and walks toward the helm. I turn and smirk when I see Alek scowling. He wouldn't look like he sucked on something sour if he didn't care. There is hope.

"Slow down the yacht. I'm going to swim toward Rodrigo."

"Are you mad?" Alek whispers, grabbing my bicep as I pass him.

"It's kinda full up here," I quip, grinning. "You need to know where we are. I'll find out."

"You don't know what's over there," he argues, keeping his voice low.

"If it means not having to see Maria's boobs ever again, then I'll take the risk."

Standing on tippy toes, I kiss his cheek. It was meant to be a ruse to conceal what I want to say, but the current which sparks between us reveals it's so much more.

"What am I looking for?" I ask, focusing on the mission at hand, and not how my body responds to his.

He grips my waist, drawing me into his chest. Being pressed together this way has every part of me melting against him. "The navigational panel or chart plotter will have the coordinates. Try to memorize them. Even if he tells you where we are, these coordinates will confirm if he's telling the truth."

I forget that we're talking and can only focus on his fingers around my hip, squeezing gently. A shiver passes over me, and I know Alek feels it. His hot breath bathes my neck, and I whimper, suddenly scorching all over.

He lowers his lips and kisses under my ear softly. "Сладкая, так бы и сьел тебя."

Groaning, I arch my neck to the left, granting him all the access he wants. I love when he speaks Russian to me. He sounds utterly sexy and sinful, and it turns me on.

My body responds how it did the other night, and I feel empowered. This is my body, mine alone, and I refuse to get lost to the ugly past where it wasn't mine. I won't let my demons win.

"Navigational panel. Coordinates. Got it," I say breathlessly, clutching Alek's shoulder to stop myself from toppling over.

This is the first time we've touched each other so openly, and all I can think is that I want more. After what happened with Santo, I never thought I'd feel this way again. But being with Alek, touching and not shying away, feels like I'm taking back my life.

Piece by piece.

I'm still a work in progress, but I'm ready.

Our faces are inches apart as I pull away slowly. I'm lost to him—entirely. I will never stop wanting him, loving him. I was naïve to think I could walk away from this. Alek is a part of me. Now and forever.

"Be safe…красавица."

Closing my eyes, I savor the way my nickname rolls from his tongue. How I've missed hearing it.

"Always," I whisper, opening my eyes.

Alek examines me closely, and I'm sure he's confused about what's going on. My hot/cold behavior is frustrating. My emotions are all over the place.

Breaking away, I make my way down the stairs toward the

platform. Alek slows the yacht down. I take off my sunglasses, sarong, and sandals and dive into the crystal blue water. The temperature is pleasant. I swim toward Rodrigo's yacht, filling my lungs as I come up for air.

He stands on the platform, offering his hand, which I accept as I approach him. He helps me up, and by no accident does he pull me toward his chest. When we collide, he laughs while I tamp down my need to knee him in the balls for touching me.

I have to remember I'm here with a purpose.

"Thanks." I chuckle, discreetly shifting out of his hold.

"American?" he says, surprised.

"Yes, don't hold it against me," I tease while unfastening my wet hair.

Rodrigo laughs, watching as I wring out my locks. "Come, let me get you a towel."

Following him, he leads me into the living space and passes me a beach towel.

Drying myself off, I subtly take a look around for anything suspicious. Nothing catches my eye. He takes the wet towel from me and tosses it into the corner of the room.

"How do you take your coffee?" Rodrigo asks, walking over the pot of already made coffee.

"Black."

He nods and reaches for a clean mug. He pours me a cup as I take a seat at the breakfast bar. "Thank you," I say as he slides it across to me.

Cupping the mug, I inhale the coffee, which smells wonderful.

Rodrigo openly ogles me, which makes me feel uncomfortable, but this was part of the plan. I just need to focus.

"Have you been at sea for long?" I innocently ask, sipping my coffee.

Rodrigo leans up against the counter opposite me. "For about a month," he reveals. "I've worked with boats my entire life, and about a year ago, I had enough money to buy this yacht. Maria and I are drifters, calling the ocean our home."

"Where did you two meet?" I honestly don't care and hope he gives me the short version, but I need to know everything I can about them.

"She was waitressing in Portugal where we're both from," he replies in a faraway voice as if reliving the memory. "It was love at first sight. Well, for me anyway. But she eventually came around.

"We both wanted adventure, something bigger than what Portugal could offer, which is why we sail with no destination in mind. Wherever the wind takes us, so to speak, is where we go. We're able to see so many different places this way."

They're go-getters—so far, no alarm bells.

"What about you? How did an American end up"—he spreads his arms out wide—"here?"

"I was working in Italy and met Olek," I say, deciding to use how I met Frank as my backstory. "It wasn't love at first sight. But Olek and I…we work."

"So, you're…together?" he asks, drawing his pointer fingers together.

Shrugging, I sip my coffee before replying, "We're something."

Rodrigo smirks, my aloof response appearing to appease him for now. I need to change the subject. "Where are we headed? The last port we were at was Latvia."

Rodrigo whistles. "You're a long way from there. We're in the middle of the Baltic Sea. The nearest port isn't known by many."

Okay, now alarm bells begin to sound.

"It's not listed on the conventional navigational charts. It's a secret, one which I was lucky enough to discover while working on the boats of the rich and powerful. Maria and I stayed on the island. It's small, but it's paradise. Untouched. I think you and Olek will love it."

No, I do not agree. I think Olek and I will hate it.

However, keeping my cool, I grin and act coy. "I hate to admit this, but I have no idea how to read the nautical charts. Do you think you could teach me?"

Rodrigo cocks his head to the side. Does he smell my deceit?

Leaning forward, I bat my eyelashes. "Please?"

Surely, this won't work, but when Rodrigo smirks, I know it has. "Okay. Follow me."

Jumping from the barstool, I follow Rodrigo as he leads the way, but a loud thud has me pausing and listening intently. I'm certain the noise came from below me. Rodrigo's sudden pallor raises more than alarm bells.

"Come, I'll teach you," he quickly says with a strained smile. When I hesitate, he reaches out and gently coaxes me toward the exit.

Every part of me is demanding I fight and find out what

that noise was, but I'm here to find out coordinates, and seeing as Rodrigo is more than eager to provide me with what I need, I follow him up the stairs and to the upper deck.

I soon forget the noise when he stands me in front of a very complicated looking screen. Alek told me to look for coordinates, but there are dozens of numbers. Which ones do I need?

"This is where we are," he says, reaching around me to point at a little dot on the screen.

We're literally in the middle of nowhere. All I see is blue. No land. All sea.

"This is the speed we're traveling." His hot breath pollutes the back of my neck, but I refrain from moving because when he points at some numbers on the screen, he's about to tell me what I want.

"These are our current coordinates." I memorize the sequence and assume the S means we're south, but south of where? "And this is where we're headed."

"Where *are* we headed?" I ask, trying my best to commit the numbers to memory as I silently repeat them over and over in my head.

I notice what looks like a portable GPS sitting off to the right. It's not switched on. I also see a satellite phone. We can call Pavel, but I know that's risky as we don't want to leave any trails behind.

"We were on the way to Romania. But now that we'll be staying a while for you to fix your yacht, we might delay our plans. You see? This is the joy of having no schedule. You can come and go as you please.

"No one knows where you are. You're invisible to the world."

Just as I'm about to ask where he'll be staying a while at, he flicks a switch and our final destination comes up on the screen.

Tura.

Tura? *That's* the secretive island? But the problem is, it's not that secretive as it's one I've heard Frank mention before. It's an island belonging to Russia.

He gently strokes his fingers down my arm, which is the perfect time to leave.

Dancing out of his hold, I try my best not to cause a scene. "Thank you for the coffee and for the lesson. I appreciate it."

Rodrigo appears disappointed as though he was expecting something to happen. His carefree approach to life seems to seep into his relationship as he and Maria clearly have no issues flirting with other people.

Just as I'm about to make up some excuse as to why I need to leave, I hear another thud, but louder this time. Rodrigo knows I heard it, so now, the question is, what's he going to do?

His Adam's apple bobbles as he swallows. "You're welcome," he says, choosing to ignore the sound we both heard.

My curiosity gets the better of me, and against my better judgment, I ask, "Can I use the bathroom? That coffee went straight through me."

I can't leave here without finding out what's below. What are they hiding?

Rodrigo quickly snares my forearm as I attempt to venture downstairs, using the bathroom as a ruse to my snooping.

"It's on the blink," he says with a forced smile. "I was just about to fix it." He turns a knob, which has the speed of the yacht decreasing. This is my cue to leave.

Torn with what to do, I nod, peering over his shoulder and down the stairs. I could make a run for it, but the problem is, what am I going to do when I uncover what they're hiding. It's apparent he doesn't want me to find out what it is, which means it can't be good.

The mention of Tura suddenly slams into me. If this island is so secretive and Frank knew about it, then does that mean Rodrigo knows of the Macrillos? He said it's small, so what are the odds everyone knows everyone?

Extremely high.

Suddenly, that unidentifiable noise is everything sinister.

I need to get off this fucking yacht. Like now.

"Okay, thank you again," I say with a wave, making my way down toward the platform. However, when I look over my shoulder, I see I have an unwanted chaperone.

Rodrigo is escorting me, ensuring I don't take any detours along the way. Something is definitely not right. I don't hesitate and dive into the water, swimming swiftly toward Alek. I get to the yacht within minutes, and when I boost myself up onto the platform, I roll onto my back and gulp in mouthfuls of air.

My heart is pounding so violently that I can feel it bounce against my chest. That was close.

"красавица!" Alek's anxious voice has me turning my cheek to see him running down the stairs.

"I'm fine," I assure him, coming into a sitting position. "I was just catching my breath."

My reassurance does nothing to soothe his worries. He drops to his knees beside me and pulls me into his arms. I go willingly. "What happened? Did he hurt you? I'll fucking feed him his spleen if he touched you."

His concern for my well-being warms me in ways I long forgot.

"I'm okay." I snuggle closer into him and wrap my arms around his neck so I can whisper the coordinates into his ear. "There is a portable GPS on board as well as a phone. They're on the way to Romania, but the port…it's on the island Tura."

Alek's body hardens, revealing he too sees the significance of this island.

"I heard a noise below deck. There is something or rather, *someone* down there. Rodrigo doesn't want me to know what it is."

Alek tightens his hold around me, and although I can barely breathe, I don't shift away. In his arms, I feel safe. I always have.

"What happens now?" I ask, turning into his neck and inhaling his scent.

He takes a moment to mull over my question before replying, "We find out what they're hiding, and then we steal their yacht."

CHAPTER TWELVE

Alek

Ella sits on the bench seat beside me, reading a magazine. She hasn't left my side since she told me what she uncovered. Maria thankfully took the hint and left. It's going to take a lot more than a nice pair of breasts to get to me.

Besides, as I sneak a peek at Ella, Maria could do cartwheels in the nude, and she still would pale in comparison to the goddess next to me.

The moment Ella swam over to Rodrigo, I wanted to chase after her. But she wants to work together, something I've not done before. And for this to work, I need to show her that I see her as an equal, which she is.

She doesn't want a Prince Charming to save her. She can save herself, and she's proved that time and time again. Today is a perfect example of this.

We now know that Rodrigo cannot be trusted. If he knows

about the island, Tura, then there is no doubt in my mind he is involved in everything illegal, and odds are, he is working for Santo. Or at the very least, he knows the Macrillo name.

Tura's motto is what happens on the island, stays on the island—and I mean that in the literal sense. There have been many mistresses who believed they were vacationing with their beau, only to never be seen again.

The Circle "vacationed" every summer on the island. I went once and was thoroughly disgusted by what I saw. Yes, I was a sick bastard, but the line between pleasure and pain became far too blurred for my tastes.

I never returned.

Tura is a place where one can be their true self without getting caught, which is why I cannot be anywhere near there. My alias of Olek will be debunked the moment I step foot on that island, and with most of my "allies" being traitorous bastards, Santo will be alerted of my whereabouts.

I need to assume I'm being hunted by every criminal Santo may have ties with. Does this include Rodrigo? I still don't know.

If he is working with Santo, taking us to Tura would be the perfect plan. But something doesn't add up—if he knows who we are, then why would he tell Ella of his plans? Yes, he didn't tell her we were headed for Tura, but surely, he isn't that careless to reveal where our destination is.

This has me believing he doesn't know who we are, and that we're safe—for now.

But I won't risk Ella's safety on a whim because if I'm wrong, we won't get off that island alive.

I have a plan, and although I have my doubts it'll work, the plan is to hijack Rodrigo's yacht and get as far away from him and Maria as possible.

Even though there is a portable GPS on board, I can't exactly steal it and be on our way without being detected. If I do that, it'll raise questions, and with Rodrigo's connections to Tura, I can't be sure he hasn't already done his research on me.

This world of ours is so infuriatingly small, so it's impossible to kill someone without it going unnoticed.

The coordinates reveal Rodrigo is right—we're headed for Tura, which means we don't have a second to lose.

I have my suspicions to what they're hiding because once upon a time, I was hiding one below deck too. It's been rumored that women are kidnapped from poorer parts of Romania, the Ukraine, and many other parts of Europe and are forced to work as slaves—in every sense of the word—on Tura.

I don't care what Rodrigo's backstory is. He needs to be stopped, and it needs to happen now.

"What's wrong?" Ella asks, interrupting my thoughts.

Turning to look at her, I smile, but it's forced. I don't want to worry her, but I know it's too late for that. "I'm worried about the situation back home," I confess. "I can't stop thinking about Irina."

She lowers her magazine with a concerned frown. "Of course. I'm so sorry. I wish I could do something."

"You have. Because of you, we know where we're headed. We're two steps ahead. If you didn't uncover this information and we arrived at Tura, things would be so different. But now, we can act."

"What do you think they're hiding?"

When I tongue my cheek, deciding whether to tell her or not, she shakes her head.

"Tell me. I need to know. We're working as a team, remember?"

She's right.

There's no way to sugarcoat this, so I state, "I think they're human traffickers."

Ella pales and places a wavering hand over her mouth. "What? *No?*"

"Tura is notorious for housing young women brought over illegally. It's quick and easy cash. It's a whole different ballgame when sailing across uncharted waters. I know," I sadly share because this is how I transported Willow to me.

"How else would someone like Rodrigo be able to afford this lifestyle? You said he told you he worked on the boats of the rich and powerful. Those men would see someone like Rodrigo as a pawn, someone they could use to do their dirty work.

"I know this because I was one of those men, Ella."

She lowers her eyes. "You're not anymore."

"No, you're right. I'm not. And if Rodrigo finds that out about me, and realizes he will be able to make a lot of money from turning me in, he won't think twice about it."

"Any other theories?" she asks, hopeful.

"Santo is riding shotgun."

She fumbles with the magazine, it tumbling to the floor.

Just the mention of him has her on edge. I wish she'd tell me what happened. Her behavior toward me has changed. I can only hope she feels comfortable sharing what Santo did, so I can enjoy torturing him all the more.

"But I don't think that's it," I assure her. "If he were hiding out below deck, he wouldn't wait this long to strike. We're at their mercy. Santo wants his revenge."

She rubs her upper arms, clearly terrified.

"I won't let anything happen to you, Ella. I promise."

She nods, but her demons won't let go. Santo broke her, and I intend to break every bone in his body as retribution.

"So what's the plan?" she asks, on board with getting us the hell away from these people.

"With Maria parading around half-naked this morning, it's clear her relationship with Rodrigo isn't solid. I will play on that."

"Play on it how?" Ella asks, almost afraid to know the answer.

"When you were on the yacht, did Rodrigo try anything on you?"

The blush to her cheeks is all the answer I need.

"So, we lead them to believe we're interested in a… foursome and invite them over for drinks. Those drinks will be laced with GHB, and once they're out, we make our move."

Her flush creeps down her neck and across her chest. It's hardly my finest plan, but it won't fail.

"And this will work?"

"Yes," I say with a firm nod. "I know it will because it worked on me."

Ella's mouth parts, stunned by my admission.

"I have Saint and Willow to thank for this plan." And I do, as this is what they did to escape me when I held them captive on my yacht.

I can't hide my shame when I think about what an insufferable bastard I was for thinking I could snap my fingers and make Willow love me.

Ella lifts my chin with her finger, coaxing me to look into her eyes. "And we can thank them when you call home."

Home.

She's never referred to Russia or me as her home before. Is she trying to make me feel better because she can read my guilt? Probably. But nonetheless, I don't overthink it and bask in how wonderful it sounds hearing her call my house her home.

"How do we…entice them?" she asks, running her finger along the stubble on my jaw.

She is driving me crazy. I want her so badly that I can scarcely think about anything but her smell and her taste. I want it all, and I want it now.

"Easy," I reply, my voice low.

She takes a step back and watches as I unfasten the buttons on my shirt, and when I see arousal, instead of disgust, my need for her grows. I take off my shirt and drop it by my feet. Her eyes focus on my tattoo.

"I like your tattoo. What does it mean?"

I want to lie; afraid my admission will creep her out. I want to pretend it has nothing to do with her, but I can't. "Even though I've forsaken my God long ago, it honors Mother

Superior and…you. The symbolism gives me the strength to face the inevitable because meeting you…it was nothing short of a miracle."

She doesn't say a word. She simply stares at me, impassive.

"I'm sorry if I've made you feel uncomfortable."

But she shakes her head firmly. "You haven't. Not at all."

The air is suddenly thick, which threatens to strangle me where I stand. I haven't felt this since we first met, when things, believe it or not, were a lot less complicated then they are now.

She's been so guarded, so hard to read, but now, I see it—she wants me. I don't know what's changed, but I will grovel at her feet for a second chance. But now, I have some seducing to do.

"Take the wheel," I instruct Ella who yelps, but quickly jumps to command.

Once she's steady, I lazily stroll out into the sunshine, stretching overhead. I know Maria is tanning, so I stroll over to the side of the yacht where she lay on a lounge chair. Gripping the railing, I tip my face to the skies and inhale deeply.

This game of seduction shouldn't be this easy, but it is.

"Do you need someone to rub lotion on your back?" Maria calls out from across the water.

With a smirk, I lower my sunglasses and reply, "Why? Are you offering?"

She sits up, falling for my ploy. Her submission is such a bore. "I'm offering."

"How about you and Rodrigo come over for a drink? Ella and I want to thank you for helping us."

She stands, nonchalant she's once again topless. "That sounds like fun. Let me go change."

Running my tongue along my upper lip, I openly stare at her breasts and grin. "Why? I like what you're wearing just fine."

She chuckles before turning and ensuring to shake her ass as she walks toward Rodrigo. She's back a moment later. "Rodrigo said we can moor up ahead. There is a beautiful cave a few miles away. We can go swimming."

"Or we can get wet another way," I counter, cringing at how sleazy I sound. But it works.

"Yes, I suppose we can. See you soon." She waves with her fingers, trying to be sexy and mysterious. *Trying* being the operative word in that sentence.

Once I have her where I want her, I turn around and make my way over to Ella. What I see has me grinning. Her stiff upper lip and flared nostrils all point at the green-eyed monster rearing her pretty head, and I cannot deny how happy that makes me. Her jealousy shows me that she cares.

"They'll be over soon," I reveal, pretending not to notice the way she clenches the wheel.

"Do you think she owns a top?"

I bite my lip, attempting to conceal my smirk. "I'll get everything organized. I won't be long."

Ella nods, still unimpressed that Maria prefers to be naked as the day she was born. I leave her and her pouting bottom lip and quickly take the stairs to the living room. Moving the coffee table and rolling back the rug, I open the safe and retrieve the liquid GHB bottle and my Glock.

It seems a rather odd necessity to have on hand, but being who I am, this is just another day in the office for me.

The liquid swishes inside the dark bottle as I shove it into my back pocket and rearrange the rug and table. I hunt for the colored disposable cups in the cupboard and place the packet onto the counter. I'd rather we drink from something a little classier, but I can't risk anyone detecting the GHB in their drink.

The potency is strong. One sip and they'll be out in less than two minutes. I just have to make sure they drink it before they sense something fishy. We can only elude their advances for so long.

Once I hide my gun in the top drawer for easy access and place the bottle into the freezer, I make my way back toward Ella, who steers the yacht like a pro. "He's slowing down," she says over her shoulder when she hears me approaching.

"Good," I reply, and on pure instinct, I bend down and press a kiss to her temple.

I'm expecting her to shy away, just how she's done in the past, but she doesn't. She peers up at me and smiles. "So, we play gracious host and drug them?"

Nodding, I try to play it cool. "Yes, exactly. The sooner, the better. Once they're out, we grab what we need, and we take their yacht."

"We can't use the GPS system I saw? Being on their boat makes me feel sick."

I understand her thoughts as my yacht is far more comfortable, and knowing how she sails does give me an advantage. But without a chart plotter, the autopilot is useless.

I need a working GPS so we know where the hell to go.

Rodrigo slows down before eventually killing the engine. I do the same.

The need to protect Ella is almost suffocating, but I keep my calm as I need a level head. Even though the distance isn't far, Rodrigo and Maria ride a Jet Ski to reach us. She dismounts from the back and jumps onto the platform.

Both Ella and I watch as Maria and Rodrigo come on board. The moment they climb the stairs, I wrap an arm around Ella's waist and draw her into my side. "This is me marking my territory," I whisper into her ear.

Before she can object, I add, "Rodrigo will see this as a competition. Trust me, he's going to do anything to challenge me. But if it makes you feel uncomfortable, I can—"

"Don't let me go," she interrupts, pressing closer into me.

"That won't be a problem, красавица."

The moment Rodrigo sees us together, he smirks, but it's not a friendly gesture. The way he hungrily eyes Ella has me wanting to rip out his eyeballs and feed them to him. But I slip my mask into place.

It's game on.

Maria wears a black dress. I'm surprised she's wearing clothes, to be honest. When she sees me holding on to Ella, she narrows her eyes.

They've been here for less than a minute, and they've already overstayed their welcome. "Come, let me show my gratitude for helping us out."

I lead Ella toward the stairs, thankful Maria and Rodrigo are following.

Rodrigo has brought a bottle of scotch, which will not be drunk by Ella and I. I can't trust that he doesn't have the same plan for us. Once we're in the living room, I let Ella go and make my way into the kitchen.

"Wow, this is even more impressive on the inside." Rodrigo whistles, looking around.

"*Eu te disse*," Maria says, which has alarm bells sounding because she just said I told you so in Portuguese.

Ella looks at me with an arched brow, but I subtly shake my head. We have to bide our time.

"What would you like to drink?" I ask, looking at Rodrigo over the counter. "I have vodka. Scotch."

"Here, I brought a bottle. Let us toast with this." He raises the bottle in question.

"Save your alcohol," I say with a friendly wave. "You've done more than enough to help us. This is the least I can do to say thanks."

Rodrigo shrugs. "Maybe for later then."

"Yes. Is scotch okay?"

Everyone nods while I calmly go about pouring our drinks.

As expected, Rodrigo is too busy gawking at Ella to notice as I open the freezer with intent to grab some ice, which I do. But I also add a few drops of the GHB to Maria's and Rodrigo's cups. Swirling it around, I smile as the drugs mix in with the alcohol perfectly.

However, when I close the freezer door, my smile is soon to disappear.

Maria is standing before me, arms folded with a smirk. I

need to think quick on my feet because I'm so busted. "Don't tell on me," I whisper with a seductive growl. "This is just going to loosen us up a bit."

Maria's smirk grows wider as she reaches for both cups before I can stop her. "Then I better have both because I bet I'm going to have to be extremely loose to accommodate you."

She makes it a point to look at my groin as she downs one cup and then the other in quick succession as I look on, helpless to stop her.

She's just ingested six drops of pure GHB, thinking it was some light party drug to set the mood. At her height and weight, she'll be down for the count in seconds. She places one empty cup onto the counter, but when she attempts to repeat the same action with the second, she misses, and it rolls along the floor.

She follows the movement, her pupils dilated as she sways on her feet. As she stumbles forward, I launch forward and catch her.

She peers up at me, trying to focus. "Whaa did yoouu—" But I silence her slurs by pressing my mouth over hers and kiss her slack lips. She's floppy in my arms, and it won't be long until she's comatose.

Ella and Rodrigo stop talking when they're aware of me mauling Maria. I can't gesture to Ella what just happened, but thankfully, she uses her smarts when I hear her purr, "How about we go outside? I want to show you something."

Their departing footsteps alert me that he's fallen for it. The moment they're gone, I remove my mouth from Maria's, scrubbing my lips to remove any remnants of the GHB.

She has passed out, so I lug her down the stairs toward the bedroom.

She's dead weight, so I try my best to place her on the bed, but she ends up collapsing onto her stomach. Afraid she's going to suffocate, I turn her cheek so her face isn't pressed into the mattress. She looks awfully uncomfortable, but her comfort is the least of my concerns when I hear something smash upstairs.

Charging up the stairs, two at a time, my heart is in my throat when I reach the upper deck to see Ella being held hostage by Rodrigo who has a knife at her throat. Instantly, I come to a screeching halt and raise my hands in surrender.

"Let her go," I demand, as he has one chance to do as I say before I end his life.

"Where's Maria?" he shouts, tightening his hold on Ella. I notice a trickle of blood seeping from a wound to his temple. Looks like Ella got to him before I could.

She mouths, "I'm sorry," but I shake my head. This is my fuckup, not hers.

"She's passed out. Your beloved can't handle her liquor."

"Bullshit! You did something. I knew we shouldn't have stopped, but Maria—"

"But Maria what?" I press, wanting to know what he was going to say.

Rodrigo begins to walk backward, taking Ella with him. "Maria knew you'd have money on board. Your yacht is worth a fortune. She wanted you to trust us so we could rob you. She found your engagement ring," he reveals, while Ella blanches.

I noticed she had taken it off but didn't think much of it

when Maria used the bathroom. Everything that is of value is locked in the safe. But Maria's snooping found Ella's ring, which is worth a small fortune. So that's why they stuck around.

To rob us.

It's a relief they don't know Santo, but now I need to get us out of this.

"But something isn't right with you two. I know you're Russian. And I'm pretty sure your name isn't Olek."

Taking in my surroundings, I search for a weapon. My gun sits uselessly in the kitchen. I need to think outside the box, and I see that in the form of my cane, resting near the helm.

Rodrigo is small-fry. He's someone's monkey boy and not the boss. So it's time I showed him who's boss.

"You're right," I affirm with a slow nod. "I am Russian. And I'm the motherfucking king of Russia. You fucked with the wrong person, asshole. Now, let her go. Otherwise, I will break every finger on your hand."

Rodrigo continues walking backward, pressing the knife into Ella's throat. "I don't think so. She comes with me."

Clucking my tongue, I slowly follow Rodrigo's moves, stopping when I'm within reach of my cane. "Bless you for thinking that was optional."

He's nothing but a little boy, playing in the big, bad world. It's time he learns what happens when you fuck with the wrong person.

Ella watches for any cues, and when I lunge for my cane and use it as a spear, she stomps on Rodrigo's foot and ducks out of his hold. The throw is wide, which was done with intent because anyone's natural instinct is to dodge something that is careening toward them, and this gives me the opportunity to storm forward and make good on my word.

I snare his wrist and bend it back until I hear it crack with a satisfying crunch. Before he can cry out, I punch him straight in the nose. He staggers back, cupping his bleeding face.

Ella dashes out of danger while I run toward it, elbowing Rodrigo in the stomach, and when he tries to fend me off, I deliver an uppercut to his jaw. He collapses onto his back, howling and wheezing for air. Placing my foot over his throat, I prohibit that from happening.

"Now, you're going to tell me what you're hiding on your yacht. And if you even think about lying to me, I'll break more than just your nose."

He tries to remove my foot with his non-broken hand, but he senses defeat and surrenders way too easily. "I was to deliver them to Tura. I don't know the specifics. I'm just the deliveryman."

I knew it.

No one would suspect what appears to be a happy couple, traveling the world, of human trafficking. It makes no difference to me if he's not the mastermind behind it. He is accountable for such a heinous act, as am I for the sins of my past.

I press down on his neck, watching his face turn a lovely shade of red as he fights for air.

"Alek, no!" Ella exclaims. "No more bloodshed. Let's just go."

Every part of me rebels, needing the violence, needing to end this piece of shit's life, but I ease off, realizing she's right. But there is no way I'm leaving him conscious.

Just as he attempts to rise, I kick him in the face, where he collapses onto his back with a thud. He's out cold, so I feel somewhat better. I would much prefer to see him stop breathing, but we're short of time.

Rushing over to Ella, I hold her out at arm's length to look over her. "You're okay?" I ask, scanning her from head to toe.

She nods quickly. "I'm sorry I couldn't distract him for longer. When he got too handsy, I broke a glass over his head."

I can't help but smile. "That's my girl. Come, we don't have much time."

Taking Ella's hand, we run down the stairs to pack the essentials. We don't have much, but pack it all, not knowing how long we'll be at sea. Ella takes what she can from the kitchen while I raid my safe clear of everything I need.

Once we're ready to go, I jump onto the Jet Ski and help Ella onto it. I need to make a couple of trips to transport everything onto Rodrigo's yacht. When we're set, I check out the controls, ensuring everything works.

It does.

Ella shifts from foot to foot. She's anxious and wants to get downstairs, but waits for me.

Not wanting her to be exposed to such evil, I cup her cheek. "I know asking you to stay here is out of the question, but I need you to be prepared for what you might see. Rodrigo used the word them, meaning there is more than one."

She nods, but I can see the terror behind her eyes.

"They're going to Tura, so I hate to think of the circumstances in which they were kidnapped. Stay behind me, okay?"

She leans into my touch. "Okay."

Taking her hand, we walk the stairs to the bottom level of the yacht. There is a bedroom, and off to the side, there is a small door. It looks like a utility closet. In vain, I open the bedroom door and see nothing out of the ordinary, which I suspected.

Which leaves door number two.

With a sigh, I turn the handle, and no surprise, it's locked. There is an ax in a glass case on a wall.

"Break in case of emergency," I say, reading over the small print on the front of the case. "Well"—I elbow the glass, it shattering into pieces—"this is an emergency."

Reaching for the ax, I gently usher Ella off to the side so I can bring the blade down onto the handle. It pops off with ease, allowing me to reach in through the hole and unlock the door.

With ax in hand, I open the door and peer inside, but nothing, *nothing* can prepare me for what I see.

There is a small lamp in the corner of the bathroom, allowing me to see three small children, huddled together on the floor. Their heads are downcast, but their dirty clothing allows me to guess what condition they're in.

I drop the ax, shaking my head at the horror before me.

Ella stands beside me, gasping and covering her mouth when she too sees the atrocities. "They're children," she whispers, expressing her surprise as we both were expecting adults.

I don't know where they're from, so I greet them in English. "Hello. We won't hurt you." But they continue crying, their emaciated frames shuddering in fear.

I need a moment because they remind me too much of Irina and the state she was in when crudely dropped off at the orphanage gates like an unwanted dog. Suddenly, I'm hit with a thought, and I rub over my chest, my heart threatening to burst free.

Ella drops to a crouch in the doorway. "Hi, my name is Ella. And this is my friend, Alek. We're not going to hurt you. The bad man and woman are gone. I promise."

The children's whimpers grow softer, and one of them lifts her face. I stagger back because she may as well be my Irina.

"Bad man gone?" she whispers, eyes wide in hope. Her accent is possibly Polish.

Ella nods. "Yes. They're gone. You're safe. Are you hungry? Thirsty?"

Her soft voice soothes the children as one by one, they lift their faces. Two girls and one little boy. I can't do this.

Turning, I walk to the railing and grip it, internally screaming at the injustices in this world. How long have they been kept this way? Where are their families? And who bought them?

I need to know.

Once I've pulled it together, I turn around and try my best to smile.

Ella knows better than to force them out, so she slides a bottle of water toward them. As well as a couple of granola bars. They look at the offering, scared and confused. Who knows when they last ate, or showered for that matter?

They are covered in filth.

Ella comes to a stand and turns to me, leaving the kids alone. They need time to adjust. They need time to see we're not here to hurt them, but that trust won't come easily…just how it didn't with my цветочек.

If Mother Superior were here, she'd say this was a sign from God. But what I have to do, what I have to unearth is surely a curse from the devil himself.

"We need to—"

"I know," Ella says, not needing me to finish my sentence.

This can't be a coincidence. These kids may as well be Irina, and if they're headed for Tura, then I need to know who bought them. I need to know who's in control of this operation because they may be my key to finding out Irina's past.

The answers have to lie here. Irina's past has always been such a mystery, and maybe that's because I've been looking in all the wrong places.

Maybe she was once like these little children, shipped off to Tura and forced to live here. It would explain her poor lingual skills because who would teach her how to speak?

But even if she wasn't, I need to put a stop to whoever is doing this.

A rage overtakes me, and my body shudders with the force. I am going to kill every last motherfucking vile cunt on that island. I can't breathe. I need to hit something before I explode.

"Alek," Ella whispers, knowing better than to touch me when in this state. "Go. I'll handle it."

I can't be near anyone when this way. I know myself. So I do as she says and march up the stairs, ready to steer us the fuck away from this hell. Adjusting all the controls, I start the engine and begin to cruise at a steady pace, not wanting to scare the children.

Lifting the satellite phone, I dial Saint. "Oh, thank fuck! Where have you been?"

"Long story," I reply. "How's Irina? And everyone?"

"We're all fine. Worried about your sorry ass, but we're okay. What happened?"

"We got caught in a storm. Lost signal to the GPS and phone."

"Whose number is this?"

"Some asshole who I choked into submission," I bluntly reply. "Any news on Santo?"

"He's still looking. He's closing in," Saint reveals, which worries me.

"Closing in how?"

"He ransacked Pavel's laundromat. Although he's not admitted it, we know it's him. He has worked it out, and it's only a matter of time now."

"скотина," I curse, clenching my fist. "Well, the asshole whose yacht I stole, he was harboring three little kids. The drop-off—Tura."

"What are you planning, Popov?"

"These kids look like Irina. We are literally in the middle of nowhere. I wish I could drop them off someplace safe— them and Ella—but such a place doesn't exist. I'm not leaving them with anyone I don't know, so staying with me is the safest thing for them at the moment," I reveal, hating how corrupt this world can be.

"I need to get onto that island to find out who's behind this. I wish it were a coincidence, but this is a select market. And you know, in our world there are rarely coincidences. There is only one person behind this, and I can't shake the suspicion that they know what happened to Irina.

"Why else can't I find anything on her? She didn't just appear into thin air. She has a past, and after what Serg said about her—" I pause, needing to center myself before I explode. "I fear she may have been at Tura. Someone has gone to great lengths to ensure she can't be traced back to them.

"I can't let this go. I have to investigate this lead. I will never forgive myself if I don't. Even if I'm completely wrong and Irina was never at Tura, at the very least, I can stop the sick asshole who is kidnapping and selling these kids to the depraved.

"I can't turn my back on them, Saint. If I don't strike now, I fear I'll never get this opportunity again."

"Jesus Christ," Saint utters, just as disgusted as I am. "So what happens when you get to Tura?"

With a smirk, I reply, "I find out who is selling these kids, what they know about Irina, and then I kill them very fucking slowly."

"You do that, and Santo will know where you are."

"That's the idea," I say, hinting at my new plan. "Those men and women on Tura are the enemy. They are the people I want to eliminate to reform Russia with my underdogs. There is no room for them, and I cannot succeed with them alive."

"You can't kill them all," Saint states, but the doubt in his voice has me grinning wider.

"I can try. But to those who are fortunate enough to survive, I will instill the fear of God into them. They'll know not to fuck with me. I wish to rule with respect, but with people like these, I must rule with fear.

"The moment I step foot onto that island, anyone who is allied with Santo will alert him of my arrival. He will come with an army, but I have my own. Who's on board with our plans?" I ask, hoping Pavel was able to convince the men I need to side with me.

"All of them," Saint replies while I sigh in relief.

"Tell them it's now their chance to rise to the top. This will blindside everyone as the elite believe the underdogs don't know about Tura, and they don't, until now. We ask whoever wants to enforce their power to come with us.

"They're sitting ducks on Tura. This is their haven where they can indulge in their perversions and not be judged. But I'm judging, and I'm going to eliminate as many of them as I can."

"This is a good plan," Saint says, excited he's able to spill some blood. "I'll see how many people we have on board and call you back."

"Excellent, but you must move soon. I'm about a couple of days away from reaching Tura. This will give us an advantage over Santo. He won't expect my plans, which allows us to ambush him. I will make him believe I'm at Tura delivering the kids as it's a lucrative deal for me.

"When I find the person responsible for subjecting these

kids to such horrors, I will make their death look like we got into an argument, and as punishment, they got the pointy end of my knife imbedded into their heart.

"This allows me to restore my ruthless reputation as this will be a very public affair. Most will be scared, but some will be pissed off, and that's when they'll call Santo. He's already put in the hard word that he's looking for me.

"This will be like stealing candy from a baby," I conclude, taking a breath.

"You know, you're a fucking evil mastermind. I'm pleased we're now on the same side," Saint says, which has me chuckling.

"Thank you, мой друг."

Saint hangs up, knowing time is of the essence, so I suspect he'll call me back soon.

The odds I'd be placed in this situation were slim to none, but my world, it's small, and it's like eight degrees of separation. I don't know who is behind exploiting children because as ashamed as I am to admit it, it wasn't a concern of mine.

I didn't meddle in business that didn't profit me, but that's changed.

Some may say this is hypocritical, considering I had no qualms about trafficking young women for my pleasure once upon a time. But never children. And now, I can make amends for all the wrong that I've done.

"Did you call home?" Ella asks, coming up the stairs. She looks exhausted.

"Yes, I've told Saint of my plans."

"And they are?"

"I fear Irina was once at Tura," I confess, a mixture of emotions overwhelming me. "Those children may as well be her."

"I think you might be right," she softly agrees.

It's nice to know I'm not overthinking this because if she too can see the resemblance, it just confirms my suspicions.

"I need to find out who this person is and what they know about Irina. And when I find that out, I'm going to take great pleasure in seeing them choke on their blood."

"We're going to announce our location to Santo then?" Ella wisely says.

"Yes, but we have an advantage. He won't know my true motives for being there and will suspect I've come alone. But Saint has informed me my plan to build a new army has worked. This is their opportunity to rise above."

"So it's going to be a bloodbath?"

Nodding, I smirk. "Indeed. The only way off that island is their boats. So, we take that away, and they either surrender to me, or they die. Santo may believe he has friends on Tura, but that'll soon change when their lives are at stake.

"He, of course, will bring an entourage from Russia and beyond to protect him, but he will lose."

"By doing this, you're just cementing your leadership. That no one fucks with you and gets away with it. This will clear up any doubt over your governance," Ella says, appearing impressed.

"Yes, in part, but this is for Irina. This is my chance to avenge her childhood which was robbed by these sick Мудак's.

It also allows me to ensure no other child suffers this way ever again. The Russia I rule will maim and destroy anyone who thinks they can defy my stance on this.

"The enemy will be herded, and I will pick them off, one by one."

"So once this is over with, you're still planning on being a Russian…mobster?" she asks, appearing to search for the right word.

"Yes," I reply honestly. "With or without me, drugs, guns, crime, it'll exist and I'd rather I ruled than someone else whose moral compass lost direction long ago. I understand how hypocritical that sounds, but being the bad guy…it's what I'm good at. It's what I know."

Ella walks toward me, and just when I think she'll slap my cheek, she touches it tenderly. "You're not the bad guy. Better the devil you know, right?"

Smirking, I wear the title with pride. "Precisely. I wish I could be happy living a simple life, but I can't. This is who I am."

I wait for disgust, anger, but I get neither. "And who you are is someone I…"

Her pause has me desperate to know what she wanted to say, but she doesn't continue.

"I'm going to check on the kids." She removes her hand and scampers away, leaving me wondering who I am to her.

CHAPTER THIRTEEN

Alek

The clock on the GPS says it's after one in the morning, and although I am way past tired, I can't switch off.

Ella has spent the day with the children, leaving me alone as I think she sensed I needed the quiet. I can't stop thinking about the plan. It'll work, but I fear there will be many casualties along the way. This *is* war, and it's to be expected, but I know Santo won't give up without a fight.

The thought of Ella being in danger eats a hole straight through me. The plan of her going to Ireland is off the table, but I think it always was. Ella deserves her revenge on the Macrillos. Denying her would be beyond hypocritical. Ireland is where she'll be safe physically, but emotionally, she'll always be lost to the past.

I'll try everything in my power to keep her safe, but before we reach Tura, I need to teach her how to fight. If she's going into this, she must be fully prepared.

"You need to get some sleep."

The yacht is on autopilot, but the moon is full and it's a beautiful night, so I decided to stay up here and think. I hoped I'd be able to feel better about what we're walking into, but I don't.

Turning over my shoulder to look at her, I do a double take because her hair is cut short.

She notices me staring at the drastic change and tugs at the strands just below her chin. "I felt like a change," she explains, not that I needed a reason. It's her body, and she can do what she pleases with it.

"I like it," I say with a smile.

Our conversation is strained because although a clear plan has been formulated as to what's about to happen, I still have no idea what's going on between us.

Before this latest bombshell, she made her feelings, or lack of, perfectly clear. But there's been a shift, and I need to know what that now means.

She pads over to the lounge near me and takes a seat, drawing her knees toward her chest. She's in sleep shorts and a tee, clearly ready for bed. So I wonder why she's up here and not there.

"The kids are terrified," she says, resting her cheek on her knee as she turns her head to look at me. "I managed to get them to eat something small. But they won't come out of the bathroom. I've given them some blankets and pillows, but they just stay huddled together, watching me with big frightened eyes."

"It'll take some time," I reply with a sigh. "Irina is only

just coming out of her shell. The damage done to these kids is irreparable. It makes me sick."

"Me too," she whispers. "Being forced against your will—"

She closes her eyes, her lower lip quivering.

"красавица?" I ask, turning around to face her. "What's the matter?"

She sniffles, and all I want to do is console her, but I don't know if it's welcome.

"Please talk to me, Ella. I can't stand to see you cry. You're"—here goes nothing—"breaking my heart."

She slowly opens her eyes and lifts her head. "I know," she starts, drawing her knees closer into her chest. "I know what it's like to be forced…against your will."

The night is still, but Ella's confession has just silenced my world for good. "What, what does that mean?" I ask, not wanting to assume because no, I don't want what I think happened to be true.

"You asked what happened with Santo, well, he…I," she falters, licking her lips quickly. "He said you, he was going to hurt you, and I couldn't, and I couldn't help you because Frank threatened to lock me in the room."

She takes a steadying breath. "It was the only way I could help," she whispers, a single tear trickling down her cheek. "I wouldn't allow everything we worked so hard for to be destroyed. It wouldn't be for nothing."

I stand, unmoving, my mind detached from my body as I hear the woman I love with all of my heart confess something so atrocious, I don't think I'll ever forget this sinking feeling for the rest of my life.

"He said he'd kill everyone that I loved if he found out I was lying, and there is really only one, only one person I love." She peers up at me with poignant eyes. "And that's you, Aleksei. I love you so much I can barely breathe, which is why when Santo forced himself on me…I didn't resist.

"He r-raped…me, and although he thought he was showing me affection and love by being gentle and telling me how good I felt, I didn't want it. I didn't want him. But I did it because I may as well be dead if any harm came to you.

"I'm sorry. I know you're probably disgusted with me. I should have fought h-harder. I should have done something, but I didn't, and now I have this ha-hatred, this bitterness"—she tugs at the loose material over her heart—"inside me, and I don't know how to make it go away.

"I lashed out at you when it was never your fault. It was m-mine. I just wanted to help." She buries her face into her palms, sobbing, while I stand utterly still, unsure if I'm breathing.

All I can hear on repeat are the ugliest words to ever be spoken—*he raped me.*

He took from her, he defiled her, and now she's the one burdened with the shame and guilt when it should be him.

"I understand if you don't want me a-anymore," she muffles into her hands. "I'm ashamed. That's why I didn't tell you. I feel so… unclean."

If this is what it feels like to have your heart ripped in two, then that's okay because I will happily give a piece, hell—she can have the whole thing—to Ella, hoping to mend her broken, wounded heart.

I can't stand to see her in pain, so I turn and walk toward the edge of the yacht. I need a minute.

I grip the railing, my knuckles cracking under the force. I look into the vast nothingness—a perfect analogy to how I'm feeling. There is nothing but pure rage coursing through me. Killing Santo isn't enough. He needs to suffer and suffer in ways unimaginable.

What I did to Serg will be nothing compared to what I intend for Santo. There will be nothing, *nothing* left of him when I'm done. I will wipe his existence from this earth. The pain he inflicted on Ella—I will return tenfold.

I want to scream. I want to kill something. But I can't. Ella needs me, so pushing my vengeance aside, with a mechanical pace, I walk over to her. Her eyes are red-rimmed when she slowly lifts her face to look at me, terrified.

I do the only thing I can—I fall to my knees before her, begging for forgiveness as I submit everything I am to her. "прости, что подвел тебя. Я никогда не подведу тебя опять. Ты любовь всей моей жизни, и скоро, когда я наберусь смелости, я скажу тебе это. Но я не могу сейчас…потому что я тебя не достоин. Мне нужно стать человеком достойным твоей любви."

I'm sorry for failing you. I'll never fail you again. You are the love of my life, and one day, when I have your courage, I will tell you this. But I can't now…because I don't deserve you. I need to become a man worthy of your love.

I wish I could say these words to her in English but not yet. I don't want her associating the first time I profess my love for her to this moment in time. And when she doesn't ask what I just said, I think she too understands the reason.

With a hesitant touch, she lifts my chin, coaxing me to look at her. But I can't. *I'm* the one who's ashamed. I failed to protect her, allowing something so vile to happen.

"Ella, I kneel before you, unworthy of your love," I declare, head bowed. "What you did, моя любовь, I don't deserve you. I wish he had killed me if it meant saving you such horrors. I will *never* be disgusted by you. You did nothing, *nothing* wrong.

"This isn't your fault. It's his. I'm the one who is begging for your forgiveness for allowing this to happen. I failed to protect you when that's all you've ever done for me. Never be ashamed because this isn't your fault," I desperately repeat because she needs to hear it.

She bursts into tears.

"I'm so, so sorry this has happened to you. Sorry is such an inadequate word however, because nothing can ever make this okay. But he's going to pay, I promise you," I vow, gripping her cold fingers in mine as I finally meet her eyes.

"You'll have your vengeance. His life is yours."

She nods jerkily.

"We're not going to just kill him…we're going to paint Tura with his blood. I will end him, his bloodline, and kill the Macrillo name forever. He will be nothing but a forgotten memory."

Tears spill down her cheeks. "Th-thank you."

"Don't ever thank me, красавица. This is only a small gesture to make up for a lifetime of regret. I'll never forgive myself for what happened to you. You have every right to hate me. I hate myself for being so weak when it comes to you.

"I should have left you alone, but I couldn't. I needed you. I still do. Every fucking moment of every single day. And my greed has now resulted in your suffering. Please let me make it right. What can I offer you? What can I give you to try to make amends for the pain I've caused? I'll crawl on my hands and knees for the rest of my miserable existence, begging for your forgiveness. Just tell me what you want."

I grip her fingers, begging she tell me what I can. Anything, it's hers.

She wipes away her tears and leaves me speechless as she reaches for the lapels of my shirt and gently tugs me toward her. I'm still on my knees, but I peer up at her, pleading she put me out of my misery any way she deems fit.

I will accept whatever punishment she wishes to bestow on me. But what she says next is nothing short of a miracle.

"I want you," she whispers. "That's all I've ever wanted. You."

Before I can speak, she bends down and presses her trembling lips to mine. I freeze, unsure what to do, but Ella leads the way when she coaxes me to open to her as she runs her tongue along the seam of my mouth.

We kiss slowly, like two lovers becoming reacquainted after years, after lifetimes apart, and I suppose in some sense, we have, in fact, been reborn.

She moans into my mouth, deepening the kiss when she adds a little tongue. I allow her to control me, unsure if this is too much, too fast after what she just confessed. But that thought is soon abolished when she slides a hand into the front of my shirt.

She runs her fingernails over my chest, backward and forward, over and over again. I want her so damn much, but I'm afraid I'll do something wrong.

She senses my retreat and stops me from moving away when she clutches the hair at my nape. "I want it to be your touch I remember," she whispers against my lips. "I want it to be your body inside me—always and forever."

Groaning, I nibble her bottom lip. "Whatever you want, but we can wait. I'm worried—"

But she won't hear of it. "No more waiting."

She smashes her lips to mine, moving off the lounge and dropping to her knees before me so we're on an equal playing field—which is what she's always wanted. Our kisses are frantic, and when I cup her ass and draw her into my erection, her moans are music to my ears.

With desperate fingers, she unfastens the buttons on my shirt, almost tearing it off my torso as she disrobes me. Her touches are impatient, and when she strokes over my tattoo, I hum into her parted mouth.

"Do you like it?"

"Yes, very much," she replies breathlessly.

It pleases me.

I need her in ways unimaginable, but when I rub over the front of her shorts, she cries out and recoils.

Instantly, I draw back, panicked as I cup both cheeks in my palms. "I'm so sorry. Forgive me."

But she shakes her head, angered at herself. "No, it's not you. It's just...I can still feel him. Hear him," she confesses in a whisper. "I want it to go away."

It never will. It will lessen, but what happened to her will always remain. Suddenly, I'm struck with an idea—this will be uncharted waters for the both of us.

"Come," I order, coming to a stand and offering her my hand.

She accepts without hesitation, following me as I lead her toward the bedroom. When we enter, I see she has changed the sheets on the bed, which pleases me. Letting her hand go, I walk over to my bag, which I haven't even unpacked and grab what I need.

Turning to face Ella, she peers at the red tie in my hand. Looping it around my fist slowly, I tug it tight. She gasps, eyes wide with curiosity.

"Power was taken away from you. You lost control, so now, I offer it to you," I reveal, extending out my hand, which holds the tie.

"I-I don't understand," she falters nervously.

"I surrender myself to you, Antonella Ricci. Do what you will. I am subservient…to you."

Ella's eyes widen in understanding. I am offering to switch roles—she can be the dominant while I submit. This is not in my nature, and I feel beyond uncomfortable when I'm not in control, but if this will help Ella associate feelings of control, instead of defeat, then I am her loyal servant.

She walks toward me while I stand perfectly still. She gazes at the tie, and after a few seconds, she accepts my offering. I wait for instruction.

She runs a fingernail across my chest along to my back

as she walks in a circle around me as if admiring her prey. When at my back, she leans over my shoulders and whispers, "Kneel."

I let go of control and do as she commands.

She remains at my back, placing her hands on my bare shoulders. "Do you remember the first time you asked me to kneel before you?"

How can I forget? The memory is singed onto my very soul.

"Yes, it's a memory I revisit often," I confess.

She gently draws my arms behind my back before binding my hands together with the tie. It takes all my willpower not to fight her, but when I think about what she endured, how even though her hands weren't tied physically, but metaphorically, I surrender.

Her bare feet pad across the carpet as she comes to stand in front of me. I peer up at her, unbelieving how lucky I am to have my queen's love.

"Me too," she reveals, biting her lip as she commences running a hand down her neck and over the front of her tee. The thin cotton allows me to see her erect nipples, and my mouth waters at the sight.

"I didn't know I liked being dominated that way, but when I'm with you, all I want to do is please you."

Swallowing before I choke to death, I watch as Ella slips a hand into the front of her shorts and begins to play with herself. Her tiny moans alert me that she's already wet, that her fingers are slipping into her sex with ease.

This is torture.

"I touched myself when I watched you shower," she admits, moaning as she increases the speed of her fingers. "I love the way you look. The way you feel. You are so fucking… hot. I know that's not the most eloquent of words, but your dominance, it turns me on."

Tugging at the tie, I pray for it to come loose before I perish. But I'm tied up tight.

"When I first met you, all I could think about was taking your cock into my mouth and making you come," she reveals, tossing her head back as she works herself feverishly. "It was so wicked. I've never had those thoughts before."

Sweet Mother of Joseph, Ella speaking dirty will surely be the death of me.

"And then when I knew you wanted me as much as I wanted you…oh god," she gasps. "I would fantasize about you at the orphanage. Late at night, when everyone was fast asleep, under the roof of God, I would think about how I wanted you to defile me in the most wicked of ways. And when you did, I wanted it never to stop."

This sight is killing me in the best of ways. Ella pleasuring herself while talking dirty is something I could easily become addicted to. But when she stops touching herself and slides her shorts down her shapely legs, there is something else I *know* I'm addicted to.

She saunters over with her bare sex on display and ripe for the picking. She removes her tee and tosses it over her shoulder confidently. I need a minute because seeing her completely naked needs to be savored, not rushed.

Her curves make her all woman, *my* woman, and when

she stands in front of me and clutches my hair in both her hands, it's time I please my woman the way she deserves.

She spreads her legs and coaxes me to take her pretty pink пизда into my mouth. But I don't need any encouragement. On my knees with hands tied behind my back, I begin to pleasure her with my tongue. She moans, spreading her legs wider, her hands still threaded through my hair.

She controls the speed, the depth, and I'm her willing subject, a tool that is there for her use. She rolls her hips as I follow her movements with my tongue. I suckle over her clitoris where it's swollen and sensitive—I flick it with the underside of my tongue.

She cries out, trembling, but wants more.

I arch my head back to get a deeper angle, and when I sink my tongue into her, twirling it around and around and side to side, those trembles turn into tiny pleasured spasms. She's close, and I can't wait to taste the sweetness on my tongue.

Her pussy clenches, sucking me into a honeyed heaven. She is all over my face, and I love it. I love her. She is it for me. If, for whatever reason, she leaves, I will never seek another because this love I feel for Ella is forever.

She is my future—in this lifetime and the next.

She grips my hair tightly, rubbing my face deeper into her pussy, and when I rub my stubble across her sensitive flesh, she whimpers, "More."

Then more she will receive.

With only my mouth to pleasure her, I suck, lick, devour as she races closer and closer to the finish line. Her flesh comes alive in my mouth, the heat driving me wild, but just as she's about to come, I pull away.

She sags forward with a frustrated grunt, her eyes popping open. "Why, why did you stop?"

"Fuck me," I order bluntly because when she comes, it'll be on my cock.

She doesn't need to be told twice when I come to a stand, and she quickly takes off my pants. My cock is standing upright, and she licks her lips, which has me grunting in pure need. I lower myself back onto the carpet and sit with my legs out in front of me.

My arms are still bound behind me, so this is now Ella's show.

Ella's pussy glistens under the soft lighting, and when I lick my lips and taste her honeyed sweetness, my cock jerks in approval.

"Do you know how fucking sexy you look right now?" she says, watching me hungrily. "I wish you could see yourself through my eyes. I know all you see is a monster, but I don't see that. I never have."

She slowly lowers herself over me, gripping my shaft with her hand and guiding me toward her entrance. She rubs the head of my cock against the outside of her pussy, moaning.

"I see a good man, a man I love with all of my heart. I love you, Alek. More than I can ever say." Just when I think this moment couldn't get any better, she takes me into her body unhurriedly.

I grit my teeth, the tie threatening to break as I clench my fists. This feels so good.

When I'm buried deep, she pauses, lips slack as she wraps

a hand around the back of my neck. "Does it feel good?" she asks softly, clenching her muscles around my cock.

"Yes, you feel incredible," I reply, the corded veins in my neck confirming the fact that I'm barely holding on.

She smiles, and thank the heavens above, she begins to move.

Her slow movements are torture, but this is all for Ella, and watching her milk her pleasure from me is a magnificent sight. She arches her back, which juts out her beautiful breasts. I bend forward and take one into my mouth, rolling my tongue over her nipple.

She moans and begins to move faster.

I want to touch her so incredibly bad, but the temptation adds to this sensual experience for us both. She rides me, shuddering each time she lifts her hips and slams back onto my shaft. Her fingers dig into the back of my neck as she moves her hips wildly, holding on.

Her eyes are squeezed shut, and a sheen coats her flushed body as she rocks against me. She is using me to help replace her dreadful memories, and although they'll never go away, now, she has this experience to revert to when the demons come out to play.

This is her show. Every action, every movement is controlled by her. No one is forcing her because what this is between us is nothing but love.

The friction between us has me clenching my jaw, desperate not to come because I won't, not before her. She bounces on my lap, slamming onto me over and over again, and when she rolls her hips, I can't help but curse.

"блять! твоя пизда прекрасна"

"Oh god," she groans, her body covered in perspiration. "Whenever you speak Russian…it makes me so hot."

More Russian spills from me because if she continues working my cock this way, I'll speak all the Russian she wants.

"What did you say?" she says breathlessly, rocking against me.

"I said I like the way you ride my cock."

She groans loudly, my words encouraging her to move faster. The way she moves is hypnotic, and I'm completely under her spell when she clenches her muscles and comes loudly and violently around me. I'm sucked into a vortex, and as she orgasms long and hard, I desperately pump my hips, wanting to give her every second of pleasure that I can.

She slumps forward, and with sluggish fingers, she reaches around to untie me.

The moment I'm free, I spring up, taking her with me as I'm still embedded deep inside her. She yelps, surprised we're on the move, and when I toss her onto the bed and dive on top of her, she realizes we're not done.

I am so hard that I'm fearful what will happen when I come. But now, I focus on giving her orgasm number two.

I slip into her pussy with ease, and now that I can use my hands, I'm all over her. Kissing, touching, fondling—I can't get enough. She kisses me back, almost tearing my hair by the roots as she tugs hard.

Pumping my hips, I sink into her heat, shuddering and grunting because she feels so good. Snaring her wrists, I raise her arms over her head and pin them to the bed. She is now bound.

But the way she squirms, matching me stroke for stroke, she's happy to pass over the reins. I grip her leg and wrap it around my waist, deepening the angle as I punish her with deliciously hard, long strokes.

"More!" she demands, arching her back and thrusting onto my cock as I sink into her passionately. And more she gets.

I am covered in sweat as I work her body over, slamming my mouth over hers, fucking her with my cock and tongue. Not a wisp of air can pass between us, but still, we're not close enough. With her wrists bound in one hand, I cup her throat with the other and begin to fuck her hard.

This act is primeval, but feeling her pulse beat frantically against my fingers is a rush of euphoria. She knows this is my go-to move, and appeases me by arching her neck, allowing me to hold on tighter. Her offering has a string of Russian curses that make no sense spilling from me because I am lost to her.

Her pussy clenches around me and when I slip my thumb into her wet mouth, she suckles it, sending us both wild. I work my thumb in and out of her mouth, thumbing over her pouty bottom lip before snaring it between my teeth.

I'm not gentle as I claim her body, but this is me, and even though Ella has been through something so heinous, to change how I am with her, I'm afraid she'd think of it as me treating her differently because of what happened. If I thought she didn't like it, I wouldn't do it, but the way she moans and writhes under me confirms she likes the rough play as well.

She uses the heel of her foot to keep me pressed to her,

and as I slam into her, she shudders and squeezes her eyes shut.

"Я так тебя люблю. Моя любовь к тебе бесконечна," I pant, feeling my impending orgasm rushing at full speed.

I love you so much. My love for you is endless.

I can't stop the Russian which spills from me, and when Ella hears my breathless admission, she screams, her body contorting as she orgasms once again.

The moment the last tremor rocks her body, I'm about to pull out, but Ella locks her legs around me. "Come inside me," she gasps against my mouth.

I'm too far gone to argue, and with two quick thrusts, I spill my seed inside her.

My orgasm is so fierce that my body is still rocked with the aftershocks minutes later. Eventually, I roll off Ella and lie on my back, still panting and covered in perspiration as I fold my hands over my stomach, attempting to catch my breath.

Peering up at the ceiling, I realize this is the first time in a long time that I am comfortably numb.

Ella groans, rolling onto her side. On instinct, I move my arm so she can nestle into me, and when she does, I hum, kissing the top of her head.

We're silent, both enjoying the afterglow of our lovemaking. I can't believe I almost lost her. But now that I have her, I'll never let her go.

"I'm so sleepy," she whispers with a yawn.

"Sleep. I'll be here when you wake."

"Promise?"

With a content smile, I press another kiss to her head. "I

promise. Красавица?"

She hums in response, already half asleep.

"We made it to a bed," I say, referring to our conversation many moons ago. How we've both changed since then.

Her steady breathing is an indication that she's finally succumbed to exhaustion.

I peer down and see a small smile spread across her lips. With that vision in mind, I join Ella, welcoming sleep because tomorrow is a brand-new day we will face—together.

CHAPTER FOURTEEN

Ella

wake after what feels like a hundred years, and the only reason I stir is because I think I'm about to come.

Opening my eyes, I do a double take when I see that I actually *am* on the cusp of coming because Alek is nestled between my thighs, leisurely going down on me.

A startled gasp turns into a moan when he peers up, and I see his beautiful steel-blue eyes.

"I won't be a moment," he says, before diving back down to finish what he started.

I clutch at the long strands of his hair, holding on as he devours me without apology. He gently coaxes me to toss one leg over his shoulder, opening me wider to him, and when I do, he suckles on my clit while circling his tongue deep into me.

"о блять!" I curse in Russian.

It's one of the only phrases I know and seems appropriate

because, with one final stroke of his tongue, I'm coming so hard, I can't stop screaming '*oh, fuck*' at the top of my lungs.

Alek muffles my cries as we're not alone on the yacht by placing a hand over my mouth with a chuckle as he crawls up to lay beside me, watching me as I come.

I bite his palm in response, which only elicits a hungry growl in response. At this rate, we'll never leave this bedroom, but honestly, that wouldn't be so bad.

After last night, it feels like I can breathe a little easier. The weight still presses on my heart, and I know that will only ever lessen when I drive a blade through Santo's chest, ending his life.

I didn't know how Alek would react when I told him the truth, but what he did, what he said, I never expected that. He didn't look at me with disgust or disappointment. He looked at me with love.

I don't know what he said to me in Russian, but for him to speak it in another language, I expect it's something he can't say in English—yet. And that's okay. I'll wait. I'm not going anywhere. And neither is he.

It took us many hardships to get here, but they weren't mistakes. I refuse to look at them in such a light. They were lessons learned. I will never forget what Santo did to me, but I won't let it rule me because that would mean he won.

Once my breathing returns to a semi-normal pace, Alek removes his hand from my mouth with a victorious smirk. He's a very good lover. He's also very generous in the bedroom.

He always ensures my needs are met before his, and what he did last night, a ruler giving up control to help me overcome my fears, that shows the kind of man he is.

"Sleep well?" he smugly asks, which also reveals he can be a dick at times as well.

I nudge him in the ribs in response.

"When did you learn Russian?"

Laughing, I brush my newly cut hair from my cheeks. I like it short. "I have a very good teacher."

He shrugs, not bothering to argue. "Saint called while you were asleep. They're going to meet us at Tura. We're a few hours away from arriving."

"You can only get to Tura by boat? No private planes allowed?" I ask as it seems odd.

"There is nowhere to land and no place close by to refuel," he explains. "It'll take Santo roughly two days to get to Tura. Saint and Pavel have a head start, so they'll arrive before him. But they must come at nightfall.

"They need to remain hidden. Otherwise, our element of surprise will be lost."

"So when we get there, we pretend we're there to deliver the kids in exchange for money?" I ask, disgusted Rodrigo and Maria were planning on doing that.

"Yes," he says, appearing just as appalled as me. "I'll think of some reason as to why Rodrigo isn't the one delivering them, and the moment I find out who is behind this, I torture them for information before killing them very publicly."

"Well, I'm sure that'll smoke Santo out."

Alek nods, appearing worried. I know that's because of me.

"As much as it pains me to say, we must get up and get

ready." He openly stares over my naked form, tonguing the corner of his mouth. "There is nothing more I want than to lay in this bed all day and feast on your body, but we cannot."

He's right, but the way he speaks with his sexy, smooth accent and those come fuck me eyes, I can't help but pout.

"Oh, my greedy girl," he says with a lopsided smirk, thumbing over my bottom lip.

I am greedy, and I realize how much so when I wanted him to come inside me. I don't know why, but it just felt right. Knowing he's inside me, a part of me, pleases me. I have an IUD, so I can't get pregnant. But having Alek's child—that doesn't scare me as much as it should.

Pushing those thoughts aside as there are three real, not hypothetical children on board that need care, I nod and climb out of bed. I have a shower, leaving Alek to get us to Tura.

I don't know what faces us because no matter what Alek has told me about Tura, I expect it's going to be so much worse. It's not just an island where it's okay for little kids and kidnapped women to be bought as slaves, but it seems murder, and other atrocities are a part of the norm.

Basically, it's Disneyland for the rich and perverted.

Anything goes, which is why when Alek kills whoever is behind the selling of innocent children, no one will think twice about it. However, no doubt word has spread about Alek being a wanted man, and it won't take long for the foes to challenge him, just how that man did at Alek's party.

I'm sure they'll end up just how he did—dead.

Once I'm dressed, I check on the children, smiling sadly

when I see a bowl of untouched cereal by the door. Alek has tried to make progress with them, but they're clearly still afraid.

They're sleeping under the blankets I gave them, which is a start. I leave them to their slumber and go on the hunt to find Alek.

He's not in the kitchen or living area, so I walk up the stairs to the upper deck. I instantly head for the helm but gasp in horror when someone comes up from behind and places their arm across my throat.

"Never let your guard down, красавица, especially when we get to Tura. You must treat everyone like the enemy. I'm going to teach you how to fight," he says into my ear, kissing the shell.

Refusing to fall under his spell, I stomp on his foot and duck out of his hold when he shuffles back a few steps.

Spinning around, I place my hands on my hips. "What makes you think I don't know how to fight already?"

He grins broadly.

"Point taken, but I want you to spar with me."

Scoffing, I can't help but tease, "An old man like you? I'd feel bad hitting a senior citizen, but if you insist."

He shakes his head before having me eat my words as he unbuttons his shirt. When he reveals an expanse of golden, hardened flesh, I swallow deeply before I drool. He is a specimen crafted by the gods because he is chiseled in all the right places, putting the statue of David to shame.

His abs ripple as he gets into position, placing his hands in front of him, like makeshift focus mitts. I'm so distracted by the light dusting of hair between his pecs and his V-muscle that when he strikes out and gently taps me on the side of the head, I almost fall on my ass.

"Focus," he orders with a smirk.

He's right. I need to get my head in the game.

Thankful I opted to wear shorts and a tank, I get into position and punch Alek's hand.

"Ow!" I cry out, dancing on the spot as I cradle my hand.

"Are you all right?" Alek frantically asks, attempting to help me, which is his error because, with *his* guard down, I'm able to punch him in the jaw.

It's a light tap, but I gloat in victory. "Focus," I say in an accent supposed to resemble Alek's.

He rubs over his jaw, unable to hold back his laughter. "Is that supposed to be me? Why do I sound like a Hollywood version of Count Dracula?"

"Because you suck," I counter quickly, which is my error because he arches a smug brow.

"Oh, there's something I wouldn't mind sucking right now."

My cheeks instantly flush because he's looking at me like I'm his next meal.

Just as I'm about to say a wisecrack remark, Alek kicks his foot out and trips me. Before I fall, however, he latches onto my arm, stopping me.

"Why do you constantly defy me?" he asks, drawing me into his chest.

Peering up at him, I can't help myself as I stand on tippy toes and press my mouth over his. "Because you love it when

I beg."

Which is what usually happens when I defy him—he punishes me in the most delicious of ways.

Humming in approval, he kisses me passionately, robbing me of everything but him, and that's okay because he's all I need. He's all I'll ever want.

He cups my behind, drawing me closer into him so I can feel his erection. I love that he's just as turned on as me. What I feel for this man scares me, but it frightens me in the best possible way.

Love isn't supposed to make sense. It's supposed to scare, consume, complete you, and with Alek, it does all of this, and then some. What we have doesn't make sense, but to me, it's perfect—two pieces of a broken picture.

He completes me—mind, body, and soul.

He whispers Russian against my lips, setting every part of me on fire.

"I really need to learn Russian," I murmur.

He chuckles in response, before slapping my ass. "Another day because now, you're going to fight me."

He kisses me one last time. I can't help but pout when he pulls away. But he's right. We're hours away from arriving at Tura. Who knows what awaits us?

He runs his long fingers through his hair, the sunshine bouncing off his bronzed flesh. His muscles look incredible—hardened and defined. I never thought I'd find an older man this attractive, but it's because of his age that I find him all the sexier.

He's so refined, dominant. He knows what he wants—

unlike men my age who are interested in playing the field—
and right now, the way his eyes are eating me up from head to
toe, he wants me.

"Красавица, I will take you over my knee and whip you
until you listen," he warns with a sultry smirk.

Placing a hand on my cocked hip, I return his grin. "Is
that supposed to be a threat?"

He shakes his head dangerously slow. "No, pet, it's a
promise."

Before I have a chance to rebuke, he advances forward,
ready to attack. I pounce into position on the defense, and
when he attempts to hit me, I jump back and duck low, jabbing
out and connecting with his flank.

He nods, impressed as he regains position.

"Didn't think I could fight?"

"I've come to learn to always expect the unexpected when
it comes to you."

We begin to spar, Alek teaching me how to duck and
weave, replacing my scrappy street fighting which I was forced
to learn in order to protect myself because it's always been just
me. I've been fine with that, until I met Alek.

I didn't know what I wanted in life until he walked into
my world and taught me that I'm not a quitter—I never have
been. Together, we're going to conquer. I refuse to accept any
other fate.

I'm breathless and covered in sweat when Alek strikes
out, tripping me, but he doesn't allow me to fall. He grips my
arm and spins me toward him so we're pressed back to chest.
His scent is amplified tenfold.

"You put up a good fight," he says into my ear, his hot breath trailing a path down my neck. "But you're weak with your left jabs. Punch harder."

Nodding, I have no idea what he's saying because all I'm focused on is the way his body is molded to mine. How can we fit so perfectly? In every sense of the word.

He draws his forearm over my throat, coaxing me to tip my head backward. I know this is his favorite move. It has to do with the fact he's so damn bossy in all aspects of life, but honestly, I like it. I like his dominance because all he would have to do is squeeze a little tighter, and he'd hurt me.

But the fact he restrains himself, the way he skates the thin line between pleasure and pain excites me.

"Ok-okay," I reply breathlessly. It has nothing to do with the physical activity and everything to do with Alek.

Looking up into his eyes, I intentionally lick my upper lip, knowing he'll swoop down and capture it into his mouth. When he does, I moan, sinking into him when he nibbles on my top lip before slanting his mouth over mine.

We kiss sluggishly, savoring the other with passion and love. Alek grips my chin and tilts my head so he can deepen the kiss. Our tongues lazily circle the other, but in the end, Alek wins as he dominates my mouth, my kisses, compelling me to submit.

But I come willingly.

With a sigh, he kisses me one last time before pulling away.

"We must get ready. Tura is just an hour away." He kisses the tip of my nose before letting me go.

I wish we had five more minutes, but it's game time. I need to get in the right frame of mind.

"How should I dress?" I ask as we still are yet to discuss my role in this.

He doesn't look impressed as he says, "Everyone on that island will assume you're my—"

His pause has me filling in the blanks. "Concubine?"

"I rather hate that word," he reveals stiffly. "Mistress doesn't sound as…sordid."

"Well, potato, potahto. They know Willow and Saint are your significant others. I'm just here for the ride, right?"

Alek shakes his head, snaring my waist and drawing me into his chest. "Even though this is all a charade, it still turns my stomach. I'm sorry."

He kisses my forehead, expressing his regret.

"It's just make-believe," I say aloud for the both of us. "Will I be expected to behave like a prized pig?"

A winded wheeze gets caught in his throat, but there is no sugarcoating this. Aleksei Popov has had many mistresses in his time, and they all were at his beck and call. If I act any different, they will sense our deceit.

He's already skating on very thin ice. We need to convince them for long enough so he can slaughter whoever is ruining the lives of countless children. No doubt, word will spread to Santo that Alek is here with a woman. But hopefully, the fact I've cut my hair may throw him off long enough that we have a decent head start on him.

We need Saint, Pavel, and whoever is on our side to get to Tura before Santo so we're able to ambush him.

It's all based on what-ifs. But it's the best shot we've got.

"You'll be expected to obey my command," he replies, and by the tone of his voice, I know things are about to get serious. "These are not good people. They'll smile and act like they're your best friend, but they're not.

"They are simply sniffing out a weakness in hopes they can use it against you for their gain. Do not trust anyone. No matter how nice they may appear, everyone is the enemy."

With one final kiss to my brow, he says, "Go now, get ready. I wish we could clean up the children. But they must arrive in the state Rodrigo would deliver them."

I hate how somber things have turned.

Nodding, I turn and head down the stairs to get ready.

When I pass the kids, I see they're still sitting in the small space, frightened as they watch me with wide eyes. Holding back my tears, I quickly have another shower as I'm sure no mistress of Alek would be covered in sweat.

Once clean and my face is dolled up to cover the healing bruising and cuts, I hunt through my bag for something "appropriate" to wear. Everything I own is far too boring and conservative, which has me cringing when I look at the cupboard filled with Maria's clothes. I won't have that problem with her attire because *nothing* of hers is conservative.

Slipping into a tight black mini dress which is too short for my liking, I arrange it as it's a little snug. She's smaller than me, but thankfully, the material is stretchy, so it fits. I run some product through my hair and style it so it's slicked back.

The turtleneck gives me some coverage, but the sleeves are cut off and the hemline practically rides my ass. Overall, I feel really uncomfortable, but we all have a role to play. Borrowing some of her jewelry, I finish off the outfit with pearl studs and a matching cuff bracelet.

Thankfully, I think I can get away with sandals as wearing heels on an island seems rather idiotic.

Once dressed, I stand back and look at my reflection. The face of a stranger stares back at me. I look the part, and when the yacht begins to turn, I realize soon, I will need to play the part.

Touching up my red lipstick, I wish my reflection luck and check on the kids. When they see me, they shift away.

But I drop to a squat and smile. "We're going to stop soon. It's only for a little while. Whatever happens, you stay with Alek or me, okay?"

They simply stare with vacant eyes.

Alek's plan to end whoever has done this to them painfully slow is a punishment they deserve. I never believed in taking another person's life, but some people deserve to be dead.

I don't know what's ahead for these three children, but I know Alek would never abandon them. He sees Irina in them, and he'll move heaven and hell to ensure no other kid suffers like that under his reign.

I'm not making excuses for Alek, as he has very openly shared that when this is done, he won't be in line to be ordained. He plans on taking out every last person who has betrayed or questioned his authority, so he's able to build a new empire where his supremacy will never be challenged again.

The way he proposes to do this is quite smart. Everyone

always underestimates the underdogs, but a desperate man has nothing to lose.

This will work, and once it does, Alek will be the ruthless boss everyone respects, and me, I'm to be his…queen?

How do I feel about that? Knowing that I sleep beside a murderer?

Looking at the tormented children, I realize I feel just fine about it. In this world, being nice gets you nowhere. You get treated like nothing but a doormat. Alek has a chance to better the lives of the unfortunates, like these children, and punish the true bad men and women in this world.

Now that I've seen true evil, I understand Alek's reasons—better he, who has a conscious, rule, then someone like Santo who doesn't. Alek is an asshole; he's ruthless, savage, and forthright, but better the devil you know than the devil with no soul.

Alek may think he's soulless, but he's not. Look at what he did to save Irina and the orphanage. And look at what he did to save me.

A thought suddenly hits me, and I sprint up the stairs, needing to tell him this, not knowing when we will get another chance alone. He is at the helm, steering the yacht to the island, which I can see in the distance.

Our future awaits.

Alek turns around when he hears my frantic footsteps. Before he can speak, I throw myself into his arms and hug him tightly. "You gave up everything for me," I whisper against his chest.

Which he has. He left Russia and everything he's worked

so hard for behind to ensure my safety. He gave it all up for me, and for that, I love him even more so.

He rubs my back, holding me close, and what he says next just cements my love, my undying devotion to this devil who holds my heart. "*You* are my everything."

"Oh, Alek," I cry, so full of emotion that I can barely speak.

"Come now, don't cry. You'll mess up your makeup. You look beautiful." He pulls me out at arm's length, only to wipe away my tears with his thumbs.

Sniffling, I nod and pull it together. "I look like I need to add a few inches to my hemline."

He chuckles, kissing the top of my head. "You perfect any garment, but my favorite is when you're Ella—the carefree, barefoot, makeup-free woman who has stolen my heart."

I blink once, as this is the first admission that could be interpreted as him declaring his love. I don't make a fuss, though. I simply stand on tippy toes and kiss his whiskered cheek.

I stand by his side as he steers the yacht toward the island. The closer it gets, the more anxious I become. We're both walking into the unknown, which is terrifying considering the circumstances we face. From afar, the island looks like paradise, surrounded by crystal blue waters and rocky caverns.

But I know what horrors hide behind the beauty. This place is hell on earth.

Alek senses my panic and wraps his arm around my waist. "I won't let anything happen to you. I promise."

"I understand if you—"

But he cuts me off. "No ifs, Ella. I will protect you with

my last breath. No one is more important to me than you are."

Arching my neck, I press my lips to his. We kiss chastely, but this kiss means so much to me because it's filled with promise. I know it's going to freak him out, but I need to say it in case I don't get the chance ever again.

"I...I love you," I whisper against his warm mouth.

He hums low, nudging his nose against mine. "Miracles do happen."

It's okay he hasn't returned the sentiment. He will once he's ready. Besides, actions speak louder than words.

Once Tura is merely a few miles away, I watch the Alek I know be replaced with the Aleksei everyone is expecting to see. His stance changes as he holds his head high. We all have masks, and this is Alek's.

Hard. Ruthless. Cold.

The luxury yachts are moored, and when we pass one, I slide down my sunglasses, wishing to hide my surprise at openly seeing a man on his knees in nothing but a ball gag being flogged by a woman in spandex.

Alek doesn't stir, but I guess this is common practice in this world.

Once we pull up at a small dock, Alek turns off the engine and prepares for us to disembark. He looks casual in his shirt and trousers, but I know he's done this with intent. He wants to create a false sense of security, so when he strikes, it'll catch them unaware.

I walk down the stairs and cautiously approach the children. "We're here," I announce softly. "Remember what I told you?"

They peer up at me, their wide eyes expressing their fear.

"I promise, we won't let anyone hurt you. But you have to trust me." I gesture for them to come to me and give them all the time they need.

They look at one another, clearly sizing up whether they should trust me or not. They have every right to be wary. Look where they are. But eventually, the girl with the blonde hair stands. Seeing her at full height has me swallowing down my vomit.

She is skin and bones.

The other two soon stand, and the vision of three little orphans will be burned into my memory forever.

"It's okay. I won't hurt you," I soothe, encouraging them to come to me.

It takes them a few minutes, but one by one, they walk toward me, eyes downcast, afraid.

"What are your names?" I ask again, hoping they answer me this time.

"Zofia," says the blonde. Nodding at her friends, she indicates it's okay.

"Lena," says the brunette girl.

"Jacob," reveals the little boy. He can't be more than five years old.

I don't know if they're related. Or where they're from. But that can wait because the sooner we get onto Tura, the sooner Alek can make those who are responsible for this heinous act pay. I almost can't wait.

Alek's footsteps down the stairs have the children gripping my dress as they hide behind me. Alek pauses when he sees the sight before him. He shakes his head, angered.

"They are so small," he says, sickened.

"I know," I reply, reaching behind me, comforting the scared little mice.

"They're all going to pay," he vows, his jaw taut. "Serg's death will be nothing compared to what I have in store for every one of these долбоёбы."

He inhales deeply, clearly needing a moment to compose himself.

"Let us go," he instructs, walking toward the ramp.

I understand how personal this is for him. I know he sees Irina in them, and in a sense, this is his way to make peace within himself for not being able to save her. By saving these kids, he is saving her. That's who Alek is—he wants to save the world.

With the children still clinging to me, I slowly follow Alek, waiting for him to arrange the platform so we can disembark. I know better than to look around—a mistress wouldn't have permission to do so until Alek gave the orders.

So I wait until he directs me to walk.

With children in tow, we slowly descend the ramp, and once we hit the dock, I wait off to the side for Alek. A small crowd has formed. I can see their feet. But who they are, I don't know as my eyes are peeled to the ground.

A man speaks to Alek in Russian, his tone light, joyful. He seems to be happy that Alek is here.

Alek replies in Russian, before switching to English. "Yes, I have the three stowaways. Who do I see for payment?"

There is no sugarcoating with Alek.

"Always business first," says a female, who I already hate.

"Always, Galina, because with business comes pleasure."

I measure my breaths as I know he has a role to play. But I still hate every single second that I'm here.

"Is this your new рабыня?" Galina asks, and although I don't know what that means, I assume she's not giving me a compliment.

"No," Alek objects bluntly. "She is more than that. Now, if you're done gossiping like a silly schoolgirl, please direct me to who these brats belong to."

I bite the inside of my cheek to keep from smiling because the tension can suddenly be cut with a knife.

Someone clears their throat. "Follow me."

"Come," Alek says, hinting that's our cue to leave.

I don't need to be told twice and slowly follow Alek, ensuring the kids are close behind me. I scan my surroundings as best I can with my chin downcast and see Tura is an untouched paradise. The tall palm trees give the island a tropical feel, as does the soft sand.

Women are sunbathing on striped lounges while drinking colorful cocktails, and the men are playing cards or sitting by the bar. Any unsuspecting guest would be forgiven for thinking this was nothing but a holiday destination.

Alek and the man he walks with speak Russian, and although I'm curious as to what they're saying, in a sense, I'm glad I don't know what they're discussing. The children latch onto me, and their trust touches my heart.

The man escorts us to a white villa, which is absolutely stunning. One thing I've noticed is that the houses here do not have any fences around their property. It's like one big resort. I don't know if these properties are owned, or if it's a free-for-all—in every sense of the word.

We stop in the tiled foyer, where a maid offers Alek a glass of something. He shakes his head, making clear this isn't a social call.

Shoes squeak along the flooring, hinting our host has arrived, and when I hear his voice, I gasp, as I recognize who this is.

"Aleksei, I knew there was more to you than meets the eyes," says Christian, the man I met the night of the poker game. The man who is involved with the Italian mafia. The man who is Santo's nephew.

I try to keep calm, but this isn't good.

"Christian," Alek calmly says. "I suppose the same can be said about you. Does your family know about your...extra activities?"

Christian laughs jovially. "Those old farts wouldn't know a modern way of thinking if it slapped them on the side of the head."

I knew he seemed out of place compared to his uncles. It appeared he wanted to embrace a new, modern way of conducting business, while they are happy operating how their ancestors once did. This means they know nothing of this "side project."

"So this venture is all yours then?"

"Yes."

Christian has just signed his death warrant.

"I knew we were like-minded when I first met you,"

Christian goes on to say. "I've come to learn the hard way why they say never work with family. I had no other choice but to branch out on my own. I couldn't exactly be my family's competition, which is why I found a niche of my own."

Alek's silence is him barely holding on.

Is he the one who ruined Irina's life? The odds are slim, but in this world, I've learned that there is no such thing as coincidences.

"Word has it my uncle is looking for you and…Ella. Hello."

The blood drains from my face. No matter if my hair is short or long, or if I refuse to look at him, I can't hide my identity from him. He knows who I am, and he knows what I did to his cousin.

To think I have ruined this for Alek has me sniffing back tears. Every corner we turn, we're faced with a brick wall, which is ten feet high. I don't know what's about to happen because I never anticipated the person behind this would be a face we both knew.

Lifting my chin, I meet Christian's eyes. I remain passive, not wanting my emotions to show. "Hi."

He looks casual in a white shirt and chinos, and to some, he may be considered attractive with his light eyes and dark hair. But to me, he is the deadliest kind of monster. His mask fools people into believing he is harmless and standing on the sidelines while his father and uncle, who run the family, allow them to believe he is under their control.

But he is a smart predator. Waiting and watching, he bides his time.

"So, did you really do it? Did you kill Frank?"

I don't know how to respond, so I don't say anything. But my silence speaks volumes.

"I'm stuck in a predicament here, you see," he reveals coolly. "I could call my uncle and let him deal with you. I could also just forget I ever saw you, I mean, you're here with the goods. Whether you delivered them or Rodrigo, it really makes no difference to me."

Those "goods" he speaks of are the lives of three innocent children. He makes me sick.

"For my silence, I think it's fair that no money be exchanged. My silence for your freedom—that's a fair trade. Or"—he runs a thumb over his bottom lip in contemplation—"or I could kill you both for taking the life of a Macrillo. Problem solved. I could deliver your heads to my uncle as an early Christmas present. I would be the town hero. Taking out the invincible Aleksei Popov and his whore."

Alek cracks his neck from side to side.

"But then I would have to explain why I'm here, and I don't want him getting wind of my affairs. The only person who knew my secrets was Frank, but he took them to the grave."

For the first time, I don't feel bad about ending Frank's life. If he knew what Christian was doing and didn't stop him, he deserved the death I delivered.

"My secret is kept safe because all my business is conducted on Tura and you know the motto…what happens on Tura, stays on Tura. But if my uncle Santo comes here, it'll be a race to see who can tell him what I've been up to.

"They're all pathetic little sheep, wanting to get in the good books with whoever they think can benefit them the most. Which is why I won't do any of the above. You're of more value to me alive."

"How?" Alek finally speaks. He's as cool as a cucumber, but I know he has mastered his poker face.

"As you could see, my family don't think much of me. I'm only in business with them because someone with a modern brain needs to know how to wire money to our offshore accounts. If I wasn't needed, trust me, it would be a two-person deal.

"This little operation I have running on the side is very profitable, but it's not enough. It's time for new blood. So I have a proposition for you."

Alek folds his arms, listening.

"You buy from me, not my family. You make up some excuse as to why their product won't work for you. I provide what you need, unbeknownst to my uncles and father."

"Won't they know their shipment is a little light every month?" Alek asks, playing this dangerous game.

Christian plans to go behind his family's back. Greed really knows no bounds.

"No, they won't. I take care of the books. They just supply. I'm the brains behind this operation. As long as they see the money, they don't ask too many questions.

"I give you what you want. And you give me what I want."

Alek cocks his head to the side, confusing me. What does he see that I don't? "And what else do you want, Christian? You're the one calling the shots because you've got me by the balls."

Christian smirks. "I was sorely disappointed my uncle backed out of the deal."

It takes me a few seconds, but I realize he's talking about winning Saint and Willow in the poker game. Or, more specifically, Saint.

"Where is your righthand man? The one who broke my nose."

The twitch under Alek's left eye exposes his fury, but he keeps his cool. For now. "Back in Russia. Looking after business for me. How is the nose by the way?"

Christian clucks his tongue. "Call him, and I won't force you to watch my men take retribution on Ella. You really shouldn't have killed a Macrillo, little one. You've started a war; one you cannot win."

"долбоёб, speak to me," Alek orders, and his tone has Christian grinning.

"Fine. He is part of the deal. You give him to me, and your word that you'll purchase my product, and I will follow through on my end. Your anonymity, your safety is guaranteed.

"Yours and Ella's. I'll forget she ended the life of my cousin." I highly doubt that.

"And what about the children?"

Christian purses his lips. "What about them?" he asks cruelly as though they are merely chattel.

Alek's hands are tied. I don't know what he's thinking because if we don't do what Christian wants, he'll kill us. We don't have the element of surprise on our side any longer.

"Fine," Alek concedes. "I look forward to doing business with you. I will go back to my yacht and call Saint."

Christian's lips twist into an amused scowl. "Oh, no need. You're my guests. *Mi casa es tu casa*. You'll stay here until Saint arrives. We have a lot to discuss."

Guests?

I scoff. We're not guests; we're his prisoners, and when three heavily armed men flank us, it's clear we're not going anywhere.

Christian steps closer to me, while on instinct, I move the children further behind me, protecting them from his predatory stare.

When he gets within a few feet, he scrunches up his nose. "*Mamma Mia*, they reek."

"That's what happens when you're forced to live in your own filth," I spit, unable to hold my tongue.

Christian smirks, unmoved. "I don't know how these kids came into your possession, but it's surely fate, and tonight, we celebrate."

I don't even want to know what Christian's idea of celebrating entails.

"Annika, see to bathing them. Their maiden voyage awaits." He clicks his fingers, and a maid springs to command.

I hold down my bile—only just.

"Let me," I quickly offer. "They trust me."

Christian peers at them huddled behind me. "Very well. Alek and I need to talk anyway."

This buys me some time. Surely, Alek has a plan. But when we lock eyes, and he shakes his head with regret, I realize that no, he doesn't.

We're so screwed.

CHAPTER FIFTEEN

Alek

A string of Russian leaves me as I fasten my bow tie. This is bad. Actually, this isn't just bad—it's far worse.

If only I didn't pursue this avenue, if only I let go of my need to uncover what happened to Irina, we wouldn't be here. But I couldn't. I couldn't stand by, knowing what I did. It would have eaten at me for the rest of my life, but now, the end may be closer than I thought.

"блять!"

The element of surprise is gone, as Christian knows our sins. If I don't do what he says, he will kill us. He won't even bother calling Santo. He'll do the job for his uncle. I was counting on some nosy asshole calling Santo in secret, so we could ambush him as he would be in the belief that we didn't know he was coming.

However, now, there is no need for Santo to know we're here because Christian doesn't need the backup. He has everything he needs. Long story short—I do what he wants. Otherwise, he will kill us, and Santo gets off scot-free.

Why couldn't it be someone we didn't know? Why did it have to be the Italian fucking mafia behind this?

Peering at my reflection in the mirror, I wonder if my luck has run out? I never believed in such a notion before, as fools believe in luck. I'm the decider of my own fate. But I begin to question everything.

The odds are not in my favor, and even though I've fought hard to get to where I am, I've never before experienced what I'm faced with. I'm outnumbered, and if I fight, I *will* die.

Once upon a time, I would have accepted my fate, but now, I can't. And that has nothing to do with me, but everything to do with others.

I leave behind so many people I love. I leave behind something I never thought I was capable of having—a family. I'm here for Irina. I'm here so Ella doesn't have to keep running.

But I've run out of options. There is no negotiating the terms.

Christian took me into his office and laid down the rules—he would sell to me for double the price and would take twenty-five percent of my profits. Basically, he wanted me to do all the hard work while he reaps all the benefits.

I killed Serg, only for another asshole to challenge my throne. A different Macrillo, but a Macrillo nonetheless.

I called Saint, playacting that I was doing Christian's bidding. I asked he come to Tura because I had some business to take care of. Thankfully, he played along, as he guessed something went wrong.

Christian is now in the belief that Saint will arrive here, clueless to Christian's plans.

Peering at my Rolex, I know that Saint will be here come tomorrow nightfall. The plan was to sneak him in so no one would be aware he was here and alert Santo that I have backup. But asking him to come to Tura has just invited him into the lion's den.

Just thinking of what Christian wants Saint for has me clenching my fists. He sees Saint as someone special to be at my side, and curiosity is a beast—one wants what others have.

Oscar already broke Saint, and although the physical scars have healed, the ones inflicted on his heart, on his soul will always remain. I'd rather kill Saint than allow that torture to befall him ever again.

Saint will have backup of his own when he arrives, but now that Christian is expecting him, that once again foils our surprise attack. I need to think of another plan and fast, but at the moment, all I'm seeing is being blackmailed by another fucking Macrillo.

Could it be such a small world, after all? I've come to learn that yes, it is indeed. No matter how many people you meet in your life, the same assholes tend to linger and resurface over and over again.

I quickly secure my bow tie and slip into my tuxedo jacket. I have no idea what awaits, but I know it can't be good. We're stuck on an island with perverts and outlaws, and this is a recipe for disaster. The hidden camera under the light fixture follows my every move.

To the untrained eye, it would go unnoticed, but I once lived in a house such as this.

Christian has separated Ella and me. She's safe—for now, as he needs her alive.

Running a hand down my face, I exhale. This is a mess.

Make no mistake, this bedroom is my prison cell because a guard mans my door at all times. So when I open the door and see some rent-a-cop standing in the hallway, all I can do is raise my eyes to the heavens.

"Take me to Ella," I demand, leaving no room for argument.

"My order is to escort you downstairs. Guests will be arriving shortly."

"Are you hard of hearing?" I question, buttoning my jacket, unimpressed. "You either take me where I want to go, or I'll throw you from this top railing. You're replaceable. I am not."

My threat isn't empty as I have no qualms about tossing him over the banister, where he can test his landing skills on the hard marbled floor.

With a huff, he leads me down the tiled hallway to a bedroom two doors away. This villa is very Mediterranean, and no expense has been spared. On any other day, I would say this place is quite striking, but now, all I can think about is burning it to the ground.

He gestures with his head that this is where Ella is, but makes it clear he's not going anywhere.

Knocking on the door with my knuckle, I say, "Ella, it's me."

The door opens seconds later, and when I see Ella, I advance swiftly and draw her into my arms.

"Are you all right?" I ask, aware that she may not be able to answer because I'm squeezing her so tight.

"I'm fine. You?"

I chuckle in response, but it's not filled with humor. "Where are the children?"

"They're sleeping in the bed. I've bathed them. They—" She doesn't need to fill in the blanks. I can only imagine the state they're in.

I never want to let her go, but we must get tonight over with.

Regretfully, I loosen my hold on her, and when I hold her out at arm's length, I can't help but run my finger along her shoulder. I need to touch her, to make sure she knows I'll never stop.

"Forgive me, we shouldn't have come." I express my regret because if I'd kept on sailing, we'd still be safe.

But she shakes her head, placing her hand to my cheek. "There's nothing to forgive."

She may think that, but I don't. She's in danger, yet again, because of me.

"Let's go," the goon barks, but when he puts his hands on Ella, ready to drag her away, I show him what I think of him and his order.

Without delay, I elbow him in the jaw, catching him off guard. Blood trickles from his mouth as he's just bitten his tongue. He staggers back, attempting to find his feet.

"Touch her again, and I'll rip the tongue from your mouth

and feed it to you."

He wipes the blood away with the back of his hand, glaring at me. But the message seems to have gotten through. He marches down the hallway, hinting we're to follow.

Ella's eyes are wide as I loop my arm around her, pulling her close to me. "Don't leave my side," I whisper as we commence walking.

"What's plan B?" she says softly.

"I'm working on it."

She doesn't press, whether that's because she knows these walls have ears, or if she knows that's code for, I have no fucking clue what to do.

As we take the stairs, I'm on high alert, taking everything in, and when we're led into an alfresco area overlooking the picturesque scenery, my senses sharpen. Before me stands, Galina—a Russian aristocrat who owns almost every nightclub in Russia, which she uses for money laundering purposes.

Sascha—he offers protection to the rich and paranoid for a hefty fee.

And then there is Christian.

Three major players all in the same room.

Galina's beauty is renowned. It's what she's used to get to the top as her kindness is definitely not a selling point. She's had five ex-husbands and counting who have died "mysteriously." I say mysteriously because everyone knows she killed them when they stopped being of use to her.

She saunters over. Now that I'm back on top, she wants to sit by me on my throne. It'll be a cold day in hell when that happens.

"I thought Tura wasn't your scene," she purrs, extending her hand for me to kiss it. I'd rather kiss a gorilla's ass.

So in response, I fist-bump her, making Saint proud. Her face twists into a confused scowl.

"It isn't." I don't elaborate because I don't want to talk to any of these assholes.

She is taken aback by my bluntness, as she's accustomed to everyone kissing her surgically lifted ass. I am not one of those people, however.

Sascha clears his throat, drinking his champagne.

Christian is the only one who seems to be thoroughly enjoying this uncomfortable scene. "Alek kindly delivered something which belongs to me. Can you imagine the king of Russia working for me?"

I'm seconds away from tossing him off the alfresco, when Ella subtly squeezes my arm, holding me back. It doesn't go unnoticed by Galina.

"You never introduced your new pet. What shall we call you?" Galina arches a brow, sizing Ella up. She thinks she's competition, that Ella is standing in her way.

Ella does what is expected of a submissive—she remains quiet until I give her permission to speak.

"Is this one an American too?" Galina asks, disgusted.

"How is that any of your business?"

She examines her nails as if bored by the conversation she initiated. "Just wondering if I need to prepare for another disaster. Their пизда must be coated in gold for you to risk so much when you can have any woman or man you desire."

I can't stand this. If I don't kill at least one of them now, I'm going to explode.

Christian senses my anger, and although he wants to assert his power over me, he does want to make sure we're on the same team. He needs me, after all.

"No politics," he says with a wave of his hand. "We're here for a good time. This is a celebration. Alek and I are going into business together."

Sascha's brow furrows. "I thought you worked alone." He's been on my ass for years to come work for me, but I had all the manpower I needed because Sascha could only wish to be half the man Saint is.

Turning slowly, I look at him. He knows about Christian's operation, which means he's become very valuable to me. He's been the righthand man to many. What secrets is he privy to?

"Alek and I are like-minded, and together, we will thrive," Christian replies, not bothering to clarify that this business venture has nothing to do with exploiting little children.

"I've still yet to see the little mice," Galina says, and by all that's holy, she's just ensured her death will be a painful one. "There is something about little hands and big men."

Ella's gags catch in her throat. I gently rub her back.

So it appears Galina is the buyer. But what would she need the children for? She owns nightclubs, and the last I heard, they weren't a front for child prostitution. How things have changed since I fell from my throne.

This would have never happened when I was in control. But that's what happens when a soulless Мудак like Serg rules. It's a free-for-all.

Russia is a fucking mess.

"Come, let us share a meal." Christian gestures we're to sit and break bread at the outdoor table.

Eating is the last thing on my mind, but I need some time to come up with a game plan. If Galina and Sascha are aware of Christian's business, then they'll have the information I need. So I follow Christian to the glass table.

We all take a seat while Ella stands behind me. I don't want her sitting anywhere near these bastards. The drop from the alfresco isn't far. If the situation calls for it, she can jump over the railing and make a quick escape.

The maids scurry outside, hands filled with an array of foods. They place everything onto the table with military precision before leaving as quickly as they came. Christian helps himself to the antipasto platter, while I reach for the bottle of vodka.

The seal is still intact, but that doesn't mean it's not been tampered with. Regardless, I crack it open and pour myself a glass. I don't fail to notice the food served is mainly finger foods, which means no knife is required. This, of course, was done with intent.

If this gives Christian a sense of security, then he has a lot to learn. The salad fork is a far better tool to use than a knife. Picking it up, I press my thumb over the pronged edge.

"Prosciutto and melon?" Christian asks, offering me the platter.

Accepting, I stab my fork into the neatly wrapped parcel, wishing it was his head. I need this to be over with immediately. "What are your plans with the children?"

Galina pauses mid-chew, clearly stunned I've openly asked her this question.

"I didn't think you'd mind, seeing as we were discussing my relationships like the weather."

"Come, Aleksei, we're all friends here," Christian says, sensing a storm is brewing.

Galina isn't a woman who is easily intimidated.

Resting her fork on the edge of the plate, she reaches for her wine. Once she takes a small sip, she replies, "You're a smart man. I'm sure you can figure it out yourself."

"I'm sure I can," I argue, leaning back in my chair and eyeing her over the table. "But I'd rather you tell me."

Smirking, she runs her finger along the rim of her glass. "Children are so carefree. So naïve. As we grow older, we soon forget a world like that exists. Many people want to capture that innocence once again."

Crossing an ankle over my knee, I steeple my fingers in front of me. "Stop talking in fucking riddles," I calmly say. "Do you sell them to the highest bidder to appease their sordid perversions?"

Galina is taken aback, but eventually, a reptilian smirk spreads from ear to ear. "I was trying to be tasteful, but when you put it like that, then yes, that's exactly what I do.

"The orphanage you hold so dear is a gold mine. Maybe we could come to an arrangement where all of us benefit?"

Galina is just like Serg—someone's misfortune is their gain. But now that I know her sights are set on the orphanage… she cannot live.

Chuckling, I shake my head as if impressed by her offer.

"And do you keep track of every child you purchase?"

Galina leans forward and purrs, "Do you remember every meal you've had?"

The blood rushes through my body, desperate to feed my organs as I attempt to calm the fuck down.

"If the meal is memorable enough, then yes," I counter, disgusted that's how she sees these kids.

Christian laughs, appearing amused by this conversation.

"I'll have to check my laptop," she says, batting her eyelashes. "If you wanted to come by later this evening, we can look together."

Whether she is lying or not, I won't let this opportunity pass me by. "Can't wait."

That wasn't a compliment, but Galina has missed the sarcasm. "I'll make sure the vodka is chilled."

And I'll make sure you suffer the repercussions for being a soulless bitch.

Now that that's been settled, I feel somewhat more relaxed.

Suddenly, the plan I so desperately was searching for appears in front of me, and I mean that literally because when I look at Sascha, I know what I have to do.

He knows the secrets of the men and women he's protected. Some of which are here. Secrets are weaknesses, and I want to know them all. And he will obey me as I know he's guarding a secret of his own.

My plan was to kill as many of these assholes as I could, wishing to replace them with my own handpicked team. And it seems I'm about to get my wish because I won't need to kill them—they'll do that for me.

With a smile, I reach for my glass. "Let's make a toast, shall we?"

Everyone reaches for their glasses, ready for me to announce what we're celebrating.

"To the future," I cheerfully say because that future doesn't include them in it. They all salute, unbeknownst they've just sealed their fate.

It's time I smoke Santo out. This plan is a suicide mission, but so is sitting back and doing nothing at all.

This really is war.

Ditching the tuxedo, I've dressed in something a little more comfortable because tonight is not going to be pretty.

Thankfully, the festivities didn't last long as Galina had to attend to some business before our "meetup." The torturous dinner was over within an hour. Christian is as happy as a pig in shit, and why wouldn't he be?

He has everything he wants in the palm of his hand.

But what he doesn't realize is that I didn't come this far to let some pipsqueak try to overthrow me. Been there, done that, and Christian's fate will be the same as his predecessors. Being a leader means you have to think on your feet, and this plan is as unpredictable as they come.

But it'll work. I'll make sure of it.

Applying some cologne, I look at my reflection, seeing the face of a man I no longer recognize. Moons ago, the prospect of going into battle, into overthrowing this land, gave me a warm feeling in the pit of my stomach.

Now, however, it makes my stomach roil.

Slipping on my pinkie ring, I give myself a pep talk. "Давай сделаем это."

Let's do this.

When I open the bedroom door and see Ella pacing the hallway, biting her thumbnail, time stands still.

"What's wrong?" I frantically ask, lunging for her and dragging her into my bedroom.

She throws her arms around me and hugs me tight. "What are you going to do?"

Rubbing her back, I inhale deeply, her scent calming my nerves. "How did you get past the hound?" I ask as I'm surprised not to see one of Christian's goons manning her door.

"Christian seems less paranoid after dinner and told the guard to take the night off. He's only this way because he thinks you've agreed to play along with their games," she whispers.

Even though we're not being guarded, that doesn't mean they don't have eyes on us.

"I'm taking care of it."

"What does that mean?" She pulls from my embrace, begging I explain.

Cupping her face, I brush my thumb along the apple of her cheek. "It means I intend to find out everything Galina knows, and once I do...I'm going to kill her."

Ella nods quickly, expecting the answer, but that doesn't make it any easier to accept.

"She cannot live," I state firmly. "Someone like her is a cancer, and left untreated, she'll spread, infecting the healthy around her. Even if she doesn't know anything about Irina, what she proposes for those children…death is a far too merciful act."

"And what else?"

Ella is smart. She knows this is only the beginning.

"Sascha knows everyone's secrets—he knows who's undercutting who, who's sleeping with whose wife, who secretly wants who dead, and I plan on unleashing those secrets and watch them spread like wildfire."

Ella arches a brow, confused.

"These people are playing nice, coexisting because they have to, but if they found out their best buddy really wants them dead, or their partner in crime is screwing their wife six ways to Sunday, trust me, alliances will be split."

Ella's mouth parts in understanding. "You can't kill them all, so you're letting them do it for you? It's like Chinese whispers, only with a lot more blood."

Nodding with a smirk, I reply, "Precisely. They'll take one another out, and I'll stand back, picking off the rest."

"You're bringing anarchy to Tura in a few hours so when Saint arrives, you're hoping everyone will be too busy killing each other to notice his arrival?"

"Yes, and with their yachts ruined, they're shipwrecked—in every sense of the word."

For this to work, I need to cut them off from the rest of the world, and that means almost every yacht needs to go down. Fear and desperation will make a man do dire things.

"Once this is done, we can leave, right? Santo won't ever need to know we're here."

But Ella's lips soon dip into a frown as she shakes her head. "Alek, no. This plan means you don't need to have so much blood on your hands. We can leave. You can form new alliances with the associates of your choosing. A new Russia awaits. It's what you worked so hard for. Tura will be bathed in the blood of your enemies."

But she doesn't understand. Once upon a time, that was what I wanted, but now, I want something more.

Her.

Thumbing over her bottom lip, I smile, but it's bittersweet. "All of that pales in comparison to what I really want."

Her chest rises and falls as she measures her breaths. "And what's that?"

"You."

Tears fill her eyes, and for once, I've elicited happy tears instead of ones laden with sorrow.

"I won't live our life on the run, and we will always be running with Santo alive. It's time we end this now. I promised to protect you, and you're not safe with him still breathing. He needs to pay for what he did to you."

Christian doesn't want his uncle here, but this isn't his show—it's mine. And what I plan to do will bring not only Santo here, but the mafia as well.

"And if we lose?" she whispers, a tear trickling down her cheek.

"Then I take as many of those motherfuckers to hell with me," I reply, gently bending forward to kiss away her tears.

"Don't say that," she cries, pressing her hands to my cheeks.

"Then I won't." Before she can fight me, before she can tell me this plan will fail, I slam my mouth over hers and kiss her avidly.

I don't want to think of this as the last kiss, but I honestly don't know what will happen once I kickstart this plan. There are so many variables, and the odds aren't in my favor, but I will die fighting if I must. I won't sit back and be blackmailed.

I'm nobody's bitch.

Ella senses the uncertainties ahead as her urgent kisses almost knock me back with their force. She tugs at my hair. She bites at my lips. Her kisses are filled with desperation because although she doesn't want me to go, she knows that I must.

I know she wants to help me, but I need to do this alone.

If something happens to those children, or Christian gets away, this would have been all for nothing. Here, she can protect the kids, and if she needs to, she can deliver Christian the fate he deserves.

She can look after herself. She's proven that time and time again. If I fail, then she will see this through. All of this is only possible because of her. If she didn't selflessly surrender herself to Santo, I wouldn't be alive.

These three children would be forced into a life of sexual slavery, and many others after them would follow suit. Tura would continue to harbor criminals, and Russia would eventually be overrun by criminals.

Our world would be destroyed, but because of Ella—she's

saved us all.

That one act of self-sacrifice has spared so many. Everyone wants a hero, and in this story, that's Ella. I'm merely a supporting character.

We kiss with passion, with love, and when I pull away, the words, words which terrified me tumble easily from me, freeing me from the self-hate I've carried for the entirety of my life.

"Я тебя люблю."

Ella smiles, making me the luckiest man alive when she whispers, "I love you too."

I hug her tightly, kissing the top of her head and committing this moment to memory because it's nothing short of perfect.

Eventually, we break apart, but saying goodbye isn't an option, so instead, I draw her hand to my lips and kiss the back of it. "Don't hesitate to kill the son of a bitch. I'll see you soon."

Nodding, she rubs her thumb over my hand, her eyes conveying so much. "Give them hell."

With a smirk, I concur, "Only the devil can."

There will never be a right time to go, so without a fuss, I turn and leave my world behind.

I do this for her, for our future and with that thought coursing through me, I confidently walk down the stairs, cane in hand, ready to give my queen the kingdom she deserves.

Christian is nowhere to be found, but he knows I'm on my way to see Galina, so we're safe for now. If he comes for Ella, she's proven she can fight. But as long as he thinks we're in cahoots, she's safe.

Once outside, I stop and tip my face to the heavens. It's a starless night, seems appropriate, as they know what's ahead. It's safer in hiding because I'm not holding back. I make my way for Galina's villa, noting how quiet it is.

But make no mistake, the silence echoes the atrocities happening behind closed doors.

When I turn a corner, I see Walter Moller, the biggest arms dealer in Germany, on a nightly stroll. He knows to keep his paws off Russia as Pavel will rip the head from his shoulders if he dares encroach on our soil. He is an arrogant asshole, so I decide to commence my tattletale with him.

"Good evening, Walter. It's such a pleasant night for a stroll, isn't it?"

He stops in his tracks, clearly surprised to see me here as I haven't concealed my hate for him and Tura. "Aleksei? I never thought I'd see you here again. What do we owe this honor?"

His smug tone has me enjoying this all the more.

"I have some business to take care of. How's Anna?"

Anna is Walter's wife, and although he believes Anna to be the perfect doting wife, we all know better. Last I heard, she had no qualms allowing her bodyguard, Dimitri, shield her with his naked body.

"She's fine. I was actually out looking for her."

This is really too easy.

"All right, I won't keep you then. Please pass my hellos onto them."

"Them?" Walter asks, turning a vibrant shade of red.

"Yes," I reply naively. "I saw Dimitri and Anna earlier by London's Cove but didn't get a chance to say hello as they looked to be—" My pause is done with intent as I wish Walter to fill in the blanks himself.

London's Cove is notorious for illicit coupling. No guessing what he'll assume they're up to.

He storms past me, fists bunched by his side.

"Nice talk," I sarcastically say with a wave, but Walter is long gone.

This island is going to self-destruct in a matter of hours, and I'll have a front row seat, applauding my efforts to destroy them all.

With no time to waste, I continue my way, and when I approach Galina's villa, I push every emotion but revenge aside. Even if she doesn't have any information on Irina, she'll still pay for the atrocities she committed.

The door is open, so I make my way inside.

The villa is similar to that of Christian's, but I'm not here to take in the décor. My heavy footsteps announce my arrival, and when I find Galina sprawled out on the sofa, sipping champagne, I can't wait to exit the way I came.

She doesn't sit up. She continues to lie on the leather couch like the queen that she thinks she is. I really am in no mood to play these games, so I stand in front of her, smirking. It's time to lay on the charm.

"Business first," I smoothly say, making a point to look at her bare legs.

She is wearing a sheer nightgown with nothing underneath. My dinner threatens to come back up, but I swallow down my revulsion.

"Of course," she replies, bringing the crystal glass to her red-stained lips. "The information is on the table."

Without delay, I retrieve the piece of paper from the coffee table and read it over. There are names of ten children—all aged between seven and ten. I don't see Irina's name.

"So this is a record of all the children who've come into your possession?"

She nods, licking her lips. "Yes. Christian has the rest. He doesn't store it electronically, however. He won't leave a paper trail connecting this to him."

"So where does he keep all of his information then?"

Galina arches her back, jutting out her breasts. "What proper Italian needs Italian cookbooks?" she poses, and if this is one of her riddles, I'm going to cut out her tongue for wasting my time.

"This is a select market as a lot of buyers like older boys and girls. But I don't discriminate."

"Where does he get the children from?"

She shrugs. "There are a lot of unwanted kids in this world and greedy parents. He doesn't have to look far."

"Is he the only one?"

"No, but he's the biggest and most discreet. His product is always top quality."

I clench my fist, the piece of paper crinkling into a tight ball with the force. Product? They are human beings.

I knew there were others out there. I wish I could stop them all, but knowing I can put a stop to one asshole gives me a small shred of satisfaction.

I don't sense any deceit from Galina, but even if I did, I have an inkling this is all she's willing to share.

"Are you thinking about taking him out?" Galina asks. Unbeknownst to her, that's exactly what I plan on doing; just not in the way she thinks.

"Maybe," I ambiguously reply.

This gains her attention.

She slowly rises, resting against the armrest as she watches me with sultry eyes. "You need a queen by your side, Aleksei. Someone you can trust. Let me help you restructure Russia into a new world where we can thrive."

She also knows that many are still opposed to me being their leader. But that's all about to change.

"I have a gift for you," she reveals, which has me arching a brow.

I don't want anything from her.

But with a clap of her hands, I realize this gift isn't returnable.

A young woman enters the room in nothing but a studded dog collar around her neck. She is thin and pale. Nothing but sadness pooling behind her blue eyes. She looks to be in her early twenties.

"I know you prefer the company of many, so this is my gift to you. Either she can join us or I can watch while you use her as you desire. Or, if you prefer, you can watch us."

All of those options are repulsive, but I smirk, playing along.

"What is your name, возлюбленная?"

She doesn't reply. She stands obedient, which has me

believing she is Galina's submissive.

"Answer him," Galina orders, looking at the young woman as though she is nothing but dirt.

It sickens me.

The young lady lifts her chin timidly. "My name is Tina. Jaqueline. Vera. I am whoever mistress Galina wants me to be."

Galina smirks at me as though I'm supposed to be impressed she's removed the identity of this young woman.

"What was your name before Galina?"

Galina's smirk soon disappears. She doesn't appreciate being undermined in her own home. "Why are you so concerned with her name? What we need her for doesn't require her name."

She reaches under the couch and produces a leather dog leash.

Inhaling, I begin to unbutton my shirt. "I wish to know her name because she was someone's daughter. Maybe someone's sister?"

"What does that have to do with anything?" Galina stands, leash in hand. She's clearly angered that I'm not grateful for my gift.

Once my shirt is unbuttoned, I slip it off, flinching when I notice the young lady recoil in fear. "Shh, it's okay. I won't hurt you."

And what I do next catches both women off guard.

I offer my shirt to the young woman, wanting her to cover up. She looks at the offering, working her dry bottom lip furiously. Of course, she believes this to be some trick.

"Aleksei, how dare you override me," Galina sneers while I grin, relishing in her anger. "Vera is mine to do with as I please, and right now, I want her to suck your cock."

Vera quickly jumps to command, dropping to her knees and fumbling with the button on my pants. I place my hand over hers, stopping her.

Peering down, I lift her chin with my finger. "No, Vera, you'll be doing no such thing ever again."

Galina comes racing over, a war cry leaving her, and when she attempts to whip Vera with the leash, I strike out and elbow her in the nose.

Stunned, she staggers back, blood gushing from her nose as she attempts to stop the bleeding with her trembling hands.

"You've gone m-mad!" she cries, frantically pulling out tissues from the tissue box on the side table.

"No doubt," I reply with a shrug.

Offering a hand to Vera, she accepts as I help her stand. This time, when I offer her my shirt, she quickly accepts and puts it on. It hangs off her small frame, coming mid-thigh. I'm thankful she's covered, but we're not done.

In Galina's haste, she dropped the leash, which I leisurely bend down and pick up.

"Is this yours?" I ask Vera, who nods shakily. "Did she keep you chained up like a dog?"

She nods once again.

"For how long?"

"Oh, why do you even care?" Galina screams, stuffing tissues into her nose to keep from staining her white rug. "You're not a saint!"

"You're right; I'm far from one. But I'm hoping to use the rest of my life to make amends for all the wrong that I've done."

"Everyone is right. You *have* lost your nerve. Your days are numbered. Someone who deserves to rule will soon rise. Mark my words. I'll tell everyone what you've done."

"Oh, Galina," I mock with a smirk. "Who said you'll have a tongue come dawn?"

Her bravado soon diminishes, and her game plan changes. She's now fighting for her survival. She peers around the room for an exit.

"Did you know that I recently became a father?" I say, walking around Vera and carefully removing the collar from her neck. Her skin is raw from where the collar chafed her.

"I did not," Galina replies, playing along for now.

"Yes, I did. I adopted a little girl. Those three little children, the ones you planned on selling like nothing but livestock, they remind me so much of her."

Galina's nostrils are stuffed with bloodied tissues, and the sight is one I commit to memory forevermore.

"She has no family, no past. It's like she just appeared into thin air." I snap my fingers, wishing to emphasize my point. "Someone has gone to great measures to ensure her history is wiped. Why do you think that is?"

Galina's eyes widen as she suddenly understands her role in all of this. "I don't know anything," she pleads, backing away. "Christian is the one who would know."

"Does this sound like Christian? Covering his tracks this way?" When she begins to cry, I curl my lip, disgusted.

"Answer me!"

"Ye-yes," she stutters, tears streaming down her face. "He doesn't want anything linked back to him. If she's young, odds are Christian is the one who sold her."

My hunch was right. I knew this was a select market. Kids as young as Irina are trafficked discreetly because it's all about having the right connections so that the operation runs as smoothly as possible.

"Where does he keep his information?" I press because a safe seems too obvious, but suddenly, her comment about cookbooks has me laughing.

Seems appropriate because Christian is about to be served a piece of humble pie.

Galina realizes her time is up. She served her purpose in this story, and now, it's time for her to die.

"Please, Aleksei, no. I beg you." She interlaces her hands, begging I show her mercy.

I toss the dog collar at her feet in response. "Put it on."

She shakes her head, but when I make it clear this isn't optional, she bends down and picks it up with quivering hands. She secures it around her neck, awaiting further command.

Turning to look at Vera, I offer her the leash. "Show me what she did to you."

Vera is hesitant, and I can understand why. God knows how long she's been held captive and all the horrors she's been subjected to. But eventually, she accepts the leash.

"Don't you even think about it!" Galina exclaims, warning Vera of the consequences for disobeying her master.

Walking beside Vera, I give her the encouragement she needs because if Galina resists, I'll be making good on my promise and cutting out her tongue.

Galina knows it's now or never, so she makes a quick dash up the stairs. Clucking my tongue, I follow casually as I was anticipating that move. When Vera and I get upstairs, I see Galina on the balcony, frantically tipping over the chairs.

Amateur move.

One should always know where they keep their hidden weapons. It's a matter of life and death in circumstances such as these.

When Galina sees me, she hurls a glass vase, missing my head by miles.

Running to the balcony railing, she screams, "Help!"

But no one is going to help her. Calls for help on Tura are so common that everyone is desensitized. She's out here, all alone; just as those poor children were at the expense of her greed.

"Shh, shh," I coo, coming up behind her and wrapping my arms around her waist.

She flails wildly, kicking and clawing at me, but her fighting is in vain. There is only one way this is going to end.

Spinning her around, I nod at Vera, gesturing she's to attach the leash to the collar on Galina's neck. I can see that she's scared, but she lets go of her fear and marches over with the leash in hand.

"You whore!" Galina screams, spitting in Vera's face. But with spittle running down her cheek, Vera attaches the leash to Galina's collar.

"Good girl," I commend Vera, letting Galina go.

She tries to make a run for it, but Vera pulls the leash, jarring Galina back two steps.

"Bad bitch, stay." Vera's revenge is within reach, and it's a potent aphrodisiac for those who have suffered. This is going to get ugly, and I cannot wait.

Galina glares at me while I reach for a packet of cigarettes on the table. With no hurry, I reposition one of the turned over chairs and take a seat. Lighting the cigarette, I savor the hit when the sharp tobacco floods my lungs.

Blowing a ring of smoke into the air, I lean back and watch Galina be forced to her knees as Vera tugs at the leash.

"You're a traitor. Bastard." Galina spits at my feet.

"A traitor? That would mean there was some sense of loyalty between us all, and clearly, there is not. I have no loyalty toward anyone because all of you, every single one of you, are dead. Russia is about to get a much-needed facelift."

"Wh-what does that mean?"

"It means, I'm going to destroy every single motherfucker who ever doubted me. It means your death won't be mourned; it'll just be another in a long line of victims. You'll be forgotten because the fate that awaits others will make your death look so mediocre."

Her eyes widen because her vanity is bruised. If she is going to die, she wants to at least be celebrated and remembered. But I'm going to take that away from her, and that's worse than death. Fading into nothingness, like you never existed, is the ultimate fuck you to any narcissist.

"No," Galina says, shaking her head. "I'll do anything you

want. Please."

Smoking my cigarette, I savor her pleas because each one brings me closer to avenging my little girl, and all the little girls and boys whose lives are destroyed because of Galina.

"You have absolutely nothing I want."

Galina knows no amount of pleading is going to change my mind, which is why she springs into action and dives over the railing. The problem with that escape route is that Vera is still holding the leash.

Vera doesn't scream when her body jars forward two feet with the weight of Galina hanging off the end of the leash. She looks at me, and with a slow nod, I give her permission to take back her life by ending the one of her oppressor.

Vera wraps the leash around her hand to get a better grip, and with a sharp yank, we both hear the snap of Galina's neck. I hum, tipping my face to the heavens. Justice has been served.

Once I finish smoking my cigarette, I stub it out in the ashtray and come to a stand. Peering over the balcony, I see Galina dangling over the edge, swaying from side to side. The sight is hypnotic, like a morbid pendulum, singing to my depraved soul.

"Should we hide the body?" Vera asks, suddenly appearing nervous.

"Whatever for?"

She watches me with wide eyes as I casually take the leash from her hands. Galina is like a dangling yoyo, hanging off my string. But there is no winding her back up. I loop the end off the railing, securing it tight. This will ensure Galina is displayed for all of Tura to see.

"What do I do now?" Vera asks, rubbing her arms, afraid.

"You pack, take all of Galina's valuables, and get the hell away from Tura."

I wish I could offer her sanctuary, but I don't know where I'll be come this time tomorrow.

Pocketing the cigarettes, I turn to leave, but Vera grips my bicep. "My name is…Yana." It's a name I'm certain she hasn't spoken for years. "Thank you for saving me."

Cupping her face, I smile. "You saved yourself."

She nods, tears streaming down her cheeks.

She begins unbuttoning my shirt, but I shake my head. "Keep it."

I leave Yana to pack her things while I leave this hellhole behind.

As I step outside, I glance overhead and see Galina's limp body hanging off the balcony. It's equivalent to tribes leaving the heads of the enemies at their front gates. This is a warning—do not pass here, but in this case, this message is a little different.

This means war.

I hear a branch snap in the distance. Turning in a slow circle, I scope out my surroundings, but the coast is clear.

Whistling happily, I make my way to the Ramonas—the couple Sascha is currently working for. It makes no sense why they would need a bodyguard on Tura, which has me guessing Mrs. Ramona needs Sascha for something else.

No guessing what.

As expected, Sascha is out front of the Villa, smoking casually. He'll only be permitted inside when Tony Ramona passes out from one too many vinos. When he sees me, he arches a brow, as we didn't make any plans to meet after I called on Galina.

Before he has a chance to react, I march straight up to him and punch him in the face. This results in him inhaling his cigarette.

As he clutches at his throat, which is most likely on fire, I walk him toward the wall and pin him to it. He tries to buck me off, which has me kneeing him in the balls. When he buckles forward, I press my forearm over his throat, shoving him back against the wall.

"Listen to me, you son of a bitch. My war isn't with you. It's with the people you protect. I want the names of every asshole who defied me. I want to know who plans to challenge me. Oh,"—I pause, as if in thought—"I want to know who's fucking who. Who's planning on backstabbing who. I want to know all their dirty secrets."

Sascha tries to buck me off, but he doesn't stand a chance.

"Why would I help you? Traitor," he wheezes, his face red.

"Again with this word," I mock, pressing down harder on his throat. "If I actually cared what you people thought, I'd be offended. But I'm not. So, you're going to give me what I want."

"And if I don't?"

Tonguing my cheek, I shake my head, amused. "That wasn't a rhetorical question. It was literal because if you don't, I'm sure Christian would be very interested to know you're the father of a cute little baby girl. And so would the man who thinks she's his biological daughter."

"долбоёб! блять!"

So it is true.

Rumor has it that Sascha fell in love with one of his clients and got her pregnant. With his chiseled looks and broody personality, it's been rumored many women have tried to tame the beast. His client of course pretended the child was her husband's, but Sascha clearly would do anything to protect his child. He gains a sliver of my respect.

I have forgotten who the family is, but they're not a threat to me. They're merely a stepping-stone to what I want. But Sascha doesn't know that, which is why he sags in defeat.

"Fine. I'll tell you what you want. But promise me you won't touch my daughter. I didn't know what Christian did until a few days ago. He makes me sick."

"You have my word."

This may be the biggest mistake of my life, but I eventually loosen my hold and let Sascha go.

He gasps for air, and even though he could fight me, as it would be a fair fight, he doesn't. A part of me wonders if he's relieved to get back at the assholes who only tolerate him because of his ability to kill a man with his bare hands.

"Come, tell me everything as we make our way to the docks."

"Why are we going there?" he asks but follows as I lead the way.

"Because we're going to play battleship."

CHAPTER SIXTEEN

Alek

"Thank you for coming to me with this information, Aleksei."

Nodding, I play coy because I didn't tell Egor Blum that his best friend and colleague of ten years was out for his blood for his benefit. But he can't know that.

Thanks to Sascha, I now know all the dirty little secrets of the men and women who picked the wrong team. If they hadn't sided with Serg, none of this would be necessary. They all think *I'm* the traitor, but where was their loyalty to me?

They jumped ship when they thought I was finished, not bothering to take into account everything I had done for them and for Russia, so now, they will pay with their lives for their treachery.

Egor deals in stolen artwork, and when his friend disagreed with who they sold their latest haul to, things turned ugly. Egor was ignorant of this fact, as he was oblivious that his baby daughter, who just turned eighteen, is fucking his best friend behind his back.

He now is privy to both bits of information.

It's all such a tangled web with unnecessary drama. But their spectacle is my gain.

"If you'll excuse me," Egor says, eager to close the door in my face so he can deal with this situation accordingly. "I have some business to attend to."

"Of course," I reply. "Please don't tell anyone where you got this information from. It was entrusted to me, but I wanted to tell you as you have a right to know."

"Your secret is safe with me."

Oh, the irony of that comment has me biting back a smile because everyone's secrets are not safe with me.

I leave Egor to stew over what I just shared and mentally tick off life number six, which I've just destroyed. I've paid a visit to my former associates, dealing out juicy scandals, which will surely end in bloodshed in a few short hours.

I can't wait.

I left Sascha to disable most of the yachts, so no one can make a quick escape. They're all stuck here, forced to either fight or die. I hope the majority choose the latter.

With the first half of my plan set in motion, I make my way back to Christian's villa. It's late, but when I see the light in Christian's office flickering brightly, I smile.

It's time.

Most wouldn't feel this level of excitement at bathing in their enemies' blood, but when I think of Irina and what may have been done to her, I walk toward the carnage with open arms.

I'm not quiet as I enter the villa, marching up the stairs to see Ella first. Her door opens, and when she sees me, she comes running down the hallway, throwing herself in my arms.

"Oh, thank god," she exclaims, wrapping her arms around me. "I was so worried. Are you all right?"

Rubbing her back, I inhale deeply, her scent pacifying the demons within. "I'm fine. Are you okay?"

She nods, which has me sighing in relief.

"What happened to Galina? And where is your shirt?"

"She is where she belongs…hanging off the end of a dog leash from her villa balcony," I reply with no emotion. "And I gave my shirt to the young lady Galina was holding hostage."

Ella slowly pulls out of our embrace, looking at me. "Did you find out anything about Irina?"

"Not from her, but I will. I know where Christian keeps his books, but there is something I need to do first."

Reaching into my pocket, I give Ella the crumpled piece of paper with the names of the children Galina sold into slavery. I will do everything in my power to track them down.

Ella doesn't ask questions and places it into her back pocket.

"Would you like to come?" I ask because even though I'd much prefer she stays locked in her room, she is a part of this too. This is her revenge as much as it is mine.

She works her bottom lip before nodding.

I quickly go into my bedroom to slip on a shirt.

I don't need to explain that things are about to get bloody because she knows. So, I offer her my hand, which she accepts, and we walk toward Christian's office. There is no hurry to our step. We will approach this with a level head because, for once, we have the upper hand.

I only hope it stays this way.

Christian's door is open, but I knock regardless, wanting to announce our arrival.

He peers up from his paperwork, smiling when he sees us. His arrogance really knows no bounds. "Come in. I was going to check on you and see how things went with Galina."

We enter his office, and both take a seat in front of his large desk.

Discreetly taking a look around, I scoff when I see the walls are decorated with the heads of his hunting kills. A trophy room full of pain. I smile when I see a pointed letter opener within reach.

"Galina needed a breather," I say, meaning that in the literal sense, but too bad for her that luxury is no longer available to her because she's dead.

Of course, Christian interprets that as something sordid, but he'll soon find out what I actually mean.

"Saint called. He'll be arriving soon," I reveal.

Ella shifts beside me but doesn't say a word.

"Excellent. I'm so pleased we could come to an arrangement which benefits us both. So, I've been dying to ask, how long have you two—" Christian gestures with his pointer finger between the two of us.

"For a while," I vaguely reply. I want this bastard to know what Ella felt for Frank was staged. She wouldn't ever be a Macrillo of her own accord.

"Is that why you killed Frank?" he frankly directs his question to Ella.

"No," she bluntly replies. "I killed him because he deserved it."

Christian doesn't hide his surprise at Ella's blunt response. "Fair enough. He always knew how to push one's buttons. I thought it was because a better offer came along."

And this is why this asshole needs to die.

I can't sit here a moment longer and pretend. "I wanted to ask you a question."

Christian nods.

"Where do you get the children from?"

Christian leans back in his leather seat, examining me closely. "Why do you want to know?"

"Call me curious," I reply with a non-committal shrug.

Christian opens his drawer and produces a gold cigar case. He opens it up and offers me one over the desk. I accept as blood, and a Cuban cigar is a marriage I adore. I light the end and slide the box of matches back to him.

We sit quietly, smoking our cigars, but an undercurrent is lapping the surface, ready to drown us all.

"I know what you're thinking, but I don't kidnap them. They're sold to me by their families. As I see it, if they don't come into my possession, they'll end up dead anyway."

They'd be better off dead than to be sold into slavery.

"Do you ever get…returns?" I have no idea what the proper term is, and phrasing it this way makes me sick.

Christian nods. "Sometimes."

"And what happens to those kids?"

"I don't know. I have a strict no-return policy," he quips as though we're talking about a Christmas sweater. "With all these questions, I can't help but think you want in. I know kidnapping older persons is more your thing, but I'd be happy to teach you what I know."

My stomach roils in disgust because he's right—a lifetime ago, I *did* kidnap women, forcing them to submit. It's what I did to Willow. But now, even talking about this makes me want to vomit. It makes what I have to do all the more imperative, not only for the children but for myself as well.

Ella comforts me, placing her hand on my thigh. She reads my inner turmoil. But I don't deserve her consolation.

Coming to a stand, I place my cigar between my lips and reach into my back pocket for my wallet. Opening it up, I can't help but smile when Irina's picture stares back at me. Running my finger over her cheeky smile, I silently promise I'm about to make things right.

"I don't wish to go into business with you, Christian."

This gets his attention.

"I want to show you something."

Digging out Irina's picture, I pass it to Christian. His desk is the only barricade between us. He accepts the photo warily, looking at it. I look for any signs of recognition, but I don't see any.

"That's my daughter," I reveal. "Her name is Irina."

"Congratulations," Christian says, confused as to why I'm sharing this piece of personal information with him. "I didn't know you were a father."

"Not many do. And there's a reason for that. You see, Irina

means everything to me, and that means she is leverage for any lowlife who wanted to gain an advantage over me. Serg learned the hard way what happens when you hurt the people I love."

Ella's steady breathing gives me the strength to continue.

"Irina isn't my biological daughter," I expose, resting my hands on the edge of the desk. "I adopted her when she was left at the orphanage, emaciated, riddled with lice, and practically nonverbal.

"Someone dumped her like an unwanted dog, making her someone else's problem."

Christian shifts in his chair. I watch for any signs that he's reaching for a weapon or pressing an alarm button to call for help. So far, so good.

"The thing is, when I stole Rodrigo's yacht after I drugged his girlfriend and found those three little children you ordered Rodrigo to deliver to Tura, I couldn't help but compare their state to Irina's."

Christian rests his cigar in the ashtray, realizing that in roughly a minute he'll need both hands. He never asked where Rodrigo was. Rookie move on his behalf.

"You see, I can't find any background information on Irina. And I know the odds are slim, but I can't shake the feeling that you've got something to do with that. So take a closer look at that picture and tell me if she looks familiar or not."

Christian does as I demand.

After a few seconds, he dismissively tosses the photo onto the desk. "Nope," he says, popping the P. "There is nothing special about her. She's a dime a dozen. Sorry."

Inhaling deeply, I turn to Ella and pass her my cigar for safekeeping as I won't waste a good Cuban on this piece of shit. Before Christian has a chance to react, I reach for the letter opener, dive across the desk, and drive the sharpened end into his left shoulder, pinning him to the chair.

He howls in agony, desperately trying to pull out the letter opener. But I don't give him a chance.

Springing to my feet, I round the desk, come up behind Christian's chair and kick it forward so he's wedged between the desk and the chair. I grip the back of his head and slam it onto the desk. His arm is still pinned to the chair, so he either shifts to give himself some slack, or he can become a contortionist.

He slumps forward, which results in the letter opener tearing through flesh.

"How about you take a closer look?" I suggest, snaring his hair and turning his head to look at Irina's picture once again.

"I don't know her, *stronzo!*" he shouts, spittle running down his chin as I can imagine a letter opener wedged in one's shoulder would be awfully painful. "They all look the same!"

"скотина, they are *not* the same. Each life you destroy belongs to someone who could be anything. Their whole life is ahead of them, but you ruin any chance they have at deciding what their future holds. You force them into a life which no child should ever experience.

"You don't know what it's like to have to fend for yourself. You were born with a silver spoon so far up your ass that it's made you think you're invincible. But guess what, you're not."

I slam his head onto the desk once, twice, before letting him go. He slumps onto the desk, slouched in a pool of blood and saliva. His discarded cigar lays a few inches away.

"Whether you know her or not, your fate has been decided. I know where you hide your secrets. Galina told me."

Christian turns his neck to look at me. I relish seeing his nose is broken—again. "Take what you want. If you're right, then you'll find everything you need in those records. I won't bother you again. I'll forget you and Ella were ever here."

I pick up his burning cigar and examine it between my fingers. "Oh, you pathetic дурак. I was planning on taking that anyway. That's not what I want from you."

Ella is incredibly silent, watching on as her beau beats the shit out of a vile human being. I wonder what she'll think of me once my grand plan is revealed.

"What do you want?" Christian screams, helpless, afraid, just how every child he exploited felt. "You want more money? Is that it? We can renegotiate terms. Split, sixty, forty. You need me, Popov! You need another distributor. Who else will sell to you?"

And he's right. I do need someone, but it won't be him.

I help myself to Christian's cell, lifting his head so I can scan his face to unlock his phone. Siri still recognizes him with a broken nose, it seems. Once it's unlocked, I scroll through his contacts and commence my descent into hell.

Vincenzo answers the FaceTime call, expecting his son to be on the other end, so you can imagine his surprise when he sees my face.

"Aleksei?" he says, switching on the light so I can see him

better. "I didn't realize you were visiting with Christian."

"It was an impromptu visit, Vinnie. Can I call you Vinnie?"

His nostrils flare, but he nods. "Where is Christian? Is everything all right?"

"No, Vinnie," I reply, cigar still in hand. "Everything is far from all right. Your son is a double-crossing asshole. Do you know he put forth a proposition to me, offering to supply me all the drugs I want while cutting you and Fausto out of the deal?"

"He lies, *Papa!*" Christian screams.

"Christian?" Vincenzo says, leaning closer to the phone, in hopes of seeing his son. I decide to give him his wish.

Flipping the screen around, I give Vincenzo a clear view of his son, impaled to the chair. If he had any pride, he'd pull the letter opener out and free himself. Yes, it'll hurt like a bitch, but at least he'd be free to fight me.

Yet here he is, pathetically crying for his *papa*.

"Christian! What did he do to you?"

Before he has a chance to answer, I walk over to Christian and press the burning cigar into his cheek. His screams are music to my ears.

Vincenzo can see it all.

"Am I lying, Christian?" I ask, forcing the cigar deeper into his burning flesh.

"Okay!" he cries, raising his hand in surrender. "It's true, *Papa*. I'm sorry."

The cigar has burned through his flesh, so I casually remove it and slowly stub it out in the ashtray.

Flipping the screen back around so Vincenzo can see my

face, I smile. "You didn't teach your son any manners. Shame on you. A parent is the most important role model a child has. So I dare say, you're in part to blame for your son being a sick son of a bitch."

"What do you want?" Vincenzo asks, understanding there is a reason for my call.

"Let's make this a family affair," I suggest, scrolling through the contacts to find Fausto's number.

I add him to the conversation, and when he sees me, he knows something is awfully wrong.

"I hope I didn't disturb you," I quip to Fausto, who is in blue and white striped pajamas. "I won't be long."

"What's going on, Vincenzo?"

I answer for him. "What's going on is that your nephew had a little side project you two were unaware of. He is selling young children to any sick asshole for the right price. And he is making quite a lot of money doing so. As you see, I cannot allow that to happen.

"My daughter's childhood is unknown, and I fear your son may have had a hand in that. He must be made an example of; all of the motherfuckers who defied me do."

Their horrified faces prove Christian was telling the truth. They had no part in the exploitation of god knows how many children.

"Let me talk to my nephew," Fausto orders.

With a shrug, I flip the screen around, and when Fausto sees what's become of Christian, he gasps, but soon pulls it together. "Is this true?"

Christian turns his cheek to look at the phone.

With pathetic puppy dog eyes, he nods. "Yes, Zio. Forgive me."

Fausto is clearly disgusted. "How could you, *bastardo*? You've brought shame to this family! If this gets out…we will be ruined!"

Vincenzo places a hand over his mouth, torn between duty and loyalty. If this were anyone else, they'd kill them. Christian betrayed them in the worst possible way and has shamed the family name. It takes a special kind of sociopath to deal in child trafficking.

"Your nephew was also planning on stealing from you and selling to me. It was to be our little secret," I say, placing my pointer over my lips.

"Vincenzo!" Fausto shouts. "This cannot be left unpunished."

"I know," he replies, his pain palpable. "But he's my son."

"You have two others," I reply casually.

"What do you want? Tell us."

Looking at both men on the screen, I smirk. "I want your drugs. You're going to deal to me at cost. We're not going to see or talk to one another. Our exchange will be made monthly, but as far as associating with you, we don't know one another."

"And what do we get in return?" Fausto asks.

"My silence, of course. I won't tell everyone what Christian was doing and you save face. I don't think your Sicilian colleagues would be too pleased to know your family was dealing in child trafficking."

Family is everything to Sicilians. They are ruthless, but when it comes to family, you don't fuck with them. So the knowledge that Christian is selling kids would have every Sicilian out for his blood.

Christian's greed could bring down their empire, and I know what that feels like firsthand. No man would ever want that to befall them.

"And what about Christian?" Vincenzo asks, peering at his son, who lay prone and broken.

"What about him?"

"What will become of him?"

Fausto looks at his nephew with nothing but disgust. Vincenzo, however, hopes I will be merciful. But I will not.

"I'm at Tura. You may come fetch him."

Vincenzo's relief is apparent, but when I say fetch him…I mean fetch his corpse.

Before they can ask further questions, I hand the phone to Ella. "You may want to look away, красавица."

With shaky hands, she focuses the phone on Christian but doesn't turn her head. We're in this together.

Gripping Christian's hair, I yank his head back at a painful angle, forcing him to look at me. "You are the vilest creature I have ever met, and trust me, I've met a lot of sickos in my lifetime."

I yank out the letter opener from his shoulder, curling my lip in disgust when he begins to cry like a baby. He slumps onto the desk, blood spurting from the wound. But I don't give him time to rest. Hauling him to his feet by the collar of his shirt, I walk him backward, anger fueling my every step.

This is for every child he sold. Every child whose life has been ruined because of his greed.

"Please, no!" he begs, but he made his choice. It's time he dealt with the repercussions.

He fights with all that he has, but it's not enough. I won't give him the luxury of having any last words. He doesn't deserve it. With a roar, I lift him high and impale him on the horns of the antelope trophy he has hanging above the fireplace.

Blood coats my face and chest—warpaint I wear with pride.

His eyes widen as his body responds to the shock of him being his own trophy. He won't die right away. I've done this with intent. I've positioned him so that he'll eventually bleed out. I could have gone for a kill shot, but that's far too merciful for scum like him.

I stand before him, watching as he takes labored breaths, feeling the horns sticking out of his body. He is fighting to stay alive. The blood seeping from the two puncture wounds in his abdomen has me smirking because no matter how hard he fights, it's all in vain.

I don't know what Vincenzo and Fausto intend to do, but I will keep my word if they do. I won't divulge what a deranged man Christian was, saving face for their family as long as they supply my drugs. I know this is contradictory, as most would step back from this world and start afresh.

But I cannot.

This is me, and I will lie, cheat, blackmail, and kill whoever I need to in order to regain my throne for good.

Blood trickles from the corner of his mouth and splashes onto the white carpet. Visually, this picture is worth millions.

While Christian is still conscious, I say, "Every person who dealt with you will suffer the same fate. I will ensure they know why I deliver them death. The Macrillo name will be cursed over and over again."

I know how superstitious Sicilians are. I can imagine Fausto and Vincenzo crossing themselves as we speak.

"You ruined your family. I want you to take that piece of information with you when you fall at the burning gates of hell. Your father and uncle will now have to pay the price for your greed for the rest of their lives."

Tears roll down Christian's cheeks, and I spit, repelled by his cowardliness. He wanted to play a big man's game when, in reality, he is just a little boy.

"Just so you know," I whisper as I don't want Vincenzo or Fausto to hear. "Your uncle Santo is going to suffer the same fate as you. You didn't want him here, but soon, he will be privy to everything that you've done."

His chin lolls to his chest, bloody spittle drip, drip, dripping onto the carpet. His breathing becomes irregular with long pauses between breaths until they eventually stop.

He's dead.

"That's for every life you've destroyed. And that's for Saint. I would never allow you to touch him, you disgusting Мудак."

This décor just became my favorite I've seen in a while.

Turning around, I face Ella, who is sitting still, her eyes wide. I walk with measured steps toward her, extending my hand, asking for the phone and cigar. She gives them to me without a word.

I wish she didn't have to see this side of me, but I can't

stop it. This violence fuels me in ways I cannot describe. If she wants me, then she needs to see the good, the bad, and the murderous sides because I won't stop now that I've fallen in love.

Looking at Vincenzo and Fausto, I take a drag of my cigar, humming in happiness. "I'll see you soon." And I end the call.

Ella's emotions are running rampant. I can see them imprinted all over her face. But what I do next will shock her like never before.

There is one person I have left to call.

Scrolling through the contacts, I inhale deeply and stop on the letter S. Without hesitation, I FaceTime the person who is about to end it all.

"Aleksei?" Santo says, stunned I have Christian's phone and am covered in blood.

Just seeing his face has every inch of my body ready to fight.

Ella covers her mouth with both hands, squeezing her eyes shut. I know this hurts, but I need this to be done.

"Let us not bother with pleasantries," I reply, blowing out a ring of smoke before stubbing out the cigar. "Word has it you've been looking for me."

"Yes. I have. You have something which belongs to me. I want it back."

Clucking my tongue, I shake my head. "*She* never belonged to anyone," I state, as I won't stand by and allow Santo to refer to Ella as a thing. "*She* chose me. She's always chosen me."

"That *puttana* killed Frank!" he screams, spittle flying

from his mouth. "She is going to pay for the harm she's caused this family."

"Call her a slut again and see what happens," I threaten, eyeing him wickedly. "And this is what I think of your family."

Flipping the screen view around, I allow Santo to see his nephew, impaled on the wall.

He squints to see who it is but soon realizes it's Christian. "*Oh, mio dio,*" he cries, crossing himself. "Fausto and Vincenzo are going to kill you."

Laughing, I reply, "They will do no such thing. They bore witness to this piece of shit's death. They're coming here to collect his body."

"You're lying," Santo spits, refusing to believe my blood won't be spilled for this crime.

"I guess there's only one way to find out. You want me… come and get me," I challenge, nodding at Ella that it'll be all right. "I know what you did to Ella, and I am going to kill you so…fucking…slow."

Santo grins. Challenge accepted. "She loved it. She loved the feel of a real man."

Clenching my teeth, I refuse to take the bait. I need a level head to beat this bastard at his own game. He doesn't know what I have in store for him.

"C'mon then, big man, come and get me. I'm at Tura…we both are." I hang up, bowing my head. I'm going to explode.

The phone crunches in my palm as I clench it so tightly, it almost snaps in half.

I need a minute. I can't be near Ella or anyone, for that matter, so I exit the room and walk toward the kitchen.

Switching on the light, I see a collection of cookbooks stacked neatly by the microwave. Functioning on autopilot, I run my finger along the spines of each one and stop when I come to the first Italian cookbook.

Pulling it out, I take a breath, unsure what I'm about to find. Recipes on how to make tiramisu and lasagna are not what I was expecting. Flicking through the pages, it all looks legit, so I toss it over my shoulder and move on to the next and the next.

Once I have looked through all the cookbooks to no avail, I sigh, needing to think like the rat Christian, and when I see an old farmhouse scale on a shelf with two cookbooks stacked on top, I scoff, disgusted. To anyone else, they may appreciate Christian's flair for decorating, but I know better.

Walking over to the shelf, I reach for the top cookbook that specializes in Italian delicacies and open it to the first page. Where there should be recipes for home cooking, there is instead a list of names, ages, addresses, and dollar signs.

I flip through the pages, feeling bile rise the further I progress.

The second book is titled *How to Cook an Italian Feast* and has the same information. Pages upon pages of lives destroyed.

These cookbooks were printed on purpose to house the sick atrocities Christian committed. The titles are not coincidental and neither was their placement. They're sitting on scales because that's how Christian sees his victims— pieces of meat he can sell to the highest bidder.

I want to kill him all over again.

Slamming the cookbooks shut, I hunt through the freezer for a bottle of vodka and make my way toward my bedroom. My steps are heavy as I know the answer to Irina's past may be within these pages. But am I ready to uncover what happened to my baby girl?

Ella sits on the end of my bed, and when I enter, she averts her eyes.

I know I may have done irreparable damage to our relationship.

"Did you find what you're looking for?" she asks in merely a whisper.

"I did," I reply, placing the cookbooks onto the dresser. "Are you…disgusted by me?"

She slowly lifts her chin. "No."

"Afraid?"

She blinks once. "Yes."

I know my methods are ruthless, but I'll never tame my ways. I kill with purpose, and I won't stop, especially now.

I watch as she reaches into her pocket and produces an envelope, one which looks all too familiar. She opens it and unfolds a piece of paper, one which was folded with care and love—I know because I was the one who folded it.

She takes a deep breath before she commences to dance in a past which will never be forgotten. "Ella, I know you hate me, and that's okay. No one can hate me more than I do myself. I wish things were different. I wish I could give you everything you deserve, but I can't. I'm not the hero in your story. But nor am I the villain. I just am me…which is why I had to let you go.

"I don't make excuses for what I've done because all I wanted to do was to keep you safe. You were the breath of fresh air I was searching for my entire life. You helped me heal, something which I thought was impossible. But meeting you proved that anything is possible."

She licks her lips, her hands shaking as she continues to read.

"I can't leave this earth knowing you'll never know the truth. I want you to know you meant something to me. I'm not asking for forgiveness; I merely wish things were different, and if they were, please know that I'd never have let you leave.

"I'd have done anything in my power to earn your trust and love because when I thought of my future, all I saw was you. You make me want to be a better man, a better man for you.

"I never meant anything with Willow. I knew if I asked you to leave, you wouldn't, so I had to hurt you. I had to make you hate me. And by doing so, you're now free. And that has me embracing death with a smile because all I want is your happiness.

"I don't want this life for you. I don't want it for myself, yet I don't have a choice. But you do. So live for me, красавица. Live your long life, knowing you were loved. And you were loved with every fiber of my being.

"We hurt the ones we love, I understand this now because you, Ella, have done the impossible…you have taught me how to love. And for this, I thank you.

"My soul, my heart is yours…forevermore. Yours eternally, Aleksei."

She ends the letter, sniffing back her torrent of tears. It's clear this is the first time she's read it.

Eventually, she peers up, her beautiful eyes drowning. She turns the envelope over and shows me Willow's handwriting.

"This was entrusted to me. It's now time you read it. Willow," she says, her voice trembling. "I found it tucked away in my bag. Willow put it in there when she packed my bag."

I nod as it doesn't surprise me that Willow would do something like this. She has always seen the good in me, even when I didn't. She knew Ella and I would face hardships, but she was hoping this letter written before all of this occurred would help Ella understand my motives and how much she means to me.

"So it's true?" she asks, her lower lip quivering. "You l-love me like this? You love me as ruthlessly as you kill?"

"Yes." Taking a breath, I offer myself to her. "I…love you. I always have. I'm sorry it's taken me a while to say it."

I'm ashamed as she's far braver than I am when it comes to confessing her feelings. She isn't afraid to be vulnerable, but this is, *was* my worst fear.

She nods, taking a moment to process what I just said. "You want to be a better man, but you're wrong," she says, making my heart drop.

But what she counters with ensures I will worship at her feet eternally.

"You *are* a better man. You always have been. And even though you scare me, even though I know you have a rage you cannot control, that's just a small part of who you are. And I love that part. I love all parts…of you."

She springs up and comes running toward me, jumping into my arms. I catch her, lifting her as she locks her legs around my waist. She slams her mouth over mine, kissing me desperately. I thread my fingers through her soft hair, angling her face so I can dominate every inch of her.

Her tongue circles mine before she bites my bottom lip. She wants it rough.

Suddenly, I remember I'm soiled in another man's blood, and that just won't do.

Still kissing madly, I walk us toward the en suite and lift the hem of Ella's T-shirt, hinting I want it off. Now. She complies, only pulling away long enough to slip it over her head before kissing me once again.

I unhook her bra as she fumbles with the buttons on my shirt. When we're pressed chest to chest, the heat of her body colliding with mine, I realize that this is what true happiness feels like. Being this way with Ella, vulnerable and exposed, was something that used to terrify me but not anymore.

I've never felt freer than I do right now.

She shimmies down my body, and we quickly undress. The moment her underwear hits the floor, I'm pushing her into the shower, allowing the rainfall of water to shower us both. I'm already hard, and when she takes my cock into her hands and begins to stroke up and down, I groan, incredulous to how good it feels.

I've been with hundreds of women, but none of them has ever felt like Ella. She is soft, hard, tender, rough—she is everything gift wrapped in this perfect package solely for me.

Our kisses are passion-filled, but as always, behind the

yearning is untainted love. She continues to work my shaft while I slip two fingers into her wet sex. She moans around my tongue, sucking it into her mouth.

Her strokes are perfect, and if she continues touching me this way, I'm going to come within seconds. So, spinning her around, I press her chest to the glass shower wall, grip the back of her neck, and sink into her sex with urgency.

When she gasps, I pause, allowing her muscles to adjust to my size.

"Are you okay, красавица?"

"Yes," she replies breathlessly. "Fuck me, and fuck me hard."

Her filthy mouth will be the death of me.

Giving her what we both want, I begin to pump my hips, my thrusts not gentle because this passion burns us to the core. I hit her deep, which has her spasming around my cock and standing on her toes to deepen the angle.

She bounces back on my length, taking everything I give as she begs for more. I spread an ass cheek so I can see where we join. I'm mesmerized by our coupling. With my thumb, I gently rub over her puckered entrance, not sure if anal play is something she likes.

She gasps and freezes, which has me retreating my thumb instantly.

With each thrust, her body slams up against the glass. She splays her hands on the screen, rolling her hips so she can feel every hard inch of me. When she arches her back, spreads her legs, and clenches her muscles—holy mother of god—my orgasm comes out of nowhere.

Pulling out, I spill my seed all over her lower back with a roar.

Ella is about to turn around, but there is no way my woman is leaving this shower without coming.

Rounding her hip, I begin to play with her swollen clitoris. The moans leaving her are animalistic, and I love it. I love that when I touch her, I provide pleasure and not pain. But what she says next has me realizing that for Ella, the line is sometimes blurred.

"Spank me," she orders breathlessly. "I want it."

My cock twitches and is given a new lease on life.

Turning off the water, I lead Ella from the shower, ripping a towel from the rack and drying her off quickly. Once I do the same to myself, we walk into the bedroom, both naked, both hungry for this.

Looking into her eyes, I want her to see the love I feel. I want her to know she's safe because this play is about to turn rough.

"On your hands and knees," I order, cupping her chin and brushing my thumb over her pouty bottom lip.

I like that she doesn't jump to command. She takes her time, making me wait. But it's so worth it because when she drops to all fours, I take a moment to appreciate this utter perfection before me. Her ass is peach-shaped, and all I want to do is take a bite.

Coming up behind her, I cup her rounded cheek and squeeze gently.

"Not with your hands," she says. "Your belt."

She senses my hesitation and looks over her shoulder.

"Please."

Unable to say no to her, I reach for my belt off the floor and tug it tightly between my hands. It snaps sharply, which has Ella's flesh prickling with goose pimples. She wants this, so who am I to deny her.

With one quick slap, I draw the belt across her ass. It leaves a red lash in its wake. The sight sings to the depraved fiend inside me, and I do it again. She buckles forward but then springs back, demanding more.

Each lash of my belt has her whimpering and writhing, always coming back to be struck again. I'm holding back, as I don't want to hurt her, but I gently kick her legs apart, coaxing her to open wider for me.

She does as I want, and when I see her inflamed pink pussy, I hum in utter delight. The light exposes her slickness.

"You know when you touched me …"

"You're going to have to be a little more specific. I've touched you everywhere, красавица," I reply cockily as I admire her pretty pink ass.

"Not everywhere," she counters. "I've never…never done that there."

"That's okay," I assure her. I don't want her doing anything she's not comfortable with. But I've misread this entire conversation.

"No, what I meant was, I want to do *that*…with you."

"Oh," I reply, almost swallowing my tongue. "Now?"

"Yes…please."

Jesus Christ. How did I get so lucky? But anal sex isn't a smooth ride. I know it can hurt, especially the first time. But it's something I enjoy immensely, and with Ella, I think it'll be a whole different experience altogether.

So with one last lash of my belt, I strike Ella in a way that caresses her clitoris. She needs to be on the pinnacle of losing control before I go near her ass.

Dropping the belt, I cup her chin and draw her face toward me, over her shoulder so I can kiss the hell out of her. She is breathless, her body quivering beneath me, which is a good start.

"Get on the bed," I order from around her wet mouth.

She seems confused, but there is no way I'm rutting into her like some sex-starved dog. I want this experience to be as comfortable for her as possible.

Lifting her, I carry her toward the bed, but this isn't going to be hearts and roses. I toss her onto the mattress, growling when her breasts bounce from the force. I crawl up the foot of the bed as she scampers away on her elbows to rest on the pillows.

Once she's on her back, I sit on my heels and take a minute to examine this woman who stole my breath the moment I met her. Her loyalty and her strength are unlike anything I've ever experienced before, and to have her affections makes me the luckiest man alive.

I don't deserve her, but I want her, so I will ensure I become the best man I can for us both.

She blushes and turns her cheek, embarrassed by the way I'm staring at her. But she has nothing to be embarrassed about. She is a goddess and deserves to be worshiped by all.

I lower my body onto hers, loving the way we fit. Kissing

her gently, I run a hand down her chest, cupping a breast and running my thumb over her pearled nipple. She moans, as I know she enjoys her breasts being played with.

So I continue kneading her while I walk my fingers toward her sex. She's so wet that my two fingers slip in with ease. I begin thrusting deeply, before circling, wishing to stretch her wide. She whimpers, cupping her hand over mine, and encouraging me to go faster.

Her wish is my command.

Her muscles are stretched wide, and I know she wants to come, but I permit her from doing so. I slowly draw back and roll off her.

"Turn onto your side."

She does as I ask, her breathing suddenly accelerated.

Shuffling up behind her, I make sure she can feel my erection. If she wants me to stop, this is the time to tell me. In response, she scoots backward, pressing her ass against me.

Reaching around her hip, I run two fingers along her entrance but don't penetrate. I just want her to feel every part of me before we commence. She whimpers, bowing back, a silent invitation that she's ready. So I continue touching her pussy, gathering her honey onto my fingers.

She wants more, gasping each time I touch her, which is good. I need her wild with need. My fingers are coated in her arousal, which I then rub over her back entrance. She freezes.

"Relax, красавица," I whisper, biting the shell of her ear.

She loosens up a little, but this won't work with her so rigid.

Cupping her breast as I massage her ass, I whisper to her

in Russian.

She moans, finally letting go so I can slip the tip of my finger into her ass.

"Wh-what did you say?" she whimpers.

"I said, you're beautiful," I reply, circling her areola as I slowly glide my finger into her. Once I'm half a finger in, I continue. "And that you feel so good."

"Oh, god," she moans, slowly arching her back to take me in deeper.

I work my finger in gradually until I hit home.

Ella clenches her muscles, but when I kiss her neck and return to touching her sex, she relaxes, allowing me to possess every part of her. She begins to leisurely bounce back on my finger, gathering momentum as I stretch her wide enough for my cock to replace my finger.

When I turn my finger, she cries out but doesn't retreat. She allows me to prepare her because if I don't get inside her within the next few seconds, I'm going to explode.

Removing my fingers from both entrances, I place my hand that was cupping her pussy seconds ago in front of her mouth.

"Spit," I command.

She does.

I then coat the tip of my cock and her behind. "And lastly, I said…" I slowly inch myself into her entrance, waiting for her muscles to slacken.

When they do, I continue. "I want you on my cock."

"Oh my god," she pants as I grip her hip and guide her back onto my cock as I slide into her ass.

Once fully sheathed, I stop, bowing my head as I need to take a breather. This feels incredible. "Is this okay?"

Hardly articulate, but I can't focus on anything other than Ella.

She nods with a whimper.

"Can I move?"

Again, she nods.

With a hand resting on her hip, I begin to move inside her, closing my eyes in utter ecstasy because this is a first for us both. It's never felt this way with anyone before. Every part of her clings to me, drawing me into her very core.

Her movements are stilted at first as though she's trying to find a rhythm, but she soon learns what feels good and rocks against me. I play with her swollen clitoris, matching the tempo to my thrusts, and before long, this becomes Ella's show.

She shifts her hips, allowing me to slide in and out, in and out, and before long, we are moving passionately. Gone are the hesitant movements as Ella meets me thrust for thrust. She writhes as I circle her clitoris.

"You're everywhere," she pants. "And I love it. I love you."

"I love you," I groan into her ear, biting along the column of her neck.

She moves her legs, deepening the angle, and when I hit her hard, she cries out, spasming around my fingers and cock as she comes. I don't let up, however. I continue pumping my hips, loving the way her snug ass fits around me.

I never want to leave.

Humming when I pull out and slam back into her, I guide

her hips, encouraging her to ride me and when she clenches around me, I explode. Biting down on her shoulder, I come inside her, long and hard. My orgasm lasts for what feels like minutes.

When we're both breathless and spent, I gently pull out of her, missing her heat instantly. I'm about to get up and clean her up, but she grips onto me, indicating she wants me close.

I nestle into her back, wrapping my arms around her body, which still vibrates with the aftershocks of our union. I'm suddenly so tired.

As I close my eyes, a faint gunshot can be heard in the distance.

Ella gasps.

I smile.

The war has begun.

CHAPTER SEVENTEEN

Alek

A distant scream has me lifting my head, but I return to reading over Christian's cookbook from hell. So far, I haven't found anything on Irina, but I won't give up.

There are pages upon pages of names, and I make sure to read each one. Even though they aren't Irina, their story deserves to be heard. I can't believe how many children are within these pages.

Ella enters the bedroom with a towel wrapped tightly around her body, a body which I have enjoyed over and over again.

I know chaos awaits me; the screams and gunshots all point to this. My plan seems to have worked better than I had hoped. I wonder how many people have acted because of me. I can't wait to find out.

Saint will be here at any moment, as will Vincenzo and Fausto. Santo shouldn't be too far away either. The end is nigh...

"Anything on Irina?" Ella asks as she gets dressed. She's opted for a white summer dress that emphasizes the golden glow of her skin.

"Nothing yet," I reply with a sigh.

"You may never find out what happened," she softly says, not wanting to upset me. But it's a reality I need to face.

And what I say next surprises me because I actually mean it. "Some things are better not knowing. One day when she's older and ready, she can tell me."

Yes, I want to wreak havoc on every person who hurt Irina, but she's safe and has a loving home. I don't want to conjure up any bad memories because she's been through enough. Once upon a time, all I'd care for is vengeance and bloodshed, but now, all I care about is Irina living a normal, happy life.

This is a big step for me. But Irina's happiness and well-being take precedence over everything.

These other kids, however...I still don't know how to proceed.

Sascha calls me from downstairs. He's proven to be a loyal ally. If he survives, I just may keep him around. "Your friends are about three miles from port."

I told Sascha to keep an eye out for Pavel's yacht, which is named after his wife. They've arrived.

Closing the cookbook, I slip it under the mattress for safekeeping and grab my cane. I'm dressed in black trousers and a white shirt. Very formal as I intend to bring down this island in my Sunday best.

Once Ella is ready, and I have my gun concealed at the

small of my back, I offer her my hand, and we make our way downstairs. Sascha waits for us, and although I blackmailed him, he doesn't seem too upset to be a part of a revolution. He knows that what I'm doing is going to change the world as we know it.

"Dimitri and Walter are dead," he bluntly informs. "It turns out, Anna was sick of them both."

Laughing happily, I mentally cross them off my list. Every person who defied or doubted me is about to face Armageddon. They're going to be forced to pick a side, as there is no way off this island. And when Santo gets here, he is going to try to convince them his side is the only one worth fighting for.

"It's a free-for-all. Your plan has worked. They are destroying one another in fear and paranoia. With no way off this island, they've all gone a little mad."

"That ship has sailed," I reply with irony. "Look after those kids. Guard them until I get back."

Sascha nods and walks toward their bedroom. They've remained in the cupboard, feeling safer, it seems, in smaller spaces. The thought breaks my heart.

As dusk approaches, we walk outside and head for the dock. I pass many villas on the way and gather an audience when I begin to whistle happily. Going into battle has never felt so good. Doors open as curiosity gets the better of most, and they follow us, interested in what's going on.

When we approach the dock, we have a large crowd in pursuit. In times of crisis, it's natural for one to look for a leader, and that is me. These traitorous bastards once sided with my brother and thought I was unfit to fill his shoes.

Now look at them. Groveling for me to save them from themselves.

I don't address them. I don't even look at them. I wait for Pavel, Saint, and Max to disembark. When I see them, especially Saint, I can't help but smile. My family has arrived.

"Well, this isn't at all fucking creepy," Saint says, kissing both of Ella's cheeks hello before offering me his hand.

Shaking it, I smile. "They don't know what to do with themselves. It turns out, they need a leader, after all. Willow and Irina?"

"They're safe," Saint assures me. "We've got men watching them."

Very good.

Pavel and Max carry two large bags over their shoulders. No guessing what's inside. "The rest will be here soon," Pavel says. "What happens to them?"

Pavel looks over my shoulder at the forming crowd.

"What's going on, Popov? We can't get off this island, and I think that has something to do with you."

Saint smirks, folding his arms smugly. He's just as excited as I am.

With a measured pace, I turn around and face these spineless assholes. A lot of these faces were at my party. They still look at me like I'm weak. But they're about to learn the truth.

"Yes, you're right, Flynn," I reply to the man who challenged me. However, I'm glad that he did.

Flynn was Henry's colleague. I refer to their relationship

in the past tense because Henry was the lippy bastard who challenged me the night of my party. He lost his life because of it.

But it seems my display has done nothing to cement my place, which is why most must die.

"I really couldn't have planned this any better."

"Planned what?" asks Tatiana.

I know she was the first woman to offer herself to Serg the moment he stole my throne. Too bad for her.

"I needed all of you together in one place, herded like sheep so I could pick you off. One by one."

Saint laughs behind me.

"None of you know what loyalty is. You were the first to turn your back on me when you believed someone better could rule in my place." I cluck my tongue. "Shame on you."

"So what, you're going to kill us all? Is that it?" Flynn questions, incredulous.

"Not all," I reveal, setting a false sense of security.

"Just the backstabbing assholes, who are"—pretending to count the heads of the masses in front of me—"wow, a lot of you."

"Sucks to be you," Saint counters happily.

"But some of you have already done the job for me. Where is Walter?" I ask sarcastically.

They quickly clue in that I'm the reason Tura has been thrown into turmoil.

"You either form an alliance with me, or you die. The choice is yours. And I mean a real alliance. If I sense any deceit from you—"

I don't get to finish my sentence because Flynn reaches into his pocket and pulls a gun on me. He hesitates, which is his error because Saint's shot him dead within seconds.

Ella jolts but stays close by me.

"If I sense any deceit from you," I casually continue from my last point like a man wasn't just shot dead. "That will happen."

I jut my chin out toward a very dead Flynn.

"Looks like I need a new precious jewels distributor," I add with a staged sigh.

Everyone is afraid, and when their attention is suddenly riveted behind me, I realize my reinforcements have arrived.

They're all mulling over what to do. But there isn't really a choice. They either side with me, or they die. There are three men and women here who will rebel, contrary to what they say, which is why they won't be leaving Tura alive.

Their replacements are on the yachts anyway. Once I replace the main players with my men and women, everyone else can be on their merry way.

"You have to understand why we're apprehensive, Aleksei," says Boris Van Stappen, who owns the main waste management company in Russia.

His business is one I'm most interested in.

"You gave everything up for your mistress. You put Russia at risk for love, and it looks like history is repeating itself." He scowls at Ella. "Serg stepped up when you couldn't. Oscar and Astra were good—"

Boris doesn't have a chance to finish his sentence because he's shot dead by Saint. I knew it was coming. Anyone who thinks Oscar was a good man deserves to die.

The crowd gasps as they soon realize I'm not playing around. There are two others who will soon follow Boris. But I decide to draw that out because I can't go too hard, too early.

There is an abundance of yachts, and when my men and women disembark, chuckles rise from the crowd.

"This is who you wish to replace us with?" mocks Tatiana, laughing. "They are hardly out of diapers. You're embarrassing yourself, Aleksei. You want to reform Russia with a bunch of babies. Good luck with that.

"No one will form an alliance with you. It'll only be a matter of time until—"

"Until you're dead?" I finish for her when she slumps to the ground, thanks to the gunshot wound to her head.

Turning over my shoulder, I see Austin reholster his gun. "Hello, Alek."

"Lovely to see you, Austin," I reply happily, unable to wipe my smile clean.

Three traitors dead in a matter of minutes. If anyone had any doubts about my rulership, then I'm sure they're rethinking their decision to defy me.

Fear is an amazing tool.

My handpicked team stands by my side, a group of misfits who were seen as nothing, but now, they're gods among men. Their loyalty to me will be strong because I have given them power, and the assholes who stand groveling will be loyal because I have taken their power away.

Their fate lies in my hands.

And then something extraordinary happens…Russia

bows at my feet once again.

"The Orloff family pledge our alliance to you."

"As do the Nikitin family."

"So do the Becker family."

One by one, men and women who defied me, who doubted me, bow their heads as they beg for a second chance. The sight is one I will forever remember because finally, *finally*, I have gotten back my crown.

Saint stands beside me. "You did it, Popov. You won."

"There is still one war left I have to win," I reply, reaching for Ella's hand.

Once all have pledged their allegiance to me, I give them permission to pack their things. It's time they left Tura and spread the word to their peers that I spared their life. But I won't be so lenient if I get wind of any rebellion.

They realize their time on top is finished, as they're to be replaced with younger, fresher blood. Those who wish to work with me, I will happily find a place for them in my kingdom. My empire is safe…for now.

I'm not naïve. I will be challenged. But I've given the opponents an inside scoop to what happens when they do. I have an army of loyal, ruthless men and women behind me now because we want the same thing. I once worked solo, but now I don't have to.

Once they return to their villas, I shake the hands of my new colleagues. They are thankful I chose them. But the truth is, we need one another to survive this.

What I've done has never been done before. I've broken tradition. Families who had a say in Russian politics for generations have just been fired. We wait and see how they respond once they get back home, but Tura was a valuable lesson for them.

You can't overthrow a realm, which is what we are. There are more of us than there are of them.

Seven of my leaders stand by me, their excitement palpable. They will do Russia good.

"The mafia is here," Pavel says, which has everyone turning to look at the yacht approaching.

My associates gasp.

"Oh yes, I forgot to mention, we now have the mafia on our side."

Our authority just continues to grow.

As the scared little sheep return, ready to get the hell off Tura, I order my colleagues to escort them onto the yachts and back to Russia. In the end, they didn't need to fight, but being here revealed to the foes I wasn't full of shit.

It also allowed them to see the faces of their new leaders.

I was hoping for more bloodshed, but they surrendered, which is just as good.

As they're herded onto the yachts like cattle, I pull Austin aside. "Feel free to throw Eriks Yahontov overboard. He is the last who I believe will give us problems. The rest, they're too scared to breathe the wrong way at the moment."

"You did it," Austin says. "Once we're back home, the IRA wants to organize a meeting."

"Excellent." I nod, as this ally is one that will benefit me immensely.

With the mafia and IRA in my corner, this only strengthens

my position of power.

"Do you really think there won't be an uprising once the dust settles? Not everyone who opposes us is here."

"Time will tell," I assure Austin. "Word will spread."

Nodding, we all know we must wait and keep our ears peeled. But today has given the traitors something to think about.

As the crowd clears, I'm faced with yet another unpredictable situation. Fausto and Vincenzo.

"Ella, stay behind Saint and me," I order.

Believe it or not, this is the safest place for her. I can't risk leaving her in the house in case Santo arrives early. I'm not expecting him to arrive until tomorrow, but I won't take any risks.

Saint and I stand side by side, protecting Ella as she stands behind us. Pavel and Max stand behind her.

Fausto extends his hand. "Let's get this over with."

Vincenzo looks like he's seconds away from ripping out my spleen. "Hi, Vinnie," I quip with a wave.

He advances toward me, but Fausto grips his bicep, stopping his attack.

They're here to collect the body of Christian and nothing more. I've made my terms clear. They don't give me what I want, then I ruin them. And Fausto won't allow the depravities of his nephew to ruin something he's worked so hard for.

Pavel quickly checks their yacht, ensuring they didn't do anything stupid like bring backup. When he returns, nodding that it's clear, I lead the way, ensuring Ella is flanked by my men. The few stragglers making their way to the port are surprised to see the mafia here on Tura. They put two and two together, realizing I have a new partner in crime.

Just another advantage I have over them. No one wants to fuck with the Sicilians, bar me, of course.

The walk toward Christian's villa has me on high alert. Fausto is on my side, but Vincenzo isn't. I cannot trust him, which troubles me. I make eye contact with Saint, but he's already clued in to my thoughts. We have to watch Vincenzo.

No one speaks. The tension can be cut with a knife.

As we arrive at the villa, I lead the way toward Christian's office. Opening the door, I allow Fausto and Vincenzo to enter first. When Vincenzo sees his son strung up like a Christmas decoration, he falls to his knees, howling.

Fausto looks up at Christian, spitting in disgust. "You have brought nothing but shame to this family."

We watch on, giving them time to grieve.

"Help me get him down from there," Vincenzo orders Fausto.

Turning around, I stand in front of Ella, blocking her view from something she doesn't need to see. The wet squelch is enough for her to draw a conclusion to what's going on.

"I'm going to the yacht to get a body bag," Vincenzo says to Fausto.

I look at Pavel and Max, hinting they're to follow. There is no way I'm leaving Vincenzo unsupervised.

Vincenzo walks past me, stopping when we're side by side. Hate is a common emotion I see reflected in people's eyes when they look at me, but this is something else. It's beyond hate.

Pavel gestures he's to get out of my face before he ends up like his son.

Vincenzo eventually complies, leaving with Pavel and Max in hot pursuit. I suddenly don't feel comfortable having Ella here.

"Will you wait upstairs with Sascha?" I ask. If she says no, then I shall respect her wishes.

She works her bottom lip before eventually nodding.

She steps into my arms and hugs me tightly. "Be careful."

"Always," I reply, kissing the top of her head. "I love you."

Saint arches a brow but doesn't say a word. We're both smitten. *Who would have thought?*

Ella hugs Saint before leaving the office, venturing up the stairs where she's safe.

I can't shift this weight on my chest. Something isn't right. Saint watches me closely, but I shake my head subtly. It's okay. For now.

Turning my attention to Fausto, I say, "Once this is done, I will arrange a meeting. I understand Vincenzo needs time to grieve, but I don't like to be kept waiting."

Fausto runs a hand down his face. "No one knows about this?"

He saw how many witnesses were here. I could have ruined him. "I haven't told anyone. But the people who Christian dealt with know."

"*Cazzo*," he curses, understanding they are witnesses he needs to deal with. "Do you have their names?"

"Yes. Your nephew kept a meticulous log. I will make a copy for you."

"Thank you."

We haven't addressed the elephant in the room.

Santo.

"Your brother-in-law cannot live," I explain bluntly, not wanting any misunderstanding between us. "He must pay for what he did to Ella."

"I know," Fausto replies. "My wife will be devastated, as Santo is her favorite brother, but we must do what we have to in order to protect our family."

His name, not the Macrillos, is on the line.

Vincenzo returns with a rolled-up bag under his arm. Pavel nods that all is well.

I decide to give them some privacy as they wrap their kin in a body bag and wait out in the hallway.

Saint stays close. "Something isn't right," he whispers, his astute eyes scanning the villa.

"I know," I reply. "But Santo can't be here already. Fausto and Vincenzo are here because they're not coming from Russia. They're closer than Santo is."

"Maybe we're just paranoid?" Saint offers, but we both know there is no such thing.

Saint peers into the room, but it's evident he doesn't notice anything suspicious.

I believe Fausto will work with me not because he wants to, but because he has to. It's not an ideal working relationship, but we will make it work because we need one another. But is blood thicker than water?

Fausto appears, closing the office door and giving Vincenzo a minute alone with Christian. We don't bother to fill the awkward silence with small talk. We wait for him to stop being such a crybaby. His son was far from being a saint. He needs to stop seeing him as anything but the scumbag that he was.

"The least you can do is come in here and help me carry out my son," Vincenzo says through the door.

Saint makes a move, but I stop him. "I've got it."

Opening the door, I see Vincenzo standing by the zipped up body bag, overcome with grief. "He was just a boy," he says while I raise my eyes to the heavens.

"A sick, twisted boy who deserved everything he got," I add, bending down to pick up a handle on the body bag.

However, what happens next is something called a motherfucking plot twist. I am blindsided in the worst possible way.

A deafening boom has me careening backward three steps. Before I know what is happening, the room erupts into gunfire. Rolling behind a sofa, I take shelter, attempting to figure out what the hell just happened.

I go to grab my gun but can't as my hand is slippery. Peering downward, I see the reason. I've been shot in the abdomen. It's a kill shot. But my injuries take a back seat when I hear Ella's guttural scream from upstairs.

"Alek!" Saint calls out, banging on the door.

He is outside as it's too dangerous to come in. I still have no idea where the shots are coming from. Vincenzo didn't have a gun. I saw his hands. Think, Alek. The shot came from inside the body bag. But Christian is dead.

So the question is, who's inside the body bag?

"Saint! Ella!" I exclaim, begging he protect her because I can't. I'm stuck in this room with a pissed-off Sicilian and a reanimated corpse. Oh, and I'm currently bleeding to death.

Shifting with a hiss, I press a hand over my wound, my hot, sticky blood streaming through my fingers. I focus on the now because I don't have much time. Peering around the chair, I curse as the mystery of the shooter is solved—it's Santo.

I have so many questions, and I refuse to die until I know how he got here so fast. Someone double-crossed me.

"Vincenzo!" Fausto bangs on the door. "You *stupido*! What did you do?"

Okay, so it seems Fausto wasn't privy to this plan. He was double-crossed by the Macrillos—no surprise there.

"I would never let this *bastardo* live!" Vincenzo screams. "He killed my son!"

"Your son was a cunt," I wheeze, the room beginning to spin.

When I hear footsteps, I grab my gun and fire around the chair. They didn't know I was carrying, so this should fend them off for a bit.

"Surprise," Santo says. His voice sounds distant, so I assume he's taking cover behind the desk.

"I hate surprises," I call out, trying to gauge where he is. I need eyes on him.

Gunshots sound from above me.

"No," I murmur, shaking my head.

There are so many people who need my protection, and I'm utterly useless to them.

This is my fault for being so certain Santo wouldn't arrive until tomorrow. I shouldn't have let my guard down. But how the fuck did he get here so fast?

"I know you're hit. I can smell your blood," Santo says pleased. "I should put you out of your misery, but you must suffer, just how Frank did."

"And Christian," Vincenzo adds.

This buys me some time, so I decide to humor him. "Give it your best shot, долбоёб."

The door bursts open, and I frantically aim my gun at the entrance, but what I see has me realizing no gun can ever protect me from this.

Saint is being led into the room at gunpoint by some goon. He is followed by Max and Pavel in the same predicament. They were only able to capture them because we were caught unaware. The perfect ambush tactic in any war.

Where are our weapons? This isn't like Pavel to come unprepared.

Ella enters, flanked by two Macrillo boys. She has her hands raised and doesn't shed a tear, that is until she sees me, bleeding out behind the chair.

"Alek!" she cries, attempting to run to me, but is dragged by her hair, kicking and screaming toward Santo.

"Let her go!" I roar, and with all my might, I come to a shaky stand.

Tossing my gun into the middle of the room, I raise my hands in surrender. "You won! You can have it all. Just let her go," I plead, locking eyes with Ella.

I know this isn't an option, but I have to try.

"This bitch killed our brother," says Lorenzo, Frank's older brother. "She's not going anywhere."

Santo's sons don't know how personal this is for their father. He would never tell them. He reaches out and strokes her cheek with the back of his fingers.

"*Bambina*, why did you have to ruin everything?"

In response, she spits in Santo's face. My brave girl doesn't cower. Santo wipes his cheek with a handkerchief, smirking.

Fausto stands by the door, watching on and probably wishing he married into a different family. Where is Sascha and the children? I can only hope they managed to escape.

All of my allies are being held captive in this room. I've never been more fucked than I am right now.

My legs threaten to give out, so before they do, I kick the chair around and take a seat, facing Santo. He knows I'm fatally wounded, but I won't give him the satisfaction of seeing me crumple.

"Don't you want to know our grand plan?" Santo mocks, relishing in the limelight.

I yawn in response.

He continues. "I knew you'd expect me to arrive tomorrow, which would make you complacent. You Russians aren't the only ones with a secret island," he reveals. "I charted a plane there and then sailed the yacht to Tura. The island is only a stone's throw away."

And I would have known that if I came to this fucking island more than once.

Clenching my fist over my wound, I flinch as I reposition myself because I can't get comfortable. Ella keeps looking at my gunshot wound, the worry etched all over her face. She knows what this is too. As do Saint, Pavel, and Max.

There is no coming back this time. This is the curtain call. What a show it's been. But if I'm going to die, I'm going to make sure I go out with a bang.

As I pondered earlier, is blood really thicker than water?

"You may have outsmarted me there, but you didn't really think I came unprepared, did you?"

The room falls silent.

"I have information that will ruin your family. When word gets out about what Christian was doing, no one will want to deal with you."

Fausto gasps. "The information, you made copies?"

"Of course, I did." I chuckle, blood trickling down my chin. "If anything happens to me, that information will be made public knowledge."

"How?" Santo questions. "Everyone you trust is here."

"Not everyone," I reply, measuring my inhales because it suddenly hurts to breathe.

"The American," he sneers, teeth bared.

"Maybe," I counter. "Or maybe it's the new army I've formed. You'll go back to Russia and be hunted. Don't believe me? Go to the port and see the three lifeless bodies of your friends. Even long after I'm dead, I'll haunt you. I'll haunt every fucking Macrillo until I drive you insane.

"So you can kill me, but the moment you step foot in Russia, you'll be maimed. You have no allies left. I killed them. And the ones left standing abide by my rule now."

"Vincenzo, we can't allow this information to get out. It'll ruin us," Fausto says, trying to get him to see reason. "We will be left on the streets like nothing!"

"He killed Christian!" Vincenzo repeats as though we need reminding.

I watch Saint closely as I know how he works. He is beyond clever, and right now, he is mapping out every escape route in his head. It's too late for me, but he can save the rest.

"Just kill her already, *Papa*!" says the other Macrillo boy. I can't remember his name. I wonder where Santo's other son is. He has, *had* four boys. Now he only has three.

"Santo, don't be stupid," Fausto says angrily. "Think of what this will do to your sister. To Mila. This will destroy everyone. Enough death has befallen this family."

Now they're stuck between a rock and a hard place. Revenge means they will be ruined. Is it worth it?

"Fine," Santo snarls. "But she cannot go unpunished. I'll let her live, but the last thing you'll see will be your little *puttana* on her knees."

I notice Saint look at Pavel as their goons are too busy enjoying the show to notice them conspiring. Taking a closer look at Pavel, I see he has something in his mouth. I subtly shake my head when I realize what it is.

It's an explosive device trigger of some sort, but the question is, where is the bomb? I won't allow him to sacrifice himself this way. I'm already dead.

"Let me say goodbye," I say, gripping the arms of the chair as I need support to stand.

"Christian didn't have that luxury," Vincenzo snarls.

"*Sta 'zitto*," Fausto scolds, as he realizes this is the best compromise where he wins.

Hobbling toward Ella, I focus solely on her because I want my last moments on this earth to be filled with her.

"Oh, Alek," she cries, shaking her head. "You're hurt r-really bad." She tries to stop the bleeding, but I won't soil her hands.

"I'm dying, красавица," I amend. She needs to know this is the end for me, but not for her. "I'm sorry I failed you."

"Shh," she coos, reaching out to support me as I sway on my feet. "You didn't. You m-made me whole. I-I lo-love you."

A pained hiss leaves Santo because regardless of what she's done, he will always love Ella. And it kills him that she'll never feel the same.

"And I love you." I press my cold lips to hers, using what strength I have left to kiss her tenderly.

"Fight," she sobs against my slack lips. I wish I could.

Inhaling her scent, I commit her to memory because when I leave this plane, it'll be knowing I was loved unconditionally by a woman who changed my life forever.

I don't want to let her go, but I must. I'm running out of time.

Shuffling over to Saint, I place my hands on his shoulders and nod. I don't need to say a word. He knows what I want to say. When he returns to Russia, he'll tell Willow that I'm sorry I left without saying goodbye.

I press my lips to his and kiss him chastely.

Pulling away, I shakily wipe away the blood smear I left behind. He grips my wrist, tears in his eyes. "Мне жаль. Я подвел тебя."

"No, my friend, you didn't fail me. You are my brother in arms."

Max is next in line, and when he allows me to kiss him, I feel forgiveness for what I did to Sara. I don't deserve it, but I take it, nonetheless.

Pavel's eyes widen, begging I don't do this. But when I press my mouth over his, forcing him to pass whatever he has in his mouth into mine, he eventually concedes.

I subtly move it to the middle of my tongue. It's metal and has a switch. Pavel is in possession of some high-tech artillery, so I know this thing will pack a punch. I think of Ingrid and how she experienced this firsthand.

Now it's my turn.

With my tongue, I push the gadget into my cheek because I'm not done yet. I have a little juice left in the tank, as Saint would say.

Staggering, I stand in front of Santo and smirk. "I thought I told you," I wheeze. "Call her a slut again and see what happens. But that's your problem. You don't fucking listen."

He cocks his head to the side, confused.

"It would have been far easier on you to kill us, but you had to get in the last word, didn't you? Or maybe you can't kill her. You can't kill her because you love her. That's the real reason you wanted her back. It had nothing to do with Frank," I say to Santo's sons.

"What?" Lorenzo gasps. "You liar."

He cocks his gun and presses it to the center of my forehead.

"Don't fucking touch him!" Ella shrieks, fighting against

Santo as he restrains her.

"No, I tell you the truth. Your father is in love with your dead brother's wife. He raped her, and your brother was going to do the same thing, which is why she killed him."

Santo swallows deeply because shaming him in front of his family is a crime like no other. But I needed them to know this vendetta has cost them all.

Fausto swears in Italian, disowning Santo for his crimes.

Pulling back my shoulders, I look Ella in the eye and shift the device so it sits on my tongue. When I open my mouth to speak, Ella sees what I'm hiding and lunges for me.

"No!"

Santo clues in to her outburst, and I smile, open-mouthed so he can see. "*This* is what happens motherfucker…you die."

He shoves Ella aside so he can dive for cover while Vincenzo raises his gun, about to end me before the bomb can.

But another explosion erupts behind me, and Vincenzo falls to the ground, dead, thanks to the bullet Fausto just fired. Fausto has no idea what's going on as my back is turned to him. He assumed Vincenzo was going to kill me as he couldn't let his son's death go unpunished.

"Alek, no!" Ella begs, but I drop to my knees, the world spinning out of control.

"Run!" I manage to push out, begging Saint to take Ella to safety.

Pavel and Max elbow their captors, who easily buckle when they too see the detonator in my mouth. Dying for the Macrillos isn't worth it.

Saint picks Ella up by the waist. She fights him wildly. "Saint, no! Please d-don't let him do this. Please let me go. I need to help h-him."

I collapse onto my side, watching the world tilt on its axis and smile at the chaos I caused. I don't know what's going to happen to Russia, but I've assembled a mass of leaders who will ensure none of these atrocities will ever happen again.

"Go! Now!" I shout, feeling my body shutting down.

Saint looks at me with nothing but love and nods. Ella claws at him, but he won't let her go. He will ensure he sees this through for me. I hear Ella's cries down the hall.

She's safe.

Santo looks at his dead brother, eyes wide as he begins to process what just happened. I've destroyed the Macrillo family. His sons will never look at him the same way again. Neither will his brother because his brother-in-law just shot him dead.

There is no coming back from this.

Santo is truly alone. He has nothing. I stole everything from him by telling the truth, and he has no one to blame but himself.

A rage overtakes him, and he steals the gun from Lorenzo's stunned hands and points it at me. Just as I'm about to embrace death, taking this asshole with me, a single gunshot rings out that has Santo dropping to his knees.

I don't know what's happening. My body has gone numb. Fausto is long gone, as his life is more important than some vendetta that doesn't involve him. So who shot him?

Santo collapses onto his side so we're face-to-face. The

gunshot was through the chest. His white shirt begins to stain red. Two fallen leaders about to suffer the same fate. How I wish Ella got her revenge, but I hope knowing I'm taking him to hell with me is enough.

I move my tongue, about to blow this villa to the ground, but surely, I'm too late. I've embraced death because a voice which should not be here resonates around me.

"Stay awake, Aleksei…Mother is here."

This is hell. I'm sure of it, but when familiar hands cup my face, brushing my matted hair from my cheeks, I realize this just may be hell on earth.

Suddenly, everything is so cloudy.

"Spit it out!" Pavel orders, putting his hand under my mouth.

Am I dreaming? Dead? In limbo?

I know it's none of the above because why the hell would I want Zoya anywhere near me.

My tongue feels swollen. I can't move. Pavel pries open my jaw and reaches into my mouth, carefully removing the device. Once it's out, he sighs in relief.

Seconds later, Ella is everywhere—her scent and her kisses as she showers me with love. "Please don't die. I n-need you. I love you so much."

I can't speak. I can't move.

All I can do is watch as Saint knocks out the two stunned Macrillo boys and yanks up Santo by the collar of his shirt. He punches him in the face, breaking his nose. He has a large hunting knife in his hand and looks at Ella, offering it to her. He understands this is her fight.

But she clutches onto me, her body protecting mine, surrendering her vengeance so she can escort me from this life into the next. "N-no, I won't leave Alek. You do it. Make that worthless son of a bitch pay."

And those are the last words Santo will ever hear.

Saint nods and looks at me. This is his final gift to me.

He rips open Santo's shirt, the buttons scattering all over the floor. He stabs him in the chest and draws the knife downward, splitting him open as he cuts him—sternum to groin. Santo has gone into shock as being gutted is as brutal as it sounds. His insides are now on the outside, but it's not enough.

In one fluid movement, Saint slashes Santo's throat and reaches into the wound, pulling out his tongue and leaves it hanging—a perfect Columbian necktie. Santo slumps forward, and within seconds, he's dead.

Saint shoves his corpse into a chair, as he knows I wish to stare at this vision with my last breath. I wish he could have suffered more, but the truth is, he could die a thousand deaths and it still wouldn't be enough.

This is for Ella. Her monsters are dead. I can now leave this earth, knowing she's safe.

My eyes begin to flutter, but Saint is determined to save me, regardless of my state. "You're his mother. Roll up your sleeve. He's going to need your blood, and so help me god, he's going to live…even if I bleed you dry."

With a smile on my lips, I slip into oblivion, leaving behind this world that I set on fire.

CHAPTER EIGHTEEN

Alek

Three Months Later

"And th-they l-lived ha-happily eva afta," says Irina, closing the book proudly. She has every right to be pleased because this is the fifth book she's read all by herself.

"Very good, цветочек. I'm so proud of you," I say, rubbing her back.

She snuggles into me because even though she can now read by herself, that doesn't mean she'll stop sitting on my lap. I have a feeling that won't stop even when she's older, and I don't mind.

Irina and I share a bond, but when I look at the three little children tucked soundly in their king-size bed, peering up at us with sleepy eyes, I realize I share a special bond with them all.

Three months ago, I was brought back to life—again.

The details were sketchy, seeing as I was dead for quite some time, but Saint, the stubborn son of a bitch wouldn't give up on me.

Pavel chased down a yacht that hadn't gotten far with Dr. Lebedev on board and gave him an ultimatum—save my life or die. The good doctor didn't fancy the latter option, so when he arrived back at Tura, he did just that; he saved my life.

The twist to this story is that if Zoya hadn't been on Tura, providing a perfect blood donor match, then I would have perished. She gave me a transfusion that saved my life.

I was unconscious for four days, and during that time, the only thing I clung to was Ella's voice. She was the only reason I didn't give up. I knew she never left my bedside, praying and begging I live. And when I wanted to give up, the pain almost unbearable, she lent me her strength, and that was how I survived.

When I woke and saw Zoya and Ella sitting by my bedside, I thought that maybe I had perished after all. But Ella explained what Zoya did. She was the one watching me on Tura. I felt like someone was watching me the night when Galina died, and they were.

No surprise, Zoya was at Tura, looking for a new beau to sweep her off her feet, but when she saw me, she said it was mother's intuition and knew I was in trouble. If my eyeballs didn't hurt like every single part of my body, I would have rolled them, but whatever the reason, I'm grateful.

She shot Santo, which meant I didn't need to blow myself up to take him with me. I never saw this plot twist coming, but I guess I should know by now to expect the unexpected when Zoya is involved.

She wanted to be a part of my life. She was sorry for everything she'd done, and although she saved my life, that didn't excuse her past behavior. One good deed didn't erase the endless bad ones she's committed throughout her life.

So I did the only fair thing—she saved my life, so I spared hers.

I allowed her to leave Tura, unharmed, but if I ever saw her again, I would kill her. I will never forget what she did to me, to Irina, but allowing her to live, alone, is far worse a punishment than ending her life.

I haven't seen her since.

We left Tura ten days later when I was able to travel. I hated being treated like an invalid but allowed Ella to nurse me back to health. She needed to do it—she needed to touch me, touch my beating heart to ensure I was alive.

When we arrived back in Russia, I honestly didn't know what to think. Word had spread about the fight between Santo and me, but the fact I was still standing and he was shark bait, well, that only helped my rise to the top.

My plan had worked. My kingdom was built with people I chose to lead. Yes, I slaughtered my enemies without remorse to get where I am and created utter bedlam, but it was a necessary evil. Anyone who ever doubted my authority was now a convert as no one had the balls to challenge me.

Those that used to be the majority are now a very slim minority. So if they value their life, they do what I say.

Everything goes through me, Pavel, Saint, and Max. I can't

do this on my own, and those three men proved their loyalty when they had every right to let me die. We rule Russia better than ever as Russia is now reformed.

Fausto also proved loyal because ultimately, he chose me over Vincenzo. It's not that clean-cut, but he shot Vincenzo when my life was at risk. Yes, he was trying to save his own ass as well, but in the end, he didn't agree with what Christian did and deemed my punishment just.

Because of this, he and I are now in partnership, and we're the biggest drug lords in all of Russia and beyond. His supply is grade A, which meant, eventually, our stuff was sought after by all. This overthrew any competition, and now, there is none.

It's just me.

Also, having the IRA in my corner has made me unstoppable. Austin has proven to be a very loyal ally.

Any respectable man would have given up this life, but I never claimed to be honorable. I have a family to feed and what a family I've come to attain.

There was no way I was handing the three children over to the police. Mother Superior offered to take them in, but I couldn't do that to them. They would be seen like Irina was—hard work—and they'd already been through so much.

So I decided to adopt them. As long as it was okay with Irina of course.

I explained they were like her, orphaned and alone, but if she didn't want them as her siblings, then I would find other arrangements for them. This was her decision as much as it was mine.

When she met them, I didn't know what she'd think. I didn't want to stir up any repressed memories.

But what she did, she simply stole my heart all over again. She removed her little pink cardigan and gave it to Zofia, saying she looked cold. She unhooked her silver necklace and placed it around Lena's neck, saying her eyes were as bright as the diamond around her neck. And Jacob, she gave him her treasured *Thomas the Tank Engine* book.

She accepted them without thought because they were her siblings. Although not related by blood, they shared a bond like no other. From that day forward, Zofia, Lena, and Jacob have lived with me.

My house has plenty of rooms, but the three little ones prefer to sleep together in the same bed. I understand and respect their wishes. I hope one day they will feel comfortable to choose their own rooms but one step at a time.

Jacob yawns, which has me realizing I'm still here, in their room. I often get lost in my head because I can't believe this is my life. With Irina still clinging to me, I bend down and kiss the foreheads of my three children.

It makes me happy that they're no longer covered in filth and are well-fed.

"Good night, маленькие ягнята. Sleep well."

"Good night," they sleepily reply in unison, huddling under the covers.

With one last look at them, I switch off the light. The night-light provides the light they need because they don't like the dark.

Leaving the door open an inch, I walk to Irina's bedroom

with her clinging to my neck. Her gentle breathing alerts me that she's already fallen asleep. Pulling back the covers, I gently put her to bed.

She shifts and gets comfy as I tuck her in.

Looking down at her, I never forget that she's the reason I have what I do. Everything is for her, for all my children, because I will protect them with my life.

Just as I'm about to leave, Irina sleepily says something which has my heart clenching in completeness. "Спокойной ночи, папа."

Good night, Papa.

Irina has always referred to me as Ski, and that has been more than okay. This is the first time she's called me her father.

But I don't want to make a fuss. "Good night, цветочек."

Leaving her door ajar as she doesn't like it closed, I wait out in the hallway, needing a minute to catch my breath. Is this what having it all feels like?

But when I hear soft footsteps pad along the carpet toward me, I realize that *this* is what a happily ever after feels like.

Ella and I haven't spent a day apart since returning from Tura. She belonged with me, and I wouldn't have her living anywhere but here. I know it seems awfully fast, but considering what we've been through, it made sense.

I didn't want to be without her, or her without me. I suppose we're one of those nauseating couples who can't spend five minutes apart, but let them judge. I don't care. This is the happiest I've been in, well, ever.

"What are you staring at?" she whispers, not wanting to wake the children.

"You," I reply frankly, taking her in from head to toe.

She playfully rolls her eyes. I spank her on the ass in response.

Taking her hand, we walk downstairs toward the kitchen as I have a few minutes before I need to leave. Everyone has gone home for the night. It's just us, and when she opens the freezer to retrieve a bottle of vodka, I lick my lips because there is something else I thirst for.

She turns around, vodka in hand, but when she sees me examining her very openly, she turns a lovely shade of red.

"Thirsty?"

"Very."

She pours us a drink, and when she offers me a glass, I reach for her wrist instead.

Drawing her into my chest, I smirk. "Hello."

"Hi," she replies, peering up at me from under her long lashes.

I still can't believe we're here. I should be dead, and she should be living a normal life, away from this. But I've come to learn that this *is* normal for Ella. Her whole life, she felt like she didn't belong, but now she does.

She belongs with me. She always has.

Lowering my lips to hers, I love the way she melts against me, allowing me to dominate her because no matter who I am, I will always need control. I can't change who I am, but with Ella, we balance each other out perfectly.

Sometimes, she likes to be controlled, and other times, she likes to take the reins. There is nothing hotter than Ella, the dominatrix. We are equals—in every sense of the word.

After what happened on Tura, Ella has made it her mission to help the children who have been exploited and sold into slavery. She's thrown herself into this project, hosting fundraisers, bringing awareness to the cause, and also helps Mother Superior out at the orphanage because thanks to me, they have the resources for many more children to reside there now.

She's found her calling in life, and it's here where she'll live that life out.

Ella knows that we can't go to the police with the information I have, but that doesn't mean I'm not dealing with it in my own way. She knows what that means. She doesn't ask questions, but she can guess.

Just as she can guess how I rule. I'm still ruthless and murderous, but I make no apologies. Russia is better for it. Some say better the devil you know, and in this case, I am the devil they all know not to fuck with.

This life is the life I choose to live. It's in the darkness where I thrive. I'm not the good guy, but I've come to learn there are worse men than me. And killing those men seems to balance out the good and bad I have inside me.

Ella loops her fingers behind my neck, kissing me deeply, always wanting more. Just as I'm about to bend her over the kitchen counter, ignoring the doctor's orders about refraining from strenuous activities, a loud clearing of a throat has me putting my plans on hold.

"You sure have a lot of energy for an old man," Saint quips, helping himself to an apple from the fruit bowl.

Ella snorts while I shake my head.

"Remind me why I gave you a key," I playfully retort.

"Sorry, Ella, but we gotta bounce," Saint says, hinting if we're going to do this, now is the time.

Where we're going excites me immensely. So I nod.

"I'll see you soon." I kiss Ella's cheek.

"Oh, before I forget, Willow wanted to know if you needed any help with the renovations at the orphanage."

Ella smiles. "That would be awesome. I'll call her now."

Who would have thought Willow and Ella would be friends? Life does work in mysterious ways.

Even though my house is a fortress and Sascha is now my personal bodyguard, I can't help but worry about Ella.

She senses my concern. "Take your time."

I forget Saint is feet away and lower my mouth to Ella's, kissing her deeply. Her hair has grown longer, which allows me to run my fingers through it and pull—hard.

"Okay, maybe hurry a little," she says from around my lips.

With a chuckle, I pull away, cupping her cheek. "I love you, красавица."

She smiles, just as she does every time she hears me profess my love for her. "I love you too."

And for that, aren't I the luckiest man alive?

Leaving my family behind, I meet Sascha, who stands at the front. "Call if you need me."

He nods with a slanted smirk. "I won't, but okay."

Saint grins as he and Sascha have become good friends. Sascha is where Saint once was—my righthand man—but everything is different now. No one is here against their will.

The three women who played my submissives now live a comfortable life away from devious men like me.

Celine still won't accept a pay raise even though she is now looking after four children. But with my house filled with friends who constantly want to spend time with them, she barely has any time alone with the kids.

All in all, my life is far from being the Russian kingpin that I am.

But when the witching hour is upon us, it's a whole different story.

Patting Sascha on the back, I walk toward Saint's black truck. My injuries are healing, but I still walk with a cane on nights such as this. We get into the truck, and Saint commences the hour drive.

As always, I scope out my surroundings because even though I killed Santo, I'm not naïve in thinking that one day, his sons and wife will be out for my blood.

The Macrillos have kept their noses out of my business as they're outnumbered. They saw what I did to their family, and after the bombshell I dropped about Santo, maybe their revenge can wait. Santo isn't worth the bloodshed.

But some people are.

I flick through the stations on the radio, stopping when I come across a classical piece. Classical music always gets me in the mood.

"Are you sure it's him?" Saint asks, sensing my murderous impulses growing.

"Yes."

Saint whistles. "Good luck to him."

Luck has nothing to do with it. His fate was decided the moment he made the wrong choice.

Cracking my neck from side to side, I decide to change the subject. "How's Willow? Settling in okay?"

Saint and Willow have decided to make Russia their home. They traveled and saw the world, but the one place they called home was Russia. It seems strange that a place that caused them both so much pain is where they choose to live.

But the good outweighs the bad. That's how Saint and Willow are—the forever optimists.

"Yes, she got a chicken," he says, while I arch a brow.

"To eat?"

Saint laughs. "No, as a pet."

"Oh, a pet," I reply, unsure what the significance of this chicken is.

The slanted smirk on Saint's lips reveals it must be a secret they're only privy to.

Once upon a time, I would have been envious, but now, I understand because I have someone who is privy to my secrets, and it feels incredible. I never in a million years would have envisioned my life turning out the way it has.

I don't know what I did to deserve this, but I'll take it.

We ride the rest of the way, discussing tactics as Saint knows my business as well as me. We make decisions together because I couldn't have done this without him. I know he still resents me for what I did to Zoey, and that's okay.

It's a reminder of what we will never become again.

But the one thing that will never change, the one thing we will always see eye to eye on is seeking revenge on those who wronged someone we loved.

Saint switches off the headlights when we're a few blocks away from our destination. This neighborhood isn't a dump, but I didn't expect it to be. It's behind the wealth and glamour where they hide.

We pull up a few houses away from the address and watch the house in question. The porch light is on. He's expecting company, but it's not us he's expecting.

"So we still stick to the plan?"

"Yes," I reply, reaching into the back seat for the bag of goodies Pavel has packed for me.

Saint nods. "Let's do it then."

With a deep breath, I calm my nerves because I have waited for this day for what feels like years. We exit the truck and make our way toward the house.

The person inside doesn't live here. He uses it when he has an itch he doesn't want his wife knowing about. And tonight, his itch is about to be scratched permanently.

Sauntering toward the front gate, I hear a train horn sound in the distance.

When we're at the front door, Saint smiles. "I love it when you get that look."

He knows things are about to get messy.

Knocking softly, I wait for the person to answer, and when he does, it takes every shred of willpower I have not to rip out his tongue. "Counselor Sagbo, sorry to disturb you at such a late hour."

"Aleksei?" he says, his surprise clear.

"May I come in?"

He looks over my shoulder at Saint as he knows I'm only asking to be polite. Either he lets me in or I'll force my way in.

"Yes, of course." He steps aside so Saint and I can enter.

I walk through the door, looking at the house of horrors.

"Come into the living room. I was just having a drink."

I gesture for Saint to take a look around to ensure we're alone.

I follow Feliks Sagbo and watch as his hand shakes when he pours me a scotch. "To what do I owe this pleasure?"

Taking a seat in the leather recliner, I lean back and smile. "I wanted to ask something of you."

"Please." He offers me my drink before taking a seat across from me.

Placing the scotch on the coffee table, I reach into my pocket and retrieve a photograph. I pass it to him and watch his face drain of color.

"Do you know that little girl?"

"I, n-no, I do not."

Tsking him, I reach for my scotch and sip it slowly. "You see, I think that you do. I think that you're the piece of shit who got his mistress pregnant, and when she didn't want to have an abortion, you permitted her and her daughter, *your* daughter to live here.

"But when you killed your mistress in a fit of jealousy, that left you with a little problem—your love child. She reminded you so much of your mistress and what you did to her…"

I need to take a breath before I fucking stab him to death.

"You're wrong. I would never." When he attempts to stand, Saint shoves him back down by his shoulders. He stands guard behind him. Feliks has nowhere to go…but hell.

"You sold that little girl to the highest bidder, you broke her, and when they grew tired of her, they dumped her at the orphanage gates like some dog!"

The whites of Feliks eyes are showing. He's afraid. Good.

"That little girl, the one you were supposed to protect because you *were* her father, is now *my* daughter. Irina Popov."

"Oh, god, no, please." Feliks drops to his knees, begging for clemency. "I didn't know what to do. Christian Macrillo said he'd take care of her."

"Well, he's now dead, so he can't take care of anyone ever again."

It's amazing the things a desperate man will tell you.

Irina *was* sold into slavery by Christian, but tracking down her father was harder than I thought. Christian had the buyer's name, whose severed body parts are cemented in a drum at the bottom of the ocean. Don't worry, he suffered, Saint and I made sure of it.

But I had to dig a little deeper to find where her roots lay.

These assholes have a code of silence because if one goes down, they all do. But what they don't know is that they're already dead, they just don't know it yet. I have their names and addresses, and I know what they did, thanks to Christian's notes.

So all I had to do was work down the food chain until I found what I wanted. I always had an inkling Irina's father was someone of importance. Which is why she took a shining to me. I was familiar in an unfamiliar world, and although I am nothing like those vile pigs, she gravitated to what she knows.

Her father is a respected man in the community, and I'd like to believe there were times when he was kind. But that doesn't excuse what he did.

Fifteen dead men and women later, I found Irina's biological father, and here we are. The man who spilled his guts—literally—told me where Feliks would be. When I searched online and saw a train station close by, I knew he was telling the truth.

The children who I have saved now reside at the orphanage. I've given Mother Superior over a million dollars to build a new wing, which is what the renovations Saint asked about are. I can't adopt them all. I wish I could. But I will provide for them until they can find good homes.

One by one, I will kill every motherfucker on Christian's list and save the children. But this one, this is personal.

I don't want to know what he did to Irina. That's not why I'm here.

I found her past, and now it's time to kill it, and kill it slowly.

Feliks continues to beg while I sit back on my throne, taking great pleasure in seeing him burn. I notice he has a gold necklace on. A praying Madonna hangs off the end.

Finishing my drink, I come to a stand, using my cane as support as I walk over to him. Looking down at him, I curl my lip in disgust. Reaching down, I yank the chain from his neck, breaking it with ease.

He yelps, but is suddenly relieved that I'm only here to rob him.

The ring on my pinkie finger, however, confirms otherwise. This chain is my new keepsake because this kill, oh this kill will outdo any others before it.

"I'll scream," he threatens while I laugh.

"Oh, I hope that you do."

Feliks knows it's now or never. He shoots up and runs through the kitchen for the back door. Saint sighs, unamused.

Before he has a chance to get within three feet of it, I pick up the crystal decanter of scotch, aim, and throw. It connects with the back of his head and he flops onto his stomach with a pained *oof*.

I cluck my tongue, shaking my head. "Such a shame to waste good scotch."

Saint smirks, reaching for our bag of tricks.

"What do you feel like tonight?"

"Let's see what Pavel packed," I reply, excited as one would be if someone packed a surprise picnic lunch.

Saint drops the bag onto the coffee table, and unzips it, and what I see sings to my little black heart. The medieval-looking tools Pavel has provided are all so appealing, but when I see a shiny device called the pear of anguish, I know I've found a winner.

If one is unsure of its purpose, let me clarify—it'll be inserted into an orifice where Feliks, if he were left alive, would never be able to sit on a barstool again.

Grabbing what I need, Saint looks over my shoulder and coos. "How sweet. Pavel packed us some protein bars."

Laughing, I catch the protein bar Saint tosses my way. "He knows it'll be a long night."

We slowly turn and look at where Feliks creeps along the kitchen floor, leaving a trail of blood from the gash to his head. He's still believes that escape is an option. But he's not going anywhere. None of them are.

I'm a bad man. And I'm okay with that.

This is *my* world. My rules. I'm the motherfucking king, and it's time to adjust my crown.

ACKNOWLEDGEMENTS

My author family: Elle Kennedy and Vi Keeland—I love you both very much.

My ever-supporting parents. You guys are the best. I am who I am because of you. I love you. RIP Papa. Gone but never forgotten. You're in my heart. Always.

My agent, Kimberly Brower from Brower Literary & Management. Thank you for your patience and thank you for being an amazing human being.

My editor, Jenny Sims. What can I say other than I LOVE YOU! Thank you for everything. You go above and beyond for me.

My proofreaders—My Brother's Editor and Annie Bugeja.

My Russian Translator and lifesaver—Lana Kart, thank you!

Sommer Stein, you NAILED this cover! Thank you for being so patient and making the process so fun. I'm sorry for annoying you constantly.

Ren Saliba—your photography is magic. Looking forward to working on more covers with you.

My publicist—Danielle Sanchez from Wildfire Marketing Solutions. Thank you for all your help.

A special shout-out to: Bombay Sapphire Gin, L.J. Shen, Christina Lauren, Natasha Madison, Willow Winters, K.

Webster, Giana Darling, S.M. Soto, Kat T. Masen, Devney Perry, Penelope Ward, Tillie Cole, Lisa Edward, Cheri Grand Anderman, Lauren Rosa, Louise, Kimberly Whalen, Christine Estevez, Ben Ellis—Tall Story Designs, Nasha Lama, Natasha Tomic, Heyne, Random House, Kinneret Zmora, Hugo & Cie, Planeta, MxM Bookmark, Art Eternal, Carbaccio, Fischer, Sieben Verlag, Bookouture, Egmont Bulgaria, Brilliance Publishing, Audible, Hope Editions, Buzzfeed, BookBub, PopSugar, Aestas Book Blog, Hugues De Saint Vincent, Paris, New York, Sarah Sentz (you're my cover go-to queen!) Jessica—PeaceLoveBooks.

To the endless blogs that have supported me since day one—You guys rock my world.

My bookstagrammers—This book has allowed me to meet SO many of you. Your creativity astounds me. The effort you go to is just amazing. Thank you for the posts, the teasers, the support, the messages, the love, the EVERYTHING! I see what you do, and I am so, so thankful.

My ARC TEAM—You guys are THE BEST! Thanks for all the support.

My reader group—sending you all a big kiss.

My beautiful family—Daniel, Mum, Papa, Fran, Matt, Samantha, Amelia, Gayle, Peter, Luke, Leah, Jimmy, Jack, Shirley, Michael, Rob, Elisa, Evan, Alex, Francesca, and my aunties, uncles, and cousins—I am the luckiest person alive to know each and every one of you. You brighten up my world in ways I honestly cannot express.

Samantha and Amelia— I love you both so very much.

To my family in Holland and Italy, and abroad. Sending

you guys much love and kisses.

Papa, Zio Nello, Zio Frank, Zia Rosetta, and Zia Giuseppina—you are in our hearts. Always.

My fur babies— mamma loves you so much! Buckwheat, you are my best buddy. Dacca, I will always protect you from the big bad Bellie. Mitch, refer to Dacca's comment. Jag, you're a wombat in disguise. Bellie, your singing voice is so beautiful. And Ninja, thanks for watching over me. To the newest addition, Wabbit; I love your apricot face.

To anyone I have missed, I'm sorry. It wasn't intentional!

Last but certainly not least, I want to thank YOU! Thank you for welcoming me into your hearts and homes. My readers are the BEST readers in this entire universe! Love you all!

ABOUT THE AUTHOR

Monica James spent her youth devouring the works of Anne Rice, William Shakespeare, and Emily Dickinson.

When she is not writing, Monica is busy running her own business, but she always finds a balance between the two. She enjoys writing honest, heartfelt, and turbulent stories, hoping to leave an imprint on her readers. She draws her inspiration from life.

She is a bestselling author in the U.S.A., Australia, Canada, France, Germany, Israel, and The U.K.

Monica James resides in Melbourne, Australia, with her wonderful family, and menagerie of animals. She is slightly obsessed with cats, chucks, and lip gloss, and secretly wishes she was a ninja on the weekends.

CONNECT WITH MONICA JAMES

Facebook: facebook.com/authormonicajames
Twitter: twitter.com/monicajames81
Goodreads: goodreads.com/MonicaJames
Instagram: instagram.com/authormonicajames
Website: authormonicajames.com
Pinterest: pinterest.com/monicajames81
BookBub: bookbub.com/authors/monica-james
Amazon: amzn.to/2EWZSyS
Join my Reader Group: bit.ly/2nUaRyi

www.ingramcontent.com/pod-product-compliance
Lightning Source LLC
Chambersburg PA
CBHW070153120726
47909CB00001B/94